Henry Henry

ALLEN BRATTON

Henry Henry

JONATHAN CAPE
LONDON

Thank you to KF, and to my earliest readers and companions.

Thank you to Brandon Taylor, Martha Wydysh, Sarah McEachern,
Željka Marošević, and everyone at Trident, Unnamed Press and Jonathan Cape.

——

1 3 5 7 9 10 8 6 4 2

Jonathan Cape, an imprint of Vintage, is part of the Penguin Random House group
of companies whose addresses can be found at global.penguinrandomhouse.com

First published by Jonathan Cape in 2024

penguin.co.uk/vintage

Typeset in 10.6/14.5 pt Minion Pro by Jouve (UK), Milton Keynes
Printed and bound in Great Britain by Clays Ltd, Elcograf S.p.A.

The authorised representative in the EEA is Penguin Random House Ireland,
Morrison Chambers, 32 Nassau Street, Dublin D02 YH68

A CIP catalogue record for this book is available from the British Library

ISBN 9781787334595

Penguin Random House is committed to a sustainable future
for our business, our readers and our planet. This book is
made from Forest Stewardship Council® certified paper.

Henry Henry

PART ONE

LAUGH NOW CRY LATER

1

At Jack's flat, he let you smoke indoors. Hal went out for a fag anyway and saw that the sun had risen; there was warm spring light on him. He walked up the road against a perpetual flow of small children in embroidered jumpers and rounded collars, and got on a bus that would take him north-west across the Thames. The sun was on his right shoulder and his temple was on the window. He struggled to fix his eyes on the back of the man in front of him. His own stink hovered about him: skunky weed, spilt Pimm's and gin, cigarettes smoked in a flat that had had a lot of cigarettes smoked in it before, the vile mix of sweat and deodorant that had congealed under his armpits and was soaking through his pale blue Oxford shirt. Sensing he was about to feel very bad, he took his aviators off the neck of his shirt and put them on his face. The bus was passing across Vauxhall Bridge; the sun was in the scummy green water, making it look almost translucent, as if it were more water than filth. Literally the most fucking beautiful thing, he thought. Here I am in London in the twenty-first century, and there's the Thames that was there when the first Duke of Lancaster was born, and there's the long-lived sun.

He got off the bus in Kensington and went into St Edward the Martyr's just as the Wednesday morning mass was beginning. He'd avoided mass since Lent began because his father had been pleading for him to go. Hal liked to have fun, he liked not to suffer. It was just that he had decided when he left Jack's flat that going to mass would be better than going back in. There was something soothing, after a night of hard drinking, about reciting, 'Lamb of God, you take away the sins of the world, have mercy on us. Lamb of God . . .' Though his throat was sore, Hal's voice was resonant, dominating the dozen others. At twenty-two, he was the youngest there by decades. He'd been avoiding glances so zealously that he hadn't been able to tell whether any of the congregation were people he knew, but he thought they must have been. The back of his neck, and the damp stains on the back of his shirt, had the feeling of being looked at. The interior of the church was cool and airy, the sunlight bright but without heat, floating above the shadows that circled the nave. Still, an overfamiliar line of sweat dripped down the inward curve of his lower back. His mouth was dry, his lips were cracked and aching from being licked.

The priest who led the mass was the particular confessor of Hal's father. Father Dyer was an old man and had known Henry since he was young, Hal since he was baptised. He had known Hal's mother. Hal was only third in the queue for communion; Father Dyer looked him in the eye as he offered him the Body of Christ, which Hal took obediently. He was going to vomit, Oh God, not here . . . oh, no, it had passed, he felt better . . . oh no, there it was again. The vivid light coming through the stained glass in the chancel vibrated at the edges. He slurred 'and with your spirit' when it was asked of him, and timed his exit so that he passed Father Dyer as he was shaking someone else's hand. There he was, one and done, state of grace achieved in forty minutes. St Augustine had said that drinking to excess was a mortal sin, but as the Church had not established a blood alcohol limit, Hal had decided that he only had to confess if he lost consciousness.

Bordering the south wall, shaded by two old lime trees and several taller, newer buildings, was a small graveyard. It had been opened some years before the Catholic cemeteries in Kensal Green and Leyton; most of the headstones were thin, leaning, illegible remnants. In a spot of sun, there was a small, white marble grave marker so brightly new that it seemed unreal, as if there couldn't really be a body underneath. The body belonged to Hal's grandfather's elder brother's only son, whose name was Richard, and who had been born the same year as Hal's father. He had died young, childless. Henry was the one who had buried Richard here. The previous dukes were interred side by side in St Michael's and All Souls in Lancaster, with the exception of the sixth duke, who had died of mysterious causes while imprisoned in the Tower of London. Hal felt he should pay his respects. If Richard hadn't been such a degenerate, Hal's father wouldn't care nearly so much that Hal was too. It was like Oscar Wilde had said: to have one queer in the line of succession was a tragedy, to have two looked like there was something fucking wrong with your family. And, in fact, the Lancasters had had three: Hal's great-great-grandfather had died in exile after going wrong with a Frenchman. Now Hal was son and heir, possessing nothing but a subsidiary title, an unignorable sense of his own pre-eminence, and a daily terror of this pre-eminence going unnoticed by everyone in the world except his father, who had rung him nine times back to back while he was at mass.

It was fine, Hal had his phone on silent. He made the Sign of the Cross, prayed for Richard's soul, and said a very genuine Our Father.

There were a lot of different ways you could vomit from being drunk. There was the tactical chunder, the unloosing of a stomach's worth of lager to make room for another few pints; the surprise puke, which was not a surprise because it would happen inevitably if you did not make it happen yourself; the takeaway puke, when you scarfed a Styrofoam box full of chips or an extra-spicy kebab and then gagged it back up again like a dog who'd pawed open the rubbish; the nightcap puke, a tidy voiding of the stomach right before you collapsed; the blackout puke, with which you were acquainted only afterwards, when you woke up in it; the night-bus puke, which probably could have been kept down if you hadn't been jerked back and forth for half an hour by an idiot sadist of a driver; the hangover breakfast puke, which suggested that baked beans and rashers did little to cure the wounds that had been incurred the night before. Then there was the most miserable of them all, the 0-per-cent-blood-alcohol empty-stomach heaving-up of bile, the body's confused and pathetic attempt to rid itself of poison that had already been pissed away. It was like doing penance when you had already been punishing yourself.

From Hal's phone on the floor beside him came Ed Poins's unconcerned drone, North London inflected with American TV: 'I've got a cousin in Australia who played rugby, and he drank so much he got a hole in his oesophagus.'

Hal said, 'I don't want to hear about people getting holes where they shouldn't have them. Can't you tell me something funny?'

He felt the weird internal grip of nausea and bent over the toilet bowl, spitting into the clear, still water. He was lucky he couldn't see his face in it; he could sort of see the silhouette of his head. Another round of puke worked its way up his throat and out of his mouth. He had to gag and gasp to get it all free. In the water it looked like a whisked egg.

Poins made a noise. 'Are you puking right now?'

Like Hal, Poins had read English at Oxford. He had talked vaguely about doing law or working in the City or whatever else would make him money – '*My* only inheritance will be my mum's semi-detached,' he liked to remind Hal – but just after they'd sat their finals he'd landed a decent supporting role in a miniseries adaptation of a First World War memoir: he played a young Tommy who'd been shot in the throat and then had a lot of homoerotic poetry written in his honour. The last time Hal had acted was with Poins, in a student production of *The Importance of Being Earnest*. Hal had been Worthing, Poins Algernon. Their physical dissimilarity – Hal fair and unusually tall, Poins dark and unusually short – had made them look amusing on stage together, and they had that almost psychic connection that enabled them to change approaches without planning or practising beforehand. Poins had asked him, after they finished at Oxford, whether he was going to keep acting, and Hal had said he didn't think so, and Poins had asked him why. He had said he was going to have to be the seventeenth Duke of Lancaster. Poins had said, 'But you can be other things too, can't you?' and Hal had said, 'No, not really,' and begun to feel sorry for himself, and Poins had laughed and said, 'Spare me.'

Hal's phone pinged; he sat back against the wall and opened his texts, having only glimpsed the notification before it disappeared.

'Oh God,' he said, 'Tom is texting me.'

'Is he complaining about your Snap story, or is your dad looking for you?'

'Oh, yeah, well, he's not even trying to pretend he's not playing go-between. He says—Here's what he says, he says: "Dad says he has something important to tell us so asked us to come to dinner at his tomorrow at-symbol seven so if you could show up it would be much appreciated thanks" passive-aggressive exclamation mark.'

'Are you going to go?'

'Why would I?'

'What if his announcement is that he's dying?'

Hal said, 'I know what he does when he thinks he's dying. He rings his solicitor and changes his will for the 500th time, then stays up all night and rings me at four in the morning telling me he can't sleep because if he does he'll die and he wants me to tell him whether he should send for a priest or try to wait a little longer. I say, "Well, if you really think you're dying, I suppose you should send for a priest," and he says, "Will you come if I do?" And then I say . . . Well, never mind, but the point is that, like, he's going to say he's going to go live in the South of France for the sake of his health or something. And I don't need to go to dinner to hear it when Tom or whoever's going to tell me anyway.'

'So, pub?'

'Is your hangover over? It's already the afternoon: come round my flat and we'll start drinking. Bring some cans of G&T, hair of the dog that bit you.'

'Yeah, okay, you know what, fine, but obviously yours isn't over, so I'm going to hang up before you make me listen to you puke again.'

Lying back on the cool tiles, Hal thought how stupid he was to talk about his father like that. It was the sort of thing you told your therapist, and after the hellish year of priests and psychologists that had followed his mother's death, he had sworn therapy off. He could get benzos from his GP in Harley Street, who was also his father's GP, and had been his grandfather's. Dr Bradmore had retained the family's loyalty through his protracted investigation for tax fraud: having been fined (not imprisoned) for tax crimes himself, Grandfather John had felt that, if anything, it made him more trustworthy. He chose his questions judiciously, and never encouraged Hal to do anything like take him into his confidence. With Poins, Hal always said more than he meant to. He supposed it was because he trusted Poins to be stupid, and to know what was best for him, which was to be stupid.

He wasn't done puking. The nausea became unbearable; he lifted himself up so that his head hung over the toilet bowl, and spat and waited for the unconscious, uncontrollable parts of his body to move.

By midnight they were with strangers near King's Cross. Hal met up with one of his dealers to buy a couple of grams, and he and Poins spent the rest of the dark hours at a warehouse club in an otherwise desolate stretch of real warehouses bordering the tracks that led out of, or into, the two stations. They went back and forth between the toilets, the bar, and the smoking section: keeping their heads rushing, bringing themselves up until they were unselfconscious enough to wade into the crush of strangers and flail about under the strobe lights, blinking out of existence in the darkness, flying straight to heaven when the lights blinked on again. They watched the sun rise from the rooftop terrace, lying back in plastic recliners and blowing smoke into the new blue sky. The trains were running again. Hal asked if Poins wanted to crash at his flat. Poins said no, he had to get home, he'd see him that evening at the pub. They walked back to King's Cross together, smoking the last two cigarettes from Hal's packet. Poins took the Northern line and Hal the Piccadilly, and Hal was alone again, coming down, hanging off a yellow pole and looking at the faces of the people around him, thinking: you don't know who I am. Well, thank God.

2

Jack Falstaff had been young, once, and handsomer than Hal, and thinner too, with dark hair rakishly pushed back. His star had risen in the early eighties, following an unimpressive adolescence at a third-tier public school, one disastrous year at Oxford, and three good years at RADA. It reached its height in 1989 with a leading role as a Battle of Britain fighter pilot who gets shot down behind enemy lines after confessing his love to a beautiful young heiress trapped in an unhappy engagement to a war profiteer. Then he was in a string of flops, and his looks went, and he got fat, and younger, handsomer men took his place, and the world went on, leaving him living on bit parts, using his talents mostly in the service of getting other people to pay for his drinks.

Hal had spent a long time deflecting Jack's advances. Then one evening last autumn Poins was gone – 'I've got a big audition in the morning,' he'd said – and Hal, stoned and chilly in Jack's unheated flat, had climbed into the warm bed and thought, It won't hurt if it's just the once. He had never in his life done a foolish thing just once. Now spring was here and they were alone together and Jack kept trying to kiss him on the mouth. He called him his 'dear boy' or his 'handsome young man', though Hal was not so much handsome as very tall and golden-haired, which overcame his blunt, droopy face to give the impression of beauty.

Leaving a splash of lager still in the can, Hal got up to piss, then came back and threw himself onto Jack's sofa, swinging his long, heavy legs up to rest on Jack's lap.

He asked Jack, 'Can you get it up, do you think?'

'Why, would you like me to?'

'No, I don't know why I asked.'

Hal had unbuttoned his trousers and taken his cock out. The lamps were on, and he thought of how his own cock looked strange in his hand, like something that didn't belong to him. He had the same sensation when he looked at his hands or feet, or his face in the mirror. As Jack took over, he thought, Thank God, now I don't have to do it any more. He recognised that he was hard and that he would come if Jack kept going, but he felt literally nothing. He watched the shadows move on the wall behind Jack's head. He heard his own hard breaths, and the lightbulbs buzzing.

'Hal,' said Jack.

Hal was staring at a spot on the wall where a length of tape seemed to have been painted over. He reached over Jack's shoulder and dug his fingernail under the edge of the tape and pulled an uneven section loose. Underneath was just an older layer of paint, a yellower white.

'Shall we just—' Jack was saying. 'Shall we just lie down for a tick?'

Hal realised he was only half-hard. It was meant to be the other way around, the old man licentious and impotent and the young man shy but coming copiously. He laid himself face-down across Jack's lap, letting Jack pull his trousers and pants down. He said, 'Tell me I'm naughty or whatever.'

'I'll tell you what to do, you naughty boy.'

Hal laughed openly, the way women weren't allowed to do with men. 'I didn't mean literally. Jack, no, look – try to act a little bit. Pretend you're my father and you're really letting me have it.'

'I was just warming up my vocal cords, and my right shoulder. There. Hal? Harry?'

'Yes?'

Jack struck him. The sensation was identifiably pain, but it wasn't frightening, or even inconvenient. There was no reason why he should want to feel it, why he should get hard from feeling it; it didn't even mimic the act of procreation.

'Are you just now coming in?' Jack began. 'Have you been out all night? Where have you been, who have you been with? What did you have them do to you? I hope they were clean. How long has it been since you've had your bloods done?'

He was hitting Hal intermittently; Hal was refusing to think about it. It would be so much more bearable if Jack didn't care so much about what Hal thought of him. Hal had had a few really good Grindr shags when he'd just moved back to London after Oxford, and that had been the best sex he'd had. Those were men who truly didn't give a damn whether Hal came or not, or even felt pleasure. All Hal had to do was to tell them, 'I want to be used.' Like a pair of pliers, or a supermarket loyalty card.

'You're embarrassing,' Jack told him. 'Do you pretend you don't know what you're doing? Do you think I'll pretend I don't know? I do. You're giving yourself up, body and soul, piece by piece, for no other reason but your sore contempt for your own inborn supremacy. Working boys at least do it for money. Still—' Oh no, thought Hal, here it is. 'Still, you must want love, if not from me. There must be someone you spend my money buying drinks for – even you couldn't drink that much alone. Is he older? Do you tell him you wish he was your father? Do you ask him to punish you?'

Hal had got somewhere close to coming in the middle of Jack's monologue, but he'd lost it again, and went limp over Jack's lap, laughing. He flung himself back into the cushions; his soft chafed cock lay against his thigh.

'Just—I'm not giving up yet,' said Hal, 'but you have to really try to pretend, or it's not going to work. Here, look. You be me and I'll be my father. Now watch.'

Hal got up and hovered over him, one knee between Jack's thighs and one hand on the cushion behind Jack's head. In a voice lower and less voluble than his own he said, 'I don't think you know quite how difficult it is, for me. Someone asks after you and I have to make excuses. People are always asking after you. They hear about you. They wonder. They're asked about you themselves, by people who don't know you. I don't think you know quite how difficult you make things for the people who can't avoid knowing you. I hope you don't know; if you did, you would be cruel. I talked to Henry Percy last week. He says his son is teaching English somewhere – I don't know where, some-where they don't speak English. He says Harry was robbed at knifepoint. Did you hear about that? I'd rather you be robbed of every penny you've got than piss it away south of the river. It's my money, you know. And your grandfather John's money, and your great-grandfather Edward's money, and your great-great-grandfather Edward's money: remember that. What do you think your grandfather would think of you now? No, don't say anything, I'll tell you: he would be ashamed to admit you belonged to him. He would cut you dead in the street, and at his club.

'I shouldn't have let you spend so much time with Richard. I see that now. I should have known. You were too young then to know what he was doing. Do you want to know now? They think they're get-ting away with it, now that the plague is over. Now they can marry each other, and be ordained in the Church of England. But that's what the Reformation did; the whole country has turned away from God. You've turned away from God. You've done worse: you've spat in God's face. God help me, but I pray sometimes to find out you were never my son.'

There, it was alright, he was coming now, it was going to be over soon. He had been satisfied; his cum dripped onto Jack's thick, hairy stomach. He shook out as much of it as he could, thankful he hadn't got to worry about getting anybody pregnant. When Henry married her, everyone thought Mary must have been pregnant. Why else would two twenty-year-olds get married? But Hal was born thirteen months after the wedding. He disgusted himself with the thought of having his own wedding, with his own impregnable bride. He was dis-gusted also by the sweat between his thighs and his arse cheeks, between his fringe and his forehead, his shirt and his lower back. His prick shrunk back into its foreskin; his breath went deep and then normal again. He thought maybe he hadn't liked it because Jack was more like his mother: blue-eyed, red-cheeked, gravid. Or because he himself hadn't pulled the likeness off.

'Hal,' said Jack, 'come here, dear, let me kiss you.'

Hal said, 'I'll pass, thanks.'

There was one cigarette left in Hal's packet. Jack had been smoking Hal's all night; he'd run out of his own and refused to go out to buy more. So they smoked the last fag together, passing it between them, and Hal hogged it, because it was his right. They set to finishing the last of the beer, then the half-empty bottle of Chartreuse that Jack had been trying to get rid of since Christmas. The stained floral sofa, the dusty fake plants, were suspended in the gentle dark of drunkenness. Hal thought of what the flat would be like when he was gone. He thought of Jack lonely, imagining the pleasures Hal took in his absence, the kinds of invitations and flatteries that had come to him when he was young and now were permanently withdrawn. Perhaps Jack knew Hal better: perhaps he imagined Hal lying in bed on the nights he slept alone, coursing with vile blood and thinking, I wish I'd been someone else, I wish I'd been someone else's son.

When Hal got back to his flat the next morning, his younger brother John was there, sitting on his sofa, watching his TV, drinking a glass of orange juice that must have been poured from the carton in his fridge. It was like he thought that, just because their mutual father paid for it, he was entitled to everything Hal had.

'Oh, okay, good, there you are,' said John. 'I just let myself in, I hope you don't mind.'

'Am I not allowed to turn my phone off? I'm an adult, I can do what I want. You literally just turned eighteen—'

'I'm turning twenty in June.'

John couldn't really celebrate his birthday: their mother had died in June, a couple of weeks after John turned five. He did boring, decent things like ask for donations in his name to charities providing maternal health resources to women in the developing world. His older relations bought him unsentimental gifts, golf clubs and leather wallets, presented without cards, which he thought wasteful. 'Every-one just tosses them,' he'd said once, only to have Blanche and Philippa insist that they kept every card they'd been given. John was at least better off than Philippa, who had been born three days before Mary died.

'I'm here,' said Hal, turning off the TV. 'You can go back and tell Dad I'm not dead.'

John had gone into the kitchen. He was making Americanos with the espresso machine Hal never used. Hal downed a glass of tap water and three paracetamol.

'Look,' said John, 'I've just come to give you the news.'

'He told you he was moving to the South of France?'

'What, no? Did he tell you that?'

'No, I thought that was what he was going to tell you.'

'No,' said John. 'The thing he told us is that he's getting married.'

'Oh, sorry, what?'

'I thought that was why you said he was moving to France, because he's getting married – apparently! – to Jeanne Valois, who I didn't even think he liked particularly, I just thought she was someone he knew. She was there, at dinner.'

Jeanne Valois was Anglo-French-Spanish-Swiss, her accent what-ever she wanted it to be, her looks vague enough that she could pass for a hundred other women in their extended social circle. She was the sort of woman people would have expected Henry to marry, if he did decide to remarry, but nobody thought he would. Hal had seen her at a wedding he had been forced to attend after Henry had begged off sick; she had dark long hair parted down the middle, and she'd been wearing a thin silk scarf and a silk jumpsuit with a plunging neckline, pale enough blue that at a distance one might have thought she was wearing white.

'They're engaged,' said John, as if Hal hadn't understood the phrase 'getting married'. Engaged was the most ambiguous word he could have used: engaged what? In a protracted legal dispute? At the moment, could you ring again later?

Scalding his tongue with his Americano, Hal said, 'I'm sure our mother will understand.'

'What about the living?'

'He has a right to get married, doesn't he? He's been alone for fifteen years. You complain about being single, and your balls only dropped five years ago.'

John said, 'It would have been decent of him to ask us first.'

Hal said, 'He didn't ask us if we wanted to be born.'

'Everyone wants to be born. He told me to tell you to come have lunch at his club today. At one.'

'It's a Friday, I've got my internship.'

'Two steps away from his club.'

'Why don't you come with me? You haven't ever been to his club, have you?'

'Yeah, well, no, because you're the only one he ever asks. If he wants to have lunch with me, he tells me to fetch him something from M&S. I can't come today, I'm just going to get my things from Dad's and then I'm going back up to Durham. I know you don't care, but the Union can't function without me.'

After John was gone, Hal stood in the front room in the cloud-dark daylight and reviewed the siblings' group chat. The last messages before the dinner had been:

🐔 20:13 is **@Hal** coming
🐔 20:14 **@Hal @Hal @Hal**
🐔 20:14 look at your phone **@Hal**
Humphrey Bogart 20:21 Haha last seen 17:36
Humphrey Bogart 20:22 He's not coming
Humphrey Bogart 20:22 Probably passed out somewhere getting bukkake'd by a bunch of homeless
Tom L 20:25 **@Humphrey Bogart** smoke after?
Humphrey Bogart 20:27 **@Tom L** you know it
Humphrey Bogart 20:28 Got the rolly on the wrist and nugs danker than your girlfriend's pussy last night

Then it started up again:

🐦 23:23 literally shattered right now like
🐝 23:23 i know
🐝 23:24 like what is happening
🐦 23:24 hahahaha **@Hal**
🐦 23:25 **@Hal** guess what

He scrolled to the most recent messages without reading the intervening ones, and found John and Humphrey talking about football. He looked at the boys' side chat and saw that the only thing anyone had sent in the last day was a link to a music video. Then he read back through the side chat that was just Hal and the girls, group name 'Single Ladies', and found his sisters engaged in an earnest discussion about how long their father had been seeing Jeanne Valois and why he had been doing it in secret, and whether Jeanne could be trusted if she hadn't at least made an effort to ingratiate herself with the family before allowing the engagement to be announced.

Hal 09:01 They were not in a secret relationship
Hal 09:02 He just asked her out of the blue because he was panicking about dying
🐦 09:02 is that what he told you
Hal 09:03 No he hasn't told me anything I just know exactly what happened
🐝 09:03 Hal where were you yesterday? Dad was a bit upset you didn't come

For April the temperature was high, and if there had been sun, the day would have been a pleasure. Instead, a maddening light rain chilled Hal's face and hands. He took the bus to Westminster, to a brown-brick building with red-brick trim around the windows, where he ascended the stairs and passed down a narrow, low-ceilinged corridor into the identical building adjacent, through white-painted wooden doors into a small office with grey nylon carpet and particle-board desks. The academics employed by the Institute seemed somehow never to be there; the only people in the office presently were the secretary – a middle-aged woman with bleached-blonde hair who commuted from Chelmsford – and the youngest real employee, a girl about Hal's age with fairly good looks and a tiresome fixation on the free market economy, which Hal suspected her to have adopted primarily in order to appeal to father figures. She issued a pained hello and he said, 'Don't worry, I'll have a long lunch.'

3

As Hal shook the rain off his umbrella, the porter on duty in the front hall of his father's club said, 'Lord Hereford, I'm afraid you've forgotten your jacket.'

This was another of the jokes Hal liked to play. He would arrive almost decently dressed, but without the requisite jacket and tie, and the porter, pretending to disapprove, would provide him with the club's spares, the tie a faded blue silk that probably dated back to about 1965, the jacket so large it would have been comical on any person smaller than Hal. Worn by someone else – an upwardly mobile millennial, habituated to informality, who had thought mandatory jackets went out with the twentieth century, or a maverick politician trying to see whether he really was above all the rules – these garments would have conferred some degree of shame. But Hal was who he was. The same rules applied to him as they did to anyone else, and he would face the same consequences as anyone else for breaking them. It was just that, on him, the consequences were charming.

The interior of Henry's club reminded Hal of one of those posh Wetherspoons that had been converted from an old bank, ballroom, or opera house, in which the original marble and gilding stood at odds with the institutional furniture, mass-produced and easily cleaned, purchased at the lowest possible price. There was a studied resemblance to a country house: the original Georgian panelling and the large gilt-framed pictures indicated that the shabby, sun-bleached carpet, the checked curtains and pleated lampshades, were not the result of poverty but of the need to distinguish this esteemed gentlemen's club, established in the time of Wellington and Napoleon, from the glitzy mixed-sex private clubs where they did not give a damn how many members you had known at school, or for how many centuries your family had been supporters of the Tories. Everyone had their place in life: you came here to be reassured that this was yours, that your presence here was a means of fulfilling your responsibility to maintain the order of the world, that you could not be faulted because you were simply doing what had been asked of you at birth.

The dining room was occupied only by a scanty few old men, and Henry. He sat at a table in the corner, tucked between a window and the fireplace. Here he looked especially young: he had recently turned forty-four and seemed, in his unfashionable black suit and blue dotted tie, as if he should be an upstart MP or City banker with one or two children under the age of ten. That was not to say that he was youthful. He had the insomniac's look of tiredness past tiredness, the widower's look of grief past grief.

Did Hal and his father look alike? Did they look like father and son? Henry's hair was darker and straighter than Hal's, parted to the side and combed back to show the grey that began at his temples and swept into the ordinary brown. He had thin, bowed lips and thin, dark eyes, and lines under his eyes and around his mouth that made him look respectable. Hal's eyes were big and blue; his mouth was fuller, his bottom lip hung foolishly. Some people – not Henry – told Hal that he looked like his mother. He didn't, he was just blond.

Henry said, 'I waited up for you last night.'

'You only told Tom to tell me to come. I thought if you really wanted me there, you'd have asked me yourself.'

'Would you have come if I had asked you?' asked Henry, guilelessly, as if he had never thought to ask before.

'No, I don't think so. But you could have just told me the news.'

'I tried to tell you. That was why I told Tom to tell you to come.'

'I didn't have to be there. You could have rung. You could have sent a postcard.'

Henry said, 'I've missed you.'

Physical revulsion started at Hal's extremities and crept inwards. Nausea passed through him, and dizziness followed. He couldn't swallow. He kept trying, and his throat kept catching. He sipped water and swallowed the wrong way and coughed. The only thing he could do was to start drinking again. He flagged down a waiter, one of the white-haired institutions who'd been there since the first time Grandfather John brought Henry as a guest, and ordered a double gin and tonic.

'We'll have wine with lunch,' Henry told Hal, as if that would somehow preclude a G&T.

Hal said, 'I should hope so.'

Lunch at the club had been elevated lately from 'public school under Second World War rationing' to a less intentionally punitive 'early noughties British food renaissance gastropub', so Hal could at least avail himself of a nice crab thermidor, which, after his second G&T and a glass of Riesling, he felt well enough to eat. Henry ordered a leek and potato pie that he didn't eat; he clawed the pastry open with a fork, pulling the innards out and pushing them about on the plate. He did drink the wine. He sometimes gave up drinking for Lent, if he felt he'd overindulged in the season before, but this year he had given up puddings and sweets, saying that at least his dentist ought to be pleased. He'd been lean at the beginning of March, and now he was thin, reporting headaches and fatigue, though not complaining: if you weren't suffering, Lent didn't count.

He said, 'I thought that this would be rather the best thing for us all. We'll get a decent injection of cash, and Jeanne will inherit property that's likely to appreciate. When she and I are dead it'll be yours, and you can do what you like without worrying about having to sell either of the houses. If I were to die before the younger ones are independent, I should hate for you to feel burdened in supporting them.'

'Are you going to have children?' asked Hal. 'With her?'

'No,' said Henry.

'What if it just happens, without you meaning to?'

'It won't.'

'Should I congratulate you?'

'You can congratulate me if you like. I don't expect it. You must know I've done it for you.'

Henry had married for love the first time, and look how that turned out. Now he was doing what he should have done all along, and marrying for money. It was the greatest blessing a man like Henry could have given to his heir: the freedom to take pleasure in his position, in the houses, in the land, in the thought of the future, in the thought of his own heir, without the fear that he might someday have to sell everything and rent a flat in SW9. Still Hal couldn't make himself thankful.

'Don't be a child,' said Henry. 'If I never married again, you'd have complained about that.'

'Well, congratulations.'

'I said don't be—'

'I'm not. I don't care. I'm happy for you to marry anyone. I'm sure she's happy.'

'Why wouldn't she be?'

'I wouldn't know,' said Hal.

He had approached the thermidor with too much confidence; he was feeling bad again. He drained his glass and let the waiter come round to pour another.

'No, thank you, that's enough,' said Henry. 'He'll have water.'

Hal said, 'No, I will have another glass, thank you.'

'No, you won't.'

'George, please, don't listen to my father, he doesn't know how to have fun.'

George politely afforded Hal a silence in which he could surrender to Henry's authority. Henry was the member; Hal, languishing on the waiting list until several more decrepit aristocrats and/or statesmen died off, was the guest, and it was not charming, even for him, to agitate against the rule of the person who had been so generous as to extend him access to this sacred seat of empire.

Hal reached across the table to take Henry's glass and finish it off for him, afterwards wiping his mouth with the sleeve of the loaned jacket. He said, 'My father needs another as well.'

Henry said, 'If you can't behave, you can go back to Camberwell.'

'You know Camberwell's actually quite posh?'

George was watching, prepared to eject Hal with prejudice, if it came to that. Having allowed his own glass to be filled again, Henry dismissed him. It was true that Henry was sometimes overfamiliar with waiters, but he would not let one of them discipline his son if he was there to do it himself.

'Come with us to the Easter Vigil,' Henry told Hal.

'Who do you mean, "us"?'

'All of you. The girls will be here on their holidays, and the boys will come down from university. And Jeanne will come.'

'I'm going to your wedding, isn't that enough?'

'If you won't come to the Easter Vigil, how will I know you'll come to the wedding? I should have thought Holy Week would be more important to you than your father's second marriage.'

'You don't know, you'll just have to see.'

'You know I've done it for you?'

'You've done it for the sake of our family. That's different from doing it for me.'

'There's more to oneself than—' Here Henry stopped, stymied by his own incapacity for language. 'There have always been things more important than ourselves,' he said. 'That's what Richard didn't understand. He was always turned inwards, looking at himself. Admiring himself for being the thing his father made him, then living in a way that foreclosed the possibility of his ever being a father himself. Instead he made a league of painted narcissists, a private army of grasping aesthetes who dressed just like he did and spoke just like he did and for all that they'd contributed to the world would have been better off stillborn.'

Could he not have come up with anything better than 'There have always been things more important than ourselves'? Wasn't that one of the things they said in Alcoholics Anonymous? Henry was so incapable, so infuriatingly unable to make sense of who he was and what he was doing, that the profoundest thing he could think to say was that there were things more important than ourselves. What was more important: heaven? England? The United Kingdom of Great Britain and Northern Ireland, which didn't even exist when the first Duke of Lancaster was ennobled?

Henry said, 'You have a brain, don't you? You didn't sneeze it out?'

'Umm, no, I didn't,' said Hal.

'You might use it. You're not waiting for your pension, you're meant to do something in the world.'

'What were you doing when you were my age?'

'I was raising you. I was managing the estate. We were in the black for the first time since about 1988.'

'You wouldn't let me take over the estate.'

'Your grandfather John was improvident. Be thankful I'm not.'

'Do you want me to get married, is that what it is? We could have a double wedding.'

'Harry, that's really enough. Please. I'd like it if you could be pleasant.'

Henry let George take his plate away. George posed no nosy questions about whether it had been to his liking, and when the little bald man in the red jacket pushed the pudding trolley around the dining room, he passed their table without stopping.

All actors smoked when they were drunk, even the ones who said they'd quit. Here, at a little house in Finchley belonging to one of Poins's more senior colleagues, the smokers had been exiled to the garden. They were standing now in a half-circle around a woman who'd had just enough wine to start gossiping about people more famous than her. Earlier she had been trapped in a corner with Hal and had had no recourse but to ask him, 'So do you act as well?' When he said he'd done a few plays at Oxford, she had gone through a list of about fifteen people she thought he might know, and when that was exhausted, she had tried, 'So what do you do now?' He had said he was at a think tank in Westminster, and her attention had gone out like a candle under a glass. Now Poins was pressing towards her, hoping that, somewhere out there, somebody at another party was gossiping about him.

Hal's phone buzzed in the back pocket of his chinos.

Tom L 00:25 Hal mate we need you
Tom L 00:25 And your good coke hookup
Tom L 00:25 Now
Tom L 00:29 A girl I've been talking to is here and she wants to know if anybody has anything decent because what her friends have got is shit please I'll pay for it
Tom L 00:29 I know you know someone
Tom L 00:30 She won't leave because her ugly friends are here alone
Hal 00:34 Ask one of the waiters, they always know
Tom L 00:35 I didn't know waiters could afford good coke lol
Hal 00:35 Are you afraid to talk to waiters? Just think of them as human beings, then it comes naturally.

Grabbing a nearly full bottle of wine, Hal said to Poins, 'Take a piss now if you've got to. We're going to Chelsea.'

'Where?'

'Come on, you've heard of it! Though I don't think they'll have heard of you . . .'

They sat on the top deck of the bus and shared swigs of the wine openly, daring the driver to boot them off. Poins's hip pressed against Hal's hip, Poins's knee pressed against Hal's knee. They were the image of masculine intimacy: two healthy young men who would look into each other's eyes and share a bottle of wine, but not kiss.

At Hyde Park Corner, they transferred buses. Hal drained the last of the wine and shattered the bottle on the pavement. Poins asked, 'Why don't you ever get an Uber, or a minicab? Or like a black cab?'

'Oh, it's so deadly expensive, I never take black cabs, and Uber drivers don't know where they're going, and I only get a minicab if I'm so drunk I don't trust myself not to end up in the bus depot.'

'But you're rich,' said Poins, making his way up the bus staircase.

As they reached the top, the bus rounded a corner and they swayed. Hal just avoided having to put his hand on Poins's shoulder.

'I never have any money. You know that. My father docked my allowance this month. I've got twenty quid in the bank.'

'You're going to be a—' Seeing the warning in Hal's face, he dropped his voice to a whisper. '*Literally a fucking duke.*'

They had had this conversation at Oxford, in Hal's rooms at Trinity, doing magic mushrooms. Hal didn't know why Poins wanted to have it again. He said, 'I'm not the Duke of Buccleuch! We're recusants: we lost everything in the Reformation, and we never really got it back. Nobody more famous than Jack Falstaff would give me the time of day.'

'Look, how much money do you spend on drugs every month? How much do you spend buying Jack's rounds?'

Hal would never, so long as he was alive, get out of being posh. He was the person his upper-middle-class acquaintances meant when they said, 'I'm not really posh, I know people who are so much posher than me.' Whether he was rich was a different matter. Rather than explain how quickly an income of £500,000 a year went when there were two houses, six children, and nearly 1,000 acres of land, he said, 'Fuck off.'

A handful of the partygoers were out on the pavement in front of the venue, smoking. Hal recognised half of them, including Harry Percy, who was the only person in the world Hal knew personally and felt inferior to. Percy was smiling at Hal. His teeth were straight and reasonably, not disturbingly, white. His brown hair was cutely curly, and he had a close-cropped ginger beard, which was new. He was shorter than Hal and taller than Poins, somewhere in that indeterminate range around five ten, and even with the beard he looked young. He would probably look like a stick of rhubarb when he was forty-five, but by then he'd be married with children, tremendously respectable. His only flaw was that he sometimes stuttered on the 'wuh' sound.

'Hal!' he cried. 'Oh gosh, it's you! I was just in there talking to Tom, but I didn't realise you were coming too. It's been so long since we've seen each other. I've been travelling – actually, I just got back from

India, yeah, I went back to Delhi for a few weeks just to catch up with friends. I'll be staying put for a while though, I'm starting an MA at SOAS in the autumn. My dad's raging about it, you have no idea, he's like, "You're throwing your youth away! You're throwing my money away!" Bit much, isn't it! I'm like, how many hours of your life have you spent watching *Top Gear*! Anyway, anyway. Hal! God, literally, how long has it been?'

They knew each other because their families knew each other: had known each other, for a long time. Percys and Lancasters had been imprisoned together during the Reformation, before the Percys cut their losses and conformed. In the 1750s, one Percy accrued such great debts gambling with a Lancaster that he had had to leave the country; he was at least a younger son. A hundred years later, another younger Percy son, an officer with the East India Company, nearly induced a Lancaster daughter to marry him. She broke off the courtship in favour of a Catholic, and he got back to India just in time for the rebellion of 1857. A hundred and thirty-five years after that, the newest Henry Percy was born, and Hal's mother wrote to Mrs Percy with congratulations, saying he and her own Harry were sure to be great friends. They might have been, if Mary had lived, but her widower found no use for Harry Percy except as a point of comparison to his perpetually disappointing eldest son. Harry Percy played rugby, Harry Percy got four A*s at A-Level, Harry Percy was elected to Pop. Harry Percy was polite, Harry Percy was hardworking, Harry Percy was charitable to the poor. Harry Percy got a place at Balliol on his own merit, while Henry had had to pull strings to get Hal into Trinity. They spent their years at Oxford trying to avoid each other, then pretending when inevitably they met at a ball or a bop or a bicycle rack that they were tremendously pleased to be seeing each other again. After they left – Percy with a 2:1 in Classics and Oriental Studies, Hal with a third in English, which he considered an accomplishment in its own right – Percy took a working tour through South Asia, teaching English and vlogging about climate justice, while Hal drank and avoided his father.

Hal pushed Poins forward and said, 'This is my mate Ed Poins, he's an actor.'

Poins said, 'Oh, no, I'm—Hi, oh, nice to—Yeah, what's up—'

'I know, I recognise you,' said Percy brightly. 'You were in that series from a while back—'

'The First World War one, yeah, I was, actually . . . Not a massive part, but so glad you had a chance to see it. What did you, uh . . . What did you think?'

'Oh, it was brilliant, it was great.' Percy's hand-rolled cigarette had burned down to the filter; he looked disappointed in it, and crushed it underfoot. 'Didn't they kill you off sort of early?'

'Yeah, the First World War killed off a lot of people early . . .'

'So what have you been up to?' Percy asked Hal. He was running his hands through his hair, shaking out his curls. 'Have you got round to doing anything yet?'

Hal said, 'Nothing so interesting as you.'

'Oh, I'm not that interesting really.'

When it was time to go in, Percy rested his hand very lightly against the middle of Hal's back. Hal didn't shake him off, but his shoulders went rigid. Maybe Percy was too drunk to notice, because he didn't let go. He put his mouth almost up against Hal's ear and yelled, 'It's so great to see you again!'

Hal yelled, 'Is it?'

'Yes,' yelled Percy. 'I hadn't heard from you in so long I was worried you were finally making something of yourself. I guess if you were, my dad would have told me about it.'

'Get your hand off my back!'

'Oh! Sorry!'

He couldn't have been too sorry. Before he withdrew his hand, he gave Hal's back three solemn pats, a devilish inversion of the penitent's three strikes to the breast: not *mea culpa, mea culpa, mea maxima culpa*, but *your fault, your fault, your own fucking fault*.

4

Hal was aware of Poins's head on his shoulder, and wondered whether they'd finally hooked up. He realised soon they were on the tube, thankfully clothed, aboveground in astonishing daylight, full and blue-green from the sky and the suburban foliage. He checked his phone and found that the screen was cracked and it wouldn't turn on.

'Poins, mate. Poins, where's your phone? I need to see what time it is. I've got my internship today.'

'Oh, oh, stop, you're shouting in my ear, that hurts. Where are we going?'

'I don't know. We're out at the end of the Northern line. Last stop was Burnt Oak, next is Edgware.' Hal fished Poins's phone out of his jacket pocket. 'It's past eight. Your phone's on 13 per cent battery.'

'Stop using it then. Literally why are we here?'

'I don't know, you're the one who lives in North London. Were you trying to take me home with you? I don't know if your mum would have liked that. By the way, you've got a lot of missed calls from her.'

'Oh, fuck, what day is it?' Poins seized his phone from Hal's hands. His panic made Hal laugh. 'Oh, I'm an idiot, I'm such a cunt. I've told Ellie I'd pick her up from Luton. Why are we on the Edgware branch? We should've gone to High Barnet.'

Poins told Hal he could go home if he liked, but Hal told him no, he didn't mind tagging along. In the passenger seat of Mrs Poins's sensible supermini, Hal plugged his phone into the adapter in the cigarette lighter socket and found that it turned on, the screen filling with the notifications he had missed the night before.

'Poins,' said Hal, slipping off his brogues and putting his feet on the dashboard. 'Do you remember much about what happened after we got to the second party?'

'The thing in Chelsea? What don't you remember about it? I thought you were lucid the whole time.'

'Did we ever meet up with Tom?'

'Yeah, do you really not remember that? He was getting his end away with some girl who I think said she's a fashion student at Central Saint Mar—'

'Don't! Don't tell me anything about Tom's freakish little relationships, he's so straight, it's unaccountable.'

'You told him all about how awful he was for bringing you there and not even wanting you any more when you got there. I had to make small talk with the girl and she was a snob, like, she was clearly like, *Who is this short cunt and why does he think he's allowed to look at me?*'

'My brothers have terrible taste in girls. I don't know why I enable them. I think I must want them to be unhappy. But did you not actually have a good time? Wasn't there an open bar?'

'Yeah, but I'm twenty-two, I'm basically a corpse. I can't drink like that any more.'

'You're still standing . . .'

'I'm sitting. Do you remember doing shots with your friend, uh, Harry?'

'I can't believe I agreed to do shots with him. Percy's not my friend. I hate him. We've known each other since we were born and I've hated him the whole time. Did he make me?'

'You made *him*. You demanded to go five for five and wouldn't shut up till he said yes. Then you had a fight in the smoking section. You went down and rolled about on the ground with him, and Tom had to argue with the door guy to make him let you back in.'

'Ah, that's class. What did we fight about?'

'No idea. I was talking to somebody else. Look, there she is. Don't say anything about drinking in front of my sister, she's innocent.'

'What? Does she not know about drinking?' As Ellie flung herself into the back seat, Hal said, 'You drink, don't you, Ellie?'

Poins said, 'How was Prague?'

'Yes, I drink,' said Ellie. 'I was drinking in Prague. Why, have you got something for me?'

'No,' said Poins, 'absolutely not.'

Smiling at Ellie in the rear-view mirror, Hal said, 'Ed and I were on the lash last night.'

Ellie said, 'I know, I can smell you, you smell really bad. He's still mad because I grassed on him once when I was twelve, I told our mum he was the one who'd been leaving fag ends in the bushes in the garden.'

'It wasn't just me, I keep telling you—'

'You were killing all the plants.'

Poins said, 'The funny thing is, Hal, I think Harry thinks you're best mates? Did you not notice he kept introducing you to people he knew? Like he wanted them to know he knew you? Even after you fought him?'

'Yeah, I saw the fifteen follow requests on Instagram. It's not that he wants them to know he knows me because he's proud of knowing me, it's so that they can compare us and find him superior.'

'You were flirting with all of them, it was embarrassing.'

'I have to show Percy I can fuck his friends if I like.'

'Stop, not in front of Ellie. So is he straight, or—'

'Oh, he's the worst, he's one of those types who's always inserting himself into discussions about gay marriage or whatever to talk about how bicurious he is. Like, "You know, I really think I could fall in love with anyone? Like, it's a person's soul I fall in love with, not what's between their legs?" But he's only ever dated girls. I think the biggest scandal he's ever had is when he dated some Russian oligarch's daughter and then she thought he cheated on her but he didn't really. He kept seeing this other girl for Hindi lessons and his girlfriend was like, "Yeah, sure, *Hindi lessons*," but that was actually what it was.'

The brief impression of Percy made Poins laugh. Feeling that doing a routine would take his attention off how much his head hurt, Hal cleared his throat and said, 'Yeah, Percy's like—Oh my God, you should hear him talk about his ethically sourced meat. He's like, "You know, I think in our society w-we've rally lost that connection with the things that we eat? Like but the things that we eat *are* us, lichrally? It's like, this pork belly, it's delicious, right? Yah, but it was an intelligent creature once, right? And it's not like I'm vegan or anything – I'm from the North, not LA, ha ha – and atchy industrialised agriculture is one of the most harmful things for the ecosystem?"'

Poins was still laughing, so Hal kept going: he never let a joke understay its welcome. 'I'm just saying w-we could stand to learn from all the people who have like, a real, spiritual connection with every meal they eat, because they've atchy killed the animal with their bare hands? You know I butchered a chicken once on my uncle's farm, and it rally does make the meat taste so much better? I just w-wish these hand-wringing PETA types would understand that eating ethically isn't just about salad? It's about how our whole society is founded on a misunderstanding of our natural relationship with the land?'

In the rear-view mirror, Hal saw Ellie staring stone-faced down at her phone. He said, 'Ellie doesn't think I'm funny.'

Ellie said, 'Impressions aren't funny unless you know the person.'

'I could introduce you if you wanted.'

'No, thanks.'

Hal and Jeanne met for the first time after the engagement at brunch. Hal disliked anything that prevented him from spending the afternoon sleeping, and Jeanne had chosen the worst sort of place, glossy and modern, patronised chiefly by foreign women who put twenty-four-carat gold plating on everything they owned. But there was a full bar, and he really hadn't got any money. He could keep his drunk going for a bit longer, and if Jeanne didn't like it, she could ask his father to foot the bill. When the waitress came, Hal said, 'A Bloody Mary, please, and double the vodka in that, if you could possibly?'

Jeanne didn't mind the early drinking; she had been one of Richard's set, she must have known what it was like, though she was above it all now. She didn't even drink coffee – she had a mucky green vegetable juice. That must have been why Henry had chosen her, because she was used to deprivation.

Without trying to hide it from Jeanne, Hal took out his phone and texted Philippa:

Hal 13:12 I was 20 min late and still here earlier than you you fucking traitor

🐓 13:13 yeh sorry im a disaster!!! im on my way give her my apologies etc xxxxx

'Philippa says to say she's sorry but she's just getting out of bed, she spent all night at the strip club.' He took the straw out of his Bloody Mary and drank from it like it was a glass of water, then tongued off the salt that had stuck to his bottom lip. 'It must be a great pain for you, actually, having to deal with all of us when what you really wanted was our father. One or two children is alright – people marry people with one or two children all the time – but six seems like a bit much these days, doesn't it? I don't know whether it's climate change or abortion that makes us feel that way.'

Jeanne took that very well. She didn't laugh, but she looked amused. She said, 'I'd like to be friendly with you all the same.'

'Me particularly, or all of us?'

'Oh, all of you,' she said, 'but I suppose you're in the unlucky position of being the only one who lives in London and has enough time on his hands to go to lunch with me. Though your father has told me you like to disappear sometimes.'

'Whatever bad things my father's told you about me,' said Hal, 'it's all absolutely true. I've been a nightmare. He's always telling me how ashamed my mother would be, and I expect that's true, but I don't think I'd be much different if she were here to tell me herself.'

Jeanne said, 'Sometimes you see fathers that are absolute mirror images of their sons. Not physically – I mean in terms of their manner, and habit. I was surprised that you and your father aren't like that at all.'

'When my father's cross with me, he tells me I'm like Richard.'

'I don't think you are.'

'You were a friend of Richard's, weren't you?'

'We knew each other. I think I admired him, and he tolerated me, but that was how he liked his friendships. Your father knew him better than I did. Of course, they were cousins.'

'When I was at school, he would come up and take me to lunch in York and make me speak French with him. He would always tell me not to tell my father, but I think he told him himself, because whenever I saw Dad, he would let me know he knew I'd seen Richard. Then he'd tell me about all the bad things Richard had done. Do you remember Edward Langley? Dad says that when Richard got ill for the last time, Edward rang Dad and told him to go to hell.'

'Henry did tell me that Richard was fond of you,' said Jeanne. 'I think that if he were going to marry anyone, after Mary, it would have had to have been someone who knew those people, and understood what things were like then. I knew Edward Langley too. He was the only one I would have said was a good friend of Richard's.'

Hal felt the impulse to tell her about Henry the way he felt the impulse to scream while the priest was saying mass, or to leap in front of trains as they pulled into the station. He felt that it was God telling him to do it, that God wanted him to do it, that in resisting he was directly disobeying Him, at great risk to his soul. Do it, do it, say it, say it – God's voice in his head sounded like his own voice, the same as any other thought. The longer he said nothing, the more impossible the thought of saying anything became. There was so much else. There was the glass on the table, the wallet and keys in his trouser pockets, the phone with its screen still cracked, the packet of cigarettes and the lighter, the ring on Jeanne's finger. There was a sore on his tongue where he'd bitten it, but besides that nothing hurt him, or bothered him at all. He was content; he would say nothing. At mass he had said, and would say again, 'I confess to almighty God, and to you, my brothers and sisters, that I have greatly sinned, in my thoughts and in my words, in what I have done and in what I have failed to do . . .'

'I'm so, so, so-o sorry,' said Philippa, settling into the seat next to Hal in a whirl of over-brushed yellow hair. 'I would give you an excuse, but the truth is embarrassing, so you'll just have to trust that I really didn't mean to be so late. Did you already order? I haven't eaten at all today, and I was in the studio for five hours this morning, so I'm like, empty. I want a cocktail too, Hal. What do you have, is that a Bloody Mary? So gross, I hate the scent of tomato juice.'

As they were parting, Jeanne asked them if they'd like her to order them a car to wherever they were going next. Philippa said, 'No, I'm just walking back to Dad's, it isn't far. Isn't that where you're going?'

'No,' said Jeanne, 'I've got a few things to take care of. Tell him I said hello.'

Philippa asked Hal to walk with her. Hal, needing an excuse to reject Jeanne's offer, agreed. It was a fine day. He took his jacket off and folded it over his arm, and Philippa, whose skin was practically unpigmented, developed a pink sheen. She looked very young, and very sweet, in her tie-dyed t-shirt and pale pink rain jacket, the hood of it flopping behind her in a rude display of its own present uselessness. The flesh of her cheeks was thick and mobile, like a baby's healthy fat. She let the people on the pavement part to accommodate her. In the sunlight, she took on a reflective brightness; in the shade of freshly leafed trees, the green seemed to soak into her skin. How could she have the same mother and father as Hal? In some ways, she had it worse than he did: Philippa was the only one who had never known their mother even slightly. Hal sometimes prayed for them to switch places, then begged God not to do it, he didn't mean it, he would never do that to her.

'So she's really—' Philippa was talking about Jeanne. 'So she's really quite wealthy actually, which I'm not sure is a good thing, even if it does mean we've got enough money to keep the houses going, because if she spends anything on us we'll have to do things for her if she asks. And is she even a Catholic?'

'Of course she is.'

'Well, if she wasn't, he'd make her convert, and that never goes well. Converting just makes people annoying. I ha-ate converts. If I marry someone, they've either got to be Catholic or not Christian at all, and then I'll convert to their religion. Like, I could marry a Jewish person, or a Hindu . . . Do they think their converts are annoying?'

They were stood at a crossing somewhere west of Buckingham Palace. There were no lights at the crossing, no cars approaching, no people on the pavement. The streets around them were mostly residential, holdovers from the Georgian era, intermittently given interest by odd businesses: a chemist with a storefront from the 1920s, a wine and spirits shop, a little independent market with a bizarre selection of food and sundries (plastic-wrapped lumps of 'fine cheeses', £25 jars of pickles imported from Germany, canned veg that was always expired, a truly subpar selection of cigarettes). Then there was the local pub, which dated back to the early nineteenth century and now was run by the same corporation that ran every other pub. This was Henry's territory. He had travelled when he was young, but his world was small now, and when he was in one of his black moods, he would refuse to go further than two streets' distance from the house.

'Will you come in and say hello to Dad?' Philippa knew he didn't want to, and she hadn't wanted to ask. She had her own little Philippa things to do, like hamsters have things to do, tearing up paper and running on wheels. She was only in London on exeat, and had to make the most of her time. So it was really a mercy to herself when she said, 'No, I won't make you, don't worry.'

She went on alone. Down the street, Hal saw his father's house, which even at that distance he could imagine himself inside and a part of, continuous with the worn stair runners and the spiderwebs in the cellar, the uneven floors and the warped eighteenth-century window glass. The house was his body outside of his body, and if he had a choice not to go into his body, he wouldn't do that either.

5

On the second day of May, the first Friday of the month, Hal's current account was overdrawn by £291.13, including £120 of fees that had accumulated with each charge past the limit. He used a credit card over the weekend, thinking that the usual £1,500 would be in his account by Monday, and then it wasn't. He made a joke of it with Jack and Poins – 'Yeah, he's terminated my contract on a morals clause' – and paid their tab on credit again. Had he not been good enough? He'd attended the Easter Vigil, sober and pious; on Good Friday he'd gone to Westminster for his internship, then stopped at St Edward's to do the Stations of the Cross.

On 10 May, Hal went to the corner shop for cigarettes and a Lucozade, and his cards were declined. He paid with the last £20 he'd got in cash, then sat on a bench on Eel Brook Common, circled by nannies pushing prams and middle-aged women walking toy dogs off-leash, while a whole lot of vocationless Sloanes (*and why seest thou the mote that is in thy brother's eye*) tried to sunbathe on the grass even though the sun was out only intermittently.

When Henry answered Hal's call, he said, 'You've been avoiding me.'

'Yeah, I've been, uh, I've been a bit . . .'

'I don't want to punish you. But I don't know any other way to get you to talk to me.'

'You're talking to me now. What do you want?'

'I'd like to see you. I haven't seen you in so long.'

'We just saw each other at Easter.'

'A few weeks is a long time.'

'I saw you once every few weeks from the ages of eight to twenty-one, I don't know what's different now.'

'You were doing what was asked of you. Now what are you doing? Don't answer, I'll tell you. 1 May: £63.46, Boar's Head Pub. £150 cash advance. £16.13, Golden Doner. £27.30, Denmark Off-Licence. 2 May: £7.17, Costa Coffee. £47.26, Boar's Head. £38.40, Deliveroo. £13.08, Denmark Off-Licence. 3 May: £4.12, Chelsea Coffee House. £36.25, Boar's Head. £29.32, Denmark—'

'What do you want me to do? I haven't had my allowance since March.'

'You and your brothers are bleeding me dry. But at least your brothers spend it decently. I'd hate to know where all those cash advances are going.'

'Fresh fruit and veg from the farmers' market. Not my fault it's five quid for one aubergine.'

'Don't be funny. Why don't you come see me this afternoon?'

'Lunch at your club?'

'No, I'm not going out, I'm not fit for it. I haven't been sleeping. Last week I took my tablets and got into bed, and when I woke up I was sitting with two policemen in the drawing room. They told me I'd gone out barefoot and tried to get a room at The Cadogan. I'd left the front door open. Thank God no one came in.'

'Did you talk to Dr Bradmore?'

'He told me not to take those ones any more, and I said I don't know what I can possibly do if I don't, I've tried all the sleeping pills there are in the world. He said that I'm not getting enough exercise. Well, how can I, when I feel like this?'

'If I come, you'll feel worse.'

'I won't force you.'

'No, of course not.'

'But I haven't got anyone else. The rest of you are at school . . .'

'You could always try your fiancée.'

'Better if Jeanne doesn't see me like this, yet.'

'I'm glad you care so much about her.'

'You aren't jealous, are you?'

Hal said, 'Not at all. There but for the grace of God go I.'

He didn't go to see Henry. He sold one of his wristwatches at a 'cash for gold' shop and placed an order with his cheapest dealer. In the evening, he went to the Boar's Head and pretended he didn't know his cards would be declined, and when the manager told him they were, he wheedled and flattered and reminded her how loyal a patron he'd been this past year and a half. Between the hours of about 9 p.m. and 4 a.m., Hal felt greater pleasure than any man on this wretched earth had a right to feel. Across the river, Henry was alone and sleepless, and Hal was here in South London, happy. Then the pubs closed, the clubs closed, the tube stopped running. Golden Doner closed, Denmark Off-Licence closed. In spring, the sun rose earlier and earlier. The night buses turned back into day buses; the tube started running again. In the twenty-four-hour Tesco, the floor was cleaned, the expired perishables binned, the shelves restocked; the night shift ended and the day shift began. What was Hal going to do with himself? Who would listen to what he said? Who would laugh?

Hal stayed at Jack's until the snoring was too much to bear, then slammed one last can of Stella and wandered out into the street to find it filled with people working to keep the world spinning: boarding buses that would take them to their jobs in Central, rolling up the shutters on their shopfronts, putting on their high-vis jackets and recommencing the never-ending roadworks. They had so little choice. There was money to be made, there were bills to be paid, children to be fed, lights to be kept on, roofs to be kept over heads. The bus was pulling away as Hal arrived at the stop, and instead of waiting for the next one he kept walking, up past Elephant and Castle, across Lambeth Bridge, from which he saw the London Eye and the Palace of Westminster looking small and dull under the grey sky. Once he was across the river, he was only one of an endless ebb and flow of blue Oxford shirts. The buildings got taller and newer and shinier; red brick broke away into green-tinted glass reflecting the façades opposite. The pavements below were empty: was there actually anybody here? Hal felt that if he broke through the glass he would find nothing behind it. He took a right onto Grosvenor Place, where a brick wall topped with concertina wire marked the western boundary of the Buckingham Palace Garden, and just like that he was faced with the brown brick and white stucco of godforsaken fucking Belgravia.

His father's house was one of the white stucco ones, with wide shallow stone steps leading up to the front door. It had not been in the family since the Georgian era. It had not been in the family fifty years ago, and was unlikely to be in the family in fifty years' time. Grandfather John had bought it in 1972, out of the pure, petty need to prove that a younger son could be grander than the eldest. Henry had spent his earliest years in a mews house in South Kensington. Now nobody owned property here but foreign governments and foreign billionaires, and Henry, bemoaning the expenses that the house thrust upon him, had little choice but to let it fall into disrepair. The black paint on the door was peeling, the brass knocker and handle were tarnished. Hal was moving towards the door like he would move towards the stench of something dead, certain of what he would find and pleading with himself to overcome the impulse to find it. He could not overcome anything: he undercame, like you did when you were swimming in the ocean and got dragged beneath by a powerful wave. He let himself in.

The scent of the house was perceptible now; it hadn't been when Hal was young. It smelled like old upholstery and old wood, and whatever sprays and polishes the cleaners used. Hal was damp under his arms and in the dip of his lower back and in the middle of his chest, and the damp was richly scented like soil, nose-curlingly ripe. He was aware, moving through the house, of the foreignness of his own scent against that of the house. Beneath the runner, the stairs creaked; Hal hadn't taken off his loafers. The door to Henry's bedroom was ajar.

Hal knocked once with the back of his hand. 'It's me,' he said.

Henry said, 'I thought it might be.'

'Had you been expecting me?'

'Stop talking at me from behind the door. Come in.'

Entering, Hal saw Henry turning away from one of the windows, having just untied the sash and let the thick dark curtains fall. A line of light shone between them. The curtains on the other window were open still, letting the raw springtime light fall across the bed. There was always the same knitted blanket; there were holes in it through which Hal saw the pinstriped sheet beneath. Henry wore a clean white shirt, ironed but not starched, tucked into pleated grey trousers. No belt, no braces, no shoes. His socks were black, so worn at the heels that the skin showed through.

'I've got a terrible headache,' said Henry. 'I was going to see if I could sleep, now that the sun is up.'

'Philippa told me you were upset I didn't come to see you when I dropped her off this weekend, so I thought I would come. Are you upset I'm here now?'

'No, I'm not, I'm not upset at all. I only wonder why it is that I have to send for you in order to speak with you.'

'You don't; I'm here.'

'After how many weeks of begging? Look at you, you look like a heroin addict on a Glasgow street corner. You've sweated through your shirt. Go, pour yourself a glass of water and drink it, and then pour another one and sip it slowly. And take a paracetamol. I won't send you away until you look decent.'

Down on the lower ground floor, in the kitchen, pouring himself a glass of water, Hal felt as if some intangible touch was bending the fine soft hairs on the insides of his arms, the nape of his neck, his cheeks. If Henry told him to be good, to stop drinking, to do something with himself, Hal would deny him, laugh at him, at his incapacity to make his son do anything. The small, gentle orders – 'Pour me a drink', 'Bring me my reading glasses', 'Brush your hair', 'Straighten your collar' – Hal obeyed. Drinking water did make him feel less unwell. He checked his phone, saw nobody had messaged him since he had last checked it, and left it on the counter next to his twice-emptied glass.

Henry was at the top of the stairs, leaning against the doorframe, blocking Hal's passage into the hall. He had undone the first two buttons of his shirt, and his vest was visible in the newly opened space. His hair was slipping down his forehead.

'I thought you must have been sneaking a drink,' said Henry.

Hal blew a gust of breath into Henry's face. 'Smell. I'm innocent.'

'You do still smell like you've been drinking. And smoking: that covers up the scent of the alcohol a bit.'

'I can't help what I've already done.'

'No, of course not.'

Hal angled his shoulder to press past Henry, and was allowed to go as far as a step into the hall before Henry, agile, caught him by the upper arm and arranged him so that his back was against the wall. The small bump of the wainscoting pressed into the backs of his thighs, and he thought of *The Princess and the Pea*. Henry's hands were strong; the points where his fingers pressed into the soft flesh of Hal's arm actually hurt.

'If I died today,' said Henry, 'which I very well might, you wouldn't have the slightest idea what to do. You would spend the very little money we have left on things that pleased you, and you wouldn't know how to replace it. You would be taken advantage of. You would put us in debt, you would have to sell Monmouth, you would have to sell this house, you would make a fool of yourself in front of people who would be deliriously happy to see you do it. And when you died, there would be nothing left for your own children. If you did have children: if you didn't leave the world like Richard did.'

Hal said, 'I'd marry a rich girl, just like you're doing now.'

Henry said, 'Who would have you?'

He had let go of Hal's arm; there was nothing holding Hal in place but a sense that he should be here, his shoulders and the back of his head against the wall, his mouth slightly open. Hal tried to look at Henry's face and saw nothing but a projection of his own as Henry saw it: the hanging bottom lip, the pale cheeks with the mottled red in them, the translucent eyelashes, the blue eyes that seemed less like windows than opaque and insensate flesh, no better at absorbing and comprehending the world than his liver or his spleen. When Hal was alone, he heard the clamour of all the voices of the people he knew, the things he had been told or overheard, things that had humiliated or troubled him, an errant remark or a play on words or a Freudian slip. Here, with Henry, it was silent, almost. The enormous, half-broken radiators clanked erratically; a car passed by on the street. No lights were on in the hall, but there was thin bluish sun coming through the fanlight above the front door. Hal looked at the door and then back at Henry. He knew this was his father, there was nobody else who could be his father, but Henry was still someone else. In dreams, other people seemed like other people, even though they were only presences you'd invented without knowing it. Was waking life like that, or was it inverted, so that your self was only a branch of the same substance that made everything else up? Hal felt like he was sleeping now. Henry was wiping the corner of Hal's mouth with his thumb.

Hal said, 'I'm going to be better than you think I am.'

'How would you know? How would I?'

'You don't trust me?'

Leaning close, Henry said, 'Never mind. I don't want to hear you promise anything. I've heard enough. I've had enough from you.'

Henry's breath touched the thin colourless little hairs that ran from Hal's nape to his collar. Hal's blood moved: his fingers and toes went clumsily numb, his face glowed hot, his prick was hard in the miserable way it sometimes had been during morning prayers at school, or when a doctor listened to his lungs with a stethoscope pressed to his bare skin. Hal was giving Henry what, silently, he had been asked for. They breathed in an alternating rhythm, one taking the breath the other had just given up; they tilted towards each other like a reflection of a reflection, always a step behind itself, fading into the green-grey of the silver mirror backing.

Whatever he felt, Hal knew, Henry felt the inverse: Henry felt the skin of Hal's neck against his lips, the click of his fingernails on Hal's trouser button. He felt the warm delicate skin of Hal's prick against his palm, and the subtle contortions of Hal's muscles as they tensed, loosened. Hal wasn't sure if what he felt was pleasure, or what pleasure was. The back of his head scraped against the wall, his heels lifted off the tiles. He came; Henry wiped his hand on Hal's shirttail and took Hal's chin in his hand.

'You can stay here,' said Henry, 'as long as you like.'

Hal badly wanted not to speak. He said, 'No, it's alright, I'll go.'

'I'd like it if you stayed.' Henry pulled his fingers through Hal's hair, setting it as straight as he could. He cupped the back of Hal's head and kissed his forehead; Hal bent to allow it.

'Sorry,' said Hal.

'No, no.' Henry was letting him loose, turning him towards the door. 'You've your own life now; I know that.'

The Saturday after, Hal went to confession at a church he'd never been to before. He picked one far from home and well attended, so that the priest wouldn't know him or any other Lancaster. He would be dealt with efficiently, given his penance and absolved and blessed and sent away. Henry would have considered this dishonest, but Hal believed that who your confessor was, and how long he spent with you, was not any of God's concern. He hoped also that God would understand why he had to lie a little bit, just by omission or misrepresentation. This was a lesson he had learnt early on. After the first few times, after several confessions had come and gone without him mentioning it, Hal told the truth to his school chaplain during the once-per-term mandatory confession. The chaplain had told him that he was being hurt, and that he should tell someone else, his house master or the school nurse. Hal was fourteen and disgusted to his very core: he had gone to be given penance, not to be told he hadn't sinned in the first place. He had let it happen, he had kept letting it happen, he had felt pleasure. When he was twelve, before it started, he had gone to Father Dyer to confess before Easter and said he'd been thinking impurely of men, and Father Dyer had made him pray a whole rosary.

This time he went to a church in Richmond. Making his way down the District line, he kept thinking: *Highbury bore me. Richmond and*

Kew undid me. Wasn't Eliot an Anglo-Catholic? Ugh! It did occur to Hal that if he weren't a Catholic he wouldn't be spending his Saturday going to Richmond, but he believed in the one true Church, like his father, like his father's father and all the fathers before him, all the way back to when the Viking invaders of Normandy gave up paganism. Hal wondered what the first Christian in the direct line would think of him: this effete, unscarred boy, kneeling before a wooden screen and making the Sign of the Cross.

It had been some weeks since his last confession, and he had all the usual sins to cover: drinking, drugs, sexual fantasies, masturbation, lies, gossip, snobbery, a lack of charity towards the poor and vulnerable, failure to attend mass, disobedience towards authority, a refusal to forgive the wrongs done against him even as he did wrong against others and expected to be forgiven. Appended to such a list, the confession that he had engaged in a sexual act with a man who was 'like his father' must have been unsurprising. So it was a little bit of a lie, but it was also more true, in its way, than it would have been if he'd said it was, actually, his father. Fathers were just imitations of God, imperfect likenesses, like Aretha Franklin was like a natural woman, like Madonna was like a virgin. And Hal was sorry: that was true. The priest gave him five Hail Marys and five Our Fathers, and Hal said the usual: 'O my God, I am heartily sorry for having offended Thee, and I detest all my sins because of Thy just punishments, but most of all because they offend Thee, my God, who art all good and deserving of all my love.'

The afternoon was overcast, but fairly warm and not yet raining. Hal walked through Richmond Park. He bought a ninety-nine from a van with a queue longer than the one for confession – state of the world, eh? – and watched the deer, who seemed, today, restless and disinclined to laze. There were a few new fawns keeping close to their mothers, small enough still that their heads barely peeked above the tall grasses, and Hal thought of how many fawns, freshly birthed, must have been hidden in the brush, waiting to be led out into the frightening, incomprehensible world.

6

The next time Hal heard from his father was in June, the day before the fifteenth anniversary of his mother's death, and he heard from him only indirectly. Hal was drunk and mildly stoned, slouching in a lumpy faux-leather booth and tearing up a paper napkin. His phone, face-up on the table, lit up and buzzed.

Tom L 20:25 Hal are you really not coming to the memorial mass?
Hal 20:27 I don't know maybe why?
Tom L 20:28 Dad wants to know if you meant it or if it's just something you're saying

The phone buzzed again:

Unknown 20:30 Heya Hal it was brilliant to see you the other night! Mate of mine is having some people over tonight at her place in Dalston and I thought you might want to stop by for a bit. Lots of alcohol and we can properly catch up so let me know. Xx
Hal 20:30 Is this Harry Percy? How did you get this number?
Unknown 20:31 You gave it to me ages ago at uni I think!!

Unable to suppress it, Hal fired back a text that just read '!!'

Unknown 21:34 Here's the address . . . I probably won't be there until past 11 as I've got a dinner thing but it would be fantastic to see you. So sorry I'm so shit at keeping up with people as I'm out of the country so often but I'm sort of trapped here as long as I'm at SOAS so I thought I should start making friends in London again haha

Hal typed, 'Have you ever thought you should go fuck yourself', then backspaced and sent, 'Ya cheers mate', and told Tom to go fuck himself instead.

The party was in a ground-floor flat in a converted terrace house from the mid twentieth century, when they had abandoned the neoclassical pretence and just gone in for the unremarkable brown-box look. There was a flag in the window Hal didn't recognise, and about eight bicycles chained to the railing in front. The flat had obviously been decorated by young people with a limited budget and an indifferent sense of interior design: multicoloured fairy lights were thumbtacked along the walls, and the bay window in the sitting room displayed a collection of well-chewed cat toys. The cat was nowhere in sight. Hal emptied the dregs from an abandoned cup, refilled it with two inches of vodka and a splash of flat Sprite, and knocked it back quickly enough that he wasn't forced to taste it, which was also how he dealt with cum.

After he filled his cup again, he went in search of the toilet, which was easily found and unsurprisingly locked. He pounded on the door and said, 'Can you please hurry up in there, I'm about to shit myself, I swear to God.'

Two girls with too-short fringes opened the door and looked him over. He loomed over them, smiling. He said, 'Just joking, I actually need in because I'm going to take drugs. But you can stay and do lines with me if you want.'

'We're lesbians,' one of them said.

'Well, I don't think that ever stopped anyone from having sex for drugs, but you're safe, I'm gay.'

'Don't take the piss.'

'I'm not! I'm actually gay. I know what Fleet is and everything. But I'm seriously gagging for a line right now. You can stay or not, just let me in.'

He doubted that they liked him any better than they did before, but nobody liked Hal when they first met him unless it was a man who wanted to fuck him or a girl who wanted to marry him. The girls let him in and locked the door again, and together they did lines off the toilet seat cover.

'So who are you?' the shorter-haired girl asked him. She had a septum piercing with a fuck-off great fake sapphire; Hal stared directly at it while she spoke to him.

'I'm Hal,' he said.

'Oh, are you Hal Lancaster?'

'Maybe?'

'No, it's just, we've heard about you from Harry Percy.'

'What, was Percy chatting shit about me? What did he say?'

'Well, Harry is one of those people who, like, never actually says anything bad about anyone, you know? So even when they're slagging someone off you can't really call them out on it without looking like a bitch.'

'Who cares if you look like a bitch?' Hal bent down and did a line through the cheap metal straw he'd bought, along with some poppers, at a head shop. The straw had been gold when he first got it, but the paint was flaking off. He wondered how much paint he'd inhaled.

'That's what she says,' said the longer-haired one. 'I always try and then it doesn't come off and people actually start hating me.'

Feeling suddenly very funny and insightful, Hal said, 'If people hate you, it means they're thinking about you, and either they spend all their time thinking about how they hate you, or they start liking you and hate that they start liking you. Either way the power's in your hands, because they secretly want your approval and hate themselves for it. Is that not true? That all the people who hate you really just want you to like them?'

The shorter-haired one said, 'Do you secretly like all the people you hate?'

'No, but I'm different.'

Someone's fist thumped on the door; there was muffled impatient speech. Hal rolled his eyes and said, 'I'm going out for a fag.'

The little garden behind the house had collected the overspill from the flat: on the small circular metal table, a dozen plastic cups lay half-empty, some with fag ends floating in the abandoned drink. The only light came from the windows facing the garden. Hal and the two girls spoke to one another's silhouettes. Smoking gave him something to do with his hands, but he was high and so restless it was uncomfortable, like an itchy jumper or an unwanted erection. His muscles twinged with tension, his nose felt like there was snot stuck in it, there was a pressure in his groin and he wasn't sure if it was arousal or the need to piss or nervousness. He ashed his cigarette so hard that the filter broke off; he burnt his thumb when he lit another. In the middle of a self-deprecating anecdote about the last time he went to a gay club, someone put a hand on his shoulder and he flinched like there had been a snap of static electricity.

Percy was there, wearing a t-shirt with a V-neck so deep it showed his chest hair, which was sparse and ginger like his beard. His arms were toned, his wrists and forearms streaked with long veins. He wore a wooden beaded bracelet on his left wrist. He said, 'Ah, I didn't know you knew Fern and Siobhan!' It was as if he genuinely found it delightful when people he knew also knew each other.

'We don't,' said the shorter-haired girl. 'He just started talking to us, and we haven't been able to get him to shut up.'

'This is Hal,' said Percy. 'Yeah, we were actually at uni together. Actually, he acts, he did a really great turn in *The Importance of Being Earnest*. Fern does theatre' – he was looking at the short-haired girl – 'but it's actually really experimental, black-box stuff, you know, not exactly Wilde, or like, wild as in jungle but not Wilde as in Oscar, ha ha. And Siobhan is a textile artist, amazingly talented, she actually has an installation up in the, uh, what was it, I'm so sorry—'

'The East London Women's Library,' said Siobhan cheerfully. 'It's only temporary, until August, so if you get a chance . . .'

'Oh, yeah,' said Hal, 'that's your favourite spot, Percy. Every time I meet you, you're like, "Sorry, got to run, need to drop by the East London Women's Library and return this copy of *The Well of Loneliness*." You two are his friends, you tell me: does this sort of thing get him laid?'

'I don't know,' said Fern, 'we try not to pay attention to what straight people do.'

Knowing that to resist was vulgar and would make him look worse, Percy bore the teasing with a smile. He said, 'Well, I'm single at the moment, so that should please you.'

'It does. I hope you're alone forever.' Fern tossed her fag end into one of the empty cups, then took Siobhan's hand and pulled her away, saying, 'See you, Harry. Nice chatting.'

Once they had gone, Percy said, 'The lesbians are ruthless.' That was how other queers talked, but in his Northern–Etonian accent he sounded unconvincing and offensive, like an MP joking about bumboys and bra-burners. Retreating into familiar territory, he said, 'Shall we get legless?'

Hal retrieved someone else's bottle of whisky: it was half-full, still a decent 300ml. He hated drinking cheap spirits straight, but he wanted to make Percy suffer. The two garden chairs were occupied, so Hal and Percy sat on the patchy grass and smoked and passed the bottle between them, unnoticed in the shuffle of guests coming out for a smoke, going back in, coming out again. Hal did what Jack did and held court, piecing together a sort of stand-up routine featuring stories about his failures, his total uselessness at the British Policy Institute, his extraordinary alcohol tolerance, the time his drug dealer told him he was spending too much money on drugs. Percy boasted about his achievements by joking about how boring he was in comparison: 'Yeah, literally all I do now is read books and write essays,' or 'I basically did a whole cleanse while I was in Sri Lanka, I didn't drink or smoke or do anything else for a month.' Hoping to embarrass Percy,

Hal told the story about the gay club that he'd just told Fern and Siobhan. Percy, trying to roll a cigarette in the dark, laughed automatically, but sank then, for the first time that evening, into silence.

'Mate,' said Hal, 'just take one of mine. Here. This is why I don't roll my own. Fucking impossible to do when you're drunk.'

'The filters are biodegradable,' said Percy, but he took one of Hal's anyway. After the first drag he said, 'So, how is it, being, uh, out?'

'What, out like *out*? I've only actually said it to a precious few people; everybody else knows because of gossip. You know because of gossip.'

'Actually, it's strange because I don't think I'd ever guess, if I didn't know? So it must have surprised people, when they found out. It surprised me when I found out. First thing I heard about you in Freshers Week. And I was like, how do you not know him at all and know everything about who he's sleeping with, and I've known him forever and never known?'

'That's the first thing people said when they talked about me? It was 2010, not fucking 1810.'

'Well, yes, but I think there was a curiosity . . . You know, it was before gay marriage, and I think people wanted to see how it was going to work, with inheritances and everything. It's one thing for a normal person to come out, it's another thing for—'

'Ugh, don't say it! Don't say it! Don't say a fucking word about it. You're not a normal person, your family's net worth is in the nine digits.'

'Yeah, it's the oil . . . Stole it from the Scots . . . Though the market's crashing like hell . . .'

'It wasn't some grand statement, you know, it wasn't—It wasn't flinging open the front door, it was sort of slipping out the side door, except the side door creaks so everyone hears it. I couldn't care less really. It did upset my father. I suppose that's why I let it happen.'

'Why are you so awful to your father? I like him. I don't think my dad likes him, but my dad hates everyone.'

'So does mine, secretly. What does it matter to you?'

'It doesn't,' said Percy. 'But isn't it a waste of time? And even if you don't get on with him, I don't see why you would do things, such enormous, life-altering things, you know, just to upset him. It's childish. It's such a waste of time and effort.'

'That's what he says about me. Waste of time and effort. Like going to a far-away restaurant that turns out to be closed, except you've spent twenty-two years getting there, and the restaurant has your exact name and it's going to get all your stuff when you die.'

'Don't you want to sort of do something – you know, do something with your life?'

'I don't know, why, what do you want to do?'

'In twenty years,' said Percy seriously, 'I'm going to be prime minister.'

Hal laughed at him, rude and unforgiving. He lay on his back in the cool moist grass and watched the stars and the tops of the trees and the houses blurring with the inwards churn of his own drunkenness. He laughed so hard he coughed. He shut his eyes and felt the earth spinning beneath him, keeping him pinned to its surface by the force of its motion. There seemed not to be anyone else in the garden any longer. In the house, there was still music playing; Hal could hear only the bass.

'I don't think it's that ridiculous of me,' said Percy.

'You're so insufferable. And my father thinks you're the second coming of Christ.'

'Well, that's an exaggeration,' said Percy, as if he were clearing up a serious misunderstanding.

'God, shut up! Prime minister of my fucking balls. Tell me again how great Sri Lanka was. "Wow, I'm Harry Percy, I've had food poisoning on five different continents. Wah-wah-wah, donate to UNICEF."'

From somewhere above – Hal looked up and saw a shape in the first-floor window – a woman who was plainly not a playwright or a textile artist shouted, 'Do you know there are people trying to sleep up here? Do you not realise how loud you are?'

Hal laughed. Percy shoved him to shut him up, fumbling to his feet.

'I'm so sorry,' Percy called up. 'We were just going. So sorry to bother you, truly.'

Hal, still on the ground, still laughing, told him, 'You're such a little bitch.' He squinted at the open window, but the woman was just a spot of blue against black. There might have been a floral nightgown.

'Do you not know,' she went on, 'that there are other people living here who've got to get up in the morning?'

Percy shouted, 'We're really so sorry! We had no idea we were being such a bother, no idea, really. We don't live here, actually, we're just guests!'

'It's half three in the morning,' she cried. 'Of course you're being a bloody bother. I don't care whether you're guests or not, you should know better than to go on like that in the middle . . .'

Once they were on the street again Hal said, 'Ah fuck, we're so far from my flat.'

'Where do you live?'

'Umm, Fulham . . . Don't make fun of me, it's where my dad decided I should live.'

'Fulham, yeah . . . It isn't – kind of boring? I mean, I'm staying at my dad's place at the moment and it's basically awful, but it's not too far from SOAS and he says if I want a flat I've got to pay for it, and I can't make enough to afford living in Central while I'm still at uni, and if I lived anywhere else the commute would be too long, so . . . You're not going home yet, are you?'

Hal would have looked up the nearest kebab shop and walked there. Percy hailed an Uber and brought Hal to a twenty-four-hour place in Shoreditch, garishly decorated, full of City boys in sweat-stained shirts who'd failed to pull and now were stuck with each other. Hal was too drunk to comprehend the menu; Percy ordered him a fry-up and a pint of lager. When their pints arrived, Percy slapped Hal's outstretched hand, saying, 'Not until you've eaten something.'

'Are you my mother?' Hal took a vigorous drink of lager, spilling it down his chin, spattering his shirtfront. He wiped his mouth with his sleeve.

'No, but you obviously need one. Oh God!' Percy's screwed-up plaintive face came into focus for a second. 'I'm sorry, I wasn't thinking.'

'No, no, keep going, that's the funniest thing you've said all night. I'm making you grow a sense of humour. Don't say sorry, say "Thank you, Hal, for the fact that I'm now capable of making jokes, it's a skill I'm sure will serve me well in future."'

'I really didn't mean it, I just said it.'

'You can do an entire tight five about my dead mum,' said Hal, 'just as long as I don't have to hear you moralising at me.'

'You just don't believe anyone actually has a conscience. You think everyone is secretly just like you. Either that or they're too stupid to be just like you, or too common.'

'You don't even know me,' said Hal. 'Our parents know each other, that's all.'

'Alright,' said Percy. 'Then we don't know each other really.'

Talking to Percy was like trying to fence with a wall. He was always himself, earnest, impassable, uncheckable, evading all attempts at – Hal thought *penetration*, and laughed. Yes, Percy was like St Sebastian if the arrows bounced off.

'It's just that it's on my mind,' said Hal.

'What is?'

'My mother—It's past midnight already, so today is the day my mother died. I'm not getting drunk to drown my sorrows, I do this most nights.'

'Oh, I'm so sorry. I didn't know it was today.'

'And this is the first year I'm not going to the memorial mass, which is a godsend, honestly. It's in Monmouth and her family drive me mad. You know the Woodstocks, don't you?'

'Of course I do, they're Mum and Dad's friends. I think they're sound enough. I mean, I'm not super keen on golfing with Thomas Woodstock, but it's mostly Dad who does that, I just get enlisted occasionally. I'm terrible at golf, by the way, never ask me.'

'I wouldn't.'

'So there's a memorial for your mother – today? In Wales? And you're out at four in the morning? Are you even going to be alive tomorrow? Sorry, sorry, bad phrasing, I keep doing it, I think it's actually sort of a psychological thing.'

If Hal wasn't there, he would be in his bedroom at Monmouth. The windows would be open, the curtains tied back, letting the damp grassy night air pass through. He would be alone, sleepless, halfway between drunk and hungover. With his ears ringing in the quiet, he would suffer the fear that reminded him how much he was like his father. He would go to Henry and beg a pill or two from his supply of pharmaceuticals, and endure Henry's concern: 'Are you sleeping badly? Are you not well? Do you need to see Dr Bradmore?' Then he would take the pill and pull his duvet up to his neck and sleep for as long as he could before Tom or Humphrey or John came banging in, telling him Dad was saying they'd got to get up or else they'd be late for mass.

When the bill arrived, Hal snatched it out of the waiter's hand with a zeal that visibly shook the man. He paid in cash and put down too much for a tip. Then he gave Percy fifty quid and said, 'Get me a cab home.'

Percy gave the fifty quid back: he tucked it into the back left pocket of Hal's trousers, buttoning the pocket so the money wouldn't fall out. He persisted even after Hal told him to stop touching his arse. He got into the cab with Hal, and when it arrived at Hal's address, Percy got out too.

Hal said, 'What are you doing? Why are you still here? Do you want me to invite you in?'

'No! I'm trying to make sure you get into your flat without passing out.'

'Do what you—Ah, fuck.' Thinking the little gate had been open, Hal had walked straight into it, bashing his knee.

Hal lived on the top floor of a very ordinary three-storey terraced house. There was a black-and-white chequered porch, a bay window, a blue door, and a flower box that the woman who lived on the ground floor neglected. Opening the door, one was confronted immediately with a carpeted staircase. Fifty years ago, someone much less grand than him owned this whole house. Now he (his father, that is) owned a quarter of it (there was a basement flat also). As Hal entered his flat, Percy came in after him, saying, 'I won't stay long. Where are the lights in here? Is there a switch? Oh, here it is . . . No, that's not it . . .'

Turning on the light in the bedroom, Percy revealed the duvet that spilled from Hal's bed to the floorboards, which were covered by dirty clothes and half-empty cups that he stepped carefully to avoid. Hal and Percy stunk of drink and cigarettes and trailed the scent about as they moved, leaving impressions of themselves in the air they had just displaced.

'You should go to the memorial.' Percy was yanking open Hal's dresser drawers, taking out trousers and shirts. 'That's the sort of thing you regret on your deathbed, you know. Your family will remember it forever, and every time you do something they don't like they'll remind you of it.'

'Percy, get out of my flat. Go home.'

Looking up, wobbling a bit, Percy said, 'Really?'

'Yes,' said Hal. 'There's a reason we're not friends.'

'Yeah, 'cause you're the biggest cunt who's ever lived, and I try to be a good person.'

'Here it is, the Percy righteousness, the privilege-guilt that demands absolution . . .'

Percy said, 'Would it kill you just to stop?'

'Stop what? If I just stopped, full stop, that would be dying. That's like saying would it kill you to die.'

'Fuck off! Shut up, shut up. I'm sick of you. Have you got a suitcase? I'm trying to do a good deed and you're ruining it. You haven't tricked me, I know you're stupid underneath the cleverness.' Ferociously, he pitched rolled-up pairs of socks into a duffel bag. 'I know about your funny little impressions of me. "Ha ha ha, I'm Harry Percy and I'm actually cognisant of how I affect other people! I'm Hal Lancaster and I'm sooo funny. Sooo funny! I'm Hal Lancaster and I'm better than everyone else because I was born without feelings. Ha ha! Laugh at my jokes! Ha ha!"'

'You don't seem to want to leave, though.'

'I do,' said Percy. 'I'm leaving right now. Don't forget to pack underpants.'

Shutting the door to his flat, locking it, Hal had that discomfiting sense of a familiar place being changed just by having temporarily contained a new person. Alone again, Hal took on the outsider's vision, and everything around him – the cracked ceiling, the Persian rug, the tiny dining table with the mismatched chairs, the bricked-up fireplace with the chipped plaster bust of the *Apollo Belvedere* in it – took on a slightly different attitude and proportion. He was ashamed to take his clothes off; it felt as though Percy had left his eyes behind.

The sun was rising. With the lights out, Hal saw that the palest blue glow came through the crack in the curtains. He was still drunk enough that the bed seemed to be moving beneath him, as if there were another person on the underside, tossing and turning, trying to fall asleep. He shut his eyes and remained completely awake. Fuck, he thought, fuck. I know, he thought. Fuck, he thought. He got up and packed his underpants as well.

PART TWO

PARACETAMOL

7

Hal's drunk only lasted him through the first hour of his journey. He fell asleep on the train and woke to the kind of root-canal headache that made it impossible to think. Each fleck of rain on the window next to him felt like a slap to the side of his head. In the little train toilet, where he did a truly grievous, painful shit, the mirror was placed just across from him, so that he was faced unavoidably with his reflection. Perched on the tiny toilet, his body looked obtrusive and enormous. His face had the bruised, hopeless look of a gin fiend in a Victorian moral tract. Under the fluorescent lights his skin was the colour of spoilt milk. Pale stubble was coming up in patches, not quite committing to fully covering his jaw. His hair was greasy, the curls weighed down, his eyes bloodshot and his eyelids puffy pink. He noticed a crust of dried spit in the corner of his mouth, which he wiped away. The smell of his own shit was so horrific he gagged, keeping himself from vomiting by a feat of willpower so great he doubted it would ever be repeated. He deepened his misery by imagining the relative comfort of his flat, the solitude in which he could descend to the depths of indignity securely. He was happy to live, but why could he not do it as a dog or a slug, something with little intelligence and no sense of shame? As he exited the toilet, the girl waiting for it made a face.

There was no train station at Monmouth; Hal disembarked at Newport and hired a cab. Starting the meter, the driver said, 'Late night?'

'Yeah, I never really went to bed.'

'Oh, well, that's what you're meant to do when you're young. Where are you going? I'll try not to take any sharp turns.'

'To Monmouth—It's, umm, there's not an address as such . . .'

'Ah, I'm from Monmouth myself.' The driver, a tall man with a long, rounded nose and the vague accent characteristic of the Marches, looked at Hal in the rear-view mirror, appraising him: so what sort of business does this boy have here, in my place? Explain yourself. Or don't, but I'll make my own assumptions.

Hal said, 'Do you know Monmouth House?'

'Yes, I do. Are you a guest of the family then?'

'Well, I've just come for a couple of days . . .'

'I've been driving for eight years, and it's very rare I take anyone up there. I have a cousin who goes up to help with the cleaning sometimes. She says they don't have many visitors; the place is closed up most of the year. I think they spend most of their time in London.'

'Yes, I think they do . . .'

'They own a good deal of the land round the town – about 1,000 acres in all, and when I was a boy the estate was larger than that. Those were the days when John Lancaster owned it. John was the one who really took things in hand: paid off the county council, started buying up businesses . . . Made better use of his wife's inheritance than others might have done in his position.'

'I suppose,' said Hal, shutting his eyes to keep his stomach from churning, absently picking a spot on his forehead, 'that things might change when the son inherits.'

'That may be true,' said the driver.

For about thirty minutes they drove in silence, making their way north through the pastures between the mountains and the mouth of the River Severn. As they broke off onto the road that would lead them to the house, passing the sign that read 'PRIVATE PROPERTY: NO RIGHT OF WAY', Hal said, 'Do you know much about him, the oldest son?'

'Who, Henry Junior? Well, he was born here in Monmouth. I think all the children were. I don't know much about them. Yes, it was a surprise when we found out he was gay. Open about it too, very open, not like the last Duke of Lancaster, who was a bit of a flamboyant character, but never actually came out. Of course, it's a different time now. I say, well, if this is what he wants, there's no reason why he shouldn't. I've got a nephew who's gay, and he gets on well enough. The world's changing.'

'Surely though it can't be changing all that much, if the Lancasters still own everything.'

The driver looked as if he thought Hal might be testing him for evidence of treasonous inclinations. Seeing in the mirror that Hal was looking at him look at him, he turned his attention back to the road. They were passing through the park surrounding the house: the grass was even, lushly green, rolling towards every horizon, undisturbed by the hedgerows or rock walls that separated one tenant's land from another. A line of trees ran along each side of the winding road, and on Hal's left, a willow-lined pond split away into a brook, which ran nearly dry during droughts but was deep with rainwater now. The car crossed over a stone bridge that had gone green with moss.

'The estate is impressive,' said the driver, 'there's no doubt about that. But things aren't like they used to be, at least where agriculture is concerned.'

The house was coming into view. It was a seventeenth-century manor house, a sandstone rectangle with a gabled roof and casement windows, quite small and plain by the standard, but embellished with a Tudor-style garden that had been put in by Hal's great-great-grandfather Edward in the late nineteenth century. The chapel, which had the crumbling, precarious look of a genuine medieval remnant, had been constructed at about the same time as the garden. They had had cash to spare, then, Hal supposed. But the estate had only come to John because it had passed the height of its profitability: it had been offloaded onto the younger son with all the generosity of a movie star passing on tat from an awards show gift bag.

'If you go round the side,' said Hal, 'just past those hedges . . .'

The cab eased into the cobbled yard between the house and the stable block, which had been converted into a garage sometime after the Second World War. One door had been left open, revealing the BMW Hal's brother John had bought off a friend without telling Henry, who had been convinced that if any of his children owned a car, they would drive the wrong way down the motorway and get flipped into the air by a lorry, smashed straight into the next life. Hal did sometimes exercise the convertible Henry had driven in his twenties, which otherwise lay shrouded and untouched. Henry would tell him to be careful, but he would let him go, as if he were encouraging Hal, specifically, to die.

Hal paid in cash and refused the offer to make change. He did accept the driver's business card. When Hal opened the rear passenger door, the driver said, 'Have a lovely stay in Monmouth, Lord Hereford.'

'Oh, cheers,' said Hal.

The Old Testament reading was one that Henry had chosen for Mary's memorial mass at least twice before, the bit in Isaiah about flesh and grass: 'What shall I cry? All flesh is grass, and all the glory thereof as the flower of the held. The grass is withered, and the dower is fallen, because the spirit of the Lord hath blown upon it. Indeed the people is grass . . .' The second time Henry had used it, Eleanor Woodstock had suggested that she and her husband might choose the readings next time, if it was too much of a burden for him. Henry told them that the passage had been a favourite of Mary's. Hal didn't know if that was true, but it shut Eleanor and Thomas up. Eleanor was sitting in front of Hal now, in a stonking black hat with a veil and feathers, like it was Goth Nite at Ascot.

Eleanor and Thomas were not Mary's mother and father. Mary's father was a baronet named Richard who used the nickname 'Dick'. He had been a bachelor of forty-three when he married Joan Fitzalan, who had been twenty-one. Eleanor was born a year later, in 1958, by which time Dick and Joan were already living separately. Mary was born in 1970, during a short period of reconciliation induced by pressure from family and clergy; she was three or four when her father left for New Zealand with his mistress. Hal had met him just once, at

Mary's funeral: all Hal remembered was that he'd had a pink nose. Lady Bohun died of cancer when Mary was fifteen. Eleanor was twenty-six at the time and had made a good marriage to one of the few English Catholics who actually had a bit of money, and so to save her father from the trouble of raising his own daughter, she and Thomas volunteered to become Mary's guardians. They approved the marriage to Henry out of plain snobbishness: what did they need the baronet for, if they could have a duke in the family? Now Mary was dead and the duke was all they had left.

Hal, next to Philippa in the back left pew, let his vision blur. He imagined arms and legs sprouting from the Brecon Beacons, grasping and flapping before going still, blackening, decomposing, soaking back into the earth. The inside of his head throbbed. His lips were dry, and he kept licking them without thinking, making them drier. He had changed shirts before the mass, but hadn't had time to bathe, and the air-freshener scent of his deodorant did nothing to mask the odour of his unwashed body. It didn't matter. His mother in her coffin must have smelled worse. What would she look like now, fifteen years dead? Hal thought of the Egyptian mummies in the British Museum. One day they would crumble into dust and disperse; they were pagans, they would not be resurrected.

Earlier, as they left the house, Henry had held Hal back. 'Go on ahead of us,' he'd told the rest. He let the door, original Jacobean oak, stand half-open, casting him in shadow while Hal stood in blue-grey light. John carried his umbrella with the ladybird pattern; the others were chancing it.

'If you were going to make a fuss about not coming,' Henry had said, 'you might as well not have come. We're meant to be remembering your mother. Now everyone is thinking about you again.'

'I only changed my mind at sunrise. I took the first train out.'

Opening the door fully, Henry had said, 'You stink like the sewer. As soon as mass is finished, you must go up and bathe.'

The New Testament reading was one Henry hadn't used before. It was from Peter, whom Hal always thought of when he was upside-down on a fairground ride. Father Price read, 'Christ therefore having suffered in the flesh, be you also armed with the same thought: for he that hath suffered in the flesh, hath ceased from sins . . '

Behind Father Price was a triple-arched stained-glass window. In the centre panel, St George stepped on the dragon as if it were a coat laid out over a puddle. The Virgin looked on from the glittering clouds, and at the top of the arch hung a dove with an olive branch in its beak. On the left was St Edmund the Martyr, filled with arrows; on the right was St Sebastian, also filled with arrows. Rays of yellow glass shot out from their near-naked bodies. When he was very young, even before his mother died, Hal had been afraid to look closely at these windows, in case someone should see him and be able to tell that he liked looking. He had been too young to understand the implications: he had had the shame without the reason for it. It was something to do with the way people talked about Edward, who had designed these windows himself. They talked the same way about Richard, who let Hal eat double helpings of pudding, and taught him to ride a pony and speak French.

'But let none of you suffer,' said Father Price, 'as a murderer, or a thief, or a railer, or a coveter of other men's things. But if as a Christian, let him not be ashamed . . '

Hal thought it was quite right to draw a distinction between the sufferings of, for instance, a boy with a deathly whisky hangover and a woman haemorrhaging after having given birth to the child of her husband. However miserable Hal was, he never claimed that his suffering was Christian. But what about Richard, shaking with chills, sweating with fever, going blind? Or Edward, who was implicated in a sex scandal in 1910, and went into voluntary exile in Tunis while the middle-class man who had been his lover went to hard labour prison? Hal's father and grandfather said that these men came to the ends they did because of how they lived. It wasn't just that they were queer: it was that they raised their favourites beyond their stations, and wasted their fortunes on frivolous things, and neglected the social equals to whom they owed favours, and disobeyed their fathers. The least they could have done was preserve the status quo. Still, Hal thought their pain meant something to God, whereas his own never had. Hal wondered whether Henry thought his own peculiar sufferings – his pains, his insomnia, his psoriasis, his depressions, his ferocious headaches – were those of a railer or a coveter of other men's things, or whether they were a sign of grace visited upon him in reward for his devotion. Henry's eyes were closed; stained-glass light shone on his face. Jeanne, in a black mantilla, was serene. With the preternatural sensitivity of a woman who is used to being looked at, she returned Hal's gaze, expressionless.

'Wherefore,' concluded Father Price breathlessly, 'let them that suffer according to the will of God commit the keeping of their souls to him in well doing, as unto a faithful creator.'

It had been a long reading, and Father Price looked relieved to be that much closer to the end of the mass. Hal's lips stung with being licked, and though he had brushed his teeth and rinsed with mouthwash, his mouth was so dry that it was going foul again. He prayed to the Virgin like a schoolboy begging to be let out of lessons early: Please save my mother's soul, please grant her eternal life, please let her not suffer for my misdeeds or my father's, please make it so that we won't have to worry about her any more. I'm sorry this is so selfish, I'm sorry I don't have the good manners even to pretend to you that I'm better than I am. But do it anyway, please, do it anyway, please.

The bathroom had been converted from a bedroom sometime in the mid nineteenth century, and the space seemed too big for what it contained: a ceramic sink, a painted-wood dresser, a clawfoot tub not quite large enough for Hal, a pull-chain toilet with worryingly low water pressure. The hardwood floor, warped and stained by over a hundred years of moisture, was insufficiently covered by a ragged old hand-woven rug. A battery-powered clock on the dresser reminded you that you couldn't forget about time even when you were in the bath, except that the batteries had run out ages ago and never been replaced.

Hal took a nude in the mirror above the sink, the reflection of his face half-covered by the reflection of his phone, and sent it to Jack, ignoring the message Jack had sent earlier. Then he put his phone on the dresser and got into the bath. He had to bend his knees to fit in, and the water didn't reach even to his nipples. Looking at the fat around his waist, he thought despondently of all the shirtless pictures he'd seen on Percy's Instagram, the unostentatious toned muscles and the confident stance. Hal's headache flared, and he remembered something Percy had said last night about how the best cure for a hangover was a shot of wheatgrass juice and a raw egg with hot sauce. The thought of it made him feel ill. He folded his legs to give his upper body space to sink into the bath, then slid down low enough to rest his head against the back of the tub.

There was a knock at the door. Hal, knowing who it was, said, 'Come in.'

Henry shut the door behind him but did not lock it. He had taken off his jacket and tie, and rolled his shirtsleeves up. Braces held up his trousers, which were the same ones he wore every year; they were looser on him now than they had been the year before.

'Do you feel quite awful?' asked Henry. 'There's paracetamol in the top drawer here, I think.' He rustled through the bits and pieces in the drawer, the half-empty tubes of hand cream and the restaurant matchbooks. 'It might be out of date . . .'

'It's easing off,' lied Hal, 'it's alright.'

'You looked awful when you came in.' Henry's gaze fell on Hal's phone; he picked it up. 'Ah, you've a message from someone called Jack. "You look scrumptious, like a little strawberry tart. I want to put my cock right between those pink plump thighs." He's sent you a picture. Was that who you were with last night?'

Henry placed the phone face-down again. He pulled up a chair to the side of the bath and sat down, resting a hand on the rim of the tub. Submerged in the bathwater, Hal's hands were shaking.

'No. Last night I was with someone you'd approve of. I was with Harry Percy.'

'Will I have to apologise to his father for what you've done to him?'

Henry turned on the showerhead and tested the water with his fingers. He told Hal, 'Close your eyes,' and soaked Hal's hair, pulling his free hand through the curls to ensure they were wet all the way through. He had never done anything like this when Hal was of an age to be bathed. Hal had learnt second hand that other parents did bathe their children, brush their hair, feed them, put them to bed, tend to them when they were ill. By the time Hal was old enough to remember things, there were Tom and John to occupy his mother's attention, and then came the rest of the children. Hal supposed that if Henry had bathed him then, he might think of it as a comfort now, a reprieve from adulthood. As it was, it only made him more aware of his body, of Henry's awareness of his body, this big ugly grown-up thing. The water was warm, trickling down his neck and shoulders. Henry was rubbing soap into his hair.

'You were right to come,' said Henry. 'I just wish you hadn't made such a production of it.'

Henry dipped a cloth into the water and scrubbed Hal's neck, his shoulders, his armpits, his back, his chest. Hal bent forwards and backwards, lifted his arms and put them down again, as Henry directed. Henry lay the cloth over the side of the tub, then dried his hands and rolled his sleeves down, buttoned his cuffs.

'Do have lunch with us,' said Henry. 'I've asked Father Price to stay. And Eleanor and Thomas will expect to see you. They're having drinks now; I'll go down and make excuses for you.'

8

Father Price, new to the parish, had not yet exhausted his store of small talk: he sustained the soup course with polite enquiries about the chimneypiece and the panelling, segueing into generic praise of the gardens, which allowed Eleanor and Thomas to describe the garden at their 'little farmhouse' (a listed building) in Oxfordshire. It was only with the fish – penitential turbot and celeriac – that Father Price, perhaps feeling he had established a meaningful intimacy, perhaps feeling that he would be remiss if he took too much enjoyment from the hospitality Henry was offering on the occasion of his wife's death, said, 'Perhaps you'd like to tell me more about Mary.'

There was a silence long enough for Father Price's face to melt with mortification, then stiffen into face-saving solicitude. Hal wished he could have told him that he hadn't said anything wrong: it was just that the usual thing was to proceed through the rituals of mourning without ever acknowledging Mary had actually once been alive.

Thomas said, 'She was a really clever . . . a really pretty girl.'

'Yes,' said Eleanor.

'Before she was married, she wanted to take holy orders. She had been speaking to the headmistress of St Mary's about it. She wanted to join the Benedictines on the Isle of Wight.'

'I doubt they'd have taken her on,' said Henry.

'Anyway, Oxford made an offer first,' Eleanor told Father Price. 'That was where she met Henry.'

Jeanne said, 'I knew her then too. I liked her very much.'

'Yes, but you didn't really know her, did you?' Thomas stuck his fork into his pile of celeriac. 'You were one of those people who hung about Richard, taking drugs and having cross-dressing parties.'

With a little laugh Father Price said, 'I had a few wild nights myself at university.'

'None that left you with AIDS . . . I presume?'

'Well, no, indeed not,' said Father Price.

It was up to Henry to say, 'Let's not count sins at the table,' after which Father Price remembered his pastoral duty and said, 'No. All we can do is atone, and sin again, and atone again.'

Slipping out of his chair, dropping his napkin, Tom said, 'I'll just be a minute. So sorry.' After a few minutes, Humphrey did the same. Hal peeked at his phone and saw that in the group chat Tom had posted:

Tom L 13:07 Going out to smoke 🌲 🌲 🌲

When Philippa rose from the table, Henry said, 'Is there some other lunch somewhere you're all attending?'

'I'm menstruating,' said Philippa haughtily.

'Philippa,' said Blanche.

'It's perfectly natural. Should I be ashamed?'

'There's a difference,' said Eleanor, 'between being ashamed and having manners,' but there wasn't, and Philippa was already gone.

Tom and Humphrey crept back in just as the poached pears were served. They had covered up the scent of the joint they'd smoked with a fresh application of nightclub-toilet cologne. Henry seemed willing to overlook this until Philippa wobbled in, doe-like on her modest heels, supporting herself with a hand on the table as she lowered herself into her seat. She had doused herself in the same cologne; getting a whiff of herself, she sneezed.

'One thing,' said Humphrey, 'one thing I remember about Mum is that she would always—'

'We've moved on,' said John.

'Oh? Why?'

With the firmness taught to him by their former nanny, a frightening Scottish Presbyterian, John said, 'We've had enough of it.'

Philippa laughed: a private snort, derisory, then genuine giggles as some inexplicable humour took her. Her own laughter seized her, and she crumpled under it, bowing her head, gasping, covering her reddened face with her hands. It became the kind of compulsive bodily freak that, though provoked by amusement, pulled its captive further and further from good spirits the longer it went on. A couple of times she wrestled herself into silence only to start again. Struggling through the laughter, she said, 'Is there anyone here who didn't know her at all, besides Father Price – and me? I'm the one who's got the most licence to be upset, and I'm the only one who's even slightly capable of acting normal.'

'That's not true,' said Blanche. 'You literally just left to take drugs with Tom and Humphrey. And I don't remember Mum any more than you do.'

The whites of Philippa's eyes were bright, and her crooked sharp teeth were bright too. She said, 'God, I don't care, Blanche. You're the one who has to cheat on exams because all you do is get drunk and give blowjobs in fields. You're never going to be head girl – that's just what the boys at the college in the village call you.'

More than one person at the table said, 'Philippa!' Henry, sitting back in his chair with his arms crossed, had a bored look that suggested a contempt all the more brutal for being under his control.

'Why would you say that?' Blanche asked Philippa. 'Why would you say something like that here?'

Philippa was sent upstairs to lie down. Humphrey said hopefully, 'I should go up and help her.'

'No,' said Henry. 'You and Tom will stay until I've dismissed you.'

Eleanor said, 'I hope I don't need your permission to leave.'

'Of course not. You're not my child.'

'Thank God for small mercies.'

She pushed in her chair so hard that the back of it knocked against the edge of the table, rattling the plates. Then she gave one of those classic rude country-girl laughs which sound like a large dog's cough. Thomas followed her out; their pears were left forlornly half-eaten in their pools of red wine sauce, like meat freshly expelled or extracted. Hal remembered how an armchair Mary had bled on after giving birth to Humphrey disappeared, then reappeared in new upholstery, then disappeared again years later. Only guests who didn't know what it was ever sat in it.

Now that he risked no contradiction by the people concerned, Henry talked at length about the Woodstocks and Bohuns. He explained the circumstances of Mary's birth, her father's departure and her mother's death, her adoption by Eleanor and Thomas. Dismissively, he sketched in Thomas's background: the gentleman's education paid for by the grandfather in trade, followed by the middling career in finance and the midlife-crisis foundation of Woodstock Energy, which in fact had made less than a million in profits last year. He explained that naturally it had been difficult for the Woodstocks to accept, when he and Mary were engaged, that Eleanor's only remaining relation was starting her own family. Naturally Mary's death had been hard on them all, especially the children, who could not be expected to act like children who did have mothers.

Father Price must have felt like he was being taken into Henry's confidences. Hal, who had heard the same stories told in many different ways by many different people, saw that Henry was offering this candour to Father Price in exchange for his loyalty: for his assurance, even if unspoken, that all Henry had done was marry a woman and have children by her, just like God had intended, and if Eleanor and Thomas Woodstock felt that he was responsible for Mary's death then they were wrong. He wasn't asking Father Price for forgiveness; he was asking him to believe that he had done nothing for which he needed to be forgiven. Father Price, dazzled by the land and the house and the marble-and-wood chimneypiece with the figures of Adam and Eve in Eden, poured too much sugar into his coffee.

While Henry was distracted, Blanche slid her phone out of her little velvet handbag and typed rapidly:

🐝 13:54 @🐦 Did you know that Daphne said everyone in your year thinks you're a bitch

🐝 13:55 When Iris asked to be moved out of your room it was just because you were such a bully she just said it was a health problem so you wouldn't be even more of a raging cunt to her

🐝 13:57 Everyone remembers year 8 when you tried to be bulimic and fainted in hockey practice and if they're nice to you it's because they think you might try to kill yourself

🐝 14:00 Now you have to be the special one who gets everyone to cry about how you're such a poor orphan as if literally all of us didn't lose our mum aswell

🐝 14:00 On the day of her memorial which is actual pathalogical narscisist behaviour I just can't tolerate it sorry

🐝 has left the chat.

Blanche was straining not to cry. Nobody was looking at her. Father Price was laughing at a story Henry was telling him. In the boys' chat, Humphrey had written:

Humphrey Bogart 13:58 Fuck I've got to poo really really badly but if I asked dad to be excused he'd belt me

Tom, smiling down at his hidden phone, responded:

Tom L 13:59 Shit yerself Humphrey!

But after flicking through his other chats, his smile dropped; he looked up at Blanche and mouthed, 'What the fuck?'

Proudly, clenching her jaw even as her bottom lip trembled, Blanche kept Tom's gaze for a moment, just long enough to assure him he was seen, then turned her head like she was posing for a portrait-ist. Hal texted Percy:

Hal 14:08 Guess where I am

H Percy 14:08 Oh did you go to Wales after all?

Hal 14:09 I wish I hadn't it's been a shambles

H Percy 14:10 But aren't you glad you were there

Hal 14:11 No

Hal 14:11 You owe me an apology for convincing me to act
   against my better judgment

H Percy 14:13 I'm sorry!

H Percy 14:13 I'll make it up to you

H Percy 14:14 It's a few months off yet and we're already
   booked for the 12th but when the season starts why don't
   you come shooting

Hal 14:15 Oh God

That night, Hal pulled rank to get into the shared bathroom first. He showered, brushed his teeth, flossed, washed his face, and took the time to swab his ears just to piss off John, who was next in the queue. In his bedroom he stripped down to his boxer-briefs, plugged his phone in, set an alarm, then collapsed on top of the duvet and fell asleep with his ineffectual little bedside lamp shining, painting the dark with a few strokes of dim gleam.

The lamp was still on when Hal woke, and the room was still dark, but the shadows were different. There was a weight on the mattress near Hal's knees; Henry was sitting on the edge of the bed. He was in the shirt and trousers he'd worn to lunch: the shirt was untucked, the top two buttons undone. Wrestling through drowsiness, Hal lifted his head to look at the old clock on his bedside table with the radium-glow hands, which said it was just past four.

'I had hoped it would go better than that,' said Henry, with an unexpected equanimity. 'It would have been better if I could have told the Woodstocks they haven't got to come back. I don't see a reason to have them here every year – not even once a year, much less three or four times. They'd been willing to spend money on the children before, but now the children are too old and uninnocent, there's a chance they'd spend it improperly. So the funds for the school fees and accommodation and the private lessons and the holidays have dried up. It was Thomas's money as much as anything else that got you into Trinity. Now Tom and John and Humphrey are complaining about being treated unequally. God only knows what will happen to the girls. Philippa has been telling me she wants to go to New York, to study ballet. I have no idea why. I expect she'll want a flat there as well. You all want flats. I can't afford six flats on my income alone. I can only hope Jeanne will help – well, I see Philippa is working on her. Philippa is a clever girl, but the boys are a bad influence. If I had only had girls, it would have been much nicer.'

'You should go to bed,' said Hal.

'I can't sleep.'

'Take a pill.'

'It won't help.' Henry leaned down and rested his face on Hal's shoulder, and put his hand in Hal's hair. 'I would sleep if I could. Sometimes I can't because I'm wondering where you are.'

The night was so heavy that it kept Hal down and in place. His head was like frothed milk, his hair curly and his thoughts diluted. Henry touched Hal's chest, then the side of his face. Hal turned his head and looked at the wall, the lamplight and shadow, the marks on the old wallpaper from tape and thumbtacks and poster putty. When Hal stayed here the summer after he finished at Oxford, he took down the ephemera he had hung up during his school years – film posters, snapshots, none of it with great meaning – and never put anything else in its place.

Before Henry left, Hal flung his arms around Henry and embraced him. He felt, in a way he couldn't remember feeling as a child, a plain and uncomplicated need for his father, whatever sort of person his father happened to be. His mother was gone and he was lonely, and he was the eldest and could not let his brothers and sisters know that he was weak. He felt what all the other small boys had felt their first night at boarding school, that misery of abandonment to which he had then been proudly immune. Henry, having never provided the comfort a child instinctually desires, could not provide it now, and held Hal without warmth.

Henry was there while Hal was falling asleep. When he woke again at about six, the lamp was off and the room dimly blue with dawn light, and Henry was gone.

9

There were some who would say that Harry Percy wasn't really Northern: he was the son of a landowner and had spent his adolescence at Eton. Simply by virtue of owning the land, the landowner somehow was foreign to it, so that the Percys seemed to have retained the exoticism of the Norman conqueror even as Northumberland became the home from which they staged their expansion into the Orient. But Percy had at least attended primary school in the village nearest the family seat, where the family occupied a small portion of the house so that the rest could be done up and opened to paying visitors. The Henry Percy who was Percy's father was an extraordinary miser and would not let the house run at a loss. North Sea oil was drying up; in ten years they might have become the kind of family who needed to figure out how to extract a profit from houses so grand they could only have been built with the profits from some other extractive enterprise. So the shooting lodge was for most of the season let to parties of sportsmen who could afford a shooting weekend but not the land itself.

Or perhaps they just hadn't any interest in owning a grouse moor. Hal found it difficult to imagine having Percy's enthusiasm for wildlife management, which he discussed on the train up from London, then at dinner, then over whisky after dinner. He might have got through his recitation earlier if his father hadn't kept interrupting, disparaging the area's environmentalist factions, whom he suspected of being either foreigners or Londoners. The locals, Mr Percy had said, were grateful for the employment. If the shoot were shut down there would be nothing else, and the young people would leave for Durham or

Newcastle, and the old people would die and their houses collapse and the villages fall into the final, apocalyptic ruin that deindustrialisation had not yet effected.

The lodge was positioned atop a slight prominence between the Cheviot Hills and the coast of the North Sea, stuck in the middle of one of those great British nowheres that the island, from a map view, seemed too small to sustain. About a mile north stood a medieval chapel that had finally been shut a few years ago; a mile south was a stone-walled pub with outdoor tables not quite protected by umbrellas bearing the Strongbow logo. One would have to travel much further to reach any of the nearest villages, which themselves were outposts along roads running between Newcastle and Edinburgh. Shadowed by clouds, the lodge's sandstone and red shingles were dull; indoors, the fresh paint and new furniture gave off a holiday-let impersonality, despite the family crest over the fireplace and the manky old stag's head in the hall. The Percys made up for this surrender of material idiosyncrasy by living with a proprietary carelessness, setting down glasses without coasters and poking the fire so that the sparks flew onto the rug. Dinner was prepared by Percy's stepmother, who impressed them all by treating excellent cuts of meat with the care that was due them. She had been married to Percy's father for less than five years, and still displayed the newcomer's urge to contribute to family life. By the time the previous marriage had ended, Percy's mother had been openly hateful of it: of having to be a Percy all the time forever, concerned with nothing so much as the continued success of the surname given to her by her husband.

The last person Hal spoke to before going to bed was Percy's little sister, Marguerite. He went upstairs and she was on the landing; it was unclear if she had been going back down for something or waiting for him to come up. She had cried a lot as a baby and her voice was permanently hoarse. She said, 'Night, Hal. Actually I'm getting up really early so I can drive out to the stables before the shoot? You can come with me if you want, I'll drive you. You haven't seen Nelson yet, have you? Nelson's the stallion. You'll love him, he's such a beast, it's so funny.'

Marguerite, assured of her comfort, allowed herself to be splendidly stupid, granting herself perpetual immunity from the petty slights of graspers and plotters. She had never once shown the slightest attraction to Hal, but he thought she would marry him in a blink if he asked. She would go to Monmouth and turn the stable blocks back into stables.

'We could ride together the morning after next,' she went on. 'I'll take Nelson and you can take Belle.'

'Gosh, I don't know, I haven't ridden a horse since Richard was alive.'

'Oh, a vegetable could ride her, she's an angel.'

'Find a nice sturdy turnip, then.'

'You don't want to come?'

'No, no, yeah, no, I mean, if I feel up to it. Depends on how much I drink tomorrow night, and that depends on how well I shoot. If I don't embarrass myself, I'll celebrate, and if Percy shows me up all day, I'll drink myself to death, out of honour.'

'No, no, don't compare yourself, it's not fair. With Harry he can't help it, it's just like, the family trade.'

'Mmm, yes, someone's got to keep the population in check.'

'Oh, no, we want the population to be high. Within reason obviously, we don't want there to just be birds everywhere all the time, like then there wouldn't be enough heather, but during the season—'

'I know, I know . . . It was sort of a joke about like, the family trade, like, colonial administration, you know . . .'

'Oh . . .' She gave him a serious, open look that got across to him how bored she was without seeming at all to blame him for it. 'Well, if you want to come see the horses, meet me in the cloakroom before dawn.'

The guest room Hal had been put in contained a twin bed, plaid curtains, and an antique escritoire of rather poor craftsmanship that had clearly been salvaged from the main house. As it turned out, his room was diagonal from Percy's; they ran into each other in the middle of the night, Hal coming back from taking a piss and Percy going. Percy, squinting and rumpled, asked if Hal was sleeping alright. Hal said, 'Great, thanks,' even though he'd been up on his phone playing online poker to keep from having to lie down in the dark in an unfamiliar bed and think his thoughts. In bed again, Hal considered wanking, gave his prick a few testing tugs, found it responsive, and stopped.

He woke to sunlight, suffering the type of involuntary erection that might have been sexy if he had been in bed with someone he liked enough to fuck in the morning. He was afraid to go take his morning piss in case he ran into Percy again, and he was afraid to wank in case he lost control of his bladder after he finished, which, he reassured himself, had never happened to him personally, though it had happened to a boy named Christian in Tom's year at school, and even now that he was at LSE his school friends still called him Chrisser the Pisser, Christian the Pisstian, the Lemonade Stand, the Golden Firehose, Pee Free. Realising he was desperate for a fag and he couldn't go out to smoke until he pissed, Hal texted Percy, 'You up?' He was prepared to own the awkward impression that he was trying to hook up with him at seven in the morning, at his family's shooting lodge. In response, Percy actually came into Hal's room, not even knocking, just thrusting his way in valiantly.

'I've been up for ages,' said Percy. 'I've set my body clock so that I wake up with the sunrise. I always do, during the season.' He yanked open the curtains; there were no hooks or ties to hold them back, so they slipped down again. 'Are you coming down for breakfast? It'll be laid out in half an hour. We won't wait for you if you miss it. We won't wait for you if you're late for the shoot, either.'

'Do you always come into people's rooms like this?' Hal pulled the duvet up to his neck, trying to arrange his legs so that his erection didn't show through. It would be alright, he thought; it was softening.

'Oh, I'm sorry, I didn't know you were shy. I thought, you know, boarding had totally eroded our expectations of privacy. I can leave . . . I just wanted to say hello on my way downstairs, and remind you about breakfast. I don't mind at all really, it's just my dad who has a thing about being punctual.'

Percy hovered half-in half-out, holding the door ajar. As he swayed, the floorboards creaked. He said, 'I'll leave you be, then. But you really won't want to miss the sausages, they're as local as you can get, there's this family farm just east of here that works with an abattoir near Newcastle—'

'Go away, stop advertising. I'll miss breakfast if you keep standing here talking to me, I've got to clothe myself and I'm not going to do it in front of you.'

Feigning irritation, Percy said, 'Gosh, I'm sorry! I'm going!'

After Hal relieved himself, he got himself hard again and wanked into the toilet. He was distracted by how red his piss had been: had he eaten beets, or did he have bladder cancer? He finished without much feeling, flushed his abject little sperms away, then locked himself in the separate bathroom and took as long of a bath as he could get away with. The bathroom was filled with plants; the scent of the soil and the fragrant, damp leaves made Hal feel like he was in a hothouse in a botanical garden, bathing in the middle of the exotic ferns, looked over by bored tourists, which made him ashamed of his body. Hal imagined Percy naked in the bath and grimaced. In shared spaces, the leftovers of someone else's presence were always hovering around you, reminding you that their owners were human too, and did all those human things you pretended not to do. When was the last time Percy wanked? It couldn't have been that long ago: he struck Hal as the kind of person who wanked regularly because he thought it was good for him to clean his ducts out. He probably watched boring porn, faceless men fucking teens or milfs in a series of impossibly acrobatic positions, the video switching back and forth between wide shots of melded limbs and contextless close-ups of cocks hammering into waxed cunts. Hal gave a repentant shudder and drained the bath.

Hal's super-traditionalist tweed had been borrowed from his father; the jacket and waistcoat fit well enough, but the plus-fours were too tight and too short. Mr Percy, dressed similarly, sat at the head of the table and ate five sausages and related to Hal that he had recently donated his great-uncle's silver to the local regimental museum. The great-uncle had been a commanding officer during the regiment's service in the Second Boer War. Percy reminded his father that the British had done terrible things in the Boers, very possibly war crimes, and his father, with the ease of one who has won the same argument many times in a row, said, 'That was a hundred years ago. And I've donated the silver.'

'But it isn't as if we've stopped fighting wars overseas. We were in Iraq for eight years! The regiment was in Iraq! And the government—'

'The Labour government? You were a child when we went to Iraq. I wasn't. And I recall the PM frothing like an animal in the House of Commons.'

'I won't defend Blair, he's no better than a Tory. But you haven't been listening if you think I'm loyal to a party that hasn't got anything to offer besides not being—'

'Oh, well, no,' said Mr Percy, mopping up grease with a piece of toast, 'I haven't been listening. I haven't since you were about twelve, I think.'

Percy was dressed like he might be intending to try to sabotage the shoot. He wore an oversized quilted jacket with hand-stitched elbow patches and a pair of corduroy trousers tucked into dirty work boots. Instead of a flat cap, he wore a black knitted one with his curls sticking out from under the folded cuff. Yet in the gun room, out with the dogs and the loaders and the shoot manager, he was a gentleman: he gave good handshakes, he was fluent in the sporting dialect, he eased Hal's way without boasting of his own ability. He could have told anyone he was the eldest son of the Duke of Lancaster and been believed. Hal fumbled with his gun and showed his ignorance about the habits of grouse. Mr Percy noticed Hal's insecurity and condescended to encourage him, knowing that his son looked better with Hal there to serve as his foil. The shoot manager approved of Percy, and it was his approval Mr Percy wanted; he was what Mr Percy passed himself off as, a stoic Northumbrian with nobly humble origins and an ancestral connection to the land.

The first wave of grouse that rose up over the crest of the hill slipped over Hal's head without his realising it. When he did react, he swung round and shot wildly at the departing birds. Another wave followed;

Hal pulled the trigger again and winced as the butt of his shotgun jerked against his shoulder. When the horn sounded, signalling the end of the drive, Hal asked his loader for the advice he was barred from giving unsolicited, and was politely chastised for shooting at the backs of the grouse.

He tried harder next time and somehow shot worse. The birds were dusty smudges against the late summer heather, and he was distracted by the picture-postcard beauty of the scene: the sky was dark and bright in variegated patches, the hills blue-brown in the distance. Hal was aware of playing his own role in the image, and felt cheated of the pleasure one projects onto the subjects in a picture. His ears were sweaty underneath the noise-reduction earmuffs, his safety glasses pinched the bridge of his nose; his tweed was scratchy, his lips were chapped, his shoes were crushing his toes.

Between drives, Percy made his way around the other shooting butts, chatting with his family and their guests and the shoot staff, with whom he was cheerful and deferent. Alone with Hal, Percy made fun of the others (though never the staff): he dedicated himself to proving that Hal was his favourite, that Hal was the most privileged and valued of guests. He fussed with Hal's sticks, then moved Hal into the correct position by placing his hands on Hal's upper arms and physically redirecting him.

'The shooting's quite good today,' said Percy. 'The breeze is a bit strong, but not bad enough that you couldn't have bagged more than that. Does handling guns make you nervous?'

'Less than riding does,' said Hal.

'Usually people perform worse the bigger the stakes are, but weirdly I've always done really well under pressure. Like to the point where I need it to thrive?'

'I think perhaps I've broken my reflexes permanently with drink.'

'That's nonsense. My uncle was a full-on alcoholic and he was the best shot in our family. He probably still would be except that he's gone full vegan for some reason. Dad kept telling him that you can shoot a bird without eating it.'

'Do grouse count as ethical meat?'

'We've raised them ourselves. It's just like a farmer slaughtering a hog, isn't it? Remember, if you've hit a bird but it doesn't drop, let it go. I've just got new fillings – if I crack a tooth on a piece of shot, I'm going to kill you.'

By the afternoon a mist had lowered, draping itself down from the farthest highest point of the sky to the closer swells of heather over which the grouse flew. The lines of the landscape, the borders of objects, fuzzed out into a formless cool-grey. Hal felt the moisture in his nose and sinuses and the back of his throat. He was clear-headed; he'd only had two glasses of sherry at lunch, downed to suppress the horror he'd felt when Marguerite asked if he'd been seeing anyone. Though soreness was starting in his shoulders, he handled the gun more easily, and each time he pulled the trigger a grouse went down. The grouse kept coming, wave after wave. Guns to the left of them, guns to the right of them – like the martyrs of the Somme! Hal could have wept for those noble birds if he didn't take such pleasure in killing them. Alas, he was a member of the ruling class . . . The birds would make a fine dinner tonight, and there would be enough left over that he could take a brace to his father.

Crossing over to Hal after the drive had ended, inspecting the line of dead birds the dogs had retrieved, Mr Percy said, 'If you practised like he did, you might be better than Harry. I understand you've got to spend most of your time in London, for whatever it is you do . . .'

'I'm at the British Policy Institute at the moment,' Hal said confidently, 'but that's just until I make my next move.'

'Your father told me you weren't serious about that at all.' He was petting his dog, rubbing her back and sides as she wagged her tail and wriggled. The dog was a yellow Labrador named Daisy. She worked as a gun dog during the season, and otherwise fulfilled the office of family pet. 'Yes,' Mr Percy told her, 'you're a good obedient girl, that's right.' Scratching her ears, he said, 'My son says he has an interest in politics, but I don't know that he's serious about that either. If he were, he wouldn't be doing what he is.'

Mr Percy looked over Hal's shoulder; Hal turned to look too. Percy was approaching, his hair frizzy in the moist air, his cheeks white and pink.

'We're talking about your career,' Mr Percy declared. 'I hear you've been saying you intend to stand for MP.'

'That's part of my five-year plan, yes.'

'I'm afraid I don't see how taking a degree in Asians is going to win over your electorate. The only migrants in this constituency have come from Scotland. Nobody here, Tory or Labour or SNP, wants someone who will use their tax to pay India reparations, or let migrants make an independent nation-state of Kent.'

'I don't think I would do that,' said Percy. 'There is a case to be made for reparations . . .'

'You've only got worse the longer you've been in the South. Didn't your sister send me a picture of you wearing nail varnish?' Looking in Hal's direction, he said, 'Well, we've all got our proclivities.'

'Dad, please, we don't say things like that any more.'

'But we do! That's just the sort of thing they say in the village, at the pub, after I've stood them all a few rounds. Those are the people you've got to look after. Ordinary people, the people whose interests you have a duty to represent. That would be true even if you never did anything but look after the estate. You might impress people in London . . . you'll find precious few radical leftists here.'

'Oh, I agree,' said Hal. 'Down with the Marxists. The only good union is the union of a man and a woman in marriage.'

'You see? Hal will get to Downing Street faster than you, if you're not careful.'

Hal wondered, as they began the last drive, if he wasn't ruining his own life for himself. He was shooting beautiful birds with a beautiful vintage shotgun on one of the best grouse moors in England. Here, rich foreigners paid thousands of pounds to feel for a day what Hal felt always: that he had a right to the land, to the things living on the land, including the people. If the tradition was to hunt humans, even bleeding hearts like Percy would do it. Percy had been born to this place. The things to which he was entitled were as much part of him as his body. His invitation to Hal had been an act of strange intimacy, a Christ-like offer to eat and drink him, to hunt and shoot him too.

The light had changed: the clouds had evened out until they were stretched thinly from horizon to horizon. The sun, which was as high in mid afternoon as it would have been an hour past noon in the dead of winter, glowed dimly enough to be looked at directly without pain. When the first wave of grouse flew towards him, Hal couldn't make out their edges. He missed the first shots he took, and his bruised shoulder ached freshly each time the shotgun jerked back. He supposed that was what he got for committing violence against fellow living creatures. He also had to put up with the pain of what he was fairly sure was an ingrown toenail. Is that not enough suffering for you high-minded voyeurs? Every day, even on the best of days, there was something hurting him. Very often it was pain he had caused himself. This made him better than Percy, who was always admitting to his own pleasure.

Hal looked fifty feet to his right, missing his shot watching Percy take his. Never mind: there was another wave of frightened birds swelling up along the curve of the hill before them, unified in flight, like the scales of a snake cascading forwards as it slithered. Finally Hal felt the gun as an extension of his own body, the way the best shots did. He pulled the trigger and the recoil passed through him. A bird dropped from the wave. He thought, *God gave man dominion over beasts; the beasts are flesh to feed the men.*

Then there was a great shift, an impact, as if he had been flung up against a stone wall. He thought first that God had struck him, then that his gunner had struck him. But his gunner looked rather as if he himself had been struck.

'What?' It took effort for Hal to speak. His face felt heavy and numb. 'Did I do something wrong?'

He touched his face; the feeling was off. There was a different texture to his right cheek, a mismatch of sensation between his hand and the flesh it touched. His fingers came away bloody. Having already dropped his gun, he took off his earmuffs and glasses. The wind cooled his sweaty ears and made him squint.

'Sorry,' said Hal, in the way he might solicit the attention of an employee in a shop. 'Did something happen?'

The gunner was sounding the alarm, consulting via walkie-talkie with the shoot manager, telling him to stop the drive and alert emergency services. Hal was distracted from what he was saying by the sight of Percy sprinting towards him, taking long leaps through the heather. Mr Percy jogged in his wake, slower than his son and straining with the effort. As Percy came into earshot, Hal heard him saying, 'I'm so sorry! I'm so sorry! Hal! Hal, Hal, I'm so sorry. I am so sorry. Oh God, Hal, I'm so sorry, I'm so—'

Percy brought the pain with him: an ache deep in Hal's head and right shoulder burst outwards and became unbearable. Hal leaned back against the inner curve of the shooting butt, trying to catch his breath.

'What did you do?' Hal asked Percy. 'Did you just shoot me?'

Percy told the shoot manager to bring one of the Land Rovers.

Hal said, 'Did you shoot me, Percy?'

'Don't talk,' Percy commanded. 'You'll make it worse.'

Percy's crisis-solving imperiousness disappeared upon contact with his father, who took him by the shoulders and shook him so hard that he might have caused brain damage. Mr Percy's whole head, from collar to crown, was red; his hands, holding fast to Percy's shoulders, were blanched white. He flecked his son's face with spittle. 'Are you a fucking idiot? Are you fucking incompetent? Have you lost your wits? Have you lost your fucking mind?'

'It was an accident,' said Percy. 'It was completely an accident, I don't know what happened, I thought I was okay—'

'There's no such thing as an accident: there's only stupidity, ineptitude, and malice. You've shot him in the fucking face! You've shot him in the neck, you've shot him in the chest. His lungs could collapse, he could bleed out. What will you do if he dies?'

'It's totally fine,' said Hal. Looking down, he realised the birdshot had put several holes through the right side of his earmuffs. 'I've got a lot of brothers.'

Percy sat with Hal in the back of a muddied old Land Rover; Mr Percy drove them to the nearest A&E, which, like everything else, was in Newcastle. Hal had been disinfected and dressed by the shoot's first aider, who looked like a doorman at a terrible nightclub and had a doorman's same comforting nonchalance. An air ambulance had been suggested, but the doctor they'd got on the phone said it wouldn't be necessary, and Mr Percy seemed deflated to hear that Hal was not in such danger as would warrant an airlift. After fifteen minutes, Hal felt like he was on a summer-holiday car trip with a school friend and the friend's mother, one of those too-long drives from the marina to the villa or the villa to the airport.

'I'll never have you on a shoot again,' Mr Percy told his son. 'I'd never offer the privilege of shooting my birds to anyone who doesn't know not to swing through the bloody line.'

10

At A&E, Hal was deposited into a wheelchair and pushed past rows of curtained beds in which he could just glimpse, though his right eye had swollen nearly shut, other people in pain. He saw no blood except his own, browning on his hands and jacket. Having set Hal up in his own curtained bed, a person whose precise role was never clarified told Mr Percy there was a private room where the relations of the patient could wait.

'I'll stay with him,' said Mr Percy, keeping himself firmly on the inner side of the blue vinyl curtain.

A line of drool came out of Hal's open mouth. He said, 'Why doesn't Percy stay?'

As penance for his wrongful deed, Percy did. He sat in a plastic chair next to Hal's bed and listened dutifully to everything the staff said about Hal's condition. In the long periods between one person leaving and another entering, he paraphrased the texts he got from his sister, who communicated with him on behalf of those who were avoiding him out of respect for his grave faux pas.

Leaning to the left to talk around the person who was irrigating Hal's wounds, Percy said, 'My dad might actually mean it, about never letting me shoot again.'

Opiates had been dispensed without Hal having to ask, and the pain settled into a deeper, less accessible part of him. He would have been tired if it were the end of a good day's sport. Right now, he was exhausted into a state of subhumanity, and only spoke to ask for water. When Percy's phone died, he suggested he should retreat to the hotel room his father had booked, and Hal felt nakedly that he wanted him there, and said he had better stay, just in case.

Once Hal was properly admitted, he was wheeled to a room whose second bed was occupied by a middle-aged man suffering some sort of digestive malady that prevented him from eating. The crunching of ice sounded from the other side of the curtain as Hal, still numb in the face, struggled with a hospital roast dinner. He couldn't chew the chicken or the enormous slabs of unseasoned potatoes, and the peas were so sorry that Percy went to the Greggs up the road and brought back a container of tomato soup, which he fed to Hal like a baby. Hal tried to refuse this undignified treatment and was overruled. The staff who came in and out on various errands let themselves be charmed by Percy; they agreed with him that the food was not precisely gourmet, and seemed to apologise for it with genuine regret. He had such a natural charisma around his social inferiors that he made Hal realise how poor a defence his own bitchy irony was. Percy didn't need to be cruel: he commanded submission through a flawless projection of vulnerability. Meanwhile, the staff talked to Hal as if, having been shot like one, he had actually turned into a bird. He groaned and mumbled and was ignored. He was being kept overnight for observation and then packed off to London, where he would have an outpatient surgery to remove the pellets that might pose problems if left in. The rest, he was told, would work themselves out of his flesh on their own.

Hal woke before dawn because someone had come to take his vitals. He saw that Percy was sleeping upright in the plastic-upholstered armchair next to the bed. Could he not let go of his own goodness long enough to let Hal pass through this indignity in private? Percy woke upon hearing Hal's complaint that he was only being given strong ibuprofen, when he had been given opiates in A&E and felt worse now than he did then. The person who administered the ibuprofen, shaking his head at the barefacedness of this drug-seeking behaviour, would not entertain Hal on the question.

'Is it very painful?' asked Percy when they were alone.

It was amazing, Hal thought, that Percy had tolerated such a long stay in someone else's hospital room. Hal had been a visitor many times, and had disliked it even on happy occasions. He said, 'It's fine. It was worse having my wisdom teeth out.'

'Ooh, I still haven't had mine out. They've said I'll have to eventually, and I'm worried it'll be terrible. I suppose I deserve it after this.'

Hal was too tired and in too much pain to say the amusing thing he had thought. He said, 'You should go to the hotel. I'll just be waiting here till they finish the paperwork.'

'No no no, I've agreed to be your escort back to London.'

'As part of your penance.'

'Because I want to. I do feel bad. I had a terrible dream last night that I actually killed you, and in the dream I thought I'd just been dreaming that I was here in hospital, with you.'

Hal knew that he had dreamt and that the dreams had been bad. Before sleeping again, he would have to piss, so when Percy refused to be convinced to go get a cup of tea, Hal dragged himself up and left the lavatory door half-open as he relieved himself of the fluids he'd been given. Their mutual physical awareness – he could hear Percy shifting in his chair – reminded Hal of school, where from noon to night one's body was under the purview of one's peers. Schoolboys never passed up an opportunity to evaluate one another, to ask: 'Is he like me? Is he better than me? Is his body better than mine? Does he use that body to do the same wicked things I do? Or different wicked things?' The ones who only thought of girls were the luckiest: they were the ones who truly didn't care about the other boys.

When Hal came back to his bed, Percy said, 'We should see each other more often, after this.'

'Uh, why is that?'

'Wouldn't it be a fucking waste if you suffered all this just so that we could go back to being unfriendly? If we become great friends, maybe it will have been worth it. Then when we're old we can tell the story of how none of it would have happened if I'd been in good form.'

'You want to be my great friend? What do you think you'll get out of it?'

'Human connection? Have you heard of it?'

'Why with me, though?'

'Sometimes I think I quite like you,' said Percy.

Upon being released, Hal led Percy just off the hospital grounds and lit a cigarette. Half of his face was covered in white bandages, and he wore the jersey shorts and Adidas slides he had picked out of the bag Mr Percy had sent on from the lodge. Percy had offered to have the bloodstained tweed cleaned; Hal told him just to pack it away.

'Fuck,' said Percy, 'can you spare one of those? I've actually not had a fag in ages, I left my tobacco at the shoot.'

'Percy, I'm single-handedly subsidising your £10,000 per annum cigarette habit.' Hal was already opening the packet again: having come close to grievous injury, he felt a greater obligation to model Christ in deed and thought.

'I'll pay you back,' said Percy, 'with interest if you like,' which caused, in the instant before Percy kissed Hal, confusion as to whether Percy recognised this as stale innuendo.

Percy was standing not quite on his toes but definitely on the front parts of his feet. His lips barely touched Hal's. Hal was holding his lit cigarette in one hand and the packet in the other. He stepped back, but not without the humiliated sense that he had lingered too long in the kiss to protest it was unwanted. He wondered who had seen them from passing cars. Nobody had rolled down their window and shouted at them, which sometimes happened in London.

'I'm sorry, I should have waited until I dropped you off.' Percy was red from his neck to his cheeks, white from the eyes to the scalp. 'I didn't know when I would get another chance. I've been wanting to do it since yesterday, but I thought I shouldn't while you were in hospital.'

'You think shooting me gave you just that push you needed to decide you might as well try it on, since you know I'm up for it?' Hal blew smoke over Percy's shoulder. 'Do you still want a cigarette?'

'I don't want to put you out, if that's how you feel about it.'

'Here.' Hal held an unlit cigarette above his head. As Percy lifted up to grab at it, Hal kissed him back – badly, because he, Hal, was smiling.

Percy said, 'I never know when you mean what you say.'

'I can't help it if you're a fool.'

'Try to forget about this, won't you? I'm used to kissing girls, and they like it when you surprise them. Even if they don't let you do it again, they're usually happy enough if you try once when you're both drunk. I thought we might be drinking on the train, and then I'd have an excuse. But that was just an impulse, just then. My dad is always telling me I don't think things through, and I'm always telling him I do, but maybe he's right.'

Mr Percy drove them to the station in his Land Rover. The blood Hal had spilled during the earlier journey still dotted the brown leather seats. It was a short drive; even drugged and exhausted Hal could have walked. Hal saw in Mr Percy his son's stubborn commitment to causing bother for the sake of doing what he felt was right, though inevitably it inconvenienced everyone else involved, who wouldn't have minded nearly so much if he had just done the thing that was wrong.

11

They drank together on the train; Percy's concern about Hal's health was not so extreme that he would advocate against the consumption of a healthy can of Heino from the cafe car. To allow Hal to rest, Percy took up the burden of talking. He told stories about India and Pakistan and Bangladesh, and the strange food he ate that was actually really good, and the signs with funny bad English, and his own spirited but hopeless attempts to learn Tamil ('actually one of the oldest living languages in the world') and Bengali ('actually one of the richest literary traditions in the world'). He sounded like he was in his Oxford interview, sweating bullets, wondering whether this would be the year the university finally followed through on their promises to boot the Etonians out and get the state school geniuses in. He sounded like Henry, telling Hal about all the places he'd gone while Mary was at home with his children.

When he ran out of things to say about himself, Percy began a tentative first-date line of questioning about the facts of Hal's life. He asked which of Hal's siblings were still in school and which had gone on to uni, and whether anything interesting was happening in Wales, and whether Hal actually knew any Welsh (only the Welsh translation of the Our Father, which Percy found inadequate). After returning from the toilet, Percy opened his third or fourth can and said, 'Aren't you like the 130th in line for the throne?'

'Who told you that? I hope not anybody I'm related to. Catholics can't rule. We've had a bit of civil conflict about it, in centuries past.'

'What, still? America had its first Catholic president in the sixties. I don't know, it must be somebody else I know.'

'Even if Catholics were allowed, I still wouldn't be in the line of succession. We aren't descended from the right branch of the family. We're just leftovers from the time of the Black Death.'

'How long has it been since you've been to the castle?'

'Which one?'

'Is there more than one?'

'There's the ruin in Monmouth, and then the one in Lancaster's still standing. I like the ruin better: it's just a nice pile of rocks in some grass. At the other one, there are people who dress up like ye olde medieval Lancasters and give tours pointing out that the toilets were just holes emptying down the castle walls.'

'Isn't it amazing it's still there? My mum's family had a house that was built in the nineteenth century and burnt down in the 1950s. It didn't even last a hundred years.'

'There wasn't siege warfare in the nineteenth century – it wasn't built to last.'

'You should take me sometime.'

'I try to avoid going.'

'I'll go alone, then, and enjoy the tour without you. I'll come back and tell you all about the toilets.'

As they passed through flat, green Lincolnshire, Hal's drunk turned into the invalid's heavy sleepiness. Percy kept trying to start conversations until Hal was short with him and said that he had slept poorly in hospital and would sleep now. He had vivid dreams about ordinary things and woke with a cramped back and knees, an aching face and shoulder. The train was passing through Barnet, where Poins lived; they would be back in Central soon. When he saw Dr Bradmore, he would ask to be prescribed something good.

'My father's going to be out of his mind.' Hal spoke low enough that only Percy and perhaps the people in the seats ahead of and behind them could hear. 'He'll go on about how I barely escaped death, and how terrible it is for him to think I could have died without true contrition in my heart.'

'He won't be terribly glad you're alright?'

'It's my spiritual condition he worries about. He'll make me go to mass before the surgery. He'll say I should move back in with him to recover. He's tried to convince me I should give my flat to John when he's done with uni. He'll be waiting at the station for me, your father said.'

Percy looked steadily at Hal. Awareness showed through his slack drunk look. He leaned over in his seat and kissed Hal, starting with a medium-intensity tonguing and, finding Hal amenable, deepening into a wetter kiss. Percy's beard scratched the skin around Hal's mouth. When he pulled back, he looked startled; Hal followed his gaze across the aisle to a salmon-coloured man in a polo shirt looking out of the window with furious focus.

Henry, waiting just beyond the barriers to the platform, acted rather like he did when one of his children got in trouble at school badly enough for him to be brought in: he was impeccably polite to station attendants and cab drivers, and silent to the offending child until they were alone together. He took Hal to the townhouse and Hal went in, knowing he wouldn't have the strength to take the bus back to Fulham. He could go once he was rested. If Henry had invited himself to Hal's flat, he would not have been easily sent away.

In the hall, having shut the front door, Henry said, 'Good God, Harry.' Hal remembered Mr Percy calling his son that. 'If I'd known the boy was such an incompetent, I'd have told you not to go. I'd really thought better of him. This isn't worth fulfilling an obligation to Henry Percy.'

'I wasn't fulfilling an obligation. Percy invited me as a friend. His father was just there.'

'Oh yes, but it's all a part of maintaining the relationship. It's better when you do these things. They don't like to see me.' He led Hal into the drawing room, tied open the curtains, and said, 'Come into the light, I want to see what he's done to you.'

On the low table in front of the sofa, a cup of tea sat next to a disordered copy of the *Financial Times*. There was a faint odour of tobacco smoke. Hal thought Henry must have smoked one guilty cigarette and then aired the room.

'I shouldn't take the bandages off yet,' said Hal.

'It needs fresh air – that's the best thing for a wound.'

Gently, Henry unstuck the bandages from Hal's face, pausing when Hal winced. Seeing the gauze poking up from the collar of Hal's hoodie, Henry had him strip to his waist and peel back the larger bandages covering the wounds to his shoulder. Henry looked and seemed himself to be in pain, as if he were knelt before a grotesque image of a martyr.

'You're lucky to have your sight,' said Henry.

'Yes, I'm lucky.'

'But you will have scars.'

'They're going to leave some of the shot in, they've said.'

'Yes, I've talked with the doctors.'

'Will I look very ugly, do you think?'

'You'll still look like yourself. I'm sure it hasn't helped that you've been drinking. You've been smoking too. Don't try to pretend you haven't, I can tell. You won't heal properly if you don't stop. Your scars will be worse.'

'I'm fine. I don't care about the scars.'

'Father Dyer will hear your confession tomorrow.'

Shirtless, with fresh wounds, Hal felt Christ-like enough to say, 'No, I'm not going.'

Henry put his hand on Hal's injured cheek. At first he was gentle, as if he were trying to protect him from further harm. Then he began to run his thumb over the wounds. It wouldn't have hurt too badly if it had been one light graze, but he kept going back and forth over the same places. He pressed the edge of his thumbnail into a spot on Hal's cheek where the shot had been left in. Through a thin layer of flesh, the nail pressed hard against the pellet, and Hal's eyes watered.

'Then you can tell him that yourself,' said Henry, and handed Hal's shirt back to him.

Hal lay down for a nap on top of the duvet he'd spread out over the sheetless bed in his old room. He woke coughing after the sun had set; he'd recovered the duvet from the linen cupboard, and it was full of dust. The coughing aggravated the pain in his face, and he went for his ibuprofen only to find he'd nothing to wash it down with. He slurped cold water from the sink in the lavatory down the corridor, squinting in the bright electric light.

Coming out again into the corridor, Hal felt his father's presence in the house, and nobody else's. It was very quiet; few cars passed down this street at night, and the radiators were off until at least October. The siblings' rooms were empty. Who would stay in these rooms in twenty years if Hal never had children?

Bare-footed, soles picking up dust from the carpet, Hal went to the end of the corridor, where low light spread from underneath Henry's door. He opened the door without knocking and saw his father knelt on the rug at the foot of his bed, praying the rosary.

Henry had stopped in the middle of a Glory Be. Looking at Hal, looking down again, he went on: 'O my Jesus, forgive us our sins, save us from the fires of hell, lead all souls to heaven, especially those who are in most need of thy mercy . . .'

It was a Friday. Henry must have been praying the Sorrowful Mysteries: the agony in the garden, the scourging at the pillar, the crowning with thorns, the carrying of the cross, the crucifixion. Hal imagined being half-dead from thirst and hunger, dripping with blood, heaving on his weak shoulders the cross to which he would be nailed. He had never understood why Christ, knowing quite definitively that he was the Son of God, would ever believe his father had forsaken him. If it were Hal, he would have just got through it, certain that in the end he'd be dragged back home.

12

Once he had run out of the good painkillers, Hal texted Percy to say he could come round if he liked. Percy arrived at Hal's flat with a re-usable bag full of groceries and an enormous bouquet of sunflowers. Hal was so taken aback that the face he made upon opening the door visibly hurt Percy's feelings.

Percy said, 'I looked up "flowers for first date" and then "flowers for illness" and I couldn't decide which was right, so I chose the sunflowers just because I liked them. Are they hideous?'

Being sober, Hal was inhibited enough not to say that he thought Percy had just come over to fuck. He hadn't agreed to this being a date: he hadn't tidied his flat since the last time the cleaner came, and all the surfaces were covered in takeaway debris and old half-empty cups of tea. His fridge was also full of takeaway, which Percy had to move aside to make room for the groceries.

'I don't really cook,' said Hal uncertainly, spotting raw chicken breasts and Brussels sprouts.

'I'm going to cook for you. You obviously need a home-cooked meal, your sodium intake must be off the charts. You'll have to start taking blood pressure pills like my dad. Don't look so grim, I've brought wine too.' Percy brandished a bottle of cheap white, then looked through Hal's flat for a suitable receptacle for the flowers. 'Do you not have a vase anywhere?'

'Why would I have a vase? Nobody gives me flowers.'

'I wonder why not.' Percy stuffed the bouquet into a large glass jar that had once contained olives. A spot on the dining table was cleared to make room for it. Wincing at the state of decomposition, he pushed the rest of the rubbish into the overflowing bin. 'And do you not clean up after yourself?'

'The cleaner is coming on Thursday.'

'What, for the first time ever? This is so much half-eaten Chinese. Does your father know your flat looks like this? Look, you've got a stain on the rug here that looks radioactive.'

Sitting on his sofa, propping his feet up on the coffee table, Hal said, 'I'm sure you came with condoms too.'

'No, should I have? I wanted to give you the chance to, umm—'

'Be a lady and refuse to fuck on the first date? Percy, this is like our third date. You invited me shooting: if you'd invited a girl shooting you'd have already come inside her. Go on and open the wine, I haven't had a drink since the train.'

'I honestly didn't know that that was what I was doing. Inviting you was my dad's idea, he suggested it when I told him I'd seen you at that party. I honestly' – he was so honest! – 'didn't have any idea about anything until you were bleeding.' Percy returned from the kitchen with two of Hal's wine glasses, enormous goblets that you could pour half a bottle into and still not fill halfway. Twisting off the twist-off cap, he said, 'And then I thought, oh no, I've ruined my chance because I've shot him.'

Hal waited for them to finish their second round before he asked: 'So have you ever even had sex with a man before?'

They had just been talking about which chain supermarket had the best wine in the £8–10 range. Percy hesitated, startled. 'It depends what you mean?'

'Anything where you had an orgasm and another man was involved, or another man had an orgasm and you were involved, and it wasn't rape. Except that "unlawful carnal knowledge of a minor" does count as sex if it was consensual. And I suppose it counts if you at least touched each other's cocks and tried to have an orgasm but failed.'

'Ohhh, well.' Hal could picture him being interviewed by a BBC correspondent after a session in parliament. 'Remember that awful ball at Corpus Christi, the end of second year? When everyone was throwing fists about because someone hadn't ordered enough alcohol and everyone was trying to take what there was before it was gone? I met this Australian boy who lived in college at Merton, and he said, "Why don't you come up to my rooms?" And then we smoked pot and gave each other handjobs. But I was really embarrassed afterwards and never responded to his texts, and then I never saw him again except once at a party last year but we pretended not to recognise each other. Why? When was your first time?'

Hal laughed. He wasn't sure how he'd answer that question if he tried to answer honestly.

'Freshers Week,' he said. 'I was introduced to this don who used to be Richard's friend, like the kind of friend he had sex with, but not more than that – not his quote-unquote "friend" friend, that was Edward Langley. Anyway, he kept touching my lower back, and I thought, Oh, he thinks he's going to have sex with me too. I suppose he thought if he could get away with it with Richard, he could get away with it with anyone. He lived in college, so he asked me to his rooms, and I gave him a blowjob and felt very smug about seducing a don in Freshers Week. He was good-looking, mind you, not the sort of don who's like a reanimated corpse from the 1880s, so I thought I had cause to feel smug, until I found out he tries it on with literally every boy who will talk to him for longer than five minutes. I felt quite confident of my technique at that point, so then I found another fresher to shag. He was the one who gave me throat chlamydia.'

'Gosh! That's awful! Is that curable?'

'Oh yes, yes, don't look so pale. I just got tested in July.'

'How many people have you had sex with since then?'

'Would you believe me if I said none? Or do you really think I go round shagging any man who looks at me? I wish I had been shagging. Those were the last days of my beauty. Now I'm only attractive to sadists who take pleasure in my suffering.'

'I don't!' The wine in Percy's glass sloshed over the rim as he gesticulated. A few drops splattered on the leather of Hal's sofa, and Percy tried to rub them away with the heel of his hand. Then he looked Hal in the eye and said, 'I wish it hadn't happened. But I do—I am, you know—You do attract me. Not because I'm taking pleasure in your suffering, just because you're still – or, I mean, not still, I mean as much, or more than before, even . . .'

Hal hated to feel Percy seeing him: the mottled brown bruises down his cheek, jaw and neck, the short lines of stitches marking the places where the shot had been surgically extracted, the localised swelling that caused a greater than usual asymmetry. He looked back at Percy, at the one eyelash that curved in the wrong direction, the fleck of whitish fluid in the inside corner of his left eye, the rash on his neck where he'd shaved the overgrowth of his beard, the reddened delicate skin of his impudently flared nostrils, out of which poked a couple of fine dark hairs. He felt for the first time the desire to possess Percy's body rather than his image. Percy, recognising Hal's look, kissed Hal first again. He put one hand in Hal's hair. With the other he set his glass down, except his eyes were closed, so he put it on the edge of the table and it fell and spilled on the rug.

'Fuck, I'm so sorry. Now I've ruined your rug too.' He tried to stand to take care of it; Hal pulled him back down.

'No, stop.' Hal put a hand on the back of Percy's neck. 'Keep going. At least it's not red wine.'

Percy didn't know how to ease into it: he just spread Hal's mouth open with his tongue and licked like an anteater probing into a promising mound of dirt. Hal enjoyed it so much. It was better than kissing Jack, who was the best kisser Hal knew. They only broke apart when Percy tried to cup the right side of Hal's face, and Hal winced.

'I'm sorry.' Percy was wide-eyed and doleful. Imagine! Here was someone who recognised when he had caused pain, and apologised. Hal didn't understand: why apologise when he knew Hal would still get off with him even if he didn't? He asked, 'Does it hurt too much? Should I stop?'

'I'll tell you to stop if I want you to.' This was a lie, but it put Percy at ease enough that he could get on with it. Hal was already close to coming when Percy grabbed his cock through his trackies. He was much less drunk than he usually was when he had sex, and the unconfident way Percy handled his cock was sexy. As Percy pulled down the waistband of Hal's trousers, Hal said, 'Be careful, I'm going to come too fast.'

'It's okay.' Percy was jerking Hal off in the rote, determined manner of a teenage masturbator. He kissed all around Hal's mouth but never on it, as if arousal had rendered him incapable of aiming at Hal's lips.

'No, I'm serious, I'm about to—'

Hal was already coming. The sensation was so acute that he squirmed in Percy's embrace, curling his toes at the pleasure-discomfort. Percy was looking at Hal's cock as it spurted, furrowing his brow, muttering, 'Yeah, yeah, come on, oh fuck yeah,' exactly like people said those things in porn. Hal's spunk was smeared over Percy's hand and his own trousers and t-shirt. He caught Percy's hands and pulled his soiled fingers into his mouth, sucking them clean. Percy looked horrified, but he was breathing heavily and his erection was obvious in his jeans, and he let it happen, and let Hal kiss him with traces of his cum still in his mouth.

Pulling his pants and trousers up, kneeling on the rug in front of Percy, Hal worried that Percy would have an attack of moralism. Instead, Percy started treating Hal the way Hal liked. As Hal lowered his head, Percy put his hands in Hal's hair and pushed him down hard, rubbing his cock against Hal's left cheek, making Hal work to get it in his mouth. He kept up a line of patter as Hal sucked him off, but the closer he got to orgasm, the more strained and incoherent he became. The muscles in his thighs were deathly taut, and his hands trembled, pulling Hal's hair hard enough to hurt. Hal's face hurt also. When he made an attempt at deep-throating and gagged, Percy made a noise so undignified that Hal understood, suddenly, the historical tradition of gentlemen conducting their affairs with working-class men exclusively. It must have been a unique sort of humiliation to know that the man sucking your cock could connect the part of you that made noises like that with the part of you that had been elected to Pop and owned a grouse moor and intended to stand for MP. But, for Hal, sex was a conscious act of humility: he let Percy fuck his throat because he was making a gift of his own debasement.

They did the same thing later that evening, after Percy had cooked the chicken and Brussels sprouts and did the washing-up and packed the ample leftovers into containers, to which he affixed sticky notes with the date and the warning 'Eat within 4 days or toss!!!' They kissed for longer the second time. Then, because they were going out for a cigarette anyway, they walked down the road to Hal's usual off-licence and picked up more cheap wine and a packet of prawn cocktail crisps.

The evening was cool enough to remind Hal that summer was ending. The sun had dropped below the horizon and the sky was twilight blue, muddied by the yellows of streetlamps and lighted shopfronts. It was the kind of weather Hal associated with killing time before going up to school for the autumn term. He had turned twenty-three earlier in August, and hadn't done anything more than get drunk with Jack, who reassured him that he was still very young, that he had no idea how young he really was. He felt younger than he was, now, walking back to his flat beneath a blackening sky. At this age he was meant to be in the full flush of confident manhood. But he wasn't ready yet, he thought. There was more living he had to do before he was a man. Someone should have stopped him before he got here. Here he was, still flying forwards into the next minute and the next, closer and closer to the terrible moment when he would have to give up and become himself. He thought: I don't want to, I don't want to, I'm scared. Then he let Percy back into his flat, and in the front room, with the door still unlocked, he kissed him, and let Percy touch the right side of his face even though it hurt.

Percy stayed over, slept in Hal's bed on his unwashed sheets, borrowed Hal's toothbrush and comb. He was the first man Hal had slept with who spent the night in his bed. Hal woke from a heavy sleep to see Percy awake, sitting up and looking at his phone. In the morning light his body hair looked especially ginger. Freckles darkened his shoulders. It was a good thing Hal's face looked so bad: it would distract from the acne that stood out distinctly on his pale back and arse cheeks.

Hal said, 'Am I the ugliest person you've ever woken up next to?'

'By far. And you've got the worst personality too.'

Hal imagined how all the other people Percy had slept with had felt afterwards: the oligarch's daughter, the boy from Merton, the half-dozen beautiful girls who appeared with him once or twice and then vanished, their relationship sealed up and buried in well-bred discretion. Earlier that week – bored and high on his legitimately prescribed opiates, sitting on the sofa with an ice pack on his face, half-watching daytime telly – Hal had scrolled through years of photos on Instagram and pages of Google search results, torturing himself with Percy's goodness. There were the marathons to raise money for charity, the petitions for world governments to act on climate change, the video walk-throughs of Lahore, Islamabad, Delhi, Varanasi, each centring Percy's own sunburnt face, catching only by accident the apprehensive glance of the subaltern.

The worst thing Hal uncovered was that Percy had been photographed for *Bystander* three times over the past several years, once with each of his serious girlfriends. There was no way it could have happened accidentally: Percy had to have refused all requests for photos at every event he attended until he had the chance to be pictured with the girl to whom he had decided to attach himself publicly. These three were the girls the tabloids would go to for dirt on Percy if his career took off. They could be trusted to say that Percy was a lovely man with whom they had had a lovely relationship, and that they wished him all the best.

Hal kissed Percy before he had a chance to go off and brush his teeth; he savoured the sugary-foul taste of a white-wine hangover. He got between Percy's legs and sucked his cock until he was fully hard, and kept going until Percy came in his mouth. When Percy recovered enough to try to reciprocate, Hal kissed him on the shoulder and said it was alright, and went to smoke the first cigarette of the day out of his bedroom window, looking down at the flowers and the bins in the forecourt below, and the shiny cars parked along the length of the kerb, and the woman in a caftan walking a terrier, and the tradesman unloading his tools from his van, and the skinny tree whose drooping yellow leaves just brushed the front of the house opposite. It was a sunny day, cool and dry, with a blue sky high-vaulted but not infinite, and a breeze that carried Hal's smoke away.

13

The Boar's Head was west facing, so that on fine summer evenings the cheap wood and grimy upholstery was covered with a flood of orange sunlight. The built-up heat of the day, ineffectually dispersed by a single air conditioning unit, had a sedative effect; the pints were pulled slowly, the conversation was ponderous. It was a day like this, a Sunday, when Hal returned, and the public's depression at the imminent work week affected even the feckless unemployed, a group to which Hal now officially belonged. He had gone that past Friday to the British Policy Institute only to be invited into the director's office and told that he would not be brought on for permanent employment. The director had given the diplomatic advice that, as a bright young man with a good education, Hal had a great deal of freedom to explore his potential, and would undoubtedly make his way towards a fulfilling vocation. He then offered to put Hal in touch with a number of contacts in other fields who might be looking to take on a junior employee. Hal thanked him warmly and did a disgusting shit in the office toilet before leaving.

Jack was waiting for him at their usual booth, halfway through what was clearly not his first pint of the evening. He had already known about the injury, as Hal had had to give a reasonable excuse for his absence, but Hal had refused to send a picture, and now Jack was taken aback.

'You don't look like the victim of a tragic accident, you look like you're in the final stages of syphilis. The one half of your face is a completely different colour than the other. You look like a Battenberg cake.

Look at you, you've got holes in your face. You look like Elizabeth I after the pox. If I thought your soul showed in your face, I'd think you must be an awful person. Of course, I've always known you are, but now other people will catch on.'

'Do you think I'm unfuckable now?'

'You're not unfuckable, just un-look-at-able, like so many other unfortunates, born or made. But for some people any warm hole will do. There's a beautiful simplicity to that, I think. Like those paintings that are just one colour. Of course, my own tastes tend more towards the baroque.'

'You don't mean you wouldn't fuck me?'

'I would consider it. So long as it was from behind, and we weren't near any mirrors.'

'The problem with you, Jack, is that you live your life like you're still good-looking. Or do you honestly think you haven't changed since 1989? You should be thankful anyone will have sex with you at all. You're so old and fat you're not even appealing to people who are specifically into old fat men. It gives me second-hand embarrassment just to think about how you still go out to clubs. Like do you not notice that everyone there points and laughs at the clapped old bloke who shows up hammered and hangs round the bar trying to pull twinks who refuse to acknowledge his existence? You're bloody lucky I haven't got anything better to do than this. If it wasn't for me, you wouldn't even get your hands on another man's arse without coughing up fifty quid first, and it's not like you would ever have fifty quid if I wasn't lending it to you.'

Merely acknowledging Jack's existence seemed to require lengthy enumeration of his failings, his age and his fatness and his skintness and his irrelevance. Jack liked it. He traded on his reputation as a grotesque, he played it up, he asked for it. And it was true: Hal was the best thing that had happened to Jack Falstaff since the turn of the millennium, which marked the last time he was cast in a feature film that wasn't straight-to-video. He'd been wasting his days at a Wetherspoons in South London, waiting to die or to be given a second chance as a character actor, and all of a sudden there had been this boy who would lend him money and let him spank him or suck his cock or play with his arsehole. If Poins hadn't introduced them, Jack might have offed himself by now. So why did Jack look like he was struggling to laugh? Was Hal not being funny enough?

'Buy us another round,' said Jack, 'and then I'll give you an answer.'

'An answer to what?'

'To all your problems, my sweet boy. Heaven knows you've got them. If you didn't, you wouldn't be here, with me.' But when Hal returned with two more pints and asked what the answer was, Jack said, 'The answer to what?'

'To my problems.'

'What makes you think I would have the answer to your problems? I don't even know what you think your problems are. I haven't ever seen you with one.'

Hal's phone vibrated in his back pocket. He looked at the caller ID, afraid that it was going to be his father asking him to come home, and saw that the screen read 'H Percy'. Looking past Jack, Hal came face to face with his reflection, sallow and unflatteringly lit, in the streaky, sticky mirror behind the booth.

'What are you ringing me for?' Hal asked Percy. 'If you want your dick sucked, you'll have to come to Camberwell for it.'

'Am I not allowed just to ring you?'

'It's 2014, Percy. I talk to my friends on Instagram and I buy my drugs on WhatsApp. The only time anyone ever rings me is if some-body is in hospital.'

'I just, umm . . . Look, I can't talk for long, I'm just on my way to something in Chelsea, and I was wondering if you were going to be at your flat so maybe I could come round after? But you said you're not at home, so . . .'

'Why am I not invited, are you afraid I'm going to tell all your friends from school you're following through on the bisexuality?'

'If you want to come, you can. It's just dinner with an old mate and his girlfriend. I'm pretty sure you'd hate it.'

Hal recognised 'You can come, but you'd hate it' as the thing he always said to put off people like Poins when they tried to nose their way into something too posh for them. He wondered which part of him Percy considered unsuitable for the event. It must have been that *he* was too posh. He said, 'So is the girl someone you dated once?'

'I haven't dated every girl in the world, Hal. I've only dated like four and a half.'

'Was the half-girl an amputee or a transvestite? Sorry, sorry, but really, did you date this girl?'

'For fuck's sake, Hal, I said you could come. Or don't, I don't care.'

'I'll be back at my flat by eleven. Come by when you like.'

Hal laughed, watching himself laughing in the mirror. He was holding his phone so that the screen pressed against his upturned mouth, crossing his free arm across his chest, like an eighteenth-century portrait of a lady posing flirtatiously with a fan. He saw that Jack had put a cigarette behind his ear in anticipation of going out.

Jack said, 'Do you love him?'

'I don't love anybody but Christ.'

'Not even your old fat Jack?'

'Especially not him.'

'You used to say "I love you" very freely,' Jack told Hal. 'You were always drunk, but you did say it, and more than once, and on more than one night.'

'You should feel lucky you got that much. I haven't told my father I love him in ten years.'

Percy was drunk when he showed up, but fairly composed, and so polite that he took his shoes off before pitching into Hal's front room, saying, 'I'm so sorry I'm so late, that took so much longer than I thought it would . . . It was just, you know, we had a lot to catch up on . . .'

It was past one in the morning. Hal had been back at his flat by ten, and had hurriedly tidied the worst of the mess and showered and cleaned his arsehole and foreskin. By eleven he'd been sitting on the sofa with the door unlocked and the lights dimmed. Not wanting to look desperate, he waited till half eleven before texting Percy, 'Come round if you like, I'm in'. Percy took twenty minutes to text back: 'Sorry still here, had to stay for pudding and scotch. Don't ruin your plans on my account'. Hal had said, 'Well I'm here. Now till whenever I leave tomorrow. Will leave the lights on and my legs open for you'.

Percy had had nothing to say to that. Hal had tidied his flat a little more, and made himself gin and tonics that were a three-to-one ratio of gin to tonic, garnished with browned, shrivelled lime wedges that had been sitting in his fridge for days. When he started to feel too drunk, he did some coke, so that by the time Percy arrived Hal felt dazzling. He slammed the door shut behind Percy and said, 'Can you still get hard?'

'Yeah, I can always get hard when I'm drunk. My erections are really persistent.'

Hal said, 'That's great, Percy.'

'Can't you call me Harry?'

'I don't know, take your clothes off and we'll see.'

Percy got completely naked – he took his socks off too – and stood before Hal, holding his half-hard dick as if he were worried he might set it down somewhere and forget. It helped that Hal had put on music: it was one of Philippa's playlists, nothing he really knew, just the kind of glossy dance music they played at H&M and Shoreditch nightclubs, with breathy lyrics about sex and drugs that made the encounter seem pleasantly idealised, as if he and Percy weren't two red-faced rahs who had sucked and wanked themselves into mutually assured destruction. Percy's body was still better than Hal's: his muscles were evenly toned, his stomach flat, his shoulders defined, his arse perfectly rounded. His pubes were the same red-brown as his beard, thick and untrimmed. He was wanking himself looking at Hal, who for now was unashamed. Hal didn't look like Percy, but Christ, imagine if he looked like Jack Falstaff! He might in thirty years, but right now he was six three and fourteen stone and blond and newly twenty-three, with enough cocaine to last him another couple of nights, and there was this handsome round-arsed scion of the landed gentry who had forsaken the profits of heterosexuality to be with him specifically.

After they had kissed for a while, Percy said, 'So are you ever going to let me fuck you?'

'I thought you were too afraid.'

'Afraid of what?' Percy laughed. 'Take your clothes off. I'll fuck you till you can't walk.'

'Ha ha! Are you joking? Have you ever fucked anyone till they couldn't walk? Look, if you think you can, you can go ahead and try, but I have had sex with other men before.' When they were in Hal's bed and Percy was looking anxiously round for lubrication, Hal said, 'There's lotion over there and actual lube in the drawer, but you can just use spit if you like.'

'Do you want it to hurt?'

Rolling onto his front, propping himself up on hands and knees, Hal said, 'If it does, then it does.' After Percy spat on his arsehole, he told him to rub it in with his thumb. He talked Percy through fingering him: 'It's not that different to doing it with a girl. Same angle, same philosophical approach.' He told Percy he could use a condom or not, it was his decision: he was willing to gamble on Percy not having any incurable diseases.

Perhaps feeling that he had been challenged to perform a dangerous feat, Percy fucked him bareback; he put one hand on Hal's lower back and used the other to force his cock into Hal's arsehole. He did, in the end, have to use the actual lube.

'How's that?' asked Percy.

Hal chose to say nothing, because if he said anything he might accidentally reveal that it felt good. He made a noise, and that was enough for Percy, who held his hips and fucked him hard. Hal didn't know why he'd been expecting Percy to be weak. Because he was shorter than Hal? He was strong, and Hal felt a blunt pain every time he thrust just a bit deeper than Hal could take. Being high made the pain exciting. Hal wasn't even fully hard; that wasn't the point.

'Percy,' said Hal, looking over his shoulder, seeing Percy's heaving figure at the outer edge of his vision.

'Seriously, you're allowed to call me Harry.'

'Henry Percy.' Hal laughed. 'When we've broken up, Henry Percy, don't pretend this never happened.'

'What if we never break up?'

'Don't try to frighten me.'

'What would I be, if we got married? Would I be the Duke of Lancaster too? The dukette? The duke consort?'

Hal said, 'You wouldn't be anything. I wouldn't marry you.'

Percy was making the noises that Hal knew from experience meant he was going to come. Under his breath he was saying, 'Oh fuck, oh fuck.' Hal had just begun to feel pleasure, a persistent and predictable swelling of warmth. His sweat was wetting his hair down against his forehead, making his spread legs prickle with damp heat.

'Ahh, I'm gonna come,' said Percy. 'Oh God, oh fuck, I'm so close.'

Hal was comforted that Percy had said nothing worth saying. Shutting his eyes, he felt how the room seemed to be flipping top over bottom around him. Percy had pulled out; Hal could feel the tip of Percy's dick pressing rudely against his arsehole as he wanked himself off. Percy was triumphant: he had done it, he had fucked another man in the arse, he had done the forbidden thing. Hal was Percy's bitch, Percy's woman, Percy's hole. He felt it when Percy's cum landed on his back.

'Turn around,' demanded Percy. 'I want to see your face, I want to kiss you. Did you come already?'

'Yeah,' said Hal. He hadn't. What they had done had been enough. He was in Percy's arms and it was lovely to be there, to be one inconstant body rubbing off on and absorbing another. 'It was great.'

'Good,' said Percy. 'It was supposed to be.'

Was Percy happy here, did he feel safe here, in private, being intimate with a person whose own position was such that he could be relied upon not to violate his trust? 'That's the problem with shagging middle-class girls,' Tom had said once, drunk after dinner, smoking in the garden of the London house. 'You're always like, "I know you're going to tell all your friends about this. Unless I make it really degrading, but you like that, so . . ."' It was funny because that was the kind of hyper-energetic misogyny Tom had picked up from his middle-class mates on his economics course, those class-insecure aspiring superyacht owners who now occupied the positions at HSBC and Barclays he had coveted and been unable to secure.

Humphrey had said, 'No, it's the really posh girls and the really poor ones who like to be degraded. The middle-class ones just want you to pay for an expensive dinner and comment on their Instagram pictures.'

A memory floated up of Percy working on some sort of sexual-consent awareness campaign at his college, pinning up posters that declared 'CONSENT IS SEXY' in bold font, with the contact details for a counselling service in smaller font at the bottom, urging the viewer to call if they had been the victim of assault. How strange that that earnest boy was in Hal's bed now, his dick still wet from fucking him, reaching shyly across the pillows to touch Hal's hair.

14

If they weren't going to hide it from the rest of the world, they could not hide it from their fathers. Percy pre-empted an accidental outing by sitting down to dinner one evening with his father and stepmother and telling them that he had been seeing so much of Hal Lancaster because he was seeing him. He was brave: he had that fatal combination of stubbornness and good intentions. His father tolerated it because he knew that to forbid it would be to start a fight with his son he might not win.

Henry found out because Percy, having told his own father, made his final gesture of commitment to Hal, which was to let them be photographed together. Percy had taken Hal as his date to the twentieth birthday party of an heiress to a newspaper fortune (on her father's side) and a banking fortune (on her mother's side), whom Percy knew through his sister. At some point Hal was swept up and made to pose without explanation. Percy said, 'Come here,' and put his arm around Hal's waist, distinctly possessive, just like he'd done with the girls before. Hal told him how he'd looked him up and seen the other photos. Percy said that he'd looked Hal up too, but could find no evidence of his ever dating anyone before. All he'd found had been a sloppily written listicle from 2011, 'Britain's 30 Most Eligible Bachelors', which featured Hal at #16 and stated that he had an estimated net worth of £20 million – 'I wish I did!' – and that his relationship status was unknown.

A few weeks later, Henry asked Hal to lunch at his club. In the middle of his Welsh rarebit, he said he'd seen the picture of him and Henry Percy's son; Eleanor Woodstock had shown it to him.

'And then I happened to speak to Henry Percy,' said Henry, 'and he told me that his son had told him you two were quite close now.'

'Yes,' said Hal. It was a Friday, and he was coming down from the night before. Percy's lesbian friends had invited them back to Dalston. When they'd arrived, Fern had flung open the door, looked back and forth between them, and said, 'What happened to your face?' He hadn't slept, he'd just drunk three double espressos from three different coffee shops over the course of the morning. Now he kept having to swallow back espresso-flavoured heartburn sick.

'If you're expecting that I've brought you here to tell you you're wrong and you shouldn't,' Henry was saying, 'I won't. You reached the age of reason fifteen years ago. I should think you've had enough practice making moral decisions.'

'Well, good.'

'You know all the stories about Richard and his friends. I've told them to you already.'

'You don't have to tell me any stories about Richard.'

'Ah, so this isn't that sort of a relationship?'

'No,' said Hal.

'He and Edward Langley did sleep together. After he was too ill for it, they pretended it had been chaste fraternal love since the beginning. But it did happen, quite often, when we were all younger. Quite blatantly too.'

If Hal were really the outrageous person he pretended to be, he would have given Henry what he was asking for, and told him exactly how Harry Percy fucked him. But he was above all self-interested, and knew when to say, 'The details of my sex life are between me and my confessor.'

'So long as you are availing yourself of the sacraments.'

'Why bring me here, then?'

'I always want to see you. Why shouldn't a man want to see his son?' This was evidently some sort of joke; Henry was smiling. He patted his mouth with his napkin, and when he brought the napkin down, the smile was gone. 'It's just Philippa.'

This was the first time Henry had spoken to Hal about Philippa specifically, rather than just 'the girls', in probably half a year. Hal said, 'What, is she throwing fits again?'

'I've been besieged by the headmistress, she kept ringing and ringing and wouldn't be put off, and as soon as I spoke to her, she demanded I then speak to a firing squad of swotty females who've told me all the ways in which Philippa's been causing trouble. They've said she's been refusing to eat, which I was always given to understand was the sort of thing girls do, meaning – I would have thought – the sort of thing a girls' school could be reasonably expected to address. I don't know what they expect me to do: I can't even get Philippa to speak to me unless she wants money, and now she goes to Jeanne for that. She likes you, Hal. She looks up to you rather – I suspect that's part of the problem. But then you really ought to talk to her. Tell her she won't get what she wants from it.'

'What do you think she wants from it?'

'Oh, to make other people unhappy.'

Hal gave a hopeful glance to George the waiter, who approached unhurriedly. When Hal asked for another glass of wine, George looked to Henry for the nod.

'You've enough time on your hands,' said Henry. 'Though that will change soon enough. I've had a chat with Thomas, and he's agreed to take you on at Woodstock. Just on a temporary basis, mind you, you won't get everything handed to you on a platter. You'll have a year, and then you'll have to figure out for yourself what to do next. He wants you to go in for an interview first.'

'And that'll be, what, once a week? How many hours?'

'Five days a week, eight hours a day, at least. You'll work late if he asks, you'll go in on Saturdays if he asks, and on Sundays you'll go to mass. You'll be drawing a salary of £33,000 per annum before tax, which works out to about £2,000 a month after tax, and that will replace the allowance you haven't been working for.'

Horrified, not quite believing it, Hal said, 'I'd rather go on a mission trip.'

'This is a kindness. I've debased myself begging for a favour from a man who would probably prefer to see me dead, because I know that when I am dead and you've replaced me, you'll need the sort of discipline I've never seen any indication of you having. I did ask others – about a dozen others – before I asked Thomas Woodstock. They wouldn't take you. Rightly so: you've spent the past five years broadcasting your deficiencies across the country. You should be grateful you're being given another chance. If you were born on a council estate, you'd be in prison.'

Afterwards, Hal met Percy for a pint at an ivy-covered pub near Russell Square. Percy had just come from a seminar on postcolonial theory. Sucking the foam off his pint of lager, Hal said, 'I do have discipline. I just choose not to use it to be a fucking, like, assistant's assistant's assistant at Woodstock Energy. Thomas wants to put me in public relations? Like, am I a girl?'

'Didn't you just get sacked from your internship?'

'I didn't get sacked. I just wasn't offered permanent employment.'

'My father was talking at dinner yesterday about how if I don't have children, it'll be Marguerite's children who get everything. He told her to keep her surname when she got married and make sure the child was double-barrelled, because I can't be trusted to pass on the name now that I'm gay. I have actually literally told him that I like girls like 75 per cent. Marguerite asked what she should do if the man she married already had two surnames.'

'I suppose he hasn't heard about adoption?'

'Ha ha, can you imagine us adopting children!' Percy realised he'd been loud, and looked about the half-empty pub to see whether anyone was staring at him. 'But, really, I don't think I could cope. I mean of course I'll have kids someday, but I've always thought there's so much to do in life before you tether yourself to this creature who's constantly wailing and voiding its bowels.'

'And then if you adopt one that's old enough to use the toilet independently,' said Hal, 'you've missed the opportunity to make it primally, instinctively in thrall to you.'

'Is that true?'

'I wasn't talking about *us*. We're twenty-three and we've been together for like three months. But you might do it with some other man, sometime.'

'I couldn't with you anyway because you're a morally inflexible Catholic. They'd come after you with pitchforks if you ever had a gay baby. I mean a baby of gays, not a baby that is itself gay. Although I suppose if sexual preference is intrinsic then you are gay when you're a baby, it's just that nobody knows yet, unless they can like, measure the amount of time a baby spends looking at men or women, and correlate that with their adult sexuality . . .'

The pub had no dedicated smoking section, so when they went out to smoke they loitered on the pavement, pressing up against the cars parked along the kerb as they stepped back to make way for the people who walked occasionally by. By their third smoke break Percy was pretty drunk, and said, 'About what I said earlier—'

'I don't remember anything you say, Percy.'

'What I said earlier about the not wanting to have children w-with you specifically, it wasn't meant to be a slight against you—'

'I'm not like my father, I'm not going to cut my youth short and start amassing infants just because I'm anxious my "O God make me good but not yet" phase is due to wrap up.'

'I didn't say you were, I was just saying—'

'Well, you don't need to—'

'It wouldn't work,' said Percy. 'Just because of, you know . . .'

'Cheer up, Percy, there are worse things than inheriting a grouse moor and significant interests in oil. There are even worse things than being PM: you could be a terrorist, or a child prostitute . . .'

'But Hal, I don't—' Noticing how he was booming, Percy protested more quietly. 'I don't dislike you . . .'

'I mean it, it's fine, don't make excuses. You think I care more about what you think of me than I do. Let's go back in. I'll get us the next round.'

It was raining when they left the pub. They stopped for a quick, indifferent dinner, then took the tube back towards Fulham, because Hal's flat was the only place they could go to have sex. The carriage was full enough that there were no two seats together, so they stood in one of the bays near the doors where tourists stowed their enormous suitcases. Percy, holding onto a pole, snuck out his other hand and took hold of Hal's. Hal jerked back as if Percy had groped him, which actually he would have tolerated better. Percy took his hand again, stroking the back of it with his thumb. The train stopped at Hyde Park Corner and a lot of people got off and on. Some took second looks when they saw that Percy and Hal were holding hands. Percy didn't notice because he was looking into Hal's eyes, trying to get Hal to look into his.

'Actually I love you,' said Percy.

Had the woman in the trouser suit in the seat nearest them heard that? For a terrible frozen quarter-second, she and Hal looked into each other's eyes: he had looked away from Percy, and she, apparently, had been looking at him. She looked away first, clutching her handbag closer. Not homophobic, he didn't think, or anyway not primarily – just upset with him and Percy for making her look a stranger in the eyes on the tube.

Earlier, between the club and the pub, Hal had nipped into a Waitrose, claimed his free coffee, and stood at the magazine stand to look through the new issue of *Tatler*. Following about a hundred pages of women's luxury fashion advertisements, he found the spread of pictures from the party, interpreted by a caption reading:

COSTUME DRAMA – The hemlines were low and the collars high at Miranda Gardiner's 20th birthday party. Don't worry, the revellers at Bagpuize Park weren't suffering from a sudden attack of modesty – the party's theme was *Downton Abbey*. As the Taittinger disappeared, so did the clothes; several guests ended up skinny dipping in the fountain. (Photographed by Miles Taylor.)

Percy and Hal were on the top left, identified as 'Harry Percy & the Earl of Hereford'. Percy looked handsome, Hal uglier than he'd thought himself capable of looking. In such a small picture, you couldn't see his scars individually, but the right side of his face did look different to the left. It distracted somewhat from Percy's hand, which was so far down Hal's waist it was nearly on his arse. Marguerite had texted Hal:

Marguerite Percy 14:37 saw you and harry in fucking bystander from miranda's party ahaaahahaaaaha
Marguerite Percy 14:37 why did u let them
Marguerite Percy 14:38 so fucking awkward honestly

An old woman in a slightly ratty fur coat bumped Hal with her trolley. Hal thought of Percy and said, 'Oh! I'm frightfully sorry. Are you alright?'

15

Hal hadn't fallen for anyone in the autumn since he was in year 10, when a young redheaded novice who had entered Mount Grace Abbey the year before was brought on to teach classics at the school. Hal's Latin was bad, his Greek terrible, but from the day they met he would have died for Brother Stephen, who tutored him specially and let him get away with smoking and sometimes at weekends went walking with him on the moors. Brother Stephen was the only person there, staff or student, to whom Hal spoke honestly and seriously. He was the only person who knew Hal. The two things Hal kept secret from him were the truth about his father and his suspicion that he was irremediably homosexual: nobody needed to know about the first thing, and he thought that Brother Stephen must have guessed about the second.

In the autumn of Hal's last year at school, Brother Stephen drove them to Howsham, and they walked up the banks of the River Derwent to the ruins of a thirteenth-century priory. They ate their wrapped sandwiches on the riverbank, sitting in view of the ruins and the car park for people visiting the ruins, and Hal lay down in the grass and let his head press up against Brother Stephen's thigh. Brother Stephen said, 'We should be getting back.' For the rest of the school year, he treated Hal like any other sixth-former. Hal cornered him at the Leavers' Ball, and he wished Hal well with a finality that suggested they wouldn't see each other again. When Hal went back to Mount Grace in the autumn of his last year at Oxford, he was told that Brother Stephen had left the monastery.

Since then, Hal had had all of his crushes in late spring, when the first warm sunny days arrived and the parks and gardens filled with people, drunk and raucous and underdressed, getting sunburns on their noses and grass stains on the seats of their trousers. It was easy for him to be generous when the days were getting longer, the nights temperate and open, inviting him out into the world. It had been in the spring of his last year at Oxford that Poins introduced him to Jack, who was staying in town to see an old mate of his from RADA lead an Ibsen play. They'd met at a pokey pub Jack knew, far out of the way of any tourists or students; the downstairs was barely a quarter full, and they'd had the upstairs room, with its worn green carpet and wooden benches, all to themselves. Hal had found Jack attractive. He remembered seeing him in movies from the eighties and nineties, and there was the way he talked and the way he looked at Hal, and the way he treated Hal as if his being the heir of the Duke of Lancaster was an understandable but ultimately irrelevant extension of his being an actor.

Now the nights were long, the sun rose late, and Hal would wake in the dark before seven, enjoying Percy in bed with him before he, Percy, had to go off and be impressive all day. By quarter-past seven, Percy would be in the shower, using Hal's soap, drying himself off with Hal's towels. Hal kissed Percy goodbye and fell back to sleep until his last-minute alarm, then pulled on his shirt and trousers, ran his fingers through his hair, and took the District line alongside all the other people going to work. It was always raining, the daylight always diffuse, rubbing away the hard edges of shadows so that every discarded carton or carrier bag was extra-visible against the wet dark pavement. The Woodstock offices occupied the third storey of an ageing concrete mid rise that seemed to have been constructed, along with several others of its type, specifically in order to put something ugly in front of Notting Hill's charming old terraces. The ground floor held modest iterations of the same chain shops found on any high street in the United Kingdom. On his fifteen-minute breaks, Hal stood under the overhang in front of the Tesco Express and smoked. He suspected Thomas of assigning him this position just so that his time would be wasted less in idle pleasure than in the torment of pointless work: it was like soft-labour prison. He imagined redeeming himself through honest endeavour – bricklaying or trauma surgery or feeding the poor – because it hurt less than his old daydreams of giving acceptance speeches at the Oscars. For the first time, Hal wondered if he could become a priest. He would go on a mission far away and fail to fully learn a new language. He would strengthen himself through willing poverty. But Percy had done that first. In the evenings, he came to Hal's flat with his gym bag and a reusable tote full of shopping, and they went into Hal's bedroom and closed the curtains, and he fucked Hal half to death. Then he cooked a lovely dinner with a plausible story of adventure attached to it: 'My mate from the Philippines taught me how to make this when we were backpacking in Hawaii,' or 'I had this at a street stall in Taiwan and it was so good I had to ask them how to make it – have you ever been?' The only way Hal could beat him would be to join the military, where he could do all that and kill people too.

Later in the night, when they were drunker, Percy would talk about his family, and about the less flattering things that had happened to him at school. Hal learned more about Percy than he had wanted to know. Stories that had been to Hal only second-hand gossip became disconcertingly immediate: he remembered Percy at eight, at thirteen, at eighteen, and felt an affronted disbelief that all that time Percy had been doing things he had neither witnessed nor imagined. He tried not to think about it because if he did, he couldn't fuck. He became too aware of his body as a continuous thing, connected physically to itself, like a long line of Hals going back to conception and forwards to resurrection. Somewhere behind him there were the ones who had touched other people besides Percy, and the pious ones who promised they'd never do this, and the ones still in his mother's arms.

Hal began to miss Percy when he was gone. Sometimes in the middle of the day Hal texted him with a mild whinge or a funny picture and Percy left him on read, and when they met face to face again Hal would say, 'Did you get my text?'

'Oh, yeah, I was just really busy,' Percy would say, and Hal would loathe him: who the fuck was Harry Percy to ignore his texts? Then Percy would put his hands in Hal's hair and say, 'I missed you so much,' or 'I can't stop thinking about you,' which was meant as an expression of devotion but betrayed, occasionally, a bewilderment at having been so thoroughly consumed.

One night in late November, Hal woke to his phone buzzing somewhere underneath the bed. He leaned down and patted the rug till he found it in the pocket of his discarded trousers. It had stopped buzzing; there was a missed call from his father, from the London house, whose number Hal knew by heart without ever having saved it.

Percy was asleep, so Hal locked himself in his bathroom to ring Henry back. He looked at himself in the smudged mirror over the sink, thinking about how unappealing he looked: his thighs were fat, his Primark boxer-briefs pinched into his waist, his nipples sort of looked like surprised eyes. His first two calls went to voicemail; he didn't leave a message, just rang again.

Slurring like he was the one who had been awakened, Henry said, 'I must be interrupting you.'

'No, no.' Hal sat down on the closed toilet seat. 'I was just asleep.'

There was a packet of interdental brushes sitting on the edge of the countertop, just within reach, so he poked one into the gaps between his teeth, flicking the bits of dislodged food onto the floor. The brush came away bloody, and he tasted iron. His dentist was always telling him he didn't take good enough care of his gums.

Henry said, 'I thought you might have been with Henry Percy's son.'

'I'm just at my flat.'

'I dreamt I choked to death. I woke up and couldn't breathe. I don't know why.'

'I'm glad you're better.'

'Come and wait with me until the morning, and then I can ring Dr Bradmore.' When Hal sighed, Henry said, 'I thought I would try to avoid waking him in the middle of the night. But if you won't come . . .'

'I'll come,' said Hal. 'I'll leave now. Do you think you might die in the next half hour?'

'I might. Anyone might.'

Tossing the bloodied brush into the bin below the sink, Hal said, 'I think you can probably hold on. I'll be there.'

Percy was still asleep when Hal came back to the bedroom. He was snoring lightly; it was cute. Hal put on trackies and an old hoodie and went outside to smoke while he waited for his minicab. He texted Percy: 'Going to see my dad, he's feeling unwell though it is almost certainly nothing. Stay in my flat if you like. There is an extra set of keys in the top drawer of my desk.'

The front door of the townhouse was unlocked; Hal accidentally locked it trying to unlock it, then had to unlock it again. The upper ground floor was dark. Only a faint residual light fell down through the central stairwell, illuminating the black-and-white tiles in the hall. He felt like it was half-term and he was sneaking back in after a night out: just because the house was quiet didn't mean Henry wasn't wait-ing. He wasn't fucked up enough for this, Hal thought. He and Percy had only shared a bottle of wine with dinner. He felt his way through the dark drawing room to the console table with the crystal on it and drank straight from the whisky decanter. Then he faced the closed double doors to the dining room and whacked his forehead against the oak till he saw stars.

'Thank God it's you,' Henry said when Hal reached him. He was sitting up in bed, wearing his reading glasses. On the bedside table, the lamp with the floral blue glass shade was lit and radiating heat. 'I thought it might be thieves, you were making so much noise.'

'Just trying to find my way round in the dark.' Hal shut the door behind him even though they were the only ones in the house.

'You might have turned on a light.'

'I didn't want to presume. This isn't my house any more.'

'It will be soon enough. Come here, sit with me.'

Hal took the uneven wooden chair from the writing desk and set it by Henry's bed, just out of arm's reach. The radiators were rattling as the heat came through. His head hurt badly. He'd wanted to speed things up; now everything was happening twice as slowly, prolonged by present pain as well as dread.

Henry said, 'Our ancestors were long-lived. Your great-grandfather Edward was long-lived. Your grandfather John lived long enough. But Richard died young, and Richard's father died before his own father. I don't know what I should expect for myself. It's wrong of me, I know, to want to know what to expect. I can't rely on looking holy just before God comes round.'

'Did you take your medication before you went to bed?'

'I'm not taking the new tablets,' said Henry. 'They're awful, they make me see things.'

'You mean like dreams?'

Henry took off his glasses to rub the bridge of his nose. He folded them shut and set them on the table. In the low light his eyes were dark: you couldn't tell pupil from iris.

'When I die,' said Henry, 'I want to know that all the trouble we've all gone to, for God knows how many years, will still mean something. Can you imagine what a waste it would have been, if it ended with you?'

'It won't end with me. You've got four sons.'

'These friendships young men have – what you have with Henry Percy's son – in and of themselves, they're perfectly ordinary. Two young men caring for each other, that in itself is ordinary. That's what I've told Henry Percy, who thinks men simply shouldn't care for one another lest they be mistaken for homosexuals. The trouble is in making sure it doesn't go too far. I made that mistake with Richard. I took him too seriously, and I spent too much time with him.'

'I thought you and Richard always fought.'

'Don't you and Harry Percy fight?'

'You know we're having sex,' said Hal.

No thrill came from saying it. It didn't bring him back into his body, like saying risky things sometimes did; he was still floating in the corners of the room, looking at the cracks in the crown moulding.

The wallpaper was a soothing blue-and-white chinoiserie, a twentieth-century take on the eighteenth. The white wood mantelpiece was grey with soot from the fireplace, and a pattern of pale rectangles marked the spots where pictures had hung for years and then been removed. A carved-wood crucifix on the wall next to the bed held a pewter figurine of an emaciated Christ, his ankles crossed and his cheek pressed forlornly to his shoulder.

Henry said, 'I had thought you must have been.'

'You and Richard didn't.'

'No, not at all. Richard would never have considered it. Even when we were close, he held me at arm's length. He always made excuses not to come to my parties. I thought they must have seemed boring to him, those ordinary parties with a punch bowl and a lot of awkward schoolboys trying to get their end away with girls who'd had to be begged to come and make up the numbers. So for my nineteenth birthday, which was the first year we were up at Oxford, I went to Jeanne and her boyfriend at the time, who gave the best parties out of anyone I knew besides Richard. I told them to do what they liked and I would pay for it. I must have spent £8,000. I had to hide it from my father. The boy Jeanne was seeing had a house in the country, about forty minutes' drive from Oxford. They did it up, you know, they cleared the dining room to make a dance floor. There were gondolas taking people round the lake. The prime minister – not the prime minister then, the prime minister now, who, mind you, absolutely nobody would have guessed would ever be prime minister – nearly drowned when he jumped out of a gondola blind drunk. They had to pull him back into it, he couldn't swim to shore. I had written Richard's invitation by hand. I told him he really should come, it was going to be different from usual.'

'So did he come?'

'He said he would look at his diary, and he never mentioned it again, and I was too shy to bring it up. Then, on the day, he sent a splendid bouquet to my rooms in college, sympathy flowers I suppose, with a note attached that said, "Sorry I can't come to your party. Many happy returns. Love, Richard." '

Hal said, 'It sounds like a ghastly party.'

'Some people said it was the best of the term. Not my sister, but she never liked the mixing of the sexes.'

'Did you ever find out what Richard was doing that night?'

Henry said, 'I never asked.'

The curtains in Henry's bedroom were a heavy dark blue that blocked light completely. When Hal left the room, he was surprised to see the landing visible in the grey morning light coming down through the skylight at the top of the stairwell. He had made it through the night. He could go out walking, or to the cinema, and then to the pub, and he wouldn't have to go back to his flat and be alone until he was drunk and exhausted. Before he left, he went out through the French doors that opened onto the terrace and smoked a cigarette sitting on the stone steps that led down into the garden proper.

How many hundreds of times, on how many mornings or evenings, fine or grey, had he sat on these steps and smoked? When he was younger, he'd only smoke in view of the house while his father was out. If there was a chance Henry might have seen, Hal would go beneath the trees. After the third or fourth time it had happened, he'd smoked on the terrace knowing Henry was in, thinking it couldn't possibly matter any more. Hal's memory was generally good; even if it wasn't, one would think that anyone would clearly remember at least the first ten or so times their father had brought them to orgasm. Why did he have to work to remember even the first time? And then it had happened maybe five times between the start of that autumn term and the end of summer term, about once every school holiday except Christmas, when Henry waited until after Boxing Day and then it happened two nights in a row, once when Hal was quite drunk and once when he was not. This third or fourth time, then, had been in brilliant spring, during the Easter holidays, and the early morning had been warm enough for him to go outside in a t-shirt and flannel pyjama bottoms, which picked up dirt when he sat on the steps. His hands had been shaking so badly that he'd broken one cigarette and had to light another. That was when it had finally felt like it was happening: before, it had felt like an inexplicable mistake, an experience he had been given by accident that would soon be taken back. There was healthy lavender beneath the steps, and pale pink hydrangeas bordering the terrace, and further off, in the garden, the blooming cherry and crab apple, the pear tree. Mary had been the one who'd done the garden. Henry had told her not to bother, nobody cared about London gardens, and she had said, 'I do.' All that life! In paradise, before the fall of man, there had been trees and flowers and clean water and fresh air, and that ought to have been enough. If he was suffering now, thought Hal, it was because someone from whom he was descended had done something wrong before he, Hal, had ever had a chance to do what was right. Now, having been punished, he was here, in the garden again.

Hal had guessed it was going to happen as soon as Henry had first rung. He was never certain, but over the years he had developed a sense. He had come here anyway, having had the sense. That third or fourth time, he had gone to his father when he'd asked for him, having had the sense. Henry kissed his hands and forehead first, or rested his head on Hal's shoulder, confusing his body into accepting it. I can't believe he's still doing this, Hal thought. I can't believe I'm still letting him. Early that morning, when it had still been dark, Hal had lain there looking at the reflection of the ceiling in the mirror over the mantelpiece in Henry's bedroom, asking himself why he didn't just say no. Why didn't I just knock him down? Why didn't I just kill him? Now that I'm tall and strong, now that I'm a man. But he wasn't a man, he was Henry's son.

He tossed his fag end into the overgrown grass at the foot of the steps, then thought of Percy and considered picking it up and putting it in the bin. Then he thought that the rubbish would go into a landfill anyway. And when the gardeners came round, they would clean up after him, and if it gave them cause to talk behind his back, who was he to care?

PART THREE

NO MORE PARTIES

16

One Sunday evening, as Hal was heating up Percy's leftovers, Ed Poins texted him:

Poins Poins 19:07 Back in LDN, shoot wrapped, don't have to diet or go gym any more, lets get fucked up!!

A moment later another text popped up:

Poins Poins 19:07 You get the ✳ & meet at your place to frontload, then we hit up the club, Tim's mate hosting ✦ EXCLUSIVE ✦ party and invited me plus one

At half eight, Hal and Poins were sitting on Hal's sofa at a suitably platonic distance from each other, knocking back the canned rum and cokes Poins had bought on his way. There was a bag of cocaine in Hal's pocket that they hadn't chopped yet, and a big packet of salt and vinegar crisps split open on the coffee table. Poins had the shine of a person who'd come up a rung on the ladder: he spoke as if he belonged to another, better world, and was visiting this lower place out of simple humble fealty to an old friend.

'And they were like, just all over each other on set,' he was saying, 'and in that really annoying way where they're always playing pranks on each other, and making fun of each other in front of other people, except other people can't join in because it would be weird? And I was just like, *Ugh, gag me!* I spent the whole time out vaping with Tim

Strong and letting him pass on his wisdom about acting, which was like, "You've just gotta feel it, you've gotta put all of yourself into the role, you've gotta let go of yourself," and I'm like, oh, cool, that's totally useless and I'd rather not.'

Hal said, 'Wow, I can't believe you know all these Hollywood stars.'

'Remember when Jack Falstaff was the most famous person I knew? Speaking of, he kept texting me in agonies about you ditching him while I was in Budapest, and he wouldn't stop, and I had to lie and say my phone got nicked and I couldn't replace it till I was back in London. Now I'm going to have to think of another excuse.'

'It's a good thing you're going to be famous now.' Hal shook the coke out onto a plastic-backed hand mirror which, when it was not being used for drug-taking, Hal used in the service of trimming the hair around his balls. 'That way when I ditch you, you'll already be on your way up.'

'That was my plan,' said Poins.

The evening was misty. The cold air pinched Hal's face and bare hands. Poins had said not to embarrass him by wearing something that made him look like he was reading PPE, so he was in a pair of skinny jeans he'd bought his first year at uni and only recently lost enough weight to fit into again. Over that he wore a puffy jacket leaking feathers from the lining. Hal didn't know why Poins was so keen not to be embarrassed by him when Poins was wearing peach-coloured trousers and a cardigan.

There was a burlesque act on stage when they arrived at the club: skinny girls with narrow waists and fashionably small breasts, costumed in latex girdles and stiletto boots, were wielding unserious little BDSM whips against empty air, backed by an uninspired remix of a song that had topped the charts in maybe 2009. As soon as he checked his coat, Poins dived into the crowd in search of Tim Strong, whom he found sitting at a table in the corner talking boisterously with a tattooed man twice his size. Hal couldn't tell if this was a bodyguard, a drug dealer, or rough trade, though Poins had assured him he knew Strong was straight because he'd made his career playing gay. When

Poins interrupted, Strong welcomed him with a tight embrace. Hal was amazed anybody liked Ed Poins that much.

'And this is my mate Hal Lancaster,' said Poins, pulling Hal forward for Strong's appraisal. 'We acted together at uni, actually. He was the one I was telling you about before, who played Worthing when we did *Earnest*.'

Having, over the course of his life, been introduced to a lot of people he didn't care about, Hal recognised Strong's look of banal geniality, the vacancy behind his eyes as he clasped Hal's hand in his hot, sweaty paw and said, 'Oh yeah? Sweet, sweet. I'm Tim, what's up.'

There was a light show in green and pink, muddled by the product of the fog machine. Hal couldn't tell whether the effects were being directed live by some dark figure in a booth somewhere, or pre-programmed and played like a movie. He didn't know why taking lots of cocaine and going to nightclubs was supposed to be fun. Possibly he needed to do more cocaine. That was how it got you: you remembered how much fun it had been those first few times, and went out and did more to try to have that much fun again, except it was never quite as exhilarating, you wanted that sense of total mastery, overstimulation even, pleasurable overwhelm, the belief that everything was in your service and everything would happen in your favour. So you made excuses, you shared looks with your mates and went to the toilets and queued for a stall, and took out your baggies or vials of coke and keys or tiny spoons and did about as much as you thought you needed, and then a little more, and then a little more. Then you were out in the smoking section with post-nasal drip and a cigarette between your shaking fingers, and if the coke was good you were as high as you were at the beginning of the night, feeling that the boring world, the rainy English night, were fascinating and good again, and you were good again, and it was all going to be perfect, and none of your problems meant anything, you had no problems at all. What a privilege, to feel that good! Even though your throat was sore and your sinuses were inflamed and you knew that some unbearable pain was always possible, in the next second or the next.

'So,' Hal asked Poins, 'are you seeing anyone?'

'I don't know,' said Poins. 'There are a few guys I've been talking to, but nothing really serious.'

They were in the club's private courtyard, where the stunted, leafless, newly planted trees were failing to shield them from the rain. They hadn't wanted to bother getting their jackets back from the cloakroom, and Hal's jumper was getting damp. There was an awning, but there were some very good-looking women under it who seemed unlikely to want to make room. Hal touched the top of his head and found it slightly wet, the rain mixing greasily with his pomade.

'No one really interesting?' he asked.

'There's this model from Amsterdam, who's like very handsome but really stupid but in a sweet kind of way, but then tall skinny guys always look like spiders when they're naked. And then there's this Hungarian guy who was an extra in the movie who I've got on WhatsApp, and we sext occasionally, but he won't show hole and he can't come to London till the summer. And then there's another guy who's a waiter that I met on Grindr, and he's really bad at sexting and has a fetish for dirty socks, but he wants me to come round his place after he gets off work next Friday, so . . .'

'And you're still meeting other guys off Grindr?'

'Don't slut-shame me, it's not like, every day or anything. And I use condoms, which I know you don't, even though AIDS like runs in your family, so . . .'

'Ugh, Percy wants to have sex constantly, it's honestly terrible. Look!' Hal showed Poins his text message history, pausing on each picture for a second as he scrolled through. 'I'm like, *Mate, once a week at most*.'

'You're still calling him Percy even though you're like, fucking every day?'

'What else would I call him?'

'I don't know, whatever he wants to be called.'

Hal tossed his fag end onto the polished stone flooring, not looking to see whether there was an ashtray nearby. Poins was still vaping;

he blew smoke out of his nose and mouth, and rain fell through it as it rose. The good-looking women were going back inside, letting a group of loud men in plain suits take their place.

'Ed,' said Hal, 'tell me something honestly, I really want to know. You've thought about having sex with me before, right?'

Poins glanced warily at the men, as if there were any chance they'd heard what Hal had said over the sound of their own drunken noise. One of them was making fun of another for wearing a gilet.

More loudly, Hal said, 'Have you ever thought about having sex with me, Poins?'

Some of the men did glance towards him then. There was a poorly stifled eruption of laughter, followed by a cringing quiet as they tried to avoid confrontation.

'Why do you care?' asked Poins. 'Yes, everybody ever wants to have sex with you, it's all they think about, and then they forget to feed themselves and die of starvation, and that's why you don't have any friends.'

'Oh, stop, don't pout, Ed, your lips are too thin to pout.'

'No, I stopped wanting to have sex with you halfway through our first conversation ever, because I found out what you were like.'

'But you love me really. We're just alike, except that you're short and Jewish and I'm tall and Catholic. We've literally worn each other's underpants. Look, let's be friends again. Let's take more drugs.'

When Hal got out of his toilet stall, he didn't see Poins anywhere. The stall next to him, into which Poins had gone, was empty now, and the door was open. In the corridor outside the toilets, with the dark wallpaper and the mirrored ceiling, Hal nearly ran into Tim Strong.

'Tim!' he called out. Tim didn't look murderous at having been stopped on his way to the toilets, so he must have actually stopped taking drugs, like he'd bragged about doing in a *Rolling Stone* profile a couple of years back. 'Hey, do you remember me from like, an hour ago? Yeah, hi, it's me again. What's up?'

'Nothing much, mate. I've had too much beer, I've got to piss like a racehorse.'

'Look, tell me now while he's not around. Do you think Ed is actually a good actor?'

'He's a great guy to work with. I'd work with him again anytime.'

'But is he good?'

Strong laughed again. Hal felt vindicated; of course it was absurd, of course Poins wasn't good. Then Strong, gesturing to his BAFTA-winning nose and mouth, said, 'Mate, I hate to say it, but you've got a bit of a problem.'

Hal touched his own nose and mouth and felt wet, and thought his nose was running, which it often did in winter. He rubbed the back of his hand along his upper lip and saw in the low light that it came away with a dark, thin smear of blood. He felt a physical thrill, a convulsion of the heart, like he should have felt in August when he realised he'd been shot. He laughed too, and Strong clapped him on the back as he went into the toilets.

Looking up, Hal saw himself in the ceiling. His pupils were so wide that his blue eyes looked dark, and there was blood dripping out of his nose. People were staring at him as they passed – he could see them in the ceiling too – but he didn't care, he was looking at himself. The swelling and bruising he'd had through August and September had disappeared; the marks he had now were more or less permanent. What seemed at first glance like small dark moles were lead pellets still trapped beneath the surface of his skin. Where the shot had been surgically removed, there were white scars at the centre of divots in his flesh that made light and shadow lay upon them strangely.

Behind the nearest of the club's multiple bars, a good-looking boy in a black shirt and apron was shaking a cocktail and pouring it out, sloppily, into a martini glass garnished with a couple of shapeless maraschino cherries impaled on a neon-pink plastic sword. Leaning forward to make himself heard, Hal asked, 'Is this an open bar?'

'Yeah,' said the bartender, laconic. As if he thought Hal might be stupid, he repeated, 'It's an open bar.'

'Hang on, are you Irish?'

'Yeah, I'm Irish?'

Hal could see it now: the boy had that particular look, with the pale freckles and the long eyelashes and the detached, heavy-lidded look of distrust. Hal asked his name. Thinking of how Percy introduced himself before asking someone's name, he added, 'I'm Hal,' but he wasn't sure if it got across.

'Francis,' the bartender said.

'Is this your full-time job, or are you like, doing gigs for cash and DJing on the side or whatever?'

'I'm studying drama at Guildhall.'

'Oh, good for you. It's no use being a bartender long-term, you end up insane and addicted to hard drugs.'

'Like all the greatest actors?'

'So you want to be the next Peter O'Toole? Well, good luck, truly. I'm a failed actor myself. Am-dram's the best I could get. I've got work tomorrow morning, at my awful uncle's awful company. Totally nepotism, just not enough that I'm allowed to show up without a tie. Francis, how open is this bar really?'

Francis looked troubled; maybe he thought it was innuendo. He said, 'I don't know what you mean, sir.'

'Don't call me sir,' said Hal, casually benevolent, smiling. 'It's Lord Hereford.'

'I don't get it, sorry?'

'Nothing, it was just a joke. Francis, could I possibly trouble you for a bottle of vodka? Not, like, top-shelf necessarily, but not anything that's total shit, either.'

'Uhh, I'm not sure if we're allowed—'

'I said, don't call me sir: it's Lord Hereford. It's a subsidiary title, the Earl of Hereford. It doesn't really mean anything. It's just one of my father's that I'm allowed to use until he dies and I get everything, until I have a son and have to give him one of my titles that he can use until I die. The joke is that it's so gauche that I'm telling you because only real cunts ask to be called Lord Whatever, like you expect to be called

139

it in posh shops and hotels but it's bad form to correct someone if they don't call you it. But I've done so much cocaine, Francis, and I'd love for you to join me.'

After a long, bewildered silence Francis said, 'Yeah, if you're offering?'

'Yes, just give me the vodka. Then show me where the staff go to smoke.'

The pulsing light gave Hal double vision. He couldn't tell where Francis's gaze was directed. Francis reached down behind the bar and opened the bottle before passing it to Hal, who drank from it with his eyes closed and his throat open. Even the name-brand vodka felt like St Anthony's fire. Francis shouted to a boy in an apron that he was going for a fag, then led Hal down the mirrored corridor past the toilets and through an unmarked door into a stockroom piled with disarrayed boxes bearing the stamps of wholesalers. Another door, scuffed and smeared with something black, led into a gap between buildings just wide enough for a delivery truck to come through. Layers of fresh and faded stains haloed overstuffed bins that let off a rancid smell. A sallow, stubbled man in a dirty white t-shirt muttered a greeting to Francis before entering the building by a different door, through which Hal glimpsed the yellow fluorescence of a kitchen. Hal passed Francis the bag. Francis took out his keys and sniffed gratefully, then lit a cigarette and said, 'So even you couldn't get any work?'

'Casting directors like public school, not so much actual lords.'

'Ahh, well. That must be crushing.'

'I know, I know, such a pity.'

After another good sniff Francis said, 'I'm not going to blow you, just so you know. But thanks for the powder.'

'I don't want to sleep with you.'

'You've got your own drugs, I don't know what else you'd want me for. If you can afford this much cocaine, you could afford your own bottle of vodka.'

'Want a drink?'

'Well, since you've opened it . . .' Francis took a drink. He winced but didn't make noise. 'My manager's going to ream me. I don't really care though. I was going to quit soon anyway.'

'To do what?'

'Oh, nothing. Just work somewhere else. Somewhere with better tips. My mates kept telling me you can make £1,000 a night at a place like this. Maybe it's my personality, 'cause the cheap fuckers here always stiff me.'

'You'll be famous someday, mate. Just like Tim Strong.'

Francis scoffed. 'He does it for the money.'

'Right, right, and you do it for art. Like Peter O'Toole, who famously did nothing for the money.'

'My theory is, there are three types of actors. The kind who do it for the art in the beginning, the kind who do it for the art in the middle, and the kind who always do it for the art. The first kind stumble into the money and get addicted and never think about art again. The second kind need art to restore their dignity before they're allowed to make more money. The third never make money and never get famous. You see, if I was someone like you, I'd do it for the art and be happy with it.'

Hal liked the way Francis talked, his accent and his indignant certainty, his charming arrogant way of looking into Hal's eyes to make sure he was getting the point. He envied the force of Francis's desire, which could have existed only in the absence of opportunity. Hal had gone for a few auditions, small-time stuff, the summer after uni, and after those rejections he had never tried again. He wanted not to be himself, but he didn't want to be anyone else either: when he pretended, it was with smirks and winks, relying on irony to save him from being seen through. Poins was a better actor. Probably Francis was better still than Poins. Sensing this, Hal felt certain Francis wouldn't make it. He would end up in an office too, or shaking cocktails at Chiltern Firehouse, complaining about the incestuousness of the industry.

Hal told him, 'This is England, darling. You can't expect anything.'

Francis said, 'I've been thinking of moving to LA.'

Hal opened his palm demandingly. Francis gave him back his drugs. Hal gave a thick, mucusy cough.

'My father—' Hal started.

'Yeah?'

'You won't believe it. You'll think it's so funny. Just wait until you hear. My father—'

But Francis was looking at him, saying nothing, waiting to hear what he said. Hal said, 'Nothing. Never mind. My father is the Duke of Lancaster.'

Hal came across Poins again only after the lights were brought up. In front of the venue, they watched hired cars ferry away the last departing guests, the hangers-on who had not been invited to the afterparty. Tim Strong was long gone, home with the wife and kids. The rain was thicker, the night colder. They sheltered under the awning of another building, having been waved out of the doorway by the doorman.

Hal said, 'Did you see that really good-looking bartender earlier? The Irish one?'

'Oh yeah, Francis?' Poins blew cherry-flavoured vape smoke into Hal's face. 'I know him. I worked with him on a short a while ago. I've been trying to avoid him because we haven't talked since then, and it's awkward because like, he's got this shit idea for his own short and he keeps trying to get everyone he meets to donate to the crowdfunder that's stuck at like two hundred quid his grandparents donated.'

'What's it about?'

'It's so bad! It's about this Irish boy – because he wants to play the lead, obviously – whose dad is in prison for this mad Irish family feud murder he didn't commit, and so he goes out and kills the guy who actually did the murder, like as revenge, and then he turns himself in because he wants to be in prison with his dad, but it turns out the police have literally just found some new evidence that clears the dad, so the boy goes to prison alone.'

'Oh, that's brilliant. You're being too hard on him. That's just the kind of thing straight men like, he'll win awards. You should have introduced him to Tim Strong.'

'Why did you ask, were you trying to shag him?'

'No, I'm not a sex addict like you.'

'It's true that he's hotter than either of us.'

'Yeah, but doesn't that make you want to shag someone less?'

'I don't know, speak for yourself, mate . . .'

'I just mean—'

Poins's phone vibrated. He squinted at the screen before swiping to answer, and said, as if he wasn't sure who he was talking to, 'Hey, this is Ed? . . . Sorry, what? Well, look, she's nineteen, she can figure it out herself. Let her regret it, it'll teach her a lesson . . . Well, I don't know, what do you mean "really bad," is that like—Yeah, okay, so just get her to stay awake and drink some water. What? No, you have to stay there and take care of her. Yes, you do. It's your responsibility. Just until she's—Look, where are you? Text me the address. Tell her I'm on my way and she's a fucking terror.'

Hal was annoyed at having to face this new solemnity when he had only just recovered from Francis. He said, 'I told you Ellie wasn't innocent.'

'She's at somebody's house in Walthamstow, her friends don't even know whose house it is, and they're leaving her there because they live with their parents and have to get back before morning. Either I've got to dial 999 and then ring my mum and tell her Ellie's going to hospital, or you've got to come help me bring her back.'

'I've got work in the morning.'

'Hal, mate. I was there at uni when you gave yourself alcohol poisoning and had to get your stomach pumped. I was there in Berlin when you got a head wound from falling over drunk in the street. I stayed with you that night you k-holed in Trinity JCR. You only met me because we were both tactically chundering in Park End. You can't come to fucking Walthamstow with me?'

'I never asked you to do any of that, you just did it.'

'Because I was your friend?'

'Well, that was your problem.' Going up to the edge of the kerb, Hal said, 'Look, you've been waiting for me to splash out on a black cab forever, so here.'

*

They arrived at a quiet street of post-war terraced houses, most bare-faced but one shaded coyly by a large leafless tree. Hal could not guess what it would look like in summer. There was ordinary yellow lamp-light in the upper window, and coloured lights flashed in the lower window next to the door. Hal paid the fare with the cash left over from buying the coke, slammed the cab door behind him, shouted an apology for slamming it, and went into the house; the front door was unlocked and ajar.

It looked like, honestly, kind of a lame party. Nobody was in the front room with the lights and the music, and Hal couldn't help thinking of how somebody obviously lived a respectable life here in the daytime. The furniture was mid-range IKEA; the bare white walls and total lack of decor suggested the presence of a heterosexual man. The kitchen was clean, no dishes in the sink, but the countertop was cluttered with bottles of cheap spirits and fizzy drinks. Through the kitchen window, he saw the remaining guests sitting at a card table in the garden, smoking. Hal took a swig of whisky before going up to the bedroom where the light was on. The light came from a lamp on the bedside table, illuminating spots of vomit on the white shag rug at the foot of the bed.

'Oh, mate,' said Poins, 'your nose is bleeding.'

At twenty-three, Hal missed eighteen and nineteen and twenty, when daytime life had just been friendly tennis matches and a bare minimum of coursework, and at night he had competed against himself to pass out as quickly and grandly as possible. He had avoided boys like Percy because they were always trying to show how much they could drink without falling over or getting sick. Hal went to Poins for a partner in semi-self-inflicted torture: 'semi' because once you set it in motion it wouldn't stop. You could drink or snort or smoke whatever you liked, as much as you liked, and the substance would dispense consequences at its leisure. But now he never passed out, he never quite got rid of himself. He binged for days; he stayed conscious; he had nosebleeds and panic-attack comedowns.

'Yeah,' said Hal, 'I got one in front of Tim Strong earlier. Do you know he went to Charterhouse? It's funny how he acts like a fucking Borstal boy. Not that Charterhouse is much better.'

'You're just jealous because I got to be in a film with him and there's never been a good actor that was also a lord.'

'Poins, is your sister here or not?'

'I don't fucking know. You know everything, you tell me where she is.'

They found her in the bathroom, which in this house was so small that Ellie alone could barely fit in it. Hal and Poins crowded in, leaving the door open because it swung inwards and they would have had to squeeze in even tighter to shut it behind them. Ellie was sitting on the floor with her knees raised, resting against the side of the yellowed acrylic bath. There was vomit on and around the toilet, and down the front of her dress. She wasn't wearing tights or shoes, and her dress didn't cover her arse fully; Hal avoided looking at her thong by staring at her feet, which were blackened as if she'd been walking outside barefoot. If he were a girl, thought Hal, he would look just like that right now.

Poins knelt beside her, his back pressing up against the rim of the toilet bowl. A bit of vomit smeared on his cardigan. While he was trying to get Ellie up and talking, Hal rang for a minicab. Ellie puked into the bath. Hal thought it was a good sign that she still had enough wits about her to aim.

Ellie said, 'I'm fine, I'm fine, leave me alone, just let me deal with it.'

'No, you can't,' said Poins, 'you're in somebody else's house. Do you know these people?'

'I don't know, yeah, they're my friends' friends. Ugh, I'm so fucking drunk. But I'm fine.'

Hal said, 'A line or two would sober you up.'

Poins said, 'Shut the fuck up.' To Ellie, he said, 'Hold my arm, try to get up—'

'Move, get out of the way, you're useless.' Hal took Poins by the shoulders and physically moved him out of the way, which he did easily even as Poins struggled. Before Poins had a chance to try shoving him back, he knelt and lifted Ellie onto his shoulder.

'Stop picking up my sister,' Poins demanded.

Hal was already in the corridor, then on the stairs, lumbering unsteadily under about eight stone of drunk girl. She was laughing. He expected it to be dawn when they got outside again, but the morning was still dark and the streetlamps were still on, making everything grey-yellow. He tried to load Ellie into the back of the cab at least a little bit respectfully.

The driver said, 'If you stain the interior, that'll be £60 for the cleaning fee.'

As they pulled away, Ellie leaned against Hal's shoulder, her barely animate body shifting with the movement of the car. He reached across her to roll down the window on her side. The cold air cut in, pulsing against their faces, ruffling their hair. The air always smelled sweeter in the early morning. The roads were mostly empty, wet with dew.

They took Ellie to Fulham: Mrs Poins wasn't too strict, she would buy the excuse that Ellie had slept over with a friend, but the Poinses were respectable people, and if Ellie was going to have any freedom in the next five years, she couldn't let her mum see her like this. Hal got her up to his flat and laid her out on the sofa with a towel beneath her and a glass of water on the end table. Here he was, Mary: chaste and continent, looking over Ed Poins's little sister like a benevolent angel, except angels were never benevolent, they were soldiers in an imperial army, and probably did as much raping and pillaging as any British regiment abroad.

Labouring to lift her head up, Ellie said, 'Ed?'

'No, it's Hal, you're in my flat. Ed's sleeping.'

'Sorry for taking up your flat.'

'Yeah, no, it's fine.'

He opened one of the windows and dragged a chair over from the dining table, so that he could sit and smoke while keeping an eye on her. Blowing smoke out the window, he found himself wishing he were less aware of the fact that he had, right now, more or less total power over her. She couldn't sit up, she could hardly speak; he doubted

146

she was going to remember any of this once she was sober. He could pick her up and put her down somewhere else; he could push her out of the window and say she jumped; he could take her clothes off and put them back on again, he could wank in front of her, he could violate her in any way he chose, and if she woke up and perceived what was happening and remembered it later, nobody would believe her. Imagining it upset him, but the actions themselves seemed, however close, however possible, to be on the other side of a line he felt certain he would never cross. Or would he? What would he get from it, even? A sense of his own power? He wondered whether his father had ever looked at him and thought this clearly about what he was going to do. He wondered if there were things his father imagined doing that he had never done. He wondered what he'd thought before the first time.

Ellie rose from what had either been a deep sleep or full unconsciousness to say, 'I'm going to be sick again.'

Recognising that he had very little time in which to mitigate the situation, Hal furnished her with a bowl from the coffee table that he had left there after eating Percy's homemade pasta out of it the evening before. She puked onto the remnants of a meal that Hal had quite enjoyed.

'That's right,' said Hal, holding the bowl for her. 'Just get it out, and it'll be over with.'

'You're so nice . . . You're nicer than I thought you were. You're so relaxing, like, you're better than doctors.'

'Do you like doctors?'

'No, that's the point, you're better than them.'

Who would say those things, Hal asked himself, having actually met him? He wasn't fooling anybody any more, not even her brother. Maybe she'd hit her head. Last spring, Poins had invited Hal up to Barnet for Passover dinner and Ellie had ignored him so intensely that their mum had reprimanded her in front of everybody. Now she liked him, because he had given her a bowl to puke in. Christ, her standards were low. He felt he should do something to live up to her expectations, so he got out an old t-shirt and the smallest tracksuit bottoms he owned, and left the clothes along with a fresh towel at the end of the sofa, next to her feet. He got her a clean bowl; he filled two more glasses of water and set them on the coffee table. He told her to sleep as long as she liked and eat what she wanted from the kitchen, only be careful with the leftovers, some of them were dodgy.

'Thank you so much,' she said. 'I'm so sorry.'

He said, 'I've got to get ready.'

The window was still open, the curtains still pulled wide, except that now instead of exposing the lamplit room to the houses opposite, it presented the houses and the trees and the lavender sky to Hal like a picture. The air was cold and Ellie had curled up to keep warm, but Hal wouldn't close the window: he would be shutting her in. He added a clean jumper to the pile at her feet and turned off the lamps. By the natural light, he showered and brushed his teeth and put on a suit and combed his wet hair and put more pomade in it and did three lines off the bathroom counter, just enough to get his head straight before he went to catch the bus.

Though he had avoided looking too closely at himself in the bathroom mirror, he got caught by his reflection in the mirror above the console table where usually he dropped his keys and wallet. As with most of the furniture in the flat, Henry had got the mirror out of storage at the London house, saying there was no reason to buy anything new when they'd already got so much they weren't using. Hal looked at himself in the tarnished silver and felt that his father was looking back at him from the other side. He saw his own fear in his face and was amazed at this evidence that he could be afraid, that even in manhood he did not always appear impervious to harm. Was that him in there, looking like that? He watched himself master his expression. The fear was still there, inside of him, but his face was opaque. He put on the aviators that were sitting on the table and went out, leaving the door unlocked.

17

The London Christmas-party season was one long seizure of embarrassment. Hal and Percy had to debut the relationship again at each party, offering themselves up to be judged by each new mix of acquaintances. It was satisfying to see Percy realise he had become an object of curiosity to his own class, like Hal had always been. Boys who might otherwise have called Percy 'Hazza' and roared their drunken goodwill were now conspicuously polite. It wasn't like they were homophobic – yes, they made gay jokes, but they also thought it was proof of Britain's moral supremacy that it was so much better on gay rights than Nigeria or Barbados or wherever – it was just like, Harry Percy, Hal Lancaster, really, out of everyone? And then the girls who had never been attracted to Percy anyway told him how good they looked together, how they should totally go for drinks with them and their boyfriends, which Percy seemed alarmingly up for.

The worst was a dinner at Percy's dad's place, with Percy's dad's friends who were also Hal's dad's friends. Nobody acknowledged that Hal and Percy might be anything more than old family friends until they were all very drunk and drinking whisky after dinner, and a man who had been the old family friend of both their fathers told Hal, very smugly, pleased that he had figured out a way to Trojan-Horse the unspeakable through what he felt would be an all-in-good-fun joke: 'I suppose you have the right. He's poked holes in you, and now you're returning the favour.'

Hal had rarely seen a group of people so incapable of burying an awkward moment. He supposed that in middle age, after the schoolboy camaraderie had withered, they were more willing to let one another's jokes fall flat. It was Hal's charge now to demonstrate graciousness, even though it would require him, in this circumstance, to undergo real humiliation, and to put Percy through it too. He only did it because Percy looked like he might be about to ask the man what he meant by that. What the hell was it like being Percy, letting everyone know how you felt all the time?

Hal forced up a laugh like he would a belch and said, 'At least I'm not adding any extra holes.'

Percy was upset for the rest of the night. Hal forgave him, for he was grieving the permanent and total loss of his masculinity. When the guests had gone, Hal followed Percy up to his bedroom, locked the door, and refused to do anything but kiss until Percy sucked his dick. Then Percy pinned him face-down to the bed and finger-fucked him until Hal said he was too drunk to finish. Percy wiped his dirty fingers down the sweaty damp back of Hal's shirt and sent him to his flat to sleep it off alone.

The night before Percy left for Christmas – he was going up to his family's place in Scotland – he and Hal went to a dinner hosted by a girl with whom they'd both been sort-of-friends at Oxford. The only thing anyone talked about was what the other people they knew were doing: where they were working, where they were living, where they'd gone on holiday, who they were dating, who they were no longer dating. Hal was aware that all of these people had talked about him and Percy in their absence. 'Hal Lancaster? Harry Percy? Gosh, wow, okay . . . I didn't think Harry was serious about being sexually fluid or whatever . . .' Talking to them now, he had that feeling he got when people were thinking about who he was. They were all so irreproachably chill about it, so definitely not vulgar. But occasionally the awareness surfaced, and their gazes locked onto him for a moment of comparison between himself and the thing he was meant to be.

When Percy went out to smoke, Hal followed him just to antagonise him, and they argued in the quiet street. Outside, at night, drunk,

Hal perceived none of the soft breaths or minute movements that reminded him Percy was a complete being. There was something ahead of him, blurred, in that uncanny violet-orange of the London night, its dark parts sparkling with the little bright pinpricks produced by Hal's own failure of vision. Hal recognised that this was how other people had seen him, as some fascinating intoxicated presence stuck between their eyes, taking up all of the space on the pavement or in the smoking section or in the queue for the toilets. But when he and Percy went to bed that night, they would listen to each other breathing, and rearrange themselves when one of them turned over.

Hal had left the door of their hostess's flat propped open for easy re-entry. Slipping in, hanging his overcoat on the rack, he put a finger to his lips to silence Percy, who was just about to say something loudly. He led him down the corridor to the first door he found, which opened onto a room that was windowless and, except for the various tiny lights of electronics, dark. Leaving the door open an inch, Hal pushed Percy back against the wall, dropped to his knees, and sucked Percy's cock. Percy pulled Hal's hair and fucked his face, which always made Hal think of *Catullus 16*. Yes, yes, thought Hal, sodomise me and face-fuck me, punish me for making light of your passions. Coming in from the dining room were voices, and the noises of silverware, ceramic and glass. Percy fought to stay silent as he came. Hal found this sexy until he remembered, as if it were projected into the room, how his own breathing had sounded one night in his bedroom in the townhouse, when he was fifteen or sixteen and had tried to keep silent and still. He had thought Henry might stop if he got nothing out of him. Maybe Henry would have stopped, Hal wouldn't know. He hadn't been perfectly silent and still: he'd shuddered a little, made a little noise, at the end.

On his knees in this dark room in somebody else's flat, he coughed, and the cum in his mouth dribbled onto his chin. He wiped it back up into his mouth and swallowed. When Percy tried to stroke his cheek, he slapped Percy's hand away, and Percy said, 'Well, fuck, okay, fuck me for trying to be tender.'

Percy came back to Hal's flat with him. In the Uber, Hal had told him that he didn't have to, that he could go back to his dad's. Percy had said, 'Ugh, no, would *you* go back to your dad's?' He pulled off his clothes and flopped into Hal's bed and fell asleep, the duvet flung over his legs and his bare back exposed, his tan from the summer nearly faded away. Hal had last done a line about an hour ago, and the nervous irritability had set in. If Percy hadn't been going away, Hal would have stayed up all night, but he wanted the sense of safety that came from having Percy next to him. He took a couple of sleeping pills and got into bed, jostling Percy enough that he half-woke and made Hal the little spoon. Percy fell asleep again, and Hal stayed awake.

The streetlamp light on the wall was fading; wallpaper pattern bloomed out of the white paint. The door was open. Henry was there, in the bed, corporeal. He had weight and warmth; he was living. Hal was clinging to him. His sleeves were rolled up to show his scaly elbows; his buttons were undone to show the lines of his ribs. Hal felt disgust for this body, his father's, and wanted it anyway. Hal was kissing Henry, touching his face and his chest, wondering silently whether Henry could be convinced to fuck him. He thought, We've done wrong before, we can do greater wrong, and feel just as sorry as we already do. Give me what I want, kiss me harder, make me come.

'What the fuck,' Percy was saying. 'Hal, stop it. Hal, stop—'

He and Hal were stuck together; Hal was struggling and Percy was holding his forearms, keeping him at arm's length, telling him, 'Calm down, wake up, Jesus fucking Christ. Let me up, just let me up. I'll turn on the light.'

Once the light was on and they were untangled, Percy wiped his hair back from his forehead and said, 'I didn't think people really did that. Like were you in Vietnam?'

'Did what?'

'Try to fucking kill someone in their sleep? Are you awake now?'

'Yeah, yeah . . .' It was strange to be aware of the soft mattress, the feather duvet. The spicy chemical scent of Percy's bar soap washed through the neroli from the cologne Hal had worn to the party. 'You can turn the light off again.'

The light stayed on. Percy said, 'What were you dreaming?'

'I don't remember. You can sleep on the sofa if you're afraid. Or go back to your dad's.'

'I'm not afraid. If you really did try to kill me, I could probably kill you first.'

'Oh, that's a relief.'

It was half four in the morning, the actual dark before the actual dawn. Percy said he wouldn't be able to get back to sleep even if he tried, so he made tea and they sat up in bed together, Percy scrolling through Instagram and Hal reading the copy of *Orientalism* Percy had left on his nightstand, amusing himself with Percy's obtuse annotations. But the unbearable fear had come again, so heavy that he felt he was trapped where he lay, incapable even of standing up or rolling over. His lips were shut onto his teeth were shut onto his tongue was shut onto his throat was shut onto his guts, where the thing had been articulated in secret, against his will. Then there was the bubbling up of dissent against that articulation, even though he had said nothing aloud. What right had he to object to being violated when he went on violating himself, body and spirit?

'You have nightmares a lot,' said Percy. 'Usually I can wake you up just by rolling over, so I don't think you notice it's me waking you up.'

Percy had nightmares sometimes too, but he always told Hal about them as soon as he woke up, and then the darkness was discharged. Hal thought of telling Percy what he'd dreamt. Instead – feeling that he was only barely attached to his body, like a severed limb clinging on by a string of flesh – he said, 'Do you ever look at me and think, you know, "Gosh, something must have happened to him"?'

'You mean to make you the way you are? I mean, I know what happened. Your mum died, and then your gay cousin died and your father inherited a title from him, and then you turned out to be gay, and you're Catholic. And didn't you start boarding when you were like eight? I don't know how people can do that to their children. My dad has literally said he doesn't want to see me for more than 20 per cent of his waking hours, and I only started boarding when I went to Eton.'

'But you don't look at me and just see . . .'

'What? Your face?'

'When I was thirteen—' Hal stopped. Saying it out loud felt so completely different to saying it in his head that it seemed actually to mean something different. 'Never mind, it'll just make you want to stop having sex with me.'

'Are you talking about rape?' asked Percy, more loudly than Hal would have liked. 'Were you raped?'

Hal laughed. He said, 'It doesn't count as rape if you're not penetrated.'

'But you were? I mean – that came out wrong, I'm not saying it as a rhetorical question, like, "But you *were* penetrated" – I wouldn't know, obviously. It was an actual question, I mean w-were you—I mean, did you—Someone did do something to you?'

'A lot of people have done a lot of things to me.'

'It was when you were thirteen?'

'And for a long time after that.'

Astounded, as if he couldn't believe this was a question with an answer, Percy asked: 'Who was it?'

'Doesn't matter.'

'Yes, it does. It must have been someone you knew, if it went on for that long. Was it at school? Was it a master? Was it a priest? Was it one of the ones that got into the papers, that they did the inquiry into? Did he go to prison?'

'No,' said Hal.

'Why not?'

'Because nobody ever knew.'

'You never told anyone?'

'No.'

'Ever?'

'No, not ever.'

Percy said, 'Why not?'

'Because I didn't want anybody to know.'

'So you let him get away with it?'

'Yes,' said Hal. 'He'd already got away with it. It happened.'

'But if you had told someone the first time—'

'I can't help it now.'

'Yes, you can. Tell someone tomorrow.'

'I'll go to the Met and tell some cunt in a silly hat who'd rather be out hunting radical Islamists or sniping migrants in lifeboats all about my child abuse sob story, and then they'll say, "Well, what boy doesn't want to get his cock touched, at thirteen? Aren't you gay? Isn't that just what you wanted?" I'll say, "Well, not exactly," and then they'll sigh and groan and go to the man who did it and say, "So did you do it?" and he'll say, "Goodness, no, never, but I'm not surprised Harry would say something like that. Have you seen him? He's a drug-addled degenerate, he's confused, there's something wrong with him." Then the police would break down my door with a battering ram and search my flat for controlled substances and arrest me for possession with intent to supply because they want to show everybody that they don't just let the upper classes do what they like any more. That's how my grandfather got done for tax fraud, you know.'

'Or you could go to the press.'

'Ha ha! I'd rather go to Wormwood Scrubs.'

'But you have an obligation. Is he still doing whatever he was doing when he was molesting you? Like is he still a teacher or a priest or whatever?'

'I haven't got an obligation to do anything.'

'Yes, you do!' Percy had that noble flush, those bright eyes. 'Why would you not at least try? Why would you want to let someone else get hurt? I mean, I know you don't care about other people's suffering generally, but what if they got hurt the same way you did, by the same person? Wouldn't that make you feel something?'

It was raining hard enough to dissuade Hal from going out to smoke, but he needed the nicotine, so he opened the window and lit a cigarette. The cold air raised gooseflesh on his bare arms.

'It was just me,' said Hal. 'I swear it was just me. I know him well enough to say at least—'

'That you're special? Is that what he told you?'

'I knew I was special. He didn't have to tell me.'

'I'm sure he made you feel that way. That's what they do. He made you feel as if you were special, special to him, better than anyone else, or worse than anyone else, or both, depending on what would get you to shut up and do what he wanted. But it was all—'

'Where did you get that from, feminism? You are so tedious. You know every time you leave a room everyone is like, "Ugh, fuck, Harry Percy, there he goes again." You know everyone laughs at you? Not even just the Tory scum you think it's a badge of honour to be hated by, I mean your little collect-them-all set of third world—'

'But it was all lies, he was lying, none of it meant anything. You believed what you w-wanted to believe because it's what you needed at the time, like to cope psychologically, that's how it always—'

Hal took a good long drag, then pressed the lit end of his cigarette down against his forearm and held it there. Percy said, 'What the fuck? What are you doing?' just like he'd done when Hal had woken up.

'I'm going to keep doing this until you shut up, so it's your choice.'

Apparently ready and willing to commit violence to preserve his right to free speech, Percy knocked the cigarette out of Hal's hand and shoved him back. Hal dived for the cigarette; Percy dived to stop him. 'Get off me,' one of them said, and the other said, 'No, fuck you, you get off me.'

There were knocks at the front door. The woman who lived in the flat downstairs was on Hal's landing in her slippers and bathrobe. She said, 'Are you moving furniture up there or something? 'Cause you're really quite loud, and it's five in the morning?'

'Having passionate sex,' said Hal.

Percy said, 'I'm so sorry, that wasn't funny.'

Neither of them were inspired, once she was gone, to resume the fight where they'd left off. Saying that it was sure to get infected if he didn't treat it properly, Percy washed the burn on Hal's arm, then dabbed it with the antibiotic cream Hal had used on the wounds from the shooting accident.

'I won't put a plaster on,' said Percy. 'I don't think you're meant to put them on burns. I don't know why you want more scars.'

'Once you've got this many, why not more?'

'So it's my fault?'

'No, Percy, it hasn't got anything to do with you. It's my body. If it's anybody's fault, it's my first nanny's. When I was about three, she got distracted by Tom and left me on my own, and I split my head open on the edge of a table, and that was my first scar. You can still see it: look, right there. But I feel sorry for her. My dad made her fear for her life.'

'I don't know why he didn't make me fear for my life last summer.'

'By then I'd done enough wrong that he knew I'd deserved it.'

The window had been left open, and the bedroom was cold. The cigarette had gone out. Hal shut the window and climbed back under the duvet to find that all of the body heat had escaped. He sucked Percy off again, and Percy made all the noise he didn't before, and this time returned the favour. It was so bizarre: it was just like all the other times they'd done this, except that there was a warm, raw pain on Hal's forearm where he'd been burned. It was as if Percy didn't know what he knew, as if Hal's body was the same body he'd known before: a body with no secrets, flesh like any other flesh, all its scars explicable and all its deficiencies forgivable. He even swallowed without making a face, and then it was over and the change had never come.

When Percy left, Hal followed him only so far as the doorstep. A cab was at the kerb, waiting to take him to King's Cross. Percy kissed Hal on the lips, but he didn't wave goodbye or look back. Going in again, Hal checked his post and discovered, tucked in among the circulars, a postcard with a William Morris pattern sent by Edward Langley from an address in North Yorkshire. The message was written in fine cursive, in blue ink:

Hal—

Happy Xmas (happy birthday also). Hope yr well. Life by the sea v. quiet if ever you desire to join us. No need to tell yr father. Of c. London offers more diversion & more boys so who can blame you.

Love from Edward & Will

18

On Christmas Eve, before midnight mass at St Mary's in Monmouth, Henry brought his children to make their confessions to Father Price, who was busy enough that, though he was definitely giving them special treatment, it was still an assembly-line confession requiring no uncomfortable elaboration of one's sins. The confessional was one of those little rooms decorated like a budget hotel, with ugly patterned carpet and two faux-leather chairs next to a simple kneeler and screen. Hal took the free chair and looked Father Price in the eyes as he confessed to disobeying his father, drinking, drug-taking, committing not a small number of unnatural acts. Forgetting himself, Father Price sighed. Then he gave Hal his penance.

They went to mass again on Christmas morning, hungover and sleepless. Afterwards, in the small drawing room, they had their usual humble ritual. Henry gave each of his children three gifts: a new ornament for the Christmas tree, a spiritual thing like a rosary or medallion, and a small thing to eat, like a box of chocolates or Turkish delight. Sometimes he gave the boys books, authored by some venerable SJ, OP or OSB, addressing some failing of theirs he had observed in the past year; sometimes he regifted Mary's things, jewellery and fine clothing, to the girls. In exchange, the children contributed a respectable sum to a charity of which they knew Henry approved. Today Jeanne had to go along with it, but Hal had seen the others talk in the group chat about how she had bought each of them some expensive thing they'd been coveting. She'd given nothing to Hal, and he'd asked for nothing. He was content with the jar of candied orange peel and the St Joseph medal.

When Grandfather John was alive, he was dictator-ringmaster of the traditional Christmas games, which included passing an orange from person to person using only the neck, or trying to fish raisins out of a flaming bowl of brandy without setting your fingers on fire. He demanded that each participant give their full spirit to the endeavour, and made merciless fun of anybody who performed poorly or without vigour. He bragged about doing the same to Henry and Henry's sister and Richard and the other cousins, but he never mentioned whether his illegitimates were ever invited. John had died a year before Richard, also in February, and while Henry lacked the sense of humour required to channel his sadism into parlour games, he honoured his father's passion for mandatory humiliation with the more usual paper crowns. Henry had never looked more ordinary than he did in his crown and tatty jumper, standing at the head of the table and carving the roast. Hal, at the other end of the table, felt he was watching his father deliver one of those theatrical performances so endearing that the goodwill towards the character is extended without question to the actor. Henry was so good that he became what he seemed to be, and the memories that had seemed to Hal to be fixed and permanent now disintegrated into the ungraspable, inexpressible inventions of an unstable mind.

On Boxing Day night, after everyone else had gone to bed, Hal and Philippa went out and met under the rowan. Philippa did look like something was wrong with her. She was showing cheekbones Hal had never seen before, and her hands were greyish from lack of circulation. Still, she hadn't crossed over into total unacceptability: in her Christmas jumper and calf-length checked skirt, with her long hair falling down her back, she looked like a fast-fashion advert in a tube station. At dinner her hair had been pulled up, and Hal saw that her hairline was drawing back. He was examining her, he knew, like the others were examining him, saying he looked tired, he must have been living too hard. He hesitated when Philippa asked for a cigarette, then gave in; he'd started smoking when he was younger than her, pilfering from the packets Henry kept hidden in his desk drawers. The air was clear and dry. It was cold, they were in their quilted jackets and woollen socks, and Hal's hands were numb. Philippa smoked his cigarette and got him to tell her everything Henry had said to him about her.

'You look a bit unwell,' he told her.

'I am unwell, I can't help it, they won't leave me alone. This is all a punishment for things they could have just let me do. If Venetia hadn't gone round showing everybody, the school wouldn't have had to intervene. But they've got procedures. They've got to safeguard me.'

'Showing them what?'

'You haven't seen it? I thought Dad must have shown you. They made him watch it and he said it was disgusting.'

'It's not a sex thing?'

'No! Gosh, no. If it was, I'd change my name and go into a convent. It was just a stupid thing we did for a laugh, but Venetia posted it on her blog, and Euphemia found it and showed it to her head of house.'

'Come on, let's see it, then.'

'I don't have it, it was Venetia's and they made her delete her blog and banned her from the internet for the rest of the year. Her parents sent her to inpatient after term ended, but she's not even really ill, she just pretends to be on the internet. She posts her calorie count every day and it's always like, 400, and I know for a fact she's eating more than that. She eats like a pig when I'm not there, and then when she eats with me she pushes her food round her plate and complains about how fattening it is. She hasn't even lost ten pounds. She's jealous of me because I've got the discipline to actually not eat.'

'What about your ballet? You can't dance if you don't eat, surely?'

'There's no point, I'm no good at it. If I were any good, I would be competing in the Prix de Lausanne. There are girls my age who do. And I'm not going to get any better: I'm in the prime of my youth, right now, and they only let me dance because my father's paying for it. When I'm not in the room they laugh at my delusions.'

'You don't want to do it for the love of it?'

'No, I only want to do it if I'm better than everyone else.'

Hal's cigarette had gone out with an inch left to go; he'd just been holding it. He scraped the skin off his thumb trying to get his nearly spent lighter to hold a flame long enough for the fag to relight.

'Living there,' she said, 'having to be there all the time, and do everything they tell you to do, is torture. But then when I'm not at school I have to be with Dad.' She shrunk herself into her jacket and enormous plaid scarf. 'Didn't you hate school this much?'

'You've just got to put up with it.'

'I can't.'

'Well you've got to.'

'Why have I got to?'

'Oh, please, Philippa.'

'Because our father says?'

Dully, Hal recited: 'I bow my knees to the father of our Lord Jesus Christ, of whom all paternity in heaven and earth is named.'

Philippa dropped her fag end into the grass and stamped on it with the sole of her slipper. She said, 'He wouldn't even care if the school weren't losing their minds about it. The problem is that everything is run by the laity now. Do you know we haven't had a nun as headmistress since the eighties? Our chaplain is the only holy person on the whole staff. I wish I'd been sent to Mount Grace. I don't see why I wasn't. They were letting girls in by the time I started senior school.'

'I don't know, I suppose because Dad was less willing to take the chance that you and Blanche might get molested.'

'I would never let myself get molested. I would kill myself first.'

'Well, quite. The point is that if you're going to do things other people don't like, you've either got to put up with them not liking it, or you've got to hide it.'

'You never hide any of the bad things you do.'

'Or maybe you just don't know,' said Hal, 'about all the things I've hidden, because I've hidden them.'

'What can you possibly still have hidden? Now that you've let the whole world know you're a practising homosexual.'

'Strictly speaking you don't know if I'm practising . . .'

Philippa's voice sprang out from the darkness: 'Are you?'

'I'm not going to tell you anything about it. I'm in enough trouble for corrupting you as it is.'

'I know all about how men have sex with each other.'

Hal laughed and said, 'Then you know too much already.'

'Did Richard corrupt you? Is that what happened?'

'No, and if anybody says that, especially Dad, they're making things up. Richard never did anything to me. I did it all to myself.'

'Me too,' said Philippa. 'You never did anything to me. I would have been like this even if you didn't exist.'

When he got back to London, Hal showered and took nudes in the bathroom mirror, comparing them to the one he'd taken on the day of their mother's memorial. He had lost a lot of weight since then: not enough that his thighs didn't touch, like Philippa, but enough that he could see his collarbone and ribs and hip bones again. His face was leaner, and the scars made him look older. In June, he had looked more like Mary; now he looked halfway between his father and Richard.

He sent the picture to Percy, who texted back:

H Percy 19:13 You're so fit xx
H Percy 19:15 Send arse pic

When Hal did, Percy wrote:

H Percy 19:17 That's so fucking hot
H Percy 19:17 I want to fuck you so badly
Hal 19:18 Come round in an hour

It was the deep-cleaning you did before getting fucked that proved the sin was committed with full knowledge and consent. The spontaneous handjobs and blowjobs and fingering were the kind of mortal sins that cascaded out of chaste proximity: they were the justification for avoiding near occasions of sin. Back in the shower again, washing out his arse, Hal thought, Well, here I am, offending God. For a terrible minute, as Percy was fucking him, Hal was kicked out of the illusion and felt how grotesque it really was. He was on his hands and knees and Harry Percy was hooked into him, mixing their fluids, merging obscenely the closed and private systems of their individual bodies.

Percy curled his hand around Hal's neck and closed his fingers. Hal felt the same kind of detached shock he'd felt when Percy shot him, only this time it dropped sharply into pleasure.

'Yeah,' said Hal, 'that's good, keep going.'

Percy laughed in a way that he'd picked up from Hal. He tightened his grip enough to actually start cutting off Hal's breath, and this soothed Hal back into mindless satisfaction.

Hal wheezed, 'Thank God,' and Percy said, 'What?'

Percy let it go when Hal didn't answer; he had other things to do. He announced he was coming, then fucked Hal hard enough to hurt, which felt good. Chivalrously, making up for the fact that he'd neglected to give Hal a reach-around while actually fucking him, he finished Hal off with a blowjob, then kissed him with the cum still in his mouth. Hal was amazed that he was here and this was happening. When he was a teenager, he'd tossed off thinking of things like this, then promised the Blessed Virgin that he would never, ever, ever actually do it. Perhaps he'd have been better if he'd been given more penance. His school chaplain told him to devote himself to healthier pursuits – sport and study and prayer and good works – and sent him away to do a few Hail Marys or Our Fathers.

Afterwards, he and Percy showered together, then drank some of the whisky Percy had brought back from Scotland. They lay together in bed, warm under the duvet, and gossiped about their families. Hal asked Percy whether Marguerite had ever tried starving herself. Percy said no, she was a country girl, she only cared about the diets of her horses. His father, he complained, was giving the Tories a great deal of money in the hopes of unseating Labour in Northumberland. Hal laughed at him, and Percy pinned him down and spat a mouthful of whisky over his face.

'Go back up North,' said Hal. 'Where you belong.'

'I missed you too. I love you.'

'Mmm,' said Hal.

Hal didn't know how Percy could have been raised as he had been and still retain the ability even to recognise he wanted love, let alone admit it, let alone ask for it. It wasn't fair, he thought, that Percy had floated along on the crest of life, through public school and Oxford, and surrendered nothing of himself in exchange for the advantages he had gained. Hal had been reasonably successful at school, devout and well liked, creditable at swimming, tennis, cricket and squash, helpful to the younger boys, respectful to the monks and to the masters, friendly with the cleaners and the groundskeepers and the servers at the cafeteria, and he had accomplished this through a conformity so painful he might as well have been breaking his bones to fit through a too-narrow passage. He'd put up with it because he thought it was what everybody did: that they had to earn their privilege through the violent extraction of their natural selves, the abortion of the people they might otherwise have been. And here was Percy, who seemed to live in a place of safety, who seemed to think Hal lived there too.

19

Richard was born on the Feast of the Epiphany, which commemorated the manifestation of God as a child, the revelation of Christ's divinity to the three kings of Orient. To Richard this had meant something: perhaps it would have been going too far to say that he was literally the second coming of Christ, but he believed he was at least touched by divinity. When he was in good health, he gave the most tremendous birthday parties. Hal had never been near one – Henry would have rather he died – but Richard, ill in bed, had shown him the pictures. By then Hal had heard enough from Henry that he could articulate, inwardly, the process of degradation that had turned the Richard in the pictures into the Richard holding the pictures. Hal still envied him: at least Richard had had the pleasure before the suffering. What had Henry had? His honour, Hal supposed; good reputation.

And on Twelfth Night Henry had his own parties, which he did allow Hal to attend, once he was old enough to make conversation with adults. Richard would have been unimpressed. The parties were just like the ones Henry had given as a teenager, adapted for his cohort's decline into middle age. Drinks, nibbles, light music, influential people with mutual interests: lowering taxes on the wealthy, raising taxes on the poor, deregulating the markets, regulating immigration, booting scroungers off the dole, increasing MP expense allowances, buying property, letting property, selling property, buying horses, breeding horses, horse shows, horse races, sailing races, rowing, polo, cricket, shooting, complaining about their wives, cheating on their wives, divorcing their wives, marrying their mistresses, cheating on the wives who had once been their mistresses, getting their sons into Eton and Oxford, golf. Henry forgave them their foibles because he believed they were his creatures. He said to them, affably, 'Surely it's in everyone's best interest . . .', 'Surely we can all agree . . .' Then they did their work; then Henry invited them to his parties, allowing them for a few hours the pleasure of feeling that the privilege not afforded to them by birth was granted now as a reward for their unmoving meanness. Henry didn't understand that he was their creature, also: that in exchange for the assurance of their fealty, he surrendered History and Tradition to the crude little upstarts who, behind closed doors through which Henry would never pass, made things really happen.

Tonight, there were no stars, only clouds like a marble slab laid on top of the skyline. As Hal walked up the King's Road towards his father's house, it began to snow. The pavement grew a white carpet that showed the imprint of his brogues. He hadn't a hat or hood, just the jacket with the leaking lining and his favourite fisherman's jumper. The tiles in the hall were stained with the sludge tracked in by the guests; the cloakroom smelled like damp wool. As he passed a mirror, he saw how the snowflakes in his hair had melted but stayed clinging in droplets, shining with refracted light. His nose dripped; he wiped it with his sleeve.

'Oh, it's you,' someone said to him. It was the elderly Dowager Countess of Milton, a small woman with dyed red hair, enveloped in a huge floral frock that was almost certainly actually from the eighties, though it must have been an old lady dress even then. He bent at the waist to get down low enough to kiss her cheek. 'I have to say, darling, you've given better parties. This is very conventional, isn't it? I was expecting to see tamarin monkeys, and people cutting the necks off Champagne bottles with swords.'

Henry had been giving the same party for about fifteen years; Hal couldn't imagine why Lady Milton would expect anything different. He said, 'I'm sorry we've disappointed you, but look, we do have Champagne.'

There was music Henry had chosen, jazz standards pared down to piano and bass parts. Hal followed the sound into the drawing room, where the bassist had set up next to the antique Bechstein grand, which, of the presently living Lancasters, only John and Henry knew how to play. The fire burned so furiously that sparks jumped through the cast-iron fireguard. As Hal greeted his father's guests, he glanced at the musicians' shiny foreheads, wondering if they always sweated that much or if the house was perhaps too hot. Blanche was here, in a glittering black dress so short Hal was surprised Henry had let her wear it, being impeccably polite to a lecherous old man Hal recognised as having been Grandfather John's friend. Before she could pull Hal in to replace her, he passed through the open doors to the dining room, where the overspill of guests flowed around the table, resting their drinks on the sideboard and the mantelpiece.

The chair at the head of the table and the chair just to its right were pulled out and turned to face each other, positioned so closely that the knees of the person in one chair came nearly up against the knees of the other. The two people whose knees were almost touching were Mr Percy and a Tory MP's wife. She was laughing at the joke Mr Percy was telling; they were ruddy-faced with drink. Mr Percy didn't stand when he saw Hal, just let his mouth narrow from an expansive grin to a mistrustingly polite upturn of lip.

'So, there you are,' he said. 'Your father thought you would desert.'

Hal said, 'You've seen me here every year since I was first allowed at grown-up parties.'

'Yes, but you hadn't got anything to distract you then, and now you've got my son.'

'Oh,' said the MP's wife, 'I thought my son had been telling lies. He and Harry didn't get on at school . . .'

Hal followed a waiter with a tray of empty glasses down to the lower ground floor and into the kitchen, where his brothers were sitting near the end of the long wooden table, eating off a tray of amuse-bouches, getting in the way of the staff.

John said, 'Here, come have some of this, I think it's salmon tartare?'

Hal asked if any of them had seen their father.

'Oh, he's here,' said Humphrey, chewing. 'He's skulking. He didn't think you would come.'

'I thought marriage was going to make him more tolerable,' Tom complained. 'He's actually got worse. He's always ringing me when I'm at work, or early in the morning, saying Hal's been ignoring him and he thinks he might be dead, and can I ring him just to see whether he's there.'

Hal said, 'I know, because you ring me.'

'Yeah, and you never answer, and then I have to tell him you're not answering, and I don't know where you are, and he throws a fit at me.'

'You could just lie and say I was there, and everything was fine. I mean, it always is.'

'But shouldn't you be the one who gets in trouble for it?'

'I am,' said Hal, 'eventually, when he does get hold of me.'

Humphrey said, 'He and Jeanne actually haven't got married yet? So maybe that's it . . .' John told him he was a fool if he thought they weren't already sleeping together, and he said, 'But they live apart. And when she comes to Monmouth, they sleep in separate rooms.'

Upstairs again, the heat and the noise sharpened Hal's high until it hurt. He said something to every person he came across who wasn't a total stranger, something cheerful and amusing he made himself forget just after he said it. Nearly all the guests were over the age of forty; anybody younger had been brought along by a parent, or by an older husband. There was a priest, a Jesuit, who could probably see the hellfire glowing around Hal, but liked Henry's wine well enough not to comment.

When Hal happened across Blanche again, he held her back by the elbow and said, 'Where is your sister?'

'I don't know. Probably in the loo, making herself sick.'

'Do you really think so, or are you just being a bitch?'

'Oh, stop, don't be rude! I'm sorry, I was just being a bitch, I don't know where she is. I've been entertaining the guests for like three hours straight because nobody else is here to do it. Dad's gone off somewhere too. I really am sorry, just don't tell Philippa I said that, or she's going to post a picture of my bare ass again.'

'You weren't the one who posted that? You didn't delete it, anyway.'

'Well, everyone had already seen it.'

Hal said, 'Better not let her take the picture, next time.'

Assuming Philippa wouldn't have gone to the guest toilet, he checked the bathroom she and Blanche used. It was empty of people but laden with female effects, make-up and creams and lotions and scented candles, hair straighteners and pumice stones and bath salts. He did a few more lines and texted Philippa: 'Are you here?' Then he rang Percy, who answered only on the fourth attempt.

'I've shown my face at the party,' Hal told him. 'Why don't you come down and meet me at my flat?'

There was noise in Percy's background. One person very near to Percy was talking to others further away, and the line picked up only the moments of high-pitched emphasis.

'Yeah, I don't know, it's a bit early for me at the moment, actually. I mean, I've just got here, and there are some people I still wanted to talk to, so, umm, I don't know . . .'

If Percy were talking to anybody else, he would have made himself seem like he was genuinely sorry. Hal had overheard him doing it before, when he was denying someone else so he could spend more time with Hal: 'Oh my gosh, I'm so sorry, I'm actually just in the middle of something right now or I absolutely would, I really want to – let's go when you're next free . . .'

Hal said, 'You didn't even tell me where you were going.'

'It's just this thing – I don't know, just this thing with one of my classmates. It's just that there are people here I should talk to . . .'

'Where is it?'

'Oh, not that far, just . . . Yeah, I just don't think I could make it down to Fulham right now, sorry.'

'Meet me after we're both done, and you can spend the night.'

'You mean there or at your flat?'

'God, my flat, obviously. You can't sleep over at my dad's house.'

'Ahh, I just can't, I shouldn't. I promised my mate I'd get up early and play a game of squash with him before he goes in to work, and then I've got to meet with one of my professors to talk about funding for this project I'm doing . . .'

'What would you rather have, a blowjob now or squash in the morning?'

'No, I've really got to go. We've been saying we'd get around to it for ages, and I need his advice. I keep losing money trying to get into day trading, but I don't want to just give up . . .'

'Are you joking? You're turning me down because you want to be fresh for a financial counselling squash game? Do you work at the stock exchange? Buy! Sell! Buy! Sell! Are you literally your father? Hello, Mr Percy, is that you, I'm sorry for asking if you wanted a blow-job, I thought you were your son.'

'Yeah, well, some of us have got better things to do than stay up all night doing cocaine.'

'You've never had a real job in your life.'

'If you add up everything I do, I've been putting in seventy-five hours a week nonstop for the past year.'

'You wouldn't even come and see me for love?'

Percy sighed so sharply it made the line crackle. 'You sound like all the girlfriends I've ever had. Like, oh my god, is my dick that good?'

'What the fuck, Percy, you snap me with a picture of your hard-on like every day. I never have to ask.'

'I mean I want to have sex with you, obviously. I just think that maybe if you pick up tennis again or something, you'd be able to take no for an answer when I tell you I can't.'

'On Friday when I was at work, you texted me saying you wanted me to think about how hard you were going to fuck me? So I would be desperate for your cock when I got home?'

'Yeah, I know, because I literally wrote it into my schedule. It was like, "four to six: Hindi conversation group, six: go to Fulham and have sex with Hal". And it was great! It was fantastic, it's just—Okay, can I be really honest with you?'

'Have you not been?'

'The Catholic thing is weird, Hal. Like, I didn't really realise how weird it was before this whole thing started, I thought it was just like being Anglican but you can't get divorced, and then that didn't matter because I didn't want to marry you. I just mean, it's w—it's w—it's so fucked to think about how literally as I'm coming on your face, you're thinking you're going to go to hell for being gay unless you go tell everything to a scary old man who's probably a molester?'

'I don't think I'm going to be sent to hell for being gay, I think I'm going to be sent to hell for having sex outside of marriage, and I'm not just telling a scary old man who's probably a molester for the sake of it, I'm telling him so that he'll tell God, so that God will forgive me for what I've done. It's better than being the kind of Protestant who doesn't believe in forgiveness at all.'

'Like, I respect your religion and everything, I understand spiritual practice is an important element in human society, and rationalist W-Western secularism is in itself a form of imperialism. It's just not fun lying there next to you while you frown at the ceiling and think about how filthy you are for wanting to have orgasms just like every other human in the history of humanity.'

'It is filthy, what we do is objectively filthy. Have you ever left the room after we've had sex and then come in again and smelled it?'

'I'm literally not going to talk to you if all you do is disagree with me.'

'I've never agreed with you once in all the time we've known each other.'

'I don't even know why I'm still talking to you. I said I'd just be a second and now I'm standing in the corridor fighting with you. I'm sure you could do it till the sun comes up because you've railed fifty lines of coke, but I'm completely sober and I've been up since five in the morning, and I w-want to go home and go to bed.'

'Yeah, okay, fine.' Hal realised his breath was echoing against the tiles. 'But I mean, Christ, Percy. What incredible sanctimony from such a useless person. It's true you aren't really good for anything but sex. Unfortunately, you've been burdened with inconceivable privilege. Have you ever considered you might be more successful chained up in someone's basement? Then you wouldn't have to do anything but fuck and enjoy being oppressed.'

'Oh, Hal, you really shouldn't throw stones from such a glass fucking house. You know I used to think your father was actually a bit hard on you? Imagine having to be him. You raise your seventy children and manage your estate and like, go to church every Sunday or whatever, and then your eldest son's this dreadful waster.'

'Didn't you say you loved me?'

'Oh, God. Look, Hal. Now I'm not going to be able to sleep, I'm going to be up thinking about like, noblesse oblige. I'm ringing off. Don't try to ring me back.'

'It's just been such a bad night. If you'll be up anyway—'

Percy had already ended the call. Hal hurled his phone down, but the daisy-print bathmat cushioned the impact, and the screen was cracked anyway. He stood and looked at himself in the mirror. He would have liked to break the glass, cut his knuckles, if he couldn't hit Percy. He wanted a wound. On impulse, he picked up one of the lipsticks lying out on the dressing table and applied it. It was a bold, glossy coral, which, upon seeing it on himself, he remembered his sisters wearing; they had been the ones to do the work of finding a shade that looked attractive with their colouring. He pulled out a tissue to wipe it off and then thought, *Fuck it*, and wiped his nose instead.

It felt enormously good, he found, to have the people who usually disapproved of him subtly disapprove of him flagrantly. One of his father's friends said, 'You never cease to amaze.' At least, Hal thought, putting as much Champagne away as possible, people weren't staring at his scars. Another of his father's friends said, 'Are you going to become a woman next?' The joke was that he wouldn't: no hereditary landowner would. Even then, Hal felt the man would have liked to say the same thing to him as he would to a transsexual who *didn't* wear lipstick: 'Come on, at least make a bloody effort before you ask for my respect.' Mr Percy was so embarrassed that he would leave a room if Hal entered it. He waited just long enough for Hal to be detained by someone else, then scuttled out. Then Hal excused himself to go see where Mr Percy had gone.

To those who would still countenance him, Hal said whatever he wanted. He explained to the Jesuit that he wished he hadn't been sent to Mount Grace because whenever somebody at Oxford asked him what school he'd gone to, the follow-up was always, 'So did you get touched up?' When he found the MP's wife helping herself to whisky from the decanter, he said, 'The thing about divorces is that nobody can ever have just one. If I were a woman, I'd say that a man who's already divorced and remarried would only be good for an affair. I mean, if he started dropping hints about making me his third wife, I'd tell him not to bother. Think how many lives would have been saved if Henry VIII had just stuck with Anne Boleyn!' People started leaving. Maybe they were going to leave anyway: they were all old, and it was approaching midnight.

In the group chat Humphrey had written:

Humphrey Bogart 23:17 Haha are you wearing lipstick Hal or having an allergic reaction to the shrimp

🐝 23:18 I can't believe you put your gross mouth all over my lipstick

🐝 23:19 You can't just use things that touch people's bodies without asking

Tom L 23:23 Don't you know Hal is allowed to do whatever he wants

Hal ascended the stairs to the fourth floor, Philippa's floor, again. He noticed, stopping on the first-floor landing, that the door to the library was open when it hadn't been before. Inside, a single lamp was on, making the darkness around it darker. Hal thought that Henry was in there, just out of view. He went on.

His nose started to bleed after the first line of that round. When he let his head fall forward, specks of blood appeared on the countertop where his lines were laid out. One drop had landed in the coke. It was his fault: he'd been too impatient, he hadn't chopped it down into a fine enough powder, he'd used his myWaitrose card instead of a razor. This was why Jack always warmed his coke on a ceramic plate heated up in the microwave. Hal's sinuses were beginning to ache again; his nose was somehow numb and in pain at the same time. It made him imagine what the inside of his face looked like, raw and inflamed and leaking blood. He dabbed his right nostril with toilet paper until the blood stopped flowing. Snorting the other two lines through his left nostril, the numbness won out, and he thought he might as well do a fourth.

He put his myWaitrose card back into his wallet, his straw and bag of coke back into his pocket, and washed his hands. He felt the sudden need to piss and did so, then washed his hands again. He'd had to pat away some of the lipstick while patting away the blood that had dripped onto his lips, and now the colour was less vibrant. At a distance he would probably just look healthy.

Knowing that when he went back out he was going to look for his father, and that he could not stop himself, he dropped a message in the group chat: 'We're all allowed to do whatever we want, it's called free will'.

In the library, there was a door to a room that couldn't be accessed from the landing. This was Henry's study, forbidden to children and staff; Hal, crossing the threshold, felt the same trepidation as he'd done when he was small, coming to ask Henry for something he had only a faint hope of actually getting. The room looked the same. There was no fire; the light came from two floor lamps on either side of the fireplace, and from the green-shaded banker's lamp on the desk. Behind the desk stood a straight-backed armless wooden chair, empty. Henry was standing by the window, looking down at the snowy garden.

'Shut the door,' said Henry. 'Come here.' When Hal did as he said, he slapped Hal across the face, backhanded. He stepped forward; Hal stepped back. The heavy velvet curtains touched Hal's shoulder. Taking the scarred side of Hal's face in one hand, smearing the lipstick off Hal's mouth with the other, Henry said, 'I don't know what I've done.'

Hal said, 'I could think of a thousand things.'

Henry pressed his thumb between Hal's lips. Hal clenched his jaw so that all Henry could do was push against his teeth.

'What is it that I haven't given you?'

Hal kept his mouth shut. Henry touched his bottom lip, gently. He could not fool Hal, who saw in Henry's face that he was so angry he had lost himself. The anger put life in him: Henry looked youthful, strong enough to win a fight, as if he'd turned back into the man he had been before Hal was born.

'You'll apologise,' said Henry, 'to every person who's looked you in the face tonight. Then you'll apologise to your brothers and sisters, for making them suffer just for having had the bad luck to be born of the same mother.'

'No,' said Hal. 'Why should you be allowed to do what you like with me, and then ask me to be good?'

'Because a childless son is still perfectible, and a father isn't. You'll find out. Once a man has had his first son, he's surrendered himself.'

'Do you forgive me?'

'Of course,' said Henry.

'For what I've done tonight? For what I've done with Harry Percy? And with all the men before him? And for being too much like Richard?'

Henry leaned into Hal's neck and breathed deeply, taking in his scent and sighing it out. His lips came just up against Hal's skin, then just far enough back that Hal couldn't tell whether he was feeling the touch or imagining it. Hal took Henry's hand and unbuttoned his cuff, pulling it down so he could sniff Henry's wrist. He half-smelled, half-tasted Henry's cologne, the intoxicating reek of amber and civet. Henry held Hal's shaking hands still.

'Yes,' said Henry, 'I do. There's nothing you could do I couldn't forgive. So you can stop looking at me like that. I suppose you can't help it – you're out of your mind. Richard was never like this. You've got to stop: you took out nearly £3,000 in cash advances last month.'

'It was worth it.'

'It isn't yours to spend.'

'Blessed are the poor in spirit, for theirs is the kingdom of heaven . . .'

'Please,' said Henry, 'speak to me seriously, or not at all.'

Because Henry had asked him to be silent, Hal was. He unbuttoned his trousers and closed his hand around the most unwilling erection he'd ever had. He shut his eyes and jerked himself off the way he liked to do in private, sacrificing this particular pleasure to Henry just for the sake of being let go sooner. Maybe this was the point: he would give up everything pleasurable to Henry, and Henry would give it back as pain, and then Hal would be virtuous. Just as long, he prayed, just as long as he doesn't touch me. But when Hal was close to coming, Henry stopped him and waited for his breath to slow, then took over. Hal bit his lip and let his head fall back against the wall, expressions of disgust that Henry could interpret as approval. Something wasn't right: Hal was supposed to have started wanting it by now. He was too hot, his sweat made his clothes chafe. 'Hang on,' he said, and pulled his jumper over his head, dropping it on the rug. There were sweat stains on his shirt, under his arms and down the centre of his chest. Carefully, Henry unbuttoned Hal's shirt from the top down. He bent to inhale the scent that had gathered between the fabric and the skin.

'I don't wish that you weren't my son,' said Henry. 'I wish that you were a child again, so that I could raise you again, better.'

'You didn't raise me, you sent me to school and fondled me on holidays.'

'I know. I'm sorry. I wish it had been different.'

Hal was conscious of thinking, in these exact words, I want to go home. He didn't know where he meant. If he was going to get through this, he decided, he was going to have to let it feel good. He shut his eyes and released the tension from his muscles. Sandalwood and vetiver sifted deliciously through the persistent animal presence of the civet. If Henry were a stranger and they were pressed up against each other in a dark room Hal would like it. But Henry couldn't be imagined as a stranger: he manipulated Hal's body with a confidence that could only have come from practice and devoted observation. Hal let himself make the noises his body wanted him to make because he found them useful as a measure of his own responses. If he heard himself make the sound that indicated contentment, then he knew he should be feeling contented, if he heard himself make the sound that indicated desperation, then he knew he should be feeling desperate. He said 'Yes', more than once, and Henry must have thought he was saying yes to him. He wasn't: he was saying it to himself, telling himself, Yes, this is happening, yes, this is your body, yes, you will feel other things again, once this is done. Henry kissed his neck, and for a moment was so rough Hal couldn't stand it, so that when he relented and was gentle Hal came, holding himself still for the five seconds of perfect sensation before the pleasure was gone and his body was left subject to its last uncontrollable responses.

He realised he'd come on Henry's sleeve, and a bit on the front of his jumper. 'Oh, sorry,' he mumbled. The sight of his own genitals hanging out of the front of his trousers was revolting. He didn't understand how this, this thing, could be the root of human life. He pulled his underpants up and buttoned his trousers.

As Henry buttoned Hal's shirt, he looked at him: Henry's shame was the kind that made him seek out a gaze. Hal looked back. Henry's face was in full colour, he was brightly alive, there was a charming flop of hair over his temple.

Turning away, pulling off his jumper, Henry said, 'I've been hiding up here, avoiding my own guests. I'll have to put in an appearance before they all leave. First I've got to change my shirt.'

The counter in the third-floor bathroom, which Hal, Tom and Humphrey shared, was up to a military standard of cleanliness and organisation. There were razors and shaving cream and acne facewash and antiperspirant and hand soap and the terrible cologne Tom and Humphrey used, and that was it. The room smelled of all those things combined. Hal took off his clothes and took a shower and then put the same clothes back on, because if he changed, somebody might ask him why. He sprayed the cologne onto the sweaty armpits of his shirt and put his jumper back on.

He felt, with the same dread as when he lay down to try to sleep, that if he wanted to avoid feeling very bad very soon, he was going to have to do more cocaine. He was so fucking bored of it, just like he was bored of Jack and Poins and the Boar's Head, having once liked nothing more. The deep insides of his face always hurt, and he kept sniffing compulsively. Percy had gone from admonishing him about the rainforest to telling him that he looked like shit and he was annoying when he was high. He was going to quit, it was just that he'd always had a prideful disdain for the people who did a few lines on their friends' birthdays, or had a few pints of an evening, then made the grand announcement that they were going to spend the next two months getting clean at a retreat in Thailand or Arizona. If a person was going to ask to be praised for being good, they should have been as bad as possible before.

Doing the first line felt like snorting ground glass while his face was full of Novocaine. If cocaine wasn't an anaesthetic it would probably have hurt so much he couldn't finish; as it was, he felt the injury without the pain. He wet his fingers under the tap and stuck them up his nose to sniff the water into his sinuses; his fingertips came away tinged by blood. Then he committed himself to hoovering up the rest of the coke, after which he lay back on the tiles and covered his face with his hands, groaning, thinking about how if this was a hundred years ago he'd be a junior officer on the Western Front, trying to sneak a look at a strapping Tommy's arse before going over the top and getting blown into mist by a high-explosive shell.

As soon as he was vertical, his nose started bleeding again. He tried to staunch the flow with a hand towel. There was a knock at the door, and from the other side Philippa said, 'Hal, are you in there?'

'Yeah, just a minute—'

She opened the door boldly, prepared to see anything. He tried to close it on her, but she was already inside, peering at the paraphernalia left out on the counter. She said, 'Are you taking drugs in here? Can I have some?'

'No, get out of here, this is private.'

'You left the door unlocked.'

'That doesn't mean you're allowed to open it.'

When she reached for the cocaine, he had to take her wrists in his hands and physically stop her. 'Let me just look,' she said, and he said, 'Absolutely not.' Having dropped the towel, Hal felt blood dripping out of his right nostril and onto his upper lip. She let him keep holding her wrists while she stared.

'Philippa, get out.' He let go of her, gesturing to the half-open door.

'Everybody was saying you'd been looking for me. Didn't you want to see me?'

'Not any more. I mean it, go, now.'

Philippa reared her head back like a swan on the offensive. She said, 'No! You asked for me, now I'm here.'

'Oh, fucking Christ, Philippa.' He wiped his nose with the back of his hand. The pain in his sinuses was returning, making his eyes water. His throat hurt when he swallowed. 'I want to be alone. That's why I'm in the bathroom.'

'Fine, then I'll just go and kill myself, if nobody wants me here anyway.'

Hal felt it when he lost control of himself; it was like that lurch you feel when your horse bolts. He said, not even meaning it, but meaning to hurt her, 'I wish you fucking would. I don't give a damn as long as you leave. I'm sick of you following me around like a dog. Get a hold of yourself.'

She was standing, literally, up to him, reaching as far as five ten and low heels would take her. She said, 'As if! You want to be blamed for ruining me, you do it so you will be blamed, because as soon as you get the slightest whiff of attention being paid to anybody else, you'll do whatever you can to make everything about you again.'

Hal stepped out onto the landing and shut the door before Philippa could follow him. She tried to get out and he held the door shut against her. He shouted through: 'Go on, take all my drugs if that's really what you want. You might give yourself a heart attack, then we would all be spared.'

'Let me out, I'm sorry, I didn't mean it.'

'Yes, you did. Well, I'll tell you a secret: our father doesn't like any of us. We're only here because he wanted to see our mother suffer giving birth to us, to punish her for original sin, and he doesn't like you because you killed her off before he was done with her. But you haven't got to feel bad about it, because it was a fucking mercy.'

'I'm sorry,' she said. Her voice was tremulous, she was sniffing loudly. 'Stop it, I'm sorry. You're my favourite brother. You're my favourite out of everybody – it's not like I like Blanche more than you. Just let me out, you're scaring me, you're not yourself.'

John and Humphrey were there, pulling him away from the door, saying, 'Stop it', 'Leave her alone', 'Let her out', 'What are you doing? What the hell is wrong with you?' Hal tried to jostle himself loose and Humphrey shoved him face-first into the wall with a palm to the centre of his back, like cops do to criminals in the movies.

Philippa swung open the door, and the edge of it whacked Humphrey in the forehead. Hal turned round and yanked the door back to whack Humphrey again, saying, 'Fuck off, Humphrey! Go away!' With her eyes bloodshot and her face full red, Philippa flung herself between them and yelled at Humphrey, specifically, to stop.

Richard had been like this: he had been brought before the headmaster for fighting at least three times in his last two years of school. They'd been afraid to expel him because by that time his father and grandfather were dead, and he was the Duke of Lancaster. While he was at Oxford, a great friend of his died in a drink-driving accident, and when a Lancaster cousin joked at the wake that he'd have died of AIDS soon anyway, Richard had beaten him about the head so badly that he'd been concussed and had to go to hospital, and had suffered from the injury ever since. Hal had been raised to believe that he existed to be a vessel, bearing the lives of his ancestors into the perpetual future. Well, what more could they want from him? As he scrubbed the blood off his upper lip, he realised Lady Milton had thought that he was Richard, that it was twenty years ago. I've got to tell her she's got it wrong, he thought, I've got to tell her he's dead. But Lady Milton was gone. The last guests were gathering their things from the cloakroom, the pianist had lowered the fallboard, the bassist was locking his instrument into its hard-shell case.

The terrace, when Hal went out for a cigarette, was frosted like it had been left too long in the freezer. The flowerbeds and bushes lay dormant under the snow. Even the footprints of the people who'd come out to smoke earlier were softened by fresh accumulation. Snowflakes fell from the black upper sky to the yellow glow of the city horizon; Hal's smoke rose up through the snowfall. He stood in the cold in his blood-speckled jumper, letting his sweat dry up and the blood oxidise.

Ellie Poins answered her phone after one ring. It sounded like she'd got company, maybe a few friends sitting together and drinking. Slurring a little, not enough to make him worry he was going to have to rescue her again, she said, 'Who is this?'

'I don't know, tell me who you think I am.'

'Oh, it's Hal. You're the only posh person I know.'

'Ah, yeah, well.' Putting on a voice to mock his own voice, he said, 'How d'you do, darling?'

'How do I do what? I do a lot of things.'

'Oh, nothing, I was just—'

'Yeah, I know, that was a joke. Is your fridge running? Ha ha. It's half two in the morning. If this is you trying to pull, I'm really not interested.'

'Gosh, no, perish the thought. I rang to ask you if you'd marry me.'

Ellie was quiet. Hal was pleased to think he'd shocked her into silence, then heard muffled voices, like she was holding the phone away so she could talk to someone. He tried to listen in and couldn't make anything out. She said, 'What was that, sorry?'

'I said, I rang to ask you to marry me. Don't laugh, it isn't a joke, you'll hurt my feelings if you laugh.'

'Your feelings, okay, uh. I don't know what to say to that.'

'You can say anything you like. I'm not here to tell you what you can and can't say.'

'Uhh.' She did laugh, hesitantly. 'I don't believe you that it isn't a joke. Like have you got all your mates listening in and laughing at me? Have you got my brother listening in and laughing at me?'

'Fuck, that would have been really good. I wish I'd thought of that before Ed left me for Hollywood. No, I just thought I'd ask because I've driven away everybody else in my life, and I need at least one person on my side. What do you think? There are only about twenty opportunities per generation to become a duchess, and probably 20,000 competing for the position. Of course, you wouldn't become a duchess straight away: you'd have to wait till my father died, though you could style yourself "Lady Hereford". But then when you were one, you could make people call you "Your Grace". Ellen Lancaster, Duchess of Lancaster: how do you like that? I wonder if there's ever been a duchess called Ellen.'

'Nobody I know would ever call me "Your Grace".'

'If they refused, you could be as rude as you liked to them, and if they were upset with you for being rude, you could tell them they were just jealous. Nobody I know would like you, but they would call you "Your Grace". The only other thing is that, of course, you would have to convert.'

Ellie laughed again, this time with certainty. 'Who in their right mind would go from being a Jew to being a Catholic? I was born with the better religion, I'm not going to give it up now.'

'Oh but it's such fun, you get to eat a biscuit at mass, and all the kneeling and rising is great exercise. And you can redecorate the country house. It's not quite as big as the family seat was, but it's still a few hundred years older than your house. My mother was too busy having children to do it, so it hasn't been done since the seventies.'

'Is that all you've got?'

'And think how happy it would make Ed, getting to say his brother-in-law is the Duke of Lancaster. He'd finally have one up on the Eton-to-RADA types.'

'I thought you said he ditched you.'

'Oh, yeah, but I know Ed, I know what he's like.'

'Umm, Hal. Can I call you that, or do I have to call you Sir Lord Monseigneur the Duke of Hal?'

'You can call me Henry if you like.'

'Yeah, okay, Henry. Henryyy. It's really sweet you'd consider me after you've seen me be sick all over myself, but like, no. Like, it wouldn't be worth it even if you were a billionaire, 'cause I'd still have to bear your children.'

'Is it so wrong to get married and have children? You know, back before they were allowed to marry down, boys used to just send girls they'd got pregnant to the workhouse. Even now, you can't expect chivalry – you'd be lucky to be given cash for an abortion.'

'You are such a creep. I'd be lucky if your mum had got an abortion.'

'Come now, have a sense of humour.'

'I do, I've been joking this whole time.'

'Oh, don't give me that. You were offended. You think I'm a—'

There was noise on the line – the phone being manhandled, a distant incomprehensible voice – then Ellie, not so distant but muffled, saying, 'Yeah, one of Ed's weird friends, I don't know.' The distant voice responded, and Ellie got cut off mid-laugh as the call ended.

In real life, behind Hal, was the sound of one of the French doors opening. By the expert handling of the door, which was likely to have stuck or scraped if opened incautiously, he could tell it had been opened by someone who lived there. He thought it must have been

Henry, and remained where he was, looking out into the dark garden. Something touched his back, and he flinched. He realised Henry was draping one of his own overcoats onto Hal's shoulders. It was beautiful grey wool, double-breasted, silk-lined; Henry had had it for as long as Hal could remember. One of the buttons had come off and Mary had sewn it back on, a little out of place.

'Go away, I'm fine.' Really, Hal had been cold. He put his arms through the sleeves of the coat and lit a cigarette.

Henry said, 'Hand that to me, let me have a puff, why don't you?'

'I thought last time you said you were quitting for good.'

'Yes, but I've got to give in once in a while.'

When Hal passed the cigarette to Henry, their hands came clumsily up against each other. The scrape of dry skin against dry skin stung. Henry took a drag with the same gratefulness as Hal drank a glass of water after waking from three hours of uneasy hungover sleep. He exhaled the same way Hal did, grandly, into the sky. Snowflakes stood out bright on his dark hair. He was wearing a different jumper.

'Are you going to smoke the whole thing? Pay me a pound for it, it's practically twenty quid for a packet now.'

'No, I'm sorry. You have it.' Henry gave the cigarette back by turning it round and putting the filter to Hal's lips, getting his fingers dangerously close to the cherry.

PART FOUR

I GET ALONG WITHOUT YOU VERY WELL

20

The smoke from the incense at Epiphany mass dimmed the sunlight coming through the windows. Half-solid, it fell over the congregation like a shroud, as if they were sheet-covered furniture in a disused wing of a stately home whose owners couldn't afford to keep the whole place going. Hal couldn't smell anything, his sinuses were totally bricked up, but the smoke got in his nose and mouth, drying his tongue and the insides of his cheeks. His throat was so sore he could only whisper 'Lord have mercy, Christ have mercy.' His coughs were loud enough to draw the censorious stares of his siblings, who were probably glad for a reason to give him dirty looks. Father Dyer never looked at Hal, or if he did, Hal never caught him looking. His disapproval of Hal and his people was exercised through the homily, in which he reminded them that Christ was the king of kings, that there could be no legitimate rule but God's, that no man, son of man, has dominion over his fellow sinners. The Magi were wise because they, though gentiles, understood this, and followed the star to Bethlehem, where they abdicated to their natural superior. Better, Hal supposed, than being usurped.

After mass, the Lancasters had lunch at a restaurant on the Strand, whose wood-panelled dining room was such a perfectly oppressive recreation of what it had been like in the 1850s that it seemed wrong for women to be there. Not that the sex segregation had ended with the nineteenth century: they hadn't started letting women in until the 1980s, and Grandfather John, who believed that restaurants were for men and dinner parties for mixed company, complained every time they went that it wasn't the same. The menu – Hal refused to call it the fucking bill of fare – was just the sort of thing John liked: roast beef, roast lamb, roast venison, roast partridge, the roasted balls of mincing Europeans. Jeanne seemed like an outsider again, wary of attracting too much attention, yet unable entirely to hide her frustration at being forced to play along with the idiosyncratic and inexplicable customs of a culture that did not in the least impress her.

When Hal coughed, she looked his way. He tried to smile at her, and she said, 'You don't seem well.'

Humphrey, who had a dark bruise on his forehead, said, 'Yeah, did you see him last night?'

Jeanne wasn't listening. She was studying Philippa now, perhaps because Philippa didn't seem well either. She had tried to order a fruit salad as her main and Henry had told the waiter she would have lamb from the trolley, which, once on her plate, she refused steadfastly to eat. Hal quite understood. Without taste, he was excruciatingly aware that he was eating flesh, chewing through the muscles that had once allowed some erstwhile lamb to move, absorbing another creature's body into his own in a grotesque reversal of birth. Nausea shivered through him; cold electric spasms flashed over the burning surface of his skin. His knife slipped out of his hand and landed on the carpet with a quiet thump. He bent down to retrieve it and his vision spotted white, and he felt so suddenly weak that he had to hang there, halfway out of his chair, the knuckles of his left hand grazing the carpet, his nose dripping onto his upper lip.

Blanche, sitting next to him, said, 'You aren't puking down there, are you?'

Leaving the knife, Hal pulled the whole hideous weight of his body back up. Wiping his nose with his napkin, he said, 'No, would you like me to?'

'Don't be disgusting,' she said.

Before anybody else could say it, Hal said, 'Too late.'

Alcohol, that trusted panacea, had let him down. After two glasses of wine, he was so drowsy that he had to support himself with an elbow on the table. His eyelids drooped, his head drooped. He only stayed conscious because Blanche kept kicking him under the table. She typed something on the phone she kept hidden on her lap, and Hal's phone vibrated in his jacket pocket, but when he tried to take it out, he dropped that too.

He braced his hands against the table and pushed out his chair. 'I will return,' he slurred, 'momentarily.'

Without retrieving his phone, he absconded to the toilets, where at least one was allowed one's indignity. Feeling that something was stuck in his nose, he blew into a tissue and saw that he'd expelled a lump of bloody snot more horrifically huge than anything that had ever come out of his nose before. He whispered, 'Oh God, what the fuck,' and took his coke through the other nostril. It was only after several bumps that he began to suspect he might actually be ill. He sat on the floor of the stall and waited to feel better, and found he was only more frightened of his body. The meat of him ached. He was shaking.

On the other side of the door, he heard footsteps and voices. It was two of his brothers, he thought, but he couldn't tell which ones.

'I'm in here,' he called out.

'Hal,' one of them said.

'Yes, I'm in here,' he said.

'Hal,' his brother repeated.

'I'm coming,' he said, and dragged himself up and opened the stall door to see that the room was empty. He saw his reflection in the mirror above the sink and felt that it wasn't his own. When he moved, his reflection moved a half-second too slow. He passed his hand in front of his face. It was still the same face. He touched his face, and the reflection touched its face. But what if the face he was touching looked different from the face of his reflection? He touched a fingertip to each visible scar, counting them up. He kept losing count, and partway through his third attempt the door was opened by a pink-nosed old man in a green knitted sweater who, seeing Hal, said, 'Oh!'

Hal glanced back at the mirror and saw his reflection pull an exaggerated face: Oops! How embarrassing! That man may not know what you're up to, but he knows it isn't normal. Hal turned on the hot water and scrubbed his hands.

He had every intention of going back to his family and finishing his lunch, but the best-laid intentions have the most ill-behaved children, as the saying goes. In the middle of the dining room, his vision succumbed again to mould-like spots of white and purple, as if his body were decaying while he was living in it. Hello! he thought, I'm still in here! The spots kept pulsing in and out, obscuring and revealing different patches of the room. Sensing that he wasn't going to make it to his table, he looked for the nearest empty chair and sat in it. He discovered as his vision cleared that he had seated himself across from a white-haired woman whose knife and fork were poised in the air above her plate. Apparently he was occupying someone else's place; there was a plate of beef and a glass of wine in front of him.

'Hello,' he said, 'I'm Hal, how do you do? I'm just stopping in on my way back to my own table. I hope you're enjoying your lunch. What have you got there, the Scottish beef? Not a vegetarian, then? I'm not either, but I daresay I shouldn't like to be served up on a silver trolley.'

'My dear,' she said (she had an American accent), 'you had better run along before my husband gets back and thinks he's been replaced.'

It was going to be alright. Henry had already come to take Hal away. He pulled Hal out of the dining room and through the revolving door, which swung them back out onto the Strand. The street was busy with midday traffic, red double-deckers and hop-on hop-off tour buses, delivery vans and black cabs. Most of the people on the pavement were tourists, less numerous than in the summer, but no less enviable in their fascination with these buildings in which so much history had happened that now they could exist only as containers for the conveniences and frivolities people demanded when they came to see where history had happened. Henry and Hal – Henry standing, Hal sitting on the low steps leading up to the deep carved-stone archway that sheltered the entrance to the restaurant – drew nothing more than passing glances. They could have worn placards around their necks displaying their titles, forms of address, and a brief family history translated into seven different languages, and the sightseers would have looked them over and shrugged and said, 'They just look sort of inbred.'

Henry gave a cab driver the address of the townhouse and sent Hal off alone. When Hal arrived, Dr Bradmore was waiting for him. He asked Hal about his symptoms, took his vital signs, looked into the back of his throat, and pronounced him a victim of flu. Real flu, not coke flu: he had a fever of 102.4 Fahrenheit, 39.1 centigrade. Doctor's orders were to rest and hydrate and wait for it to be over, unless his fever went any higher, in which case ring again.

Just as Dr Bradmore was packing up his things, Hal said, 'Could you, umm . . . Could you look at my nose too? Like, the inside?' When asked why, he said, 'I'm so sorry, but I think I've done too much cocaine.'

Hal sat back in an armchair and Dr Bradmore looked up his nostrils through an otoscope. With the long plastic bit still up Hal's right nostril, Dr Bradmore said that his septum was perforated. The hole was small enough that it was likely to be manageable with saline sprays and the cessation of the use of the irritant. If he didn't stop, his septum might erode, his palate might collapse, and then he would have to undergo a very unpleasant surgery indeed.

Once the otoscope was removed, Hal touched the bridge of his nose, thinking of the little hole that had been hiding in there somewhere. He said, 'I'm not afraid of having facial surgery. In August I got shot in the face.'

Dr Bradmore said, 'I remember. Healing was delayed because you wouldn't stop smoking. Now you've taken enough drugs that you've damaged your septum permanently. I don't know how a hypochondriac like your father can stand it.'

'Permanently?'

'The perforation won't heal. You'll just have to manage it.'

'Oh. Well, my father *can't* stand it. He's very, very upset about it. That's why you've got to prescribe him so many pills.'

Mildly, Dr Bradmore said, 'I won't discuss my care of another patient with you.'

Hal felt so bad that he thought he would rather have been shot again, at closer range. When it hurt too much, he ran a hot shower, sat down in the bath, and let the scalding water fall onto his upturned face. He breathed through his mouth because he couldn't through his nose. Heaps of tissues piled up on his bed. His face was tight and swollen and unhealthily pink. His eyelids were puffy, his hair matted, his skin covered in sticky perma-sweat. He fell asleep in the middle of the day and dreamt he woke in the dark, and woke for real in the sun; or he fell asleep at night and dreamt he woke in the morning, and woke for real before the sun had risen. He half-imagined, half-hallucinated visions of his own sin. I know, he thought, I'm going to stop, I'm going to stop just in time. Let me be bad for another five years, and then I'll do my bit, I'll have the wife, I'll have the children, I'll make the money, I'll oppress the tenants, I'll buy back all the land we lost. Then I'll die by thirty-five, before I break and start sinning again.

When the worst was over, Henry let Hal out onto the terrace for a cigarette. His sense of taste and smell hadn't come back yet; smoking felt like eating ashes out of the fireplace. Henry stayed with him, leaning back against the stone balustrade, resting his hands on the edge.

'I did take my share of cocaine when I was up at Oxford,' said Henry. 'I haven't totally forgotten what it was like. Will you be able to keep out of trouble if you stay in London?'

'Where else would I go?'

'I'm sure my sister would have room for you, if you fancied leaving the Occident.'

'If I went to Asia, Harry Percy would follow me.'

'Monmouth would be cold and damp, but remarkably free of temptation. The closest thing you'd get to a monastery, only we don't brew our own beer.'

'Am I meant to go alone?'

'I was going to go up for a couple of months to sort some things out about the house before the wedding.'

'Shouldn't Jeanne go with you, if it's for the wedding?'

'Oh no, the plans for the wedding are more or less in hand. But the roof of the chapel needs mending, and the boiler, and something's got to be done about whatever is living in the attic.' He repeated what he said every time he complained about the houses or the land or the tenants: 'This is what you've got to look forward to someday.'

'Not if I sell Monmouth to an oligarch. I'll sell it to Percy's ex-girlfriend's father. I'll give him a "friend of the family" discount.'

'Don't joke about it, or you'll start thinking about it seriously.'

'Even if I did, it wouldn't matter. Nobody would take Monmouth if they had the money to buy something grander. That's why Richard let us keep it.'

That night, Hal rang Thomas Woodstock to tell him he had to take leave. Thomas said, 'Good God. I don't know why he's demanded I employ you only to turn around and prevent you from working for me. But that's what Henry is like: he impinges on you, he demands things from you, he gets upset that you won't give him what he demands, he reminds you of how long he's known you, he reminds you of the favours he's done for you, he convinces you it would be wrong to deny him. Then he makes you regret your own Christian kindness.'

21

In the summer, south-east Wales was a temperate escape from London heatwaves, mild at midday and cool enough for a jumper at night. In midwinter, once the glitter of the Christmas season was gone, there was only wind and rain. Coming back to the house after two weeks away felt like coming back after ten years and finding the place abandoned. Everyone was gone but the housekeeper and the gardener, a married couple who lived in a cottage near the outskirts of the park. Henry had told Mrs Fletcher not to make a fuss, just have the cleaners round once a week to take care of the rooms that were being lived in, and keep the pantry stocked, and cook them simple dinners with portions large enough that there would be leftovers for lunch. He inquired after her children and grandchildren, each of whom he knew by name, and gave Christmas gifts more lavish than the ones he gave to his own children.

Hal was still weak from his illness, and in agony at not having drugs. At night, when he was most energetically self-loathing, he stayed up and drank whisky and watched movies. During the day he moved from soft surface to soft surface, napping for thirty minutes at a time. There were so few distinctions between the days that it was Tuesday when he realised Henry hadn't gone to mass the Sunday before. He didn't go the next Sunday either. He spent the morning in his study, going over, he said, the accounts. Hal said that sounded like work, and Henry said, 'No, it's not, I'm not doing anything with the money, just looking to see where it is at the moment, or where it isn't.'

It wasn't, Hal thought, a crisis of faith. Henry prayed the Divine

Office eight times a day, like a Benedictine. Did he do this in London when Hal wasn't there? If Hal got up early enough, he'd catch him saying Prime at the breakfast table. They said Vespers together before dinner, and Compline after.

One evening, as Hal and Henry sat together drinking sherry before dinner, Percy texted:

H Percy 19:23 Your place tonight?
Hal 19:24 I thought you were bored of me
H Percy 19:24 No I was just not bothering you because you were upset
Hal 19:25 I wasn't upset, you'd decided to express all the deeply-held resentment you'd been repressing since we started fucking and I responded in kind
H Percy 19:25 I just needed to sleep

When he didn't get a quick response, Percy added:

H Percy 19:29 Let me make it up to you, are you at home now?

The clock on the mantelpiece struck once to mark the half hour. Hal and Henry went down to the kitchen, where Mrs Fletcher was setting out beef stew. Henry sat at the head of the table and Hal sat on his right. They enjoyed each other's company. Henry laughed at Hal's jokes. Hal texted back only after dinner, as Henry added a log to the fire:

Hal 20:52 I'm at Monmouth actually
H Percy 20:53 When are you back
Hal 20:53 I don't know possibly in a month
H Percy 20:55 A month??
H Percy 21:02 It's a bit of an overreaction to run away to Wales for a month because I was short with you when you

rang me in the middle of the night isn't it? I'm sorry you
were so bothered but I don't see why you couldn't have
told me you were leaving

Hal 21:03 And anyway I've got to help my dad with a few
things up here. Don't you always say I should be learning
how to manage the estate

Henry said, 'How is Harry Percy?'

'Why do you think I'm talking to Percy?'

'You've got a certain look on your face.'

'What kind of look?'

Henry said, 'I couldn't say.'

Hal's hangover the next morning was not even from having had
too much to drink, just from having failed to drink enough water. His
headache was so tolerable he didn't feel the need for paracetamol. He
woke to Henry knocking on his door and opening it at the same time,
saying, 'It's nearly noon.'

'I'll get up,' said Hal, 'and pray with you.'

Disliking English rhyme, Henry sang the hymns of the Divine
Office in Latin. This time it was 'Rector Potens, Verax Deus', and Hal
just barely murmured along, so that his poor pronunciation and indifferent singing wouldn't overpower Henry's fine and gentle voice. But
Hal was the better speaker, and he read the psalms: 'Blessed be the
Lord, who hath not given us to be a prey to their teeth. Our soul hath
been delivered as a sparrow out of the snare of the fowlers.'

That afternoon, Henry said he needed to look again at the accounts,
and told Hal not to disturb him for an hour or two. Hal went up to the
study after an hour. He opened the door at the same time that he
knocked, and stood by the desk and used the landline to ring the
Percys' London house. Henry, sitting at the desk, watched Hal with
restrained incredulity. If he hadn't been at least a little amused, he
wouldn't have let him do it.

Percy's stepmother answered. When Hal asked to speak to Harry

Percy, she asked who it was, and he said, 'Henry Lancaster,' marvelling at how strange it was to identify himself with his own name.

She said she would get Harry, then put her husband on the line. Mr Percy said, 'What is it now, Henry?'

Hal said, 'I won't keep you long, but I rang to apologise for how badly I behaved the other night. I'd had too much to drink, and I'm unused to wine.'

'Oh, it's you. "Marquis's son unused to wine," is it? Don't think you can slip that one past me – we all watched *Brideshead* in the eighties. Is Henry there, holding a gun to your head?'

Letting the phone cord stretch out, he came round to stand behind Henry and pick lint off the shoulders of his jumper. Henry reached back to slap Hal's hand away, and Hal caught his hand and held it still. He said, 'No, this is genuine remorse.' He touched the back of Henry's neck, where the slightly overgrown hair at his nape spread over his shirt collar.

'You'd better watch yourself,' said Mr Percy. 'Some people drink themselves under the table and never make a fool of themselves. They're less entertaining than the fools, but I'll give you a piece of advice: the more you entertain people, the less they'll do what you tell them. It's better to force a man to laugh because he's afraid of you than make him laugh genuinely and give him the impression that you're there for his amusement.'

Once Hal rang off, the heaviness appeared. Henry wasn't going, and Hal stayed too, seated on the edge of the desk, his feet touching the rug. Henry was thinking about it now, maybe wanting it, maybe not. If Hal was already in a state of mortal sin, if Henry's soul was none of Hal's concern . . . The presence of the people to whom Hal had been talking remained in the room, but what did that matter, if at the party it had happened when those same people were there in the flesh? When Henry went out, Hal thought it must have been either because he was a coward or because he did not yet want the punishment to which he would submit himself afterwards.

Henry left the door open. He went downstairs; Hal heard the stairs creak. Ponderously, without purpose or secrecy, Hal sat in the chair and looked through Henry's desk, flipping through the stacks of documents, opening the drawers to find piles of old pens, fountain and disposable, notepaper, stamps, receipts, manila folders full of papers that had yellowed with age. Scattered throughout this detritus were individually wrapped boiled sweets. Hal unwrapped a pear drop and put it in his cheek, fanning through Henry's leather-bound diary:

Dermatologist 14 Dec. 8 am
SORT PRESCRIPTIONS
TABLETS DAILY—AS PRESCRIBED
Liudmila cheque Xmas

Monmouth
– Ring back catering tenants dinner
– Ring back D Lewis
– Boiler 27 Jan
– Roof chapel late Mar/Apr
– Roof house Apr/May
– Drainage quotes

Let them give praise to thy great name for it is terrible and holy and the king's honour loveth judgment.

An old photo of Hal was tucked into the pocket inside the back cover. It was printed on glossy paper, with the supply company's logo in a repeating pattern on the back. Sometime, more than a decade ago, someone must have had the film developed in a shop. In the picture he was sitting on the deck of a sailboat, backed by blue sky and open water. He must have been twelve or thirteen. His face was fat and spotty but his limbs had begun to broaden, and his white t-shirt was loose because he was growing so quickly that if he bought clothes that fit him they would be too small in three months. His hair was thick with salt and moisture, his fringe blown away from his forehead by the same breeze that rippled his shirt.

Hal wished he could have looked at that picture and been able to see, transparently, that he had been innocent, or that his innocence had been lost and he was lacking it. But it was funny, he couldn't remember whether that was the summer before or the summer after it had all started. By the time he was fifteen or so, Hal had become fairly confident that he could look at another young person and tell immediately whether they had been interfered with. Why now, with so many years of experience, could he not look at a picture of himself and tell whether it had happened yet? It didn't matter, he supposed. He would have always been what he was.

It was nearly seven, Hal realised. If he was going to have anything to drink before dinner, he would have to go down now. Hal spat into the centre of the photo and folded it in half, spit side in. He put it back into the diary and left the diary where he recalled its being before.

22

On the anniversary of Grandfather John's death, Henry brought in pest control to look at the attic. They reported that the things living there were grey squirrels, an invasive species they were under strict orders to exterminate. They reassured Henry that they were professionals and killed humanely. Also, they would have to treat the attic for fleas. The traps were set and baited. Each morning and evening, a specialist came to check the traps and kill the squirrels that had been caught. One time he let Hal follow him out to the long grass beyond the garden and watch him dispatch three in a row. It was the first hour of daylight, and in his corduroys and Barbour, Hal was bitterly cold. He kept adjusting his scarf to keep his face warm, and the wind kept blowing it askew. The specialist, surprisingly fit and young, wore a flannel-lined jacket and fingerless gloves, and had tucked his uniform trousers into insulated work boots. His face was reddened and dry. He took more care with the killing than Hal had expected: he aimed the air pistol between the bars of the metal trap and waited for the moment the creature was right where he wanted.

They had to vacate the house while the attic was fumigated, so Henry got Hal up early, said Prime, and let Hal take him on a day tour of his own land. They took the old Land Rover up the narrow dirt roads that led through the pastures where sheep grazed, then down to flatter, lower ground and the greening fields of winter barley, saying hello to the tenants they passed. For lunch they stopped at Henry's favourite country pub, a half-timbered Jacobean survival with a ceiling so low Hal had to duck under the central beam. An old married couple shared the duties of the publican and innkeeper, pressing their children and grandchildren into service as waiters and cleaners and cooks and porters. Some of them lived on the Lancasters' land, some didn't. That day, the only people working were the wife and a girl Hal hadn't seen before. The wife made a great fuss over Henry, who did the same in return. He said how nice the place looked, how well the recent restorations had come off, how glad he was to be out of the cold and in front of a nice wood fire. He asked to be introduced to the girl, who turned out to be a cousin named Catrin who helped sometimes when she wasn't busy with her veterinary course.

If Hal had been alone, he would have been able, if not to charm Catrin, then at least to make conversation with her. Being with Henry, being brought out to strangers as Henry's son, made him ashamed of himself. When Catrin looked at him, he could feel the landownerish-ness, the public-schoolboyishness, the lordishness, radiating off him like cartoon stink lines. He could see that she was thinking, *These fucking English snobs*, and felt desperate to endear himself to her, and found that his father's presence had emptied him of everything but his Englishness and snobbery. Hal and Catrin stood meekly silent while their elders talked.

'I forgot to congratulate you,' the wife said to Henry, 'on your engagement. My best advice, after forty years of marriage, is that a man should get used to his wife knowing better than him.'

Sweetly, smiling and humble, Henry said, 'I promise I'll do what-ever she tells me,' knowing bloody well that he believed a wife's purpose was to obey.

As a young child, Hal had been devoted to his father as stupidly and intractably as if he were in unrequited love. He watched him talk to other adults and was amazed at how he seemed to exceed good man-ners and arrive at genuine graciousness. At school he was always telling the other boys what his father said, what his father did, where he had travelled and what he had brought back. The devotion was greatest in the year after his mother's death: Henry seemed so brave and unshakeable that Hal prayed every night he would grow up to be like his father. Then, when Hal was ten or eleven, the family went to lunch after Easter Sunday mass, and Henry engaged a waiter in a long conversation, and Richard, sitting next to Hal, said to him, 'Henry thinks they like him.' Hal began to notice when an attendant's proclamations of pleasure – 'That's no trouble at all, sir', 'We're happy to do it, sir' – were strained with the effort to conceal the displeasure Henry had caused. He began to prefer Richard, whose snobbery was at least straightforward; he began to rely on his pride at being associated with Richard to make up for the shame he felt at being associated with his father.

When he was fourteen or fifteen, submitting to the demand he turn into a man, Hal learned to be ashamed of Richard too. Henry hadn't seemed to notice that Hal had fallen out of love with him, but when Hal fell out of love with Richard, Richard understood at once what had happened. He began to speak to him as if he were making pronouncements from a pedestal. By then he looked fragile and underfed: his hair had thinned and lost some of its curl, and the skin of his long fingers had shrunk down over the swollen joints. But he dressed more beautifully, in women's silk blouses with big bows at the neck and the heirloom rings his mother had left him when she died. Wherever he went, he flung himself out past the boundaries of the space allotted, forcing other people to squeeze past or step over or duck beneath him. He asked the most impertinent favours of the staff who served him, and seemed never to be denied. One weekend, he went up to Mount Grace and took Hal to York for tea, and a boy from Hal's year was there with his parents, and they were sat in view of one another. The boy leaned over to say something to his mother, who looked over, caught Hal's eye, then pretended she hadn't been looking. Hal was humiliated at being seen with Richard, humiliated that Richard could tell, humiliated to know the thing that made Richard so intolerable was something Hal possessed too, independently; something Hal would have to keep even after Richard was dead and could not embarrass him in public any longer.

So he came to understand Henry. It was less painful to live if you acted like the person other people wanted to see, if you made other people the unwitting fathers of the bastard selves you bear for the sake of creating a thing that resembles the observer enough to secure their kindness, or at least their mercy.

Hal woke choking, like he'd swallowed his spit wrong in his sleep. He felt the terror of mortality, the total willingness to repent of his sins, then realised he wasn't dying. It was four in the morning. He tried to go back to sleep and was kept awake by the sound and sensation of his own breathing. He thought that when he breathed hard through his nose, he could feel the air coursing through the hole in his septum. Maybe that was how breathing had always felt. But Dr Bradmore said the hole was there, and permanent, like the scars on his face, and Hal wanted, with the petulance of the conscious sinner who has just been given cause for remorse, to be put back into the body he'd been given when he was born, and have another chance to keep it pure.

But whose body, besides the Blessed Virgin's, was pure? If it hadn't been these holes, he'd have had others: pitted scars from bad spots, cavities in his molars, gashes in his side that he could let his friends finger. His mother had given birth six times in eight years. His father had patches of psoriasis that he scratched until they bled openly, leaving scars that he then tried to hide. Henry's joints swelled when he overexerted himself, and the pain kept him up at night, like Hal was up now, only Henry didn't blast his eyes blind by holding his phone too close to his face in the dark.

Philippa hadn't said anything in the group chat since Twelfth Night. Blanche had been in and out, teasing Humphrey about the girl he was seeing, responding with the laughing-crying emoji to mediocre comedy videos Tom or John had linked. Since Blanche wouldn't worry about Philippa, Hal worried about her twice as much. Once every few days he tapped out half a text message or the first two sentences of a subjectless email, then deleted it.

Struggling to hit the right letters on the cracked screen, he typed, 'I'm sorry that I behaved', then stopped and hit send. He found the sentence funny as it was. It reminded him of what their father said when one of them acted against his will: he gave them a serenely derogatory look and said simply, 'Behave.'

The message was marked as read. Hal waited for a response, and there was none. Philippa didn't even start typing.

He needed, he thought, to take a pill that would knock him out until the afternoon. Then he could be normal again. Flinging on a bathrobe, he walked down to the far end of the long corridor, to Henry's bedroom. Henry looked perfectly usual: his bedside lamp was on, and in that circle of weak light he was sitting up in bed, wearing a jumper too moth-eaten to be seen in public and a pair of reading glasses, which he put away along with his copy of – what was that? – an old edition of selected works by Montaigne. Hal remembered writing an essay on Montaigne in the Trinity library, so drunk he could barely sit up; it had been about four in the morning then too.

'Come in or stay out,' said Henry, 'but please, shut the door. You're letting the cold air in.'

Hal didn't know why it mattered when the windows were draughty. He shut the door, then began rifling through the top left drawer of the dresser, where Henry kept his prescription bottles and blister packs. Henry got out of bed and tried to pull him away, saying, 'Don't, Harry, you'll end up killing yourself.'

'It doesn't count, spiritually, as suicide, does it, if you cause your own death by accident?' Yanking himself out of Henry's grasp, Hal opened a bottle and got two pills under his tongue before Henry could stop him.

'That's enough,' said Henry, shutting the drawer.

'That's all I wanted.'

'Well, goodnight, then.'

'But let me stay with you. It's been such a bad night.'

'I'm sorry I passed it down to you. I thought you might have been spared.'

'The only thing I've been spared is the psoriasis.' Hal fell back onto Henry's bed, his arms flung out, his legs hanging over the edge.

Henry's mattress was so much softer than his, and the linen so much smoother, and he was wreathed in the scent of Henry's night sweat and cologne. 'How can you not sleep? Your bed is so much better than mine. I'd never be able to get up.'

'You'll have to. You can't sleep here.'

This was the first time Hal had been in Henry's bed while Henry was there. Henry had been the sort of father to send a child back to its own bed if it came to him complaining of nightmares. 'When you're away at school,' he'd say, 'you'll have to get through it on your own, so you had better learn now.' Later, Hal would sneak in while Henry was away and go through his things, just like Henry went through his things.

Pulling up the duvet and tossing it over his upper half, covering his face and leaving his legs exposed, Hal said, 'Will you pick me up and carry me out if I don't go?'

'What did you take?'

'Just diazepam, nothing serious.'

Henry pulled the duvet away from Hal's face, and the low light for a second was disturbingly bright. He told Hal, 'Two tablets of diazepam aren't going to keep you from getting up and going to your own bed.'

'Have you thought about how this is the longest we've been alone together, ever? I think our last record was two weeks, when we went to France.'

'I hadn't thought.'

Straining muscles he rarely exercised, Hal lifted himself till he was sitting on the edge of the bed, facing Henry, less than an arm's length away from him. He was looking up at Henry, which he didn't do when they were standing. Why did he feel so calm, when an hour ago he was insane? Why was it comforting now to be the sole subject of Henry's attention? Where did the terror go, where was the shame? He didn't think it had gone away forever, but he couldn't summon it up. It was like when he'd had his wisdom teeth out and his jaw had been numbed, and in the hour after the surgery, still drowsy from the sedation, he'd probed the sites of extraction with the tip of his tongue so vigorously that he'd pulled the stitches out, having had no pain to tell him he should stop.

Hal pulled Henry forwards and down. To stabilise himself Henry put his hands on Hal's shoulders. Their faces came close; Hal leaned back so they were just distant enough to look at each other. He recognised the spearmint scent of Henry's toothpaste. He laughed, quietly, with a flirtatious, insulting asymmetric smile. He had made that face during a hook-up at uni once, and the boy had said, 'There's a smile that wants wiping off.'

Henry put his lips against Hal's and let them rest there, rather chastely, like the kiss of peace. The noise Hal made, little more than a vocalised exhalation, tipped the scales weighing Henry's desire and his fear, and he put his hand in Hal's hair to keep him in place. It was delicate at first, open-mouthed but slow, punctuated by moments of stillness. How many people had Henry kissed since Hal's mother? Perhaps none. He was gentle, as if appealing to a shy and unforthcoming woman; Hal imagined that this was how he must have kissed Mary, the first time. Just when he felt Henry might give up, Hal began to mirror precisely what Henry did, so that neither of them was fully at fault when their tongues touched.

Hal knew all the things he could be thinking and chose not to think any of them. The church, the law, the world, the ancestors, the family, the self, the soul, were behind a closed door that Hal passed by. The apprehension floated out of him and he was light and loose, unburdened, blank. He felt the pleasure of the vessel, which bears no responsibility for what has filled it. Having lost the fear that had been keeping him up, he was sleepy, and seemed, even as he kept himself upright and responsive, to be going back and forth over the threshold of sleep.

He let go of Henry and fell back into the duvet. He dragged himself up until his head was on Henry's pillows, where the cologne–soap–body smell faded and the fragrance of his hair began to dominate. Henry didn't follow him down.

*

The curtains were open, the daylight grey, the rain noisy. It was nine or ten, not too late, and Hal was alone in Henry's bed, without even an outline of a figure next to him. He worried for a second that he had become Henry, but his body was unmistakably his own. He searched for Henry and found him asleep on the sofa in the drawing room, where the curtains were also open. A tartan blanket was tangled around Henry's legs; his bare feet were out, his slippers on the rug. His sleeves were pulled back to show his wrists, his fingers curled loosely into his palms, his eyelashes were long and dark. Hal felt the same swelling impulse to cry as he sometimes did at mass, when the beauty struck him in the right spot. His body mastered itself before he even had time to think whether he wanted it or not. He breathed in and then breathed in again before he exhaled, and there was the single twitch of his bottom lip, and then it was gone.

23

In London you could go out at night: there were clubs, off-licences, twenty-four-hour Tescos, friends of friends who were having a party and said they didn't mind you dropping by. At Monmouth, there was only the house and the land, empty roads and shuttered shopfronts, people asleep in their own houses. Hal woke one night after a terrible dream and drove out to a petrol station on the A40 just to reassure himself that he had not been left alone in the world. He filled the tank of the Land Rover and bought a packet of cigarettes even though he'd just bought a packet the day before. He smoked in the driver's seat, sitting in the car park with the engine off, listening to the radio, thinking how decent he would feel if only he were in London, full of cocaethylene, taking the night bus back to his flat.

When he went back to the house he went to Henry's bedroom. There was no light coming from under the door, but he knocked anyway, and when Henry didn't answer, he let himself in. He turned on a lamp to see Henry lying on his side, the duvet only half-covering him, as if he hadn't been able to finish pulling it up. There was whisky still in the glass on the table, and a bottle of pills with a label that made Hal raise his eyebrows, then put a finger under Henry's nose to check that he was still breathing.

'Dad,' he said, and then again, louder: 'Dad!'

Henry was deeply asleep, or perhaps unconscious. Hal rolled him onto his back and lay down on the other side of the bed. He said Matins. He prayed for the souls of his mother and his grandparents and Richard, and Richard's mother and father and grandfather and great-grandfather and his great-grandfather's lover, Piers, and his wife Isobel and her lover, and Grandfather John's mistress and his illegitimate children, and Edward Langley and his boyfriend Will. He prayed to St Philomena for Philippa's unhappiness to end. Then he reached across Henry to turn out the light. The darkness made Hal feel Henry's presence more strongly. He heard Henry breathing; he felt, even without touching him, the warmth of his body. It was good to have someone there, living. Henry must have suffered, not having had someone there for so long. Hal shifted until he was flush up against Henry, holding him, his head on Henry's chest. Henry was soft and unthreatening, pleasant to lie beside. Hal hoped that if Henry didn't feel it consciously, his body knew, at least.

In the morning Hal was alone in bed, but Henry was there, beyond the shut door of the en suite, drawing a bath. The running water sounded the same as the rain. Hal entered the bathroom and shut the door behind him and leaned back against it.

'Good morning,' he said.

Across from him was a large window identical to the one in the bedroom. Originally it had all been one room: when the occupants had wanted to wash, their servants just plonked a tub down next to the fire. Now there was a clawfoot bath in the centre of the room, and Henry was in it, his knees sticking out of the water. He was washing his hair. The damp air smelled like sandalwood.

'Yes?' said Henry, as if he thought Hal had come to say something urgent.

'Did you sleep well?'

'I was surprised to find you there.'

'Why didn't you wake me?'

'You were sleeping.'

As Henry rinsed his hair, Hal came to sit on the edge of the tub, testing the water with his fingers, finding it scalding. Now that Hal was close, he saw how Henry's knees and shins were patched over with rashes, scaly white in some parts and pink in others. Dark scabs marked the places he'd been scratching, drawing blood, picking the scales off. The rashes that started on his elbows reached down to his wrists. His chest was unblemished and nearly as white as the bathtub. The rest of his body was blurred out by rippling water. He'd stopped washing; he was looking at Hal, waiting for Hal to be finished looking at him. Hal wondered if this was the first time since Mary died that anyone besides a doctor had seen Henry naked, and if last night was the first time since then that anyone had slept next to him. This is what it must have felt like to be Henry's wife, thought Hal: to have the preeminent right to his body, to be allowed the privilege, or given the burden, of total intimacy with a man other people only saw giving out prizes at agricultural shows.

Hal stayed as Henry drained the bath. In a white robe with dried bloodstains on the elbows, Henry combed his wet hair and shaved his face and dabbed cologne on his wrists and neck, the same scent he'd been wearing on Twelfth Night. Freshly applied, it smelled overwhelmingly of leather, with sharp citrus at the edges and musk at the centre. Hal said, 'Let me try,' and touched the atomiser to his inner wrist without spraying it.

Percy rang Hal just as he was falling into bed. He let it go to voicemail and Percy rang again, and Hal, stupidly, thinking it must be important if he was ringing twice at one in the morning, answered. He put Percy on speaker and laid his phone down next to him, remembering how it had felt to lie on his side and have Percy there holding him, resting his forehead against Hal's back, getting an erection from having his prick nestled against Hal's arse.

'I miss you,' Percy told him.

'Do you really?'

'Yeah, I do. Are you alone?'

'Yeah, I'm in bed.'

'Me too. I was just thinking about you . . .'

'You must have been, if you rang me.'

'If I was there,' said Percy, 'what would you do?'

'Tell you to leave.'

'Oh. What? Are you still angry with me? I'm trying to have phone sex.'

'No, it's fine, I'm sorry, it's just weird to think about you being here at Monmouth. Don't hang up, I'll try to be serious. If you were here I'd totally have sex with you.'

On the other side of the line there was rustling. Hal thought of how embarrassing it would be if someone was tapping their phones, or if there was someone in town who just happened to pick up the call on his ham radio. Percy said, 'So what would you do?' but Hal was distracted searching 'can ham radio pick up mobile phone'.

'Umm, yeah,' said Hal, 'so how would you want me?'

'On your knees,' said Percy, so quickly it was clear he'd been thinking it already. 'Choking on my dick, and not even being able to take it all, and begging for more, and you would be hard too, and you would keep trying to touch yourself, and I'd say "No, you can't, you're not allowed." And I'd fuck your throat so hard you'd be hoarse the next day, and everybody would ask you if you were sick.'

'That literally happened two months ago.'

'Yeah, I know, I've been wanking over it ever since.' Percy was breathing heavily, and the rustling had become rhythmic: apparently, he was wanking over it now. 'Next time I'm going to make you suck my dick before I fuck you, and then you're going to have to take me with nothing but your own spit, and then I'm going to make you fucking beg for my cum.'

Hal was laughing almost silently, letting his little snuffles pass for noises of abject arousal. But he was hard, so more fool him. He said, 'Okay, and what would you do with it? Arse or mouth, inside or out?'

'I don't know. I miss everything. I want to do it all.' Percy's heavy breathing stopped, and after a second of silence he swallowed and let out an irritated groan. 'Are you w-wanking?'

Hal wasn't yet, just holding his prick through his pyjama bottoms. He said, 'Yeah, are you?'

'Yeah,' said Percy, then: 'Are you just touching your dick?'

'Yeah, why? Is that not enough?'

'I want you to fuck yourself, since I'm not there to do it for you.'

Being commanded made Hal harder than he'd ever get from solicitations about his desires. This was dangerous: now his shame had turned away from him. He pulled his pyjamas and pants down to his thighs and put his first two fingers in his mouth, thinking, Wow, I would have killed myself if I'd been told five years ago that I'd be fingering myself because Harry Percy told me to. He had to take them out again to say 'yeah' when Percy asked him if he was doing it.

'Good,' said Percy. 'Don't be gentle.'

Too lazy to get on his hands and knees, Hal flopped over onto his stomach, crushing his nose into the pillow and muttering a plaintive 'ow'. He turned his head to the side, facing his glowing phone, and forced both fingers into himself at the same time, feeling the pain without letting it stop him, wishing, when he hadn't before, that Percy really was here, and could take control of his body for him.

'Okay,' Hal slurred, 'I'm doing it.'

'I want to hear you,' said Percy, trying to sound sexy.

'What, do you want me to moan?'

'Well, don't fake it. I want to hear you make the same noises you do when I'm actually fucking you.'

'What noises do I make?'

'Like you can't help it. Like you're getting fucked hard and you're about to come, and I'm about to come, and you're telling me to come inside you, and I'm going to, because I want you to know you're mine.'

'You've got it the wrong way round,' said Hal, trying to come and not quite getting there. He was rubbing his prick against the mattress like he used to do at school, late at night, trying not to alert his roommate to the fact that he was wanking. 'You're always going on about marking me and claiming me and making me yours and wanting everyone to know that I'm yours, and you think it's true because you fuck me, and I let you come inside me, and that's what a woman does, and that means I'm subordinate to you by nature, that you're my master, and you've planted your flag in me, like I'm the New World and you're Sir Walter Raleigh. But you're the one giving yourself up to me.'

If this had upset Percy, he would have interjected by now. He was just breathing, rustling, making noises he didn't know he was making, the ones he made when he was fucking Hal, who went on. 'You think you're not like me. But what if you are? Do you know that when my father was our age, he'd already got two children? You could die tomorrow and you'd have wasted yourself on wanking and fucking girls who were on the pill and fucking me. That's a bit pathetic, isn't it? But you're vain, and it flatters you when I say I want you, so you'll bugger me and then roll over satisfied that you've shown Hal Lancaster who's in charge, and now he's going to have to clean your priceless ancient English cum out of his arse. You don't realise—'

Hal could feel an orgasm just out of reach, graspable if he really worked for it, so he shut up and fucked himself imagining it was Percy, and then came, turning his face into the pillow to muffle his noises. Just like he did when they were really fucking, Percy announced that he was coming. Then there was a silence long enough that Percy, recovered, said, 'Are you still there?'

'Uh-huh,' said Hal. He rolled onto his back and pulled his pyjama bottoms up with his left hand, holding his right hand out as if it were infectious.

'God, I just came harder than I have in months.' Percy sounded worried, like he wasn't sure what that said about him. 'Did you come?'

'Yeah, yeah, before you.'

'Oh, that's good . . .'

'Well, I've got to, umm, clean up, so . . .'

'I thought we could stay on and talk? But if you've really got to go . . .'

'You haven't got a badminton match with the home secretary?'

'Are you still upset about that? That was like a month ago. And it was one night. Clearly you've done without me for a lot longer than that now.'

Hal's right hand was starting to ache from being held up. He reached over the side of the bed and wiped his fingers on the shirt he'd been wearing, then used it to scrub at the damp spot on the bed. He said, 'It's not like I'm having fun. I hate it here.'

'So come back to London.'

'I will,' said Hal, 'soon enough.'

After they rang off Hal became aware, lying alone in the dark, of the last traces of scent coming off his wrists, even though he'd got up and washed his hands. It was like seeing a face out of the corner of your eye and starting, thinking you'd been alone, then realising it was only a spot on the wall, or the shadows cast by the trees outside your window, or your own reflection.

24

On 14 February 2007, Hal was in year 10, studying for his GCSEs, taking lessons in French, Latin, history, physics and Roman Catholic ethics, playing tennis in the afternoon and swimming in the evening, bullying the most susceptible boys in his house, pretending not to care that the sixth-form boy he pretended not to fancy wouldn't shut up about how he'd snuck out to the woods to get off with a sixth-form girl. Hal was fifteen, Philippa was seven, Henry was about to turn thirty-seven, and Richard died aged thirty-seven years, one month, and nine days. Or eight days, if you didn't count the day he died. Hal thought it should be counted if he died at least twelve hours after the time he was born, but he didn't know what time Richard was born, or what time he died.

He only found out when he and his brothers went up to London for Easter. It was the last day before they returned to school; Hal had spent his holidays anxiously considering whether he should try to slip away and pay Richard a visit. He wasn't sure if Richard was at home or in hospital, he would have to ring to find out, and by that time Edward Langley was the one who took Richard's calls. Saturday morning after breakfast, Hal went into the garden and used his mobile to ring Richard's London house.

Edward said, 'Who is this?' When Hal said it was him, Edward said, 'It's just like Henry not to have told you.'

Late that night, after the other children had gone to bed, Hal drank a cup of whisky under Henry's supervision. He asked if Henry had gone to Richard's funeral and Henry said that he'd organised it.

Hal said, 'Why didn't you tell me he was dead, so that I could pray for him?'

'I've been praying for him. Now you can too.'

'Why didn't you ask me if I wanted to come to the funeral?'

'Because you've been at school,' Henry said.

Hal had last seen Richard a month before, in January, the day after Richard's thirty-seventh birthday. He let himself into the house because Edward wouldn't leave Richard's side. He looked at himself, at his dishevelled hair and the spots on his chin and the mustard-yellow socks exposed by trousers he'd grown too tall for, as he passed between the mirrors in the hall. The purpose he possessed when he was with his father had gone; the thing in the mirror was his double's double, memoryless. Approaching Richard's bedroom, he heard Edward speaking solicitously. Richard responded with a sharp dismissal, which was characteristic, then an apology, which was not.

Richard's bed was an antique four-poster with a canopy of blue embroidered silk. It was Richard's favourite blue, that perfect lapis lazuli, the colour of the sky in the *Très Riches Heures*, the colour of the Virgin's robes. He sat propped up against his white pillows, wearing a white dressing gown; his hair was brushed soft and parted in the middle, tucked behind his ears, falling to his shoulders. The house, which had always been full of beautiful things, was nearly empty. The pictures that had been on the walls were gone; the surfaces were bare of all the china and glass and ivory, the enamelled snuffboxes and majolica plates and crystal bowls filled with costume jewellery. All that was left in Richard's bedroom were the bed, the bedside table, the armchair, the dresser, and the dressing table with the oval mirror, on top of which was a silver-backed hairbrush and a few bottles of scent.

Edward was standing just next to the bed, his hands resting on the mattress, as if what he really wanted was to be touching Richard. Looking at the two of them together, looking at the bed, Hal thought that they must have had sex there, and was so ferociously ashamed of thinking it that his contrarian subconscious forced the images into his mind's eye. He thought they must have known, and hated him for it, supposing he was working himself up just to give greater force to his excoriation of them. He thought they wouldn't believe him if he said, 'I think I'm like you,' or if they did believe him, they would be angry at him for choosing to follow in their suffering. Now he wished, as hopelessly as he wished his mother was alive, that he could go back and tell the truth, and ask them, 'What should I do? How should I live? What do I have to do to survive?'

Richard had said, 'Take something. Do. Edward will show you what's left. Whatever you like.'

'Why would you give me something now,' asked Hal, 'when I'm going to inherit what's left anyway?'

'Do what I tell you,' said Richard. His hands were folded in his lap. His right hand was shaking; his left was still.

Not wanting to take anything too precious, Hal chose a gilt silver teaspoon with a mother-of-pearl handle. When Richard explained that it had been part of a set given to his parents as a wedding present, Hal said, 'Oh, sorry, I didn't realise, I'll choose something else.'

'No,' Richard had said, with such severity that Hal was frightened of him, this dying man, this object of pity. 'Now that you've chosen it, you have to take it. Edward, bring me the . . .' He waved his left hand, as if the gesture could finish his thought for him. Edward only looked expectant. It was incredible, really, how Richard could make the degeneration of his own mind seem like a failure of the people who surrounded him.

'Water?' Edward guessed. 'Or do you want a cigarette?'

'No! For Christ's sake, I mean for Hal, he's got to have something else . . . From my mother's things . . .'

Edward brought out a black lacquered box that opened with a key. Hal, standing near the foot of the bed, couldn't see what was in it: he saw only the ring Richard withdrew. It was his mother's wedding ring, he said, which had been passed down from his father's mother, who'd had it from her husband's mother. She had given it to him before she died even though she'd known about the disease. She had hoped he might still marry a woman, perhaps a widow with children, someone more unfortunate than himself.

'Am I supposed to give this to my wife,' asked Hal, 'when I get married?'

Richard said, 'Do what you like. Throw it in the gutter. It's just a thing.'

Hal kept the ring in a safe deposit box, thinking he could sell it if he ever needed. The teaspoon he took with him to Mount Grace and Oxford, keeping it in a desk drawer or pencil cup, mixed in with biros and matchbooks and novelty swizzle sticks. Sometime after he finished uni he realised he didn't know where it was. He tore up the flat he'd only just moved into; he went to the London house in the middle of the night and looked through the boxes he'd never unpacked after bringing them home from Oxford. He spent a whole Christmas looking through every drawer and cabinet at Monmouth, behind and underneath every piece of furniture. He interrogated his siblings, who said they didn't know what he was talking about, and anyway they'd already got more antique silverware than anyone could possibly need.

Before Hal left, Richard told him to come closer, so that he could look at him. His vision was nearly gone in his right eye, deteriorating in his left. When Hal was near enough, Richard took Hal's hands in his and Hal got a headrush like he was about to faint, for no other reason than because someone was touching him lovingly. Hal thought: Don't leave me here, with them. Or at least hold me before you go. But when his lip trembled, he was humiliated and turned abruptly, saying that if he was gone any longer his father would start looking for him.

14 February 2015 was the last Saturday before Lent. For dinner that night, Mrs Fletcher had left a foil-wrapped shepherd's pie in the fridge, with handwritten instructions for heating it up in the oven. When Hal came downstairs in the morning for coffee, he saw no sign that Henry had been down yet. He left his dirty cup on the kitchen table and drove into town; he stopped in St Mary's to light a candle and pray for Richard's soul. After he finished his prayers, he sat for a long time in a

back pew, looking up at the crucifix above the altar and thinking nothing. It was a cold, wet day and the stained glass was dim. Just when he'd decided to leave, Father Price appeared and was guilt-inducingly friendly, and Hal asked, on a whim, if he would hear his confession. Father Price said he would.

Hal didn't see Henry again until it was past midnight. Alone, Hal heated up the shepherd's pie and ate it all himself. What if Henry was dying, or dead? Well, far be it from Hal, mere sinner that he was, to interfere with life and death. And anyway Henry wasn't dying. When Hal went out onto the porch so that he could smoke a cigarette without getting rained on, he found Henry there too, doing the same thing.

'Sorry, I'll leave you alone,' said Hal, and Henry said, 'No, don't,' so he stayed, thinking, like he always did, that maybe this was the time it would be worth it.

Hal said, 'I've told Thomas I'm going back to London.'

'I've got to stay on,' said Henry.

'Stay, then.'

'It's just that I get so frightened, thinking of what might happen to you. Or what you might do. I'm better off not thinking about it. But if I could choose what I thought, I'd be the perfect man.'

The porch was illuminated by two lanterns mounted on either side of the door. Spiderwebs fuzzed over the inner surface of the glass. Hal could see the insects that had been caught, the curled-up bodies hanging suspended, wobbling with the faint swaying of the webs, unmistakably dead even in motion. There was a common-looking spider, long-legged and brown, resting inside the glass of the left-hand lantern. Hal flicked the glass and the spider scuttled over a couple of inches; he flicked the glass again and it hid in a crevice.

'Leave the poor thing alone,' said Henry.

'Are you going to mass tomorrow?'

'No. You can go without me if you like. You should.'

'Why won't you?'

Putting out his cigarette, Henry said, 'It hasn't got anything to do with you.'

'Yes, it does. You've been waiting to work up the courage to do what you want with me before Lent begins and you've got to repent. Why don't you? We're here, we're alone. If you're afraid I'll say something, you haven't been paying attention. You know I won't, and you know nobody would believe me if I did. So just do it, do whatever it is you want, and then go back to London and get Father Dyer to absolve you for it, like he always does. Tell me what it is you want from me; I want to know.'

'Please, stop,' said Henry. 'I don't want anything from you.'

'Or you can just do it, you haven't got to tell me what it is you're going to do, you haven't ever told me before. You can't hurt me, I'm already irredeemable.'

Henry said, 'I'm sorry, I'm sorry, I'm sorry. I wish to God I'd never let myself.'

'But you did.' Hal took a long drag off his dwindling cigarette and exhaled into Henry's face. 'So why not do it again? You've gone too far already, why not go a little further?'

'Because we'll all have to pay for the things we do, one way or the other. And I owe too much already.'

'Is that all?'

'Because I'll be sorry for it,' said Henry, 'and I've been sorry enough.'

'It stays with you, doesn't it? Even after you've been forgiven. So why not at least let yourself have the thing you always feel sorry for?'

'Go back inside, go to bed. I don't want to hear it.'

'No, I'm sorry, you're right,' said Hal. 'I'll go back in.'

But Henry would not be contented, now, merely to have Hal follow his command. A command could be obeyed or disobeyed. The issuing of it, even reinforced by a threat, allowed its subject a choice. Henry hated to rely on speaking in order to assert his will: that was what Richard did, and Hal. He had spent too long speaking earnestly, like Percy did, and getting undercut by people who lied. Henry's domain was the body: against Richard he had always been the purer, the healthier, the better athlete, the earlier riser, the more virile, the more tolerant of pain. Even that, now, was taken from him. He was in pain all the time, and hated the heir he had fathered.

'Stop it,' said Henry, 'stop talking, stop looking at me.'

He seized Hal by the shoulders and turned him round, shoving him up against the front door. Hal's cheek hit the wood. While he was still dazed by that first pain, Henry took a fistful of Hal's hair and knocked his face forward into the door again. It was the sort of thing that Henry could have let himself do only if he thought of it as retribution.

'I know,' Hal said.

He became aware of the sound of the rain and the pungent, sweet scent of wet earth. The wind stirred up the dust that had settled in the porch. From behind him came the sound of unbuttoning and unzipping, fabric wrinkling and shifting. Henry had let go of his hair; his scalp was pleasantly sore. He couldn't tell if Henry had got his cock out or just put his hand down his trousers. He rested his forehead against the door and listened as Henry's breathing mounted, exhalation by exhalation, into the unconscious expression of quiet, innocent noises. Henry's left hand, on Hal's shoulder, stiffened and released in time with the other exertions of his body: his right hand pulling his cock, his diaphragm contracting and his lungs swelling, his vocal cords drawing open and shut. When he fucked Hal's mother for the first time, he must have been just like that.

Hal did nothing. There was nothing it occurred to him to do; there was nothing inside or outside of him telling him to act. He was breathing, his hands rested loosely against the door. He became what Henry had made him that very first time, an assemblage of parts that lacked that final thing to bring it alive, a space that a human being had just stepped out of, leaving a sign on the door saying 'be back soon'. Henry was moving unpredictably now, frenzied for as long as he could keep it up, then barely perceptible, then forceful and controlled. He was whispering something that Hal couldn't hear. Hal wished he could have heard him; he wished he could have seen his face.

When Henry did finish, Hal knew. There was something about the noise he made, the holding-back of breath and the grateful release of it, that reminded Hal of what he was like when he came. Henry did his trousers up again. He leaned against Hal, his face in Hal's neck, the warmth of his breath bringing feeling back to skin numbed by the cold. There was a slight shaking, and Hal realised it was Henry weeping, and was sorry for him, and wanted him not to be unhappy. Life had come into Hal again, he had reoccupied himself, and he wondered whether he should do something to help Henry. He thought that if he did, Henry would turn him away. Henry let go of Hal and stepped back. When Hal turned around, Henry let his son look at him.

As a very, very young child, having just developed the faculties of coherent speech and consciously directed movement, Hal used to play a game: he approached whatever he saw nearby, a mannequin or statue or stranger, and asked, 'Are you my mother?' He wasn't so stupid that he genuinely believed any of these things might really be his mother, but when he asked the question there was always a thrilling uncertainty as to what the answer might be. Perhaps he was mistaken: perhaps the thing in front of him was his mother, and the thing he thought of as his mother was something else. Looking at Henry, Hal felt the impulse to ask, 'Are you my father?' As if Henry were a mannequin or statue or stranger, as if Hal expected the answer to be 'no' and feared the answer to be 'yes'.

Henry said, 'You had better go to bed now. You can have something to help you sleep, if you need it.'

'No, I'm alright, thanks,' said Hal. 'I think I'll stay and have another cigarette.'

At the hour of Lauds, just before dawn, the rain froze into flecks that chimed when they were blown against the windows. Hal had stayed up: the exhaustion was safer than opening himself up to the possibility of dreams. He checked to see if the trains were still running. He folded his dirty clothes and packed them into his suitcase alongside the clean clothes. He zipped his toothbrush and safety razor back into his little bag of toiletries; he put his cigarettes and phone charger and the book he'd been reading into his backpack. He put his things in a pile next to the side door and rang for a cab to Newport.

The door to Henry's bedroom was left open just a crack. After he was sure he was ready to leave, Hal went back up to look in. Henry was still in the smart woollen trousers and white shirt he'd worn the night before, lying on his side on top of the duvet, his knees bent, his cuffs unbuttoned. The lights were off, but the curtains were open, letting in just enough light for Hal to see Henry's face. Snow fell.

When Hal lay down on the other side of the bed, Henry woke. He sat up and ran a hand through his hair. He said, 'I don't remember coming to bed.'

'It's because you're still dreaming,' Hal told him.

'No, I'm not. I can read the clock – that's how you can tell. It's past eight. Get out of my bed, Harry.'

'Will you look at me?'

Henry touched the scarred side of Hal's face with his fingertips. He said, 'You've got a pellet coming up, here. It's just broken the skin. The metal is shining.'

In London it was just raining. Hal took a shower and stood afterwards in his robe in front of the bathroom mirror, trying to squeeze the metal out of his cheek like the pus from a spot. When that didn't work, he tried tweezers, which pinched and poked but wouldn't keep hold of the pellet. He stopped and drank a can of beer, then came back with the sharpest knife he had in his kitchen and used the tip to cut into the skin just deeply enough that he could pop the pellet out.

A little ooze of blood came out after. He wiped the wound clean, dabbed it with an antibiotic cream, slapped on a plaster, and put the pellet in an envelope, so that he could look at it again sometime and remember it had once been inside him.

PART FIVE

LATE SPRING

25

On the first Sunday in May the sun came out and London was beautiful. The trees that for the past couple of months had been struggling to put out foliage now looked splendidly alive. The blue sky and crisp shadows made the streets look real again, as if Hal had stepped out of a flat medieval illustration and into a Renaissance masterpiece, vast and virtuosic, laden with detail, rendered in the most expensive pigments, leaving him no opportunity to accuse the artist of technical incapacity. The ordinary disappointment of a Sunday, the anticipation of having to go back indoors and start making money again, became more tolerable with a fine spring day's promise of future pleasure. Holy Week had come and gone: why seek you the living with the dead? Labour a while longer and then you'll have the summer, you'll go to the seaside, you'll lie all day in the sun. And what about afterwards, what about the autumn, the winter? Well, the wheel of fortune always turns.

After mass, Hal jogged with Percy in Richmond Park, working up a sweat while the deer grazed unhurriedly in the tall grass. The general election was less than a week away. Percy kept saying he was going to stop talking about it, then starting up again five minutes later when he thought of something else.

'What I don't understand,' said Percy, panting lightly, 'are the people who vote against their own interests. I understand why everyone I knew at school is a Tory, I understand why my family are Tories, I understand why your family are Tories. The thing is, just numerically speaking, the party wouldn't come close to winning an election if nobody but the elite were voting for them. That's the point of the elite, that there aren't that many of us. But there are people who are voting to reduce their own benefits! There are pensioners voting to privatise the NHS! Maybe some of them aren't bright enough to see trickery and propaganda for what it is, but all of them? Think of all the millions of people who make £12,000 a year at a call centre and vote to give their own landlords tax breaks! I want to shake them until they know what's good for them.'

Even with his longer stride, Hal was lagging behind Percy. He'd given up drugs for Lent, so he'd been drinking twice as much to make up for it, and had gained back the weight he'd lost while he was on cocaine, plus nearly an extra stone. Now his thighs chafed, and he had a bit of a double chin. If he'd wanted, he could have pushed himself to catch up, but he liked to look at Percy's arse in his clinging running shorts.

'At least the Tories don't shake them,' said Hal.

'Yes they do! They shake them upside down until all the coins fall out of their pockets, then turn them right side up again and slap them in the face when they apply for a council flat. But people like you tell them, "At least we aren't shaking you," and they believe you, and beg for more.'

'There are a lot of people in the world,' said Hal, 'who are willing to forfeit the means of their own happiness for the sake of seeing others unhappy.'

'Like you?' Percy threw a cold look over his shoulder and caught Hal looking at his arse, which deepened his reproach. 'You're just a hypocrite. Jesus was an immigrant.'

'Do you know, my dad is against an EU referendum because he says that if the UK leaves the EU, we'll actually get more migrants, not less? Anyway, the Christian migrants he's alright with. He likes the Poles and the Romanians because he thinks they're all good Catholics. And he says the real problem with the Muslims is that we're getting an inferior class. It used to be that they were all nice doctors and engineers. Now we're stuck with these horrid little boys in tracksuits who've come over from Calais. He's surprisingly pro-Islam, you know, for a man who wishes he could go on crusade. I suppose he'd be perfectly happy to see sodomites stoned in the streets.'

'He wouldn't let you be stoned in the streets.'

'He would. That's the difference between your father and mine. Yours would go down the line and stone each of the sodomites until he got to you. Mine would only do it if I was first.'

'Don't be such a martyr. At least your father reads the *Financial Times*. Mine's always talking about things he read in the *Sun* – you know, "Nuke the lifeboats and let the irradiated corpses fall into the seas like soft rain." He just likes to fuck me off and then accuse me of being sensitive.'

'Have you considered being less sensitive? I don't care about anything my father says.'

'You still fight with him, though.'

'And I always win, because I don't care. Your father always wins because he doesn't care. Haven't you realised that you can't score a point against a hypocrite by calling him a hypocrite? All you're doing is letting on that you're the sort of person who means what he says. How embarrassing for you.'

'No it's not! Nothing is embarrassing for me.'

'Not even being a good-looking wealthy Englishman?'

'Oh, that's not embarrassing,' said Percy, 'that's shameful of me. Don't worry, I do still have shame.'

In the group chat, Humphrey asked if they should be the ones organising a stag do for Henry. John said, 'No absolutely not, I am not going to organise a party just so Dad can shag.' Tom said, 'He is probably having one and just not telling us about it', and Humphrey said, 'Yeah but is he shagging?'

Philippa was privy only to what Hal reported. Every other evening, after he was finished with work, she FaceTimed him from the communal iPad at her rehab facility, which she referred to as a re-education camp for unfuckably thin rich girls. Really it was a farm in Sussex where each girl had her own bedroom and they all got up at five in the morning to feed the animals and cook communal meals with veg fresh from the garden.

'I would rather be force-fed,' she told him, 'like a suffragette. Did you know Jeanne went to hospital, twice, when she was younger? It was her idea for me to come here. Dad said he wasn't going to pay £3,000 a week for me to work on somebody else's farm, so she said she would. She said she didn't want me to suffer the way she did. If she had asked me what I wanted, I would have told her I'd rather suffer.'

On Sundays, Hal went with Jeanne to visit Philippa in person. They took her to mass at the small Catholic church in the village, then walked back to the farm through country lanes, swatting away insects, peering over fences at other people's horses. Week by week, Philippa recovered the look of psychological soundness. Her cheekbones disappeared into her cheek fat, her hands changed from blue to pink. She strained to put on the performance of strength and good humour through which she purchased her release. 'And I can't believe,' she said to Hal, 'that I've still got to sit my GCSEs.'

They let her out at the end of May. Jeanne and Henry agreed she could stay that week in London and finish out the summer term after the wedding. Henry had said that he would be the one to fetch Philippa from Sussex, but when the day came, he said he was unwell.

The Thursday before the wedding, Jeanne met Hal for lunch at a penthouse restaurant with a terrace overlooking Kensington Gardens. She said she wanted to thank him for being so good with Philippa. She was asking, pridefully, without admitting she was asking, whether she and Henry still had his blessing. Jeanne was soft, Hal thought. A more Machiavellian second wife would have got rid of the children and convinced Henry to move with her to the Riviera, or LA. But sometimes when she talked about Henry, her composure slipped just enough to reveal a smile, innocently self-satisfied, like a child who has won a game of chance.

'Was it your idea to get married,' Hal asked, 'or was it his?'

'Why do you ask?'

'I thought that I should . . .'

He didn't know what he was trying to tell her. Even if he did tell her everything, what did he want her to do with it? If he had wanted to stop the marriage, he could have done it a thousand other ways. Beneath them, flecks of unnatural colour – a magenta t-shirt, a yellow picnic blanket, somebody's aquamarine hair – showed through the trees bordering the park. A tiny unidentifiable insect crawled up the stem of Hal's wine glass. He tried to push it off gently and crushed it by accident anyway.

Jeanne was amused at his incapacity. 'If I had thought you were unhappy,' she said, 'I would have tried to set things to rights.'

'I just wonder if you know what my father is really like.'

'I know things about Henry that you don't.'

'Things you would tell me?'

'I refuse,' she said, pleasantly, as if there were nothing particularly bad she might have told him, 'to gossip to you about your father.'

'I just think . . . He can be frightfully unpleasant sometimes.'

'He hasn't been to me.'

'But he could be.'

'Anyone could,' she said.

When their plates were taken away, Hal said something about getting back to the office, and Jeanne beseeched him to stay for another glass of wine. She seemed to have something yet to say. For a while they talked about nothing – how Humphrey was getting on at uni, how Blanche was getting on with her A-Levels – and then she was silent, holding her glass without drinking from it, studying Hal's face as if she were preparing to pronounce judgment.

She said, 'In first marriages, the question is usually, "What are the husband's intentions?" Does he really intend to love and cherish, does he really intend to provide for her? Or does he think of her only as a conquest, to be put aside for other, younger, better women once she's given him his son. In second marriages, the assumption of ill motive falls on the wife. Does she really love him, or is she enriching herself with the spoils of someone else's life? Will she care for his children as her own, or will she see them as unwelcome competitors for his affection? I think I've been spared this speculation because people think they know what we're exchanging. Nobody minds whether or not there's love. I prefer it that way. I don't like to be asked to make a show of my private feeling. But I think he shouldn't be alone.'

'Even if he was the most miserable sinner of them all?'

'Yes,' said Jeanne. 'I wouldn't say that the worst of sinners deserved death. Being alone is a sort of death, so why would I say that the worst of sinners should be alone?'

Hal said, 'Nobody is ever alone.'

'Oh, because God is always with us? Yes, well, of course. But if the love of God were enough for a solitary man, Adam would still be alone in Eden. Whether he would have been happier there, alone and without sin, I couldn't say.'

Hal was down in the gardens that evening, meeting Percy for beer and takeaway. They sat on the sun-warmed grass and watched the sunset lighting the gold on the Albert Memorial. All around them were people happier than they'd been since last summer; ghosts lived in the shadows, sharing in the pleasure. Tomorrow Hal would leave work early and go up to Monmouth in time for dinner. He and Percy kept their hands off each other until they were back at Hal's flat, then took off each other's clothes.

Hal said, 'I'm going to miss you.'

Percy laughed and said, 'I'll only be a day.'

Yes, thought Hal, but I'm going to miss you again, when this ends. Hal felt for Percy what his father must have felt for his mother when he proposed: this fixed and abiding desire to have this person he loved forever, a consolation for all the terrors and tedium of earthly life, a body to have beside you in the dark. He missed Percy now, with Percy heavy on top of him, and Percy's tongue in his mouth.

They fucked face to face, Hal on his back and Percy on top of him.

Percy leaned forwards and kissed Hal when the mood struck him, or breathed into his face. He'd brushed his teeth after they'd got back from dinner and his breath smelled like mint. Hal kissed him as deeply as he could, as often as he could, so that he could transfer the taste of lager and rice back into Percy's mouth. As they got close to the height of it, Percy sat back on the mattress and looked down at Hal, and Hal covered his face with his hands.

'Stop that,' said Percy, 'I want to look at you. I'm always fucking you from behind and staring at your back wondering what your face looks like.'

'You know what my face looks like.'

Percy, prying Hal's hands away, said, 'No, I don't.'

Hal looked Percy in the eyes. He imagined what Percy was seeing: his hair damp with sweat, his cheeks blotchy red, the right side of his face dotted with the scars Percy had put there, his expression . . . What was his expression like? The imaginary image fell away. Hal thought, He's inside of me, his body is part of my body, I'm looking at myself. Percy came without saying anything; Hal could only tell because his eyebrows were drawn together in a foolish expression of overwhelm. Hal kept Percy inside of him until he was finished too.

The noise of cars on the road below came in with the breeze through the half-open window. Hal stared at the ceiling and listened to Percy breathing. He said, 'I'm not thinking about going to hell.'

Percy, lying beside him, asked, 'What are you thinking about, then?'

'Nothing.'

'Nothing?'

'I'd have thought you were familiar with thinking nothing.'

'Oh, no,' said Percy, 'if anything I think too much.'

'Yes? What about?'

'I forget how lucky I am to have had what I've had at all. Then I get greedy and start wanting everything I always want. Then I think of all the people who've lived and died without ever having the things I've had, and I think, Oh God, how could I have ever wanted all of that?

How could I have ever thought I deserved it? And then that feeling goes away, and I want everything again, and I think I deserve it too.'

'Of course, I am thinking about going to hell, a little. But just in the way I usually do, not in any extreme self-reproaching way.'

'You're not going to run off to the confessional?'

'I haven't made confession in ages. I've got heaps of sins piling up. But I'm not afraid. Richard wasn't: that's why I think his faith was stronger than my father's. My father's the kind of Christian who's afraid. The thing is that God wants you to be brave when you know you should be afraid. That's what makes a real martyr.'

'Umm, well, yes, but you realise this is all just symbols?'

'Ugh, do you know what's not a symbol? Your fucking jizz, this is disgusting. Doesn't a pussy sort of absorb the cum?'

'What? No. If you're shagging a girl, it's even wetter. They're like a big dog who drools.'

'I'm getting up, I'm going to have a shower.'

'Have you really never had sex with a girl? I assumed you did it when you were at school just to fit in.'

Percy got in the shower with Hal, then complained that Hal was blocking all the water with his enormous body. Hal got out and let Percy shower unimpeded, and took a bath afterwards while Percy stood in his pants in front of the sink and trimmed his beard. Hal looked at Percy looking at himself in the mirror, and for the first time found he couldn't read his face.

In bed again, Percy said, 'The thing I think you don't realise about all that is that your family were the ones who really hated Richard. Like, my father was a bit infuriated by him, and he thought the whole thing was embarrassing, you know, he thought it was a pity, but he's known worse eccentrics than Richard. He thinks you all drove Richard insane.'

'Oh, your father has been airing his views on my family? Does he have an opinion of my mother?'

'Yes, he liked her.'

'Richard couldn't have been helped,' said Hal. 'He had been mad at least since I was born.'

'My dad said he used to be different. He said Henry and Richard both did. And do you know what else he said about your mum? That he didn't know why she got to go in the family crypt when Richard went into the landfill.'

'It's a graveyard in Kensington. Our family paid to have the church built. If I weren't going to be one of the dukes, I'd be happy to be buried there.'

'But you're going to be buried in Lancashire?'

'Very likely.'

Percy put his head on Hal's chest. He said, 'I hope I just get buried in the ground. I don't want to be embalmed and put in a coffin, that's a sick thing to do to a body. I don't want to be incinerated either, unless I actually die in a fire. I want to get eaten by whatever wants to eat me. It's really beautiful, isn't it, that there are living creatures who would want to eat our corpses? That way you don't have to wait to be resurrected, you just carry on with life straight away.'

26

The children began turning up at Monmouth in the late afternoon. They burst in through the side door, shouted at one another in the corridors, dragged their rolling suitcases up the staircase. They made frantic conversation with Monsieur and Madame Valois, bellowing 'Would you like to see the library!', 'Would you like to see the gardens!', 'Would you like something to drink!'

'Oh, so this is the son,' said Jeanne's mother, in French. She took Hal by the shoulders and looked him up and down as if he were a fruit she was checking for bruises. She was a petite, dark-haired woman, who had augmented her meticulously plucked eyebrows with the bold application of a black cosmetic pencil. In English she said, 'You are all much taller than I thought you would be.'

'Eugenics,' said Hal, and she said, 'Come again, I'm sorry?' and Henry said, 'Come into the drawing room, we'll have drinks.'

Henry had the warm innocence of a virgin bridegroom, floating aimlessly, dreaming of the future. Jeanne attended to the practicalities: 'What would you like to drink?', 'Sit on the other sofa, Mummy, this one's uncomfortable', 'So how are you finding England, I mean Wales?' She was wearing a backless dress and seemed to regret it: she kept looking in mirrors, shaking out her hair so that it covered her bare back more completely. In front of her parents and the Woodstocks, she and Henry were like a pair of thirteen-year-olds on a supervised first date, glancing at each other shyly across a considerable distance.

'I love weddings,' said Blanche. 'I've been planning my wedding since I was twelve. I just don't know who I'd ever want to marry.'

'The Irish one from One Direction,' said Philippa, and Blanche, pleased a little to have her crush brought up, said, 'No! Shut up!'

The two of them had, without Hal's knowledge or intervention, made up. Maybe it was because Blanche had started planning her gap year, and now their school seemed like an irrelevant backwater she was just killing time waiting to leave. Tonight, she and Philippa were both wearing that coral lipstick. Blanche had drawn on contour, and Philippa had daubed big circles of blush onto her powdered cheeks. When Philippa had come down, Humphrey had said she looked like a clown, and Blanche had told him that he looked like one too.

Henry sat at the head of the table. Jeanne's father, one of those very wealthy men who wear shabby suits, sat at his right. There was such a quantity and variety of wines, and such a grateful enthusiasm that the alcohol was there to soak up the awkwardness of a family reunion, that Hal could drink as much as he wanted without being singled out for his indulgence. Every time he looked up from his plate somebody was upending their glass into their mouth. M Valois, diffident when sober, became boastful, and regaled the table with unlikely tales from his family's past: his father, a captain in the French cavalry, staged an escape from a German prison camp by dressing up as a priest; his Swiss grandfather went missing from his cocoa farm in Côte d'Ivoire and reappeared eight years later in Hanoi, having only been discovered because he'd seduced the wife of the governor-general of Indochina. Thomas Woodstock countered with recollections of his own family history, which had reached a peak of excitement when their department store was bombed in the Blitz. He persisted in the face of the Valoises' unconcealed boredom until Eleanor mentioned that her half-brother had gone on mission to Vietnam, and Mme Valois, looking directly at Henry, said, 'Then you must have seen the beautiful cathedral of Phát Diệm.'

Jeanne, in French, said, 'Mum, that's not Henry's sister, Henry's sister is the one who lives in Hong Kong—No, she's not here, she's not coming—I don't know—No, I've never met her, they're not close.'

Mme Valois set down her Cognac and looked at Eleanor as if she were a stranger who had just entered the room. Seeming to assume none of the English knew French, she asked Jeanne, 'Who is this one, then?'

'Mummy, I explained this. Don't you listen?' Jeanne spoke too quickly for Hal to make everything out, but he understood the gist of it: wife, Henry's wife, sister, husband, Henry's wife . . .

'His dead wife?' said Mme Valois, still very much in French. 'Why are they here?'

Henry was actually smiling. In English he said, 'They're the closest thing the children have got to living grandparents. And since Jeanne will be the children's mother, I thought we should all get to know one another.'

Thomas must have had the feeling that Mme Valois had not been complimentary, but if Henry was the one defending him, did he want to be defended? As if he were providing the solution to some intractable problem he said, 'I'm afraid I don't speak French.'

Humphrey said, 'There was a lot of talk about "la femme". I know that one. Cherchez la femme.'

John told him, 'They were talking about wives. When you say "Cherchez la femme," you're talking about a woman, not a wife.'

'A wife is a woman,' said Humphrey.

'A wife is always a woman,' John corrected, 'but a woman isn't always a wife.'

'Yeah, she could be a nun. But a wife isn't always a woman. I mean, what about prison wives?'

Tom said, 'I'm sure Hal has viewed some relevant films.'

The other brothers laughed. Henry said, 'If you haven't learnt to get on by the time I've died, you'll spend your inheritance suing one another. Don't be flippant – I've seen it happen.'

*

By midnight, the adults were upstairs and the children were alone. Humphrey jabbed Tom and said, 'Come on, let's go rolling in the deep.'

Blanche said, 'Sorry, where are you going?'

'He means he wants to take drugs,' said Hal.

Humphrey said, 'I was trying not to mention it in front of you.'

'Am I on probation?'

'Well, after Twelfth Night . . .'

'I was on cocaine then – that's different. A little bit of MDMA never set anyone off on a killing spree.'

Philippa said, 'Yes, let's do it! You are going to let me do it too?'

Hal was prepared to refuse, but Tom was the one with the drugs, and he said, 'Only because it's Dad's wedding, and only on the condition that you swear you never tell Dad, on pain of death.'

Philippa replied, 'Yes! On pain of death!'

Watching Philippa put the capsule on her tongue, Hal thought, There goes her innocence. Then he remembered the first time he'd taken cocaine, at the birthday party of an acquaintance from school, the August before they started year 11. He had been about Philippa's age, and he hadn't been innocent then. Anyway, none of them had ever been innocent, not even when they were born. Hal demanded three capsules on account of his body mass, and after half an hour felt glorious. He sprung up from the armchair and said, 'We can't stay indoors, let's go out.'

So they went out, the boys in their dinner jackets and the girls in their light gauzy dresses, walking through the dew along the banks of the brook, smoking as they walked, sharing drinks from the bottle of Champagne they'd taken from the crates brought in for the reception, insensible to the chill that had set in after dark. Soon they reached the pond where they swam in summer, in opaque blue-green water that under the moonlight looked silver, blackened at the edges by the shadows of willows and hawthorns. When Hal walked to the edge of the dock, his reflection stretched forward over the water's surface, quivering with its faint movement, waiting for him to move also.

Tom stripped down to his boxer-briefs and leapt into the water, and Hal's reflection disintegrated. Humphrey handed the Champagne to John, who said he would keep his clothes on and be the lifeguard. Blanche, in her plain white slip, with her shoes and stockings and dress and earrings piled on the grass, dived and disappeared, and reappeared with a splash, crying, 'Oh, God, it's so cold!'

Hal pulled off his clothes and slipped in feet-first, wanting to go quietly. The cold water shocked him for a few seconds, then felt the same as his skin. He let air out of his lungs until he dropped far enough down that his bare feet touched the mud at the bottom of the pond; he sprang up and was freshly shocked when the air made his wet skin cold again. Humphrey was trying to push Tom under. John shouted, 'Hey! Hey! Don't drown each other!'

Philippa sat on the edge of the dock with her feet in the water and the hem of her dress pulled up to her knees. Hal paddled towards her, thinking she needed reassurance before she would get in, but when he was close to her she leapt onto him, driving him down, clinging so that he couldn't keep his head above water.

'Ah, get off me, let me live,' he cried. 'Can't you swim?'

'No, you've got to carry me.' She climbed up to sit on his back, the skirts of her dress floating around him like a cloak. He held her by the legs to keep her up; she held onto him by his hair, saying, 'Now I'm taller than you.'

The frogs croaked in the bushes; the plants that grew out of the pond bed brushed against Hal's feet as he kicked to stay afloat. When Philippa got bored and flung herself back into the water, Hal looked up at the stars. How did mariners make sense of it? Hal couldn't even tell which one was the North Star. The longer he stared, the brighter the stars shone, until he was bathed in light and looking through the doorway to heaven, straight into the face of God, whose manservant said, 'Excuse us, please,' and closed the door.

They shared the rest of the Champagne on the walk back, and the alcohol and MDMA and high spirits kept Hal from feeling the cold until they were indoors and the heat from the radiators made his skin burn. Philippa had walked back in her wet dress, shivering so badly that Hal had given her his jacket. 'At least my shoes are dry,' she said. Instead of giving up and going to bed, they put on their pyjamas and drank hot whisky in the kitchen. They kept looking at their phones and saying, 'Oh gosh, it's late,' and agreeing to go up in a minute, then after a minute looking at their phones again and seeing an hour had passed. By the time they really did go, it was late enough that if they worked the land they owned they would just be getting up.

The sky outside Hal's bedroom window had some early sunlight stirred into it, bringing it up into a brighter blue. He opened the window and let in the cool country air, the scent of damp trimmed grass. Along the interior walls, the blue bled into the yellow light of the lamp beside the bed. As Hal looked over the clothes he'd put out for the wedding, Henry came in, shutting the door softly behind him.

Henry looked so young. He was in his scratchy wool dressing gown, with his face flushed and his hair in disarray. He said, 'I heard you all coming up. I haven't been able to sleep. I had been saying Lauds just because I was awake. I thought I should tell you goodnight.'

Hal was violently sorry, then, that Henry was doing this. He didn't want to go forwards; he wanted to go back, and have again all the things he had lost. He said, 'Okay, goodnight.'

Henry stood before Hal and took Hal's head in his hands. He looked at Hal, his eyes, his mouth, back and forth across his face. He doesn't know I'm in here, Hal thought. Henry was leaning forward to kiss his reflection; Hal, on the other side, felt motion sick.

The creak of a floorboard in the corridor gave them just enough time to step back from each other before the door opened. It was Philippa; she was barefoot, wearing a jumper she'd stolen from Hal, standing straight up and wide-eyed, saying, 'Oh! I'm sorry.'

Hal thought of a time one of the monks at school had nearly caught him smoking. He'd thrown away the fag just in time, and the monk had known, and told him, 'You look like the cat that got the cream.'

Hal said, 'Go to bed, Philippa.'

'I'm not sleepy,' she said. 'That's why I came to talk to you.'

'I was just saying goodnight anyway,' said Henry.

Philippa stepped aside, out into the corridor, so that Henry could pass her. She watched him down the corridor, then looked at Hal, confused about why she was confused, expecting to see something in front of her that would explain what she felt. She said, 'Are you okay?'

'Yes,' he said, 'I'll see you in the morning. Don't be clever and say it is the morning: that's the oldest one in the book. Just go.'

27

Thirty years ago, fifty years ago, a hundred, 200, 300 years ago, in spring and in winter, in fine weather and wet, contented or thwarted or hateful or in love, other people slept and woke in this room. In thirty years, in 300 years, who knew who would be here, or whether here would be here at all? It was Hal's turn now. He bathed and shaved and applied cologne, then put on his morning suit and the shoes he hadn't had polished. His waistcoat was pale pink, his tie yellow-gold, the lining of his tailcoat a saturated blue that caught the eye when exposed. He got his top hat out of its box, then thought, No, fuck that, absolutely not. He pomaded his hair and parted it to the side and combed his fringe out of his face, and left his head bare.

At eight o'clock, two hours before the mass began, the children walked over to the chapel, where Father Price heard their confessions. The adults had confessed the evening before, but the children, knowing they would be bad right up until the last minute, had insisted on doing it in the morning. They went in reverse order of birth. Humphrey took the longest, and Hal wondered how many sins his little brother Humphrey could have possibly committed. As Tom exited the chapel, he waved Hal in, saying, 'He's all yours,' and Hal went in and told the truth.

Mary had shown Hal her wedding photos when he was five or six, learning for the first time about the things that happened in the world. He didn't look at them again until he was fifteen or sixteen and missing her. She and Henry looked so young, he thought, like teenagers at a debutante ball, like children play-acting bride and groom. Her dress was so enormous that you couldn't be quite sure she had a body: she was just a beaming pink face pinned into the centre of a monumental sculpture of white silk. Richard was in the pictures too, drinking Champagne, smoking cigarettes with gold filters.

At Monmouth that winter, Hal had looked again and found Jeanne in the background of two shots from the reception. She seemed too attractive and fashionable, too cosmopolitan, to be a guest at an English Catholic wedding, so seemed, in her obvious superiority, to be committing a deliberate infraction. In one picture, she was barely visible over Edward Langley's shoulder. In the other, she was standing some ways behind Henry, and another man was talking to her while she looked at the back of Henry's head. She looked at Henry the same way as her father walked her down the aisle. Again she was so beautiful that she seemed to be wrong for it. Henry had had a new suit made, but he looked just like he had when he'd married Hal's mother, when he couldn't have guessed what sort of a man he would be, and would have said, if you'd told him, 'I couldn't, I wouldn't, I won't.'

Together they knelt at the altar, and Father Price, in his green and gold vestments, assisted by a crane-like acolyte, performed the sacrament of matrimony. 'I, Henry Lionel St Michael . . .' – What a name! Hal was only Henry John Edward. – 'I, Jeanne Marie Dolores . . .' Saying their full names, they seemed to be making their promises on behalf of someone else. Father Price regarded Hal for a long second, as if he thought Hal might stand up and put an end to it. O ye of little faith, thought Hal. You're a priest: you know what kind of secrets people keep. He said nothing until the mass began and the witnesses repeated, 'Kyrie, eleison, Christe, eleison, Christe, eleison, Kyrie, eleison.'

Hal felt nothing. He didn't even feel hollow. He knelt at the rail and opened his mouth and Father Price placed the Host on his tongue. Christ's body dissolved into Hal's spit. In Latin, Father Price said, 'And the word was made flesh, and dwelt among us, and we saw his glory, the glory as it were of the only begotten of the Father, full of grace and truth.'

And Hal, and the others begotten of Henry, and Henry's second wife, and all the rest of the witnesses, who were here because they believed in grace and redemption, life everlasting, the world without end, said together, 'Thanks be to God.' Hal said it like someone politely accepting a terrible gift: Thank you, but I didn't ask for this. I don't want it. Will you take it back? If you really loved me, you would have given me something else.

Pictures were taken outside of the chapel by a fashion photographer who had known Jeanne since she was fifteen. Philippa tried to avoid being photographed entirely, and the photographer said, 'No, don't hide, you're very beautiful, an English rose,' which distressed her so much that she said she felt ill and went back to the house. Presently she texted Hal, 'There is a MAN here for you'.

On the lawn in the rear of the house there was the marquee of all marquees, with a glass-panelled ceiling and faux-hardwood floors and arrangements of flowers attached to each supporting pole. Chiffon curtains were tied back to reveal three long tables cut down the centre by white-rose garlands, shrouded in tablecloths that floated in and out with the breeze. The cobbled yard between the stable block and the house had filled with cars; in the distance another car made its way over the bridge. Seeing no Percys among the guests on the lawn, Hal started down the path to the car park and was met by Jack Falstaff, sweaty and pink, wearing a bottle-green velvet blazer and a pair of embroidered velvet loafers that Hal had known him to wear while taking out the rubbish.

Jack appeared to expect Hal to be happy to see him. He said, 'I haven't come too late?'

'Did someone ask you to come?'

'I invited myself. Don't worry, I'll sing for my supper. I combed my hair – did you notice? Took a train, two buses, and a cab. Roused myself at five in the morning, hungover! See what sacrifices I've made for you. You do look good in the morning suit.'

Over Jack's shoulder, Hal saw the Percys coming up the path from the car park. Hal said, 'You've got to go, Jack. Is the cab still here?' He got his wallet out of his pocket, took out the £200 or so he had in banknotes, and thrust them towards Jack, saying, 'Here, this is more than enough to get back to London. You can get a first-class ticket. Or a coach ticket and enough beer to keep you from delirium tremens.'

The Percys could have walked around the obstruction, but they stopped. Maybe they thought they had to keep off the grass. Percy's stepmother and sister hung back, and the men approached as if they were the first colonists of the savage outer reaches of the empire, protecting their womenfolk from a predatory animal or native, which probably was how they thought of being in Wales. Hal might have convinced Mr Percy to boot Jack out if his wife hadn't said, 'I don't mean to be rude – I know celebrities don't like it when you do this sort of thing – but I can't help it, I'm sorry: Aren't you Jack Falstaff?'

'My dear,' said Jack. 'I haven't been recognised in so long I thought I'd finally become unrecognisable.'

'I should think I ought to recognise you. All my friends at school had pictures of you in their notebooks. I stole a *Tiger Squadron* poster from the cinema. I scribbled out the girl's face and put a lipstick print on yours.'

'You know he's gay,' said Hal.

Mrs Percy said, 'I'm not surprised! The only two straight men I've ever fallen for, I've married.' She said, 'Pamela,' and held her hand out to shake, and Jack, savouring his own humility, said, 'Jack.'

Hal said, 'You don't know him. He's the worst guest you could have. He'll finish other people's drinks, and make up stories about himself, and try to get a leg over any man under twenty-nine, and then fall asleep. I tried to tell him he wasn't invited, but he didn't take the hint, or he did and he thought he'd try it on anyway. It's my fault, I've let him do it to me for years. I don't think there was a single night we've spent together that I didn't pick up the tab.'

Jack said, 'I never work for free.'

'I'd bet everything I own that you've rung all your enemies and told them you were going to this wedding.'

'You don't really own anything,' said Jack. 'Or have I misunderstood what you've been complaining about, all this time?'

If Hal had met Jack alone, Jack would have gone away. He always did what Hal wanted, in the end. But the Percys had it in their mind that whatever Hal wanted must be the opposite of what was right, and this was a conviction so strong that it overcame their upper-class tribalism. They circled around Jack, they turned their shoulders to Hal, threatening to turn their backs on him altogether. Mr Percy called out across the lawn: 'Henry! Come here!'

Jack shook Henry's hand, congratulated him on the happy occasion, and introduced himself as a good friend of Hal's, explaining that he was terribly sorry for the mix-up, dreadfully ashamed, but he had been under the impression that Hal had extended him an invitation.

Henry said, 'A friend of Harry's! Well then you must stay. Harry never lets me meet any of his friends. He doesn't even tell me about them. I've no idea what he gets up to in London. Perhaps you'll tell me.'

M Valois's toast was blessedly brief and anodyne. Hal took the opportunity to drain his glass of Blanc de Blancs and get a refill, murmuring to the waiter, 'Just fill it up all the way, thanks.'

When Henry stood, he was silent for so long that people started to get nervous. The nervousness didn't subside when he started to speak. He said, 'Most of you have known me for a very long time. Most of you were there for my first wedding, which remains one of the happiest days of my life. In fact, Jeanne was there, though I'm afraid she was so beautiful that I took pains to avoid her.' The guests duly laughed. 'After Mary's death,' he went on, forcing everyone to look solemn again, 'I felt quite certain I wouldn't remarry. But two years ago, Jeanne and I met again, quite by accident, and I began to think differently. Now I'm very happy I did, and extraordinarily happy that Jeanne would have me. To be here, today, with you, is a greater gift than I could have envisioned, or asked for, and one for which I thank God, and thank you all, for coming to celebrate with us, today.'

When Henry sat down, Jeanne put her hand over his. For a second, before welcoming it, Henry seemed to resent the touch.

From the far end of the table, Jack called out, 'Why doesn't Hal make a toast?'

Hal tried to refuse, and everyone took it as the false modesty of someone so egotistical he insisted on making it seem that he was grudgingly fulfilling others' desires when in truth he was fulfilling his own. Now if he didn't, it would seem like he was trying to punish them all for not demanding his contribution effusively enough. He stood and raised his glass.

Looking at everyone looking at him, Hal felt he had finally run out of lies. He had used them all up on frivolous things, and now that he really needed to say something untrue, he could only think of the true things he couldn't say. You would hate my father if you knew him like I know him. You wouldn't be able to look at him if you had seen him like I've seen him. I know him, I know him better than anyone else in the world, I know him better than he knows himself, I know him better than I know myself. I don't even know if I have a 'myself'. Maybe I'm just my father, and he's just his father, and on and on, all the way back to Adam, so no one has ever really died, and no one has ever really lived.

'Come on,' said Jack, 'I know you haven't got stage fright. Give us a show.'

Hal gave the best performance of himself he could muster. He told the story about how he'd missed the dinner at which Henry and Jeanne had announced their engagement, and his phone was off for so long that eventually John had to break into his flat to tell him the news. He said that as the eldest of the children he knew more than any of them how difficult it had been for Henry when Mary died, and how hard he had worked to give them a happy childhood regardless, and how wonderful it was to know that he had, now, a helpmate in Jeanne, who had been so kind to them all. He said that he was honoured to be here, with them, celebrating the beginning of a long and happy marriage, the first day of the second spring of his father's life.

The first course was a cold pea soup, which, under the direction of Jeanne's French chef, turned out delicate and refreshing, with sprigs of mint and creamy fresh chèvre. Hal excused himself and went back to the house, into the tiny, low-ceilinged toilet on the ground floor near the kitchen. He splashed water in his face and tried to avoid looking in the mirror over the sink.

There was a knock at the door and Hal said, 'Just a minute,' and Percy said, 'It's me.' Hal considered telling him to fuck off, then let him in.

'I'm fine,' said Hal, 'I just needed a minute. I'm not taking cocaine.'

'That's not why I'm here. I just wanted to, you know . . .'

Hal did look at himself in the mirror then. He noticed another pellet coming close to the surface of his skin. He said, 'Was the mask slipping?'

'No, no, I mean . . . Well, that's the thing. You're always disingenuous, I didn't think it would be that weird to see you actually faking it.'

'It couldn't have been that good, if you could tell.'

'I know you better than you think.'

Hal smiled at Percy, a little disdainfully, a little lovingly. He said, 'Move, so I can open the door.'

As they were walking back, Percy stopped and tugged at Hal's arm and said, 'Let me kiss you,' and Hal said, 'No, not here.'

28

The main course was rack of lamb, roasted in herbs after the fat had been trimmed to expose the bones, which were dried and blackened by the heat. Each plate was arranged so that one pair of ribs was interlaced with another, like the fingers of two hands. A line of bone ran from one end of the table to the other, from Henry to Jack, who exclaimed that he hadn't seen anything like it since a dinner at the French ambassador's residence in 1998. M Valois asked his wife, in French, if she could remember who had been the ambassador to the UK in '98, and she said something like, 'Who knows? If I met him and liked him, I would remember him. I've never known a politician to give a really good dinner, but I suppose an Englishman can't tell the difference.'

Laughing, M Valois said something like, 'Don't antagonise them, darling, we're stuck with them now.'

Henry had been distracted by the Woodstocks, but Jeanne, staring down at the lamb on her plate, made a series of aggrieved expressions that she realised too late Hal was observing. Politely he looked to the other end of the table, where Jack was regaling Mrs Percy with the story of his almost-marriage to the actress whose face she had scribbled out. Hal couldn't hear anybody else that far down the table, but Jack projected.

By the time pudding was served, Philippa was silly drunk, Freshers-Week drunk, eighteenth-birthday drunk. She had knocked over a glass of Bordeaux, soaking the tablecloth and spotting her pale pink dress with red. Blanche took her into the house to apply hydrogen peroxide, and while they were gone Henry instructed the waiters to cut

Philippa off. Discovering her wine replaced with water, like a cruel inversion of the wedding at Cana, she said, 'I should be allowed to get drunk at my own father's wedding.'

'You just did,' said Humphrey. 'But you're not allowed to puke or pass out.'

Philippa wasn't the only one. Eleanor Woodstock had been drinking since the first bottle of Champagne had been opened, and had eaten only a couple of bites of each course. While Philippa had become boisterous, Eleanor had withdrawn, and sat with her hands folded in her lap, her eyes unfocused. Between lunch and the evening party, there were a few long hours of leisurely socialising, and Hal, having lost track of Percy, went upstairs to see if he was in his room. Instead he heard Eleanor in the room next to Percy's, crying. The door was ajar, not enough for Hal to peek in, just enough to let the sound out.

'You've had a year to get used to it,' Thomas was telling her. 'He's done it as decently as he possibly could. He's waited for fifteen years, which is really longer than the children should have gone without a mother. Look at Philippa – surely all that could have been avoided.'

'You don't have to justify it. I don't disapprove at all. It's all perfectly suitable. I'm perfectly happy.'

'Then buck up.'

'But I miss her,' said Eleanor.

On his way back downstairs, Hal stopped by Philippa's room. He knocked and announced himself, and she shouted at him to come in. It was incredible how much of a mess she'd made in just two days: her suitcase lay unzipped in the middle of the floor, and the wardrobe doors were flung wide open, while the clothes that should have been located in these receptacles were strewn instead over all the furniture whose purpose was not to store clothes. An iridescent plastic case sat open on the stool in front of her dressing table, spilling out brushes and compacts and pencils and palettes, and the mirror was covered in various shades of lipstick kisses. She lay in her dress on her unmade bed, awake and scrolling on her phone, pulling one earbud out in acknowledgement of Hal's presence.

'Just wanted to see if you had everything you needed,' Hal said. 'Have you got paracetamol?'

'Blanche gave me some. Don't tell me to drink water, I am.' She gestured to the glass on her bedside table, sweating condensation onto an issue of *L'Officiel* with another thin blonde girl on the cover.

'Fine, then I won't bother you.'

But when he went to open the door, she took her other earbud out and said, 'No, wait.'

'What?'

She said, 'What did Dad want, this morning, when he was in your room?'

'I don't know.' He sat on the edge of her bed; she shifted to make room for him. 'Look, Philippa. I can't promise I'll never do anything unkind, because I've been so unkind to you before. But whatever you tell me, I'll never tell anyone else.'

'I'll never tell anyone else what you tell me, either. May God strike me down if I do.' Still lying down, she made the Sign of the Cross.

'You see—Umm. What should I say . . . I think—Well, no. I know our father hasn't been—I know he's been unkind to you, as I have been . . .'

'Yes?' she said.

'But if he ever did anything very bad, will you tell me?'

'Very bad . . . Has he ever done anything very bad to you?'

'I suppose it depends . . .' He looked at the dress she'd worn last night, hung over the wardrobe door, the light fabric discoloured by the muddy pond water. 'I suppose I'm alright, more or less.'

'Are you?'

'Whatever's happened to me, it hasn't been too bad.'

As Hal was changing out of his morning suit, Percy knocked on his door. Hal felt obliged, since Philippa had let him into her room, to let Percy into his. Percy was deep red and hazy-eyed. He tried to cling to Hal, and Hal pushed him off.

It seemed to disappoint Percy that there was so little of Hal's stuff for him to examine. Hal thought of Percy's bedroom in London, the art prints and framed vinyl and stacks of books and old festival wristbands, cinema tickets, plane tickets, all the objects he accumulated to remind himself of who he had decided to be. Besides the clothes and the few souvenirs Hal had kept from school, there was nothing here that hadn't been owned by somebody from whom he was descended. Unfailingly polite, except for when he wasn't, Percy took off his shoes before throwing himself onto Hal's bed. Hal thought, Now you've lain in the bed where it happened. How does it feel? He didn't want to tell him. Just by being there, not knowing, he was making the place clean again.

'How much time have we got before the party starts?' asked Percy.

'If I won't kiss you here, what makes you think I'll sleep with you?'

'God can see you just as well in London as here.'

'Yes, Father Percy.'

'It would make more sense to me if you were just repressing everything. It's just that everybody knows already.'

'They don't know everything,' said Hal, folding his pocket square.

'Well . . .'

In the mirror, Hal saw Percy staring at the ceiling, thinking, not saying what he thought. He looked so serious and innocent. Hal was devastated by fondness. This time next year, thought Hal, they would be apart.

The fairy lights bordering the marquee, the chandeliers that hung from the ceiling panels, were lit up before the sky was darker than the trees below. Waiters bore platters of drinks and hors d'oeuvres: grilled oysters, caviar on toast points, foie gras with truffles, crudités and fruit and cheese as a concession to those pernicious vegetarians. If anybody was sober, Hal couldn't pick them out. Jeanne had done well: she looked tired, a little dishevelled, but pleased with herself and unashamed of being so. The party went on splendidly around her, and she sat at a table out of the way of the crowd, sipping her drink and talking to her husband, who sat next to her.

As twilight ended, Hal went for a fag and found Jack doing the same. 'I've got something special for you,' Jack told him, and produced a baggie of coke, probably about three grams, from the inside pocket of his blazer. Hal told him no thanks, and Jack said, 'What? Hal Lancaster, saying no?'

'It'll just trick me into thinking I'm enjoying your company.'

'So is it your new boyfriend or your father who's turned you to the other side? I didn't think it would happen so soon. It's such a pity. The Earl of Hereford, heir to the dukedom of Lancaster, handsome, clever, rich, and tall, putting on his sackcloth and anointing himself with his cigarette ashes. Truly, what for? Any unfortunate can be virtuous, if they've got nothing else, but why would you?'

The night they met, they had stood in the quiet street outside the pub in Oxford and Jack had told him, 'Live, while you've got your youth, while you've got your health and your looks and your money. Someday the world will end! What will it matter then whether you've gone to mass and made prudent investments and married a good girl and put an heir in her? Heaven is a gay club in London.' Hal had pitied Jack for thinking that once youth was gone there was only the slow decline towards death, and then nothing. Now it was night again, and Hal was a little less drunk than he'd been then, and it felt like the manager was coming round their table at the Boar's Head, telling them, 'Hurry up, please . . .'

Hal said, 'At least I'm not giving up smoking.'

'If you did, I'd leave you for dead.'

There was the sense, by half twelve, that the height of the party had passed. You were never aware of it when the noise was the loudest, the drinks disappearing the fastest, the bodies crushed in most tightly. It just happened that you looked round and thought, Where did he go, that man I was talking to earlier? You noticed that others had gone too, and there was ice melting in glasses left untouched, and you began to feel the sadness of the inevitable end, even if the music was still playing and you intended to stay up till dawn.

Hal knew it had been a good party because strange new alliances had revealed themselves. Thomas Woodstock had discovered in Mme Valois a fellow horse-racing enthusiast. John and Jack were trying to bounce coins into glasses, mostly just breaking the glasses. M Valois and Mr Percy agreed that the government's capitulation to political correctness sounded the death knell of the Enlightenment values upon which the free world had been founded. Jeanne was saying something funny to Eleanor, making her laugh, pushing the joke further, making her laugh harder. Eleanor wasn't faking it: she seemed to have ventured out onto that precipice of grief upon which life, in its precariousness, becomes precious again, and suddenly it's enough to be alive on a warm spring night with a nice cocktail in your hand.

Earlier Tom had been sitting with Marguerite Percy, proving his decency by looking at her face as she talked. Now Philippa was trying to get Marguerite to dance with her, shouting, 'Come on! Don't be intimidated just because I do ballet! I do modern and jazz sometimes too!' Marguerite had been smoking weed with Hal's brothers; she moved twice as slowly as Philippa, who dragged her about with the same manic glee as Grandfather John playing snapdragon at Christmas, telling the children to be brave and put their hands into the fire.

'I'm sorry my little sister is bothering your little sister,' Hal told Percy.

'We should dance together,' said Percy, 'I mean you and me.'

'My desire to degrade myself has limits.'

'Come have a cigarette with me, then.'

The rowan was thickly leafed; clusters of white blossoms, reflecting the light that shone out from the marquee, glowed like dim lanterns floating in the dark. Away from the heat of the other bodies, Hal found the night cool and still.

Percy said, 'Mind if I steal one? I've lost my tobacco somewhere.'

'You know you can just buy a pack of Marlboro at the shops?'

'Yeah, but I want yours.'

'So you fucking admit it!'

Hal kissed Percy because he could. He meant it to be a quick press of closed lips; Percy put his arms around Hal's neck and they kissed so hard for so long that it gave Hal vertigo. He kept thinking they had to stop, and it kept going.

Hanging from Hal's neck, Percy said, 'Let's go up to your room.'

Over Percy's shoulder, Hal saw that Henry stood on the path leading through the lawn to the back of the house. He must have been going in, or coming out. Like a benevolent father, loath to cut playtime short but gravely aware, as the children weren't, of the constraints and necessities that governed them, he said, 'That's enough. You can do what you like in London, but not here.'

Hal would have let Percy go; he would have told him that they really did have to stop. It was Percy who broke away from Hal. He said, 'Not here? All day long he's been telling me, "Not here." But it's not Hal, it's you. You own the land, you don't own us, you can't tell us "Not here."'

Hal said, 'Leave it.'

'I've had enough of this, I can't fucking stand you people, it drives me fucking mad. Do you really believe in God, or is it all just an elaborate excuse to punish everybody for being a human being? We can do what we like with ourselves, and if we're damned for it, send us straight down, and we'll see you there, and we can laugh at each other in between the screaming. Is the earth not opening and swallowing us up? You'll just have to live with the knowledge that your son would rather get off with me than kneel in front of a crucifix whipping himself. I know he hasn't made much of himself, but that's just because he spends twenty-three hours out of every twenty-four trying to forget he's your son, so that in the one hour when he really does forget, he can fucking live.'

Henry let Percy talk. There was just enough light to see how his face changed. First he was surprised, even having known him, at Percy's lack of self-preservation; then he was graciously entertained; then he was really quite annoyed that Henry Percy's son was standing here talking to him like this. Then he was just bored, waiting for the boy to tire himself out. All this was conveyed through subtle movements around his eyes and mouth, minute adjustments of his bearing, well-worn phrases in the gentleman's native language of plausibly deniable passive-aggression, expertly deployed to create the illusion that a kind and honourable man was in fact the enemy of kindness and honour.

'You're the one who's made him like this,' Percy said. 'If his mum had lived, he'd have—'

Yanking him back, Hal said, 'Shut up, Percy, just shut up, you don't know what you're saying.'

Eleanor had come up the path behind Henry. Displaying the open palm of the peacekeeper, she said, 'He's drunk, Harry. Why don't you take him up to his room and let him sleep it off?'

'I'm only saying it' – Percy wriggled in Hal's grasp – 'because you're too afraid to, because you're too afraid of them.' Looking at Henry and Eleanor, he said, 'You don't know the first thing about Hal.'

Hal put his hand over Percy's mouth and Percy bit it so he'd drop it. Then Percy said, 'Has he ever told you he was abused?'

'Percy, shut *up*! Shut up, shut up! Shut—It's my fucking—God! Fuck off! You don't—You're not—I could fucking kill you—'

'Oh, kill—Kill me, then! Try! Fucking try! What are you—What do you think—Oh, go on, yeah, kill me—You fucking—'

Henry and Eleanor were telling them to stop, but Hal and Percy were brawling now like common drunks, dragging each other down into the grass, gasping towards each other just like they did when they fucked. They pressed their hands to each other's faces, kneed each other in the gut. Percy's fingers poked Hal's eyes; psychedelic spots flashed across Hal's vision. They might have really hurt each other if it had gone on longer than about fifteen seconds, but Henry pulled Hal off Percy and shoved him away, saying, 'Stop it, you're hurting him,' letting Hal stumble and struggle to right himself.

Henry held out a hand to Percy and was rebuffed. He told Percy, 'If you know him at all, you know that the one thing he does well is lie to his advantage.'

Percy said, 'I do know him.'

'I'm sure you think you do.'

They had drawn close to each other. Henry was looking down and Percy was looking impudently up, shaking, red, gloriously beautiful. Henry only seemed unkind.

'You're a good boy,' said Henry. 'You are. I know I haven't seemed to think so, lately. You're self-indulgent, you don't know when to keep your mouth shut, but you are brave. I don't think you know how much you're giving up. If you could stand to limit yourself to your better qualities, you could have anything.'

Percy, being praised, lost his resolve. That was what praise was for: to force the submission of the people who resented you, to plunge right through the pride and the sense of self to stroke the soft childish inner need that would not rest without total encompassing approval. Hal understood so well that he wished he was the one who had been praised and had given up.

Reaching the second-floor landing, Hal heard footsteps on the stairs he'd just ascended. Henry had followed him up. He took Hal by the arm and said, 'What have you been telling him?'

'He doesn't know anything. You know he doesn't know anything.'

'He thinks he knows whatever you've lied to him about. There must be some poor man you've falsely accused.'

'Nobody will believe me. I could tell the absolute truth, and swear to God it was the truth, and everyone who heard me would say, "Oh, Hal Lancaster, that fucking liar." '

'Who have you got to blame for that? Harry Percy would say it was my fault, but you know what your own failings are.'

'My failings have saved you. You haven't got anything to fear but God and the possibility that once you're dead I might leave the church, sell up, and marry a man. If you died right now, you'd know how they'd remember you: devoted husband, loving father, humble aristocrat, generous landlord, went to mass every Sunday, except for that one month he wouldn't go because he couldn't stop thinking of—'

'I'll put you out on your arse. You can make your own way in the world.'

From somewhere beneath them came the noises of footsteps and voices. 'Philippa, don't,' Jeanne was saying, and Philippa was saying, 'Let me go! This is my home, I live here. You can't stop me from going up the stairs just because you're married to my father.'

When Philippa appeared she said, 'Do you know I used to be jealous of Hal?'

Henry told Jeanne to take the girl back downstairs. He said, 'You shouldn't have let her up here.'

The clown car wasn't empty yet: Mme Valois, wobbling a little, looked imperiously surprised at having come up the stairs to face a domestic disturbance. It was as if she'd arrived at a hotel to find the staff still hoovering in her suite. She and her daughter argued in French too fluent for Hal to translate. Henry tried to assuage them in English: 'It's alright, nothing's the matter. Harry's drunk, they're all drunk . . .'

When Hal started down the stairs, Henry followed him. 'Harry,' he was saying, 'Harry, stop, come here, look at me. Henry!'

He didn't follow him out of the house. Whether he stood to watch him out of sight, Hal didn't know. Just outside the side door, Eleanor was smoking a cigarette. She asked if Hal wanted one.

Hal said, 'Sorry, can't, my father's looking for me,' and Eleanor said, 'Oh, in that case, go.'

The key to Henry's convertible was on Hal's keyring. He turned the key in the ignition, hit the clutch, and shifted into reverse. He thought that perhaps he should have looked back. Lot looked back, Orpheus looked back, and the people they looked back at disappeared. Perhaps it wouldn't have mattered. Perhaps God only did away with people you looked back at out of love.

29

The motorways were wonderfully clear. Hal rolled the windows down, turned the radio up, and drove just a little bit over the speed limit, as fast as he thought he could manage without being pulled over and arrested for drink driving. He passed Cheltenham and Gloucester, then skirted Birmingham, watching the countryside run past in a black blur, finding a new radio station each time the one he'd been listening to faded out. If he knew the lyrics he sang along.

When he stopped for petrol, his credit card was declined at the pump. He tried another card, and that was declined, and the next one too, and even his bank card. He tried the next pump and the same thing happened, so he went into the shop and told the attendant there was something wrong with the card readers, and the attendant ran all of his cards again and said 'No, it's just that your cards were declined.' Hal laughed; the attendant watched him boredly. He paid for fifty quid's worth of petrol in cash and kept going.

His phone was full of notifications he didn't read. He only had about 15 per cent battery left, so he rang Philippa.

'Oh, thank God,' she said. 'I thought you'd killed yourself.'

'I'm not that dire of a sinner. Are you alone?'

'Yes, I'm just in my room. I couldn't sleep.'

'I'm sorry to have made you worry.'

'Dad's cancelled your cards.'

'I've noticed. I'll be fine. I'm not running away, I'm just getting some fresh air. Philippa?'

'Yes?'

'I love you,' he said.

'Oh gosh. Are you sure you're alright?'

'I'm fine, I promise, I swear to God. Everything will be fine. I know I'm a liar and you don't believe me—'

'I believe you,' she said. 'Just don't be weird.'

He kept north-east, passing York, cutting through the hills. If he took the country roads north-west, he would end up at Mount Grace; if he went south he would find the ruins he'd seen with Brother Stephen. He kept straight up the A64 and watched the sun rise over the lovely pale hills of God's own country.

His phone had died by the time he reached Robin Hood's Bay. He drove until he reached a view of the sea and the sky, the early morning sunlight reflected in the bay, the white walls and red roofs glinting where they faced the light. He stopped in at a newsagent, bought a packet of cigarettes, and asked directions to the address he had memorised.

The house took some finding: he had to backtrack inland, then follow a narrow country road till he reached the white brick cottage with the ivy spreading out from the west wall. The flowers in the garden were in bloom. As Hal was going to the door, a man came from around the back of the house and said, in a perfect public school accent, 'Hello there. You must be one of the Lancasters.'

'I'm Hal.'

'Oh, I see.'

The man was about Henry's age, but softer, with dark hair and a slight paunch and horn-rimmed glasses. He was taking off his gardening gloves. He introduced himself as Will and welcomed Hal in through the back door, saying that Edward wasn't up yet, but they could have a cup of tea while they waited. He sat Hal down at the table in the kitchen. Copper pots hung over the old stove, and the china cabinet displayed blue-and-yellow majolica Hal thought he'd seen in Richard's London house.

Will filled a creamer and set it out with the sugar cubes. He offered breakfast – Eggs? Sausage? Avocado toast? – which Hal politely declined, thinking the offer had just been a formality, except that Will looked hurt Hal hadn't accepted. He said, 'I'll go see if I can drag Edward out of bed, then.'

Edward, when he came down, seemed unsurprised to find Hal in his house. He sat at the kitchen table and told Will to make breakfast, something filling for Hal, he looked like he'd been up all night. Edward looked like he had just been made fresh that morning. He looked his age – his freckled skin was finely lined, and his reddish hair was thinning – but he seemed to have shed some inward heaviness, leaving himself open and unprimed. He hadn't looked that way with Richard, but it had been a long time, and Hal's vision was different.

'I'm assuming that if Henry had sent you,' said Edward, 'you wouldn't be here at seven in the morning in a suit.'

'The wedding was yesterday,' said Hal.

'Oh, was it. I'm still amazed – think of Jeanne Valois, getting what she wanted after twenty years. Well, I wish them all the best.' Seeing Hal's face, he said, 'Sorry, is it too early for gossip? Have a sausage, they're fresh from the butcher's. Then you can tell me why you're here.'

'I don't want anything.'

'You've got to have something. Some fruit at least? What about blueberries?'

'I mean, from you. I haven't come here because I want something from you.'

'Yes, you have. It isn't anything to be ashamed of. Wanting things is perfectly natural.'

Hal put a sausage and a couple of fried tomatoes on his plate. He intended to say nothing, and said almost everything. He explained about the shooting accident, and Poins's movie, and the septal perforation, and Woodstock Energy, and Philippa going to the farm: all the recent gossip about himself and his family, told in enough detail to satisfy a prurient biographer or priest. He told him about the wedding.

'Harry Percy's son?' Edward was laughing. 'You know, Harry Percy liked Richard. Then your father made it clear it was Richard or him, and Harry chose your father, because he was the one who would live. I've never been good at self-preservation, so I suppose that's why I admire it in others. Some people are loyal to other people, some people are loyal to themselves, and either way you've just got to keep at it. You can't change once you've chosen one or the other.'

'Dad says that, right after Richard died, you dragged yourself in to apologise for how badly you had treated him. Dad, I mean, not Richard. He thought you didn't treat Richard badly enough.'

'That's what Henry says? If I apologised, it was only for being unchristian.'

'Did he apologise to you?'

'Oh yes, that's Henry's great thing: apologising so well that he makes you feel you're the one who's done wrong. Of course, he never means it.'

'He said Richard hurt him.'

'Richard did bully him rather. But only because Henry thought he was superior: "I'm a red-blooded Englishman, you're a perfumed imitation Frenchman." At school he'd always say, "If I were you", and say all the things he thought he would do better. He was insufferable, and everybody else either loved him or feared him. So, you see, it fell to Richard to put him in his place. Don't feel as if you've got to defend him. If you hadn't wanted to hear what I have to say about your father, you wouldn't have come here.'

'I do think he means it sometimes,' said Hal.

'Not in the way I mean "means it". When you're really sorry, it makes you kinder. That's all guilt is for. If you go on being unkind then it means nothing.'

'He said you're a heretic and a blasphemer.'

'Why don't you lie down? Will can put fresh linen on the bed in the guest room.' As Will got up, Edward said, 'And put out a towel for him so he can bathe, darling, and let him borrow some of your clothes. I think your measurements are closer to his than mine are.'

Will served Edward like Edward had served Richard. It was as if

Edward was being Richard so he wouldn't have to miss him. The likeness wasn't exact. Hal remembered Ed Poins, during a dress rehearsal a few days before opening night, stopping in the middle of 'Well, I can't eat muffins in an agitated manner. The butter would probably get on my cuffs,' and saying to Hal, 'It's not that you're not convincing. The problem is just, like, you make me worry I'm not convincing.' Hal had said, 'That's what the play is about.'

Lying on the fresh linen in the bed in the guest room, Hal felt the breeze from the open window stirring his hair. The white lace curtains flowed in and out; their pale watery shadows wavered along the wallpaper. His exhaustion was so profound that he lay unmoving with his eyes open, thinking of nothing, remembering nothing, fearing nothing. His body had decided for him that he was safe. He heard Will working in the garden below, snipping with his shears, singing bits and pieces of the well-known Child Ballads. How came that blood on your shirtsleeve? Oh, dear love, tell me. Oh, it is the blood of the old greyhound that chased the fox for me.

Hal woke in the evening to the noises and aromas of dinner being cooked. The sun wasn't visible from the east-facing window, but the sky was still light. The breeze was chilly enough that Hal burrowed into the duvet, releasing fresh waves of the unfamiliar scent of Edward and Will's bedding. Downstairs they were talking, lightly and teasingly. They had been here, thought Hal, just like this, for years. Living in sin: trimming the rosebushes in sin, buying antiques in sin, going to the farmers' market in sin. Walking along the bay at low tide, in sin, unrepentant, offending God. Happy, whatever that means; in love.

After he'd had a cigarette, Hal joined them in the kitchen, and Edward poured him a glass of red wine to drink while Will finished dinner. He was making Persian food: lamb on a bed of turmeric rice, diced tomatoes and cucumbers. Hal made a joke about nostalgia for the height of empire. Will said, 'Mmm, well, the Pahlavi dynasty, not that that was much of an empire . . .' He explained that his family had left Tehran in '79, when he was ten. Three years later, they lived in

Surrey, and he was at Winchester. Hal asked if he missed Iran and Will said, 'As much as anyone misses their childhood.'

They made Hal do the washing-up. Then they opened another bottle of wine and sat at the table in the garden to watch the sunset. Edward said, 'Why don't you stay with us for the summer?'

'Yes, do,' said Will. 'You're young and healthy, I'll put you to work. I was thinking of putting in a fish pond, with a waterfall and a wooden bridge. And possibly stepping stones, if I can have both those and the bridge. Edward says I'm too ambitious . . .'

'All I said was that the grander your plans are, the more you tempt fate. You spend enough time on the garden as it is.'

Will put his hand on Edward's shoulder as he walked past, going in for the night. He bent down and kissed Edward on the lips. Hal looked away. When Will was gone, Edward looked around and said, 'It's so dark all of a sudden.'

He and Hal sat in silence, and agreed, through mutual inaction, that they wouldn't go in just yet. There was wine left to drink. Hal refilled their glasses and Edward struck a match to light the candle in the Moroccan lantern that sat at the centre of the table.

It was past midnight by the time they said goodnight. They had sat and talked in the garden, sipping their wine until the bottle was empty, smoking Hal's cigarettes. Edward had told him about Richard, and about Henry. Hal watched the lantern's patterns flickering on Edward's face as the flame shifted. Edward looked straight into the light. Now and again he opened the lantern door and brought his fingertips close to the flame, drawing back when the heat was too painful, then going in again.

'If you won't stay the summer,' said Edward, 'at least stay the week. We won't really make you work. If Will tries, send him to me, and I'll see to him.'

'You just want an excuse to keep smoking.'

'Very possible.'

'It's just that I've got responsibilities,' said Hal.

Edward said, 'Fewer than you think, darling. But if you'd ever like to come up again, do. You haven't got to ring ahead. There's a spare key beneath the pedestal next to the side door.'

After Edward had gone to bed, Hal took a long hot bath and used the Acqua di Parma that had been left out in the guest bathroom. He lit the candles on the windowsill and turned the lights out and soaked in the dark, listening to the wicks popping. His body was a shadow beneath him. The reflections of each flame doubled and tripled as he stirred the water, then resolved back into one as he went still.

He woke, still smelling of Acqua di Parma, at dawn, and went downstairs to find that nobody else was up yet. Quietly, with the duplicitous caution that comes from being the first up in an unfamiliar house, he put on the clothes Will had lent him and crept out through the front door. He walked along the country roads until he reached the public path that followed the cliffs north to Whitby and south to Ravenscar. He kept north until all he saw before him was the rough green pasture, absent of any creature grazing, and the faint, high clouds, and the open sea, so far below him that the crashing of great waves looked like motes of dust on the long mirror in which the rising sun looked at itself.

He stepped over the crumbling stone barrier that separated the path from the cliff's edge and sat in the tall grass, which bent, like him, towards the sea. He watched the waves break below. Movement in his periphery brought his head up and he saw, dark against the sunlit water, an osprey beating its enormous wings, hovering for a moment in one spot, then cruising ahead again, then circling back. Hunting, Hal supposed, unless birds of prey flew for pleasure, too. It was so beautiful that he was moved almost to tears. Stupid, he thought. And for no other reason than because he was too tired to stop it, the tears came up, soaking his eyelashes and falling out over his cheeks. His chin trembled so hard that his mouth opened. Then the tears and the noises and the shudders stopped renewing themselves, and the wind coming off the sea dried his face, and the osprey dropped out of sight.

30

How old are you now? Twenty? Oh, twenty-three. The years do go by. So you were how old when Richard died, fifteen? I would have guessed you were younger, you looked so . . . I don't know, I wanted to say 'innocent', but that's not what I mean.

You've probably seen pictures of me when I was fifteen, though probably you didn't know I was in them. I mean school photos and so on. I was shiny and spotty and ginger, and I wore these little round wire-framed glasses. I thought they made me look like I was from the 1920s. I suppose they made me look like an ugly teenage boy from the 1920s. I wasn't innocent either. You stop being a child when you first understand human cruelty. I was just tremendously stupid, and I had the worst flaw anyone can have, which is the need to be liked.

Richard—No, I should talk about your father first. It's strange to me that I'm sitting here talking to Henry Lancaster's son. Because it feels sometimes as if we're all still fifteen, bunking off class, pretending to have adult lives. You must know what Henry was like; everyone at school will have told you. What a legend. They don't make boys like that any more. He went through his awkward phase at about age eleven, and then he was Sir Galahad in rugby kit. Pious and clean-living, a scholar and an athlete. Always getting caught committing good works, however much he tried to keep his left hand from knowing what his right hand was doing. Unfailingly polite to charwomen. And everything that happened with his father only happened once we were at Oxford, so the whole time we were at school he was fabulously wealthy. He was always going somewhere improbable over the holidays – Saint Petersburg or Cairo or Cape Horn or . . . Well, he's told you about Jerusalem.

Richard was a nightmare. From the time he inherited, he made everybody call him 'Your Grace'. Of course, all the other boys with titles thought he was ridiculous, but he was the Duke of Lancaster, so what could they have done? And he brutalised any boy who crossed him, and neither the head nor the abbot could do anything but give him stern talkings-to. Henry knew he couldn't keep up, so he made himself look like he had the upper hand just by being plain-speaking and decent. Richard never missed a chance to humiliate him. Part of the humiliation was just in how easy it was. Richard could say 'How do you do' and get Henry to make himself look like a fool. This of course made everybody like Henry better, and Richard less. All the love that was there for Richard in the world was concentrated in the very smallest handful of people. So, whatever love Richard had to give, he gave it to these people who loved him, as a reward for their loyalty. I was a follower. I couldn't help it. To the day he died, I was a follower. I would have been even if he'd never paid me any mind at all.

Well of course he didn't, at first. I followed him about everywhere, I mean literally followed him, and laughed at all his jokes. If he dropped a pen, I would scurry over and pick it up. He used to – I mean, before he died, I mean once we were together – he used to tease me about it, and tell me how obvious it was that I was madly in love with him. He'd tell me he used to – I mean, when we were at school – he used to invent little chores for me to do, just to see if I would. Then he'd say – when he was teasing me, he'd say – 'I'd never do that to you now, darling.' And then he'd tell me to make a pot of tea or run out and buy cigarettes.

There was only one boy Richard really loved, when we were at school. His name was Robert. He was two years above us. He wasn't handsome, and he wasn't very wealthy, and his family wasn't particularly illustrious, and he wasn't especially well liked . . . So that was how I knew, I suppose, that it was love, because there was absolutely no reason for it. For about a year, I was their go-between. I had a cousin in Robert's year, so I had reason to mix with the sixth-formers. Sometimes I would peek at the notes they sent each other, and it would make me so jealous I'd lie in bed after lights out and cry, just out of pure misery that Richard loved someone who wasn't me. Poor Henry wanted Richard to love him too – not in the same way I did, but just as much. He would have done anything for it, I think, except the one thing he needed to do, which was to submit.

Oh, but about Robert. Your father hasn't told you about any of this, has he? When we were in year 11 and Robert was in the upper sixth, one of the monks caught him and Richard out in the grass behind the house, in the middle of the night, *in flagrante*. Apparently, he was just trying to catch them smoking: he had no idea what he'd see. But I rather think that if that was all he was up to, they would have just been disciplined for smoking. You only start a sex scandal if you want there to be a sex scandal. They let boys get away with those things all the time. It wasn't even as if it were outright buggery: Richard told me later that all they were doing was wanking each other off. And because they couldn't punish Richard, they expelled Robert. Richard nearly left school over it. Henry was the one who convinced him to stay. I think that was the first and only time Henry convinced Richard of anything.

So he stayed, but he spent the last two years of school in mourning for Robert de Vere. That was when he finally started paying attention to me, just because I was there and Robert wasn't any more. The summer before our last year, we went on a driving tour of France. We started in Paris and made our way down to the Riviera. We did it again the year before he died, but . . . No, no, I'm too tipsy, I keep distracting myself. I was going to say that Robert went to spend some time in Quebec, he'd got an uncle or somebody who owned land there, and then as far as anyone knows, he just stayed. I'm sure someone could look him up. I don't know how many Robert de Veres there could possibly be in Quebec. Richard went to visit him after he was diagnosed. He sent me a postcard, it said: 'Bonjour de Montréal!'

So, the diagnosis . . . I've got to tell you the story, because I do think you ought to know. It's just that I don't know how to tell it. At the time, I hardly knew anything. Richard told me everything afterwards. And not straightforwardly, either: he said lots of mysterious things and let me puzzle over what it all meant. I used to think he was just putting me in my place, like he did with Henry, but now that I'm telling you, I don't know. It's not just one story.

No, I do want to tell you now. But give me another cigarette, won't you? Thank you, you're an angel.

So, the diagnosis. We were twenty. It was our second year at Oxford. Be patient, I'll get to your parents in a second. We were twenty, and I'm sure your father has told you a great deal about what Richard was like then. I'm sure you expect me to tell you that none of it was true: that Richard was innocent and clean-living, and Henry told you what he wanted to believe. I don't know that it matters. The virus enters you, at some point. Then you find out. That was 1990. There was nothing anybody could do about it then, really, except make dying a bit less painful. The first person he told was his mother. He said it would have been easier if she'd disowned him, but she couldn't, she loved him too much. The second person he told was Henry. I don't know why. He never said. Henry would have been the last person I'd have told. He was too busy being in love with Mary Bohun. All the straight boys were in love with some girl or other, but it's different when you're waging a campaign to marry her. It was like Henry was the one who was going to die, and he wanted a church wedding first.

Richard said Henry was kinder than he could have imagined. They stayed up all night together, the night he told him, and then they went to mass. I didn't know anything until I went home for Easter and my parents were talking about it. They said they were telling me in confidence, as it had been told to them in confidence by Thomas and Eleanor Woodstock. I only found out about ten years later that the one who'd told Thomas and Eleanor was Henry. I thought Richard had told them himself. Well, I had to go to the loo and fucking weep and then come back and pretend I was just sad for his family that he was putting them through it. I was so upset that when we went back up for the new term I went straight to Richard's rooms and told him a lot of things I'm embarrassed to remember now. It was amazing that he was so gracious to me when I was telling him, essentially, that he had been betrayed.

Henry did it for himself. Why does he do anything? His father had been disgraced, they'd lost all their money, and the Woodstocks were telling Mary she couldn't possibly marry him, she'd be throwing her life away. He was the son of a younger son, he was downwardly mobile. He was going to have to become a barrister, or join the army. But once they knew he'd be the Duke of Lancaster, they thought differently. They quite liked to think of Mary being a duchess. Shame about Richard, but what did he expect? And I couldn't help thinking – Oh, God, he's going to know I said this, somehow. Every time I thought it, I'd pray to the Blessed Virgin to help me be kinder, though I suppose I wasn't trying hard enough because I don't think she ever did. I thought sometimes, Why couldn't you not have got it? Why couldn't you have been safe? It wasn't '83 – we'd all seen the tombstone advert. So I thought, You're proving them right. You're proving your family right, you're proving the Church right, you're proving the tabloids right. You could have just not done it. Why did you? And Richard always knew what you were thinking, and he'd be so hurt, and act so badly, or else he'd be so kind to you that you'd hate yourself for crossing him. But all that is just to say that, when I think about that summer, I think it was one of the happiest of my life. At the time I had the sense of having fallen from grace. Now I think . . . I wasn't innocent, I had learnt about the world. Still, I think I had a sort of purity. I was in love. I didn't want anything. That's how you know you're happy, that's what happiness means.

I remember thinking, at your parents' wedding, that they pitied us. I thought, At least we've got freedom. Which your father doesn't believe in: he thinks free will only exists so you can prove your commitment to suffering. There had never been any question, ever in their life, of how they should live, and Richard and I did what we liked.

Once we dropped acid at the house in Lancashire, and Richard said he could see the first fourteen dukes standing round him in a circle, telling him whether they were in heaven or hell or purgatory. He said he saw a vision of his great-grandfather Edward shot full of arrows like Sebastian, with a halo over his head. He thought it was a genuine vision, he thought God was trying to show him that Edward had in fact been a saint. We got into an absolute screaming row about it, because I was stupid enough to say that it would have been a surprising coincidence if God had decided to speak to him at the exact moment he happened to be on acid. I didn't realise until he was really dying that it hadn't just been, you know, the vanity of a Catholic with important ancestors – it *was* that, but he also wanted to know that a person who had sinned as gravely as he'd done could still someday be holy.

No, I don't believe, any more. I wish I did. I would be happier, thinking that all I've got to do to earn forgiveness is just to follow the rules. Or maybe I wouldn't. Your father believes, and it deranges him. If ever I have the urge to return to the fold I think of Henry. When the rumours started going round about you, I thought, Serves him fucking right. Sorry, I've got to stop telling you all of the most unadmittable thoughts I've ever had. You'll go away thinking Henry was right about me.

So they let Richard come to your christening, but Henry wouldn't let him hold you. Mary apologised to us later, in private. She said she didn't mind at all, it was just Henry. Who knows whether she was telling the truth? She told us she was the one who convinced Henry to let you know Richard, but that was only after five years of keeping Richard from coming within spitting distance of you. Couldn't she have tried harder? But she was always so apologetic, she was always so extra-kind to Richard and me and all our degenerate friends. Oh, she was modern, she was open-minded, she was thoroughly reasonable, she was saintly, even. She thought sinners should be shown more kindness than anyone. The first time Richard had to go to hospital, she sent him hyacinths because she knew they were his favourite. She kept lists of things people liked, so she could give them good presents. Of course, neither she nor Henry would visit. They said they couldn't risk it, with so many young children at home.

That first time it was pneumonia. It was pneumonia the last time too, a different kind. It was . . . What year was it, '94, '95? It must have been '94, the first time. He was in hospital for about five days. After he recovered, he seemed quite well again, and for another couple of months we lived like we'd been doing, and then in the winter he caught flu and was ill again. We had been planning to go to India. We were meant to be leaving in two weeks, and he kept saying it was fine, we would still go, he would be fine by the time we left, it was just flu, people do catch flu in winter. And just as he was starting to feel better, he was ill again. His fever was so high he was seeing things. I had to take him to A&E in the middle of the night. I remember sitting next to his bed and looking at him and thinking, Oh, God, I'm not ready for this part. I thought I would know when it was going to happen, and feel that we'd lived enough that he could go and we wouldn't feel he was missing anything. Actually it just felt like . . . I don't know what it felt like. I want to say it felt like dying, but it didn't. What Richard felt was what felt like dying.

It was the sort of situation in which one prays for a reversal of fortune, knowing it's quite impossible, still hoping that you, against all odds, will be the one lucky person for whom the impossible happens. Then it did happen, in '96. You do know what I mean, don't you? Oh, of course not. I've been telling Will, young people don't know. I'm not chastising you. I quite understand. If I didn't have to know about it, I wouldn't want to know about it either. I've overlooked a great deal of suffering myself: a lot of wars, a lot of famines, earthquakes and floods and wildfires, carpet-bombing, state-sanctioned torture. When Richard was ill, I'd look at other people and think, *You have no idea what it's like*, and I'd hate them for it. Then I'd think of how many other people must have looked at me and thought the same thing. I'm not unaware. But I never want to think about CD4s or enzymes or nucleosides or nucleotides again. There's something so horrific about having to learn that the person you love is made up of all these little things. You go to sleep with him, and you wake up with him, and you think, There he is, he has blond hair, he has blue eyes, he's got a heart and lungs and a nose and mouth, his fingers are—Did you ever notice how long his fingers were? Slightly upsetting. His toes too. Then he's ill and you have to think about how inside every part of him there's a set of smaller parts, and then in each of those parts there's a set of smaller parts, and in each of those parts, so on and so on, getting smaller and smaller, and you don't know them like you know him, and you can't get them to do what you want. You're just a pile of specks in a bigger pile of specks. Richard had the wrong specks, then he didn't have the right specks, which changes all the other specks, and then they go on changing until you can't have the man you love in bed with you any more because he's a corpse. Sometimes I wish we still believed in the four humours and bloodletting and miasma, so that I wouldn't have to think about what really goes on.

No, I am grateful for modern medicine, though, it's given us so much. General anaesthesia, blood transfusion, oral contraceptives, contact lenses, liposuction, amphetamines, LSD, and combination antiretroviral therapy. He'd been taking AZT before, and spending a lot of money on it, but that alone wouldn't have saved him. And then after '96 they started telling people who got diagnosed that they could expect to live quite normal lives. And it didn't just stop them from getting ill in the first place: it made people who had already got ill better again. Being simple-minded, having no greater desire than to keep Richard for as long as I could, I was just thankful he was living. If we had been born five years earlier and lived exactly the same lives, he would have died aged twenty-six or so.

Richard wasn't thankful. He spent ten years going back and forth about whether he should live or die. Yes, no, no, yes. Going quite violently from one end to the other. He would never have jumped out of a window or taken an overdose – even at his least pious he wouldn't have risked it – but sometimes he felt he needed to put himself in the way of death and see whether it would take him. He would stop taking his tablets and wait to see what happened. Then, when he changed his mind and decided to live, he would start it up again. It had to be his choice, I had no power over him at all. He hated the thought of my having power over him, so much so that if I told him to do what the doctors told him, he'd refuse, just to show me I couldn't make him do anything. Like when we went to Greece for the summer: once we were settled in, I found out he hadn't brought his medication with him. The only thing he'd brought was paracetamol. I actually smashed a plate, I pitched it onto the floor near his bare feet and he stepped on a shard. He said, 'Clean that up,' and I said, 'No, you do it,' and he said, 'I'll send you back to Hertfordshire,' and I said, 'No, you won't. If you did you'd have no one left.' It's amazing to feel something and then let it out of you. There was the most beautiful sunset over the sea, and we were saying we hated each other. He slept in our bed and I took the spare bedroom, and then we both woke at five in the morning and went out onto the terrace for a cigarette, and then we had the best—some of the best sex I've had, anyway, I couldn't speak for Richard. It must have been strange, being Richard, and having that power over people: making it seem, even when you're clearly, demonstrably in the wrong, even when you're being horrible beyond belief, that the first and best thing in the world is to please you. Making people feel as if they're worth nothing, then making them feel, when you've decided they deserve your grace, that they're the sole recipients of the purest and most powerful love.

But Richard did get ill again. In '95, I thought we could have one more good year and then we'd have lived enough. Well, I was about your age then: I was twenty-five. The treatment failed when we were thirty-five. He'd gone on and off it too often. His body had finally decided that he must not really want to live. So we'd had ten years, and I still kept asking for longer. Oh God, the nights I used to lie awake, praying, Just not now, just let us have another spring, no, no, just let us have another summer, and that's all, I promise, and we'll be good.

Wait, I'll go back. Because your mother died while Richard and I were being happy. Your father thought it was so unfair: there was

Richard, living when he deserved to be dying, and there was Mary, dead. What had been the point of it, of finding a nice Catholic girl from a good family and marrying her before even so much as kissing her with tongue, if she was going to die before she was finished raising your children? Now you've got to raise the children yourself! Richard told me Henry told him they had wanted more: they thought perhaps they could make it four boys and four girls. It makes me shudder, but I expect that's because I'm a godless sodomite with a fundamental disrespect for the perpetuation of human life. Look at me and Richard: what came out of us, before he died? A lot of pretty pictures? A lot of diseased semen?

He didn't tell Henry, by the way, when the treatment failed. First or second or at all. He didn't tell anyone. They found out what was happening the way you did, just by seeing it. I don't think any of the Lancasters knew that he wasn't meant to be dying yet. They just thought, Oh yes, here he is, dying, like we've been waiting for. They didn't know why he hadn't died ten years ago. Henry had been willing enough to be a good Christian when it was just for a year or two, but every year past '96 he felt was another year he, I mean Henry, had been cheated out of.

Richard talked about you a great deal in those last years. He adored you. He had such great fun testing you. But he still – you must know this, he didn't make any secret of it, so I hope I'm not letting you down – he never wanted you to be his heir. He didn't think it was right. I always thought he would change his mind, but he said, 'No, not Hal. I would have had him as an heir if he were my son, but it's too late now, he's Henry's.' He loved you. He wanted the best for you. He loved Henry, he wanted the best for him too. But he would've only forgiven Henry if Henry had been sorry, and he wasn't. He'd got what he wanted. He'd got Mary Bohun and the six children, he was going to get the title and the . . . Well, he didn't get either of Richard's houses, at least.

He should have been glad Mary was spared the long decline. Watching someone die is so fucking deadly boring. Everyone else goes on living, and then for you it's this awful dream where you're trapped in a waiting room trying to remember the names and the side effects and contraindications of 500 different medications, and the precise dates and outcomes of his last 500 appointments, and you're dredging up money for the 500 outstanding bills – for all the wrong Richard did do, he at least tried not to burden the NHS. And I did the paperwork, and I took him to his appointments, and I took his phone calls, and I found things he would eat, and I went and fetched them and cooked them for him, and I read him the gossip columns and the theatre reviews, and I played fucking Bezique with him, even though he was such a sore loser. I entered his credit card number when he bought things online, and I made him hot water bottles when he was cold, and I brushed his hair, and filed his nails and ran his baths and cleaned up every bodily fluid a person could possibly produce, which is what people who haven't done it say love is. That part wasn't love: it was obligation. It was fear of the embarrassment of being seen to be selfish. Even though Richard was the most selfish person in the world. And so at odds with his own body. He understood everything, in perfect detail, but he kept asking what was happening to him. Sometimes he would tell the doctors, 'Cure me, I don't care how you do it, I don't care how much it costs, I don't care how much it hurts.' When they told him they couldn't, he said he'd ruin their lives, he'd get their licences revoked, he'd make their wives divorce them. Then I would have to apologise to them on his behalf. Then he would tell me about the flowers he wanted at his funeral. He said on no account should there be roses. He would only take roses if you clipped them off your own bushes, he said getting roses from the florist was common.

By the very end, he had decided he did want to die. Why wouldn't he? He was pious again, he had repented, he was assured of eternal salvation. He was barely living: what did he want life for? By the very, very end he couldn't speak, he couldn't lift his head. It was like his soul had slipped out through the cat flap. But he stayed alive longer than they thought he would. They told me to prepare, and I thought, Fuck you. Then I had to get the priest in to do the last rites while he was still at least conscious. Then he lived for another day. If he hadn't taken so long to die, Henry wouldn't have been able to clear his conscience. You see they hadn't met except at mass since before we found out the treatment had failed. I rang him as soon as Richard went to hospital that last time, and I rang him when they said it was doubtful he'd survive this one, and Henry said, no, he wouldn't come, Richard had made it clear he didn't want to see him, he wouldn't go against Richard's own wishes. I said I thought Richard did want to see him, really, and he said Richard wasn't known for making a secret of who he did and didn't want in his company. I said Richard didn't know what he wanted. Henry told me to stop ringing him, and I told him to go to hell. So that part, at least, is true. Then, the day before Richard died, Henry appeared at the hospital saying he was sorry and he needed to see him. He told me to leave him alone with Richard for a moment, and I told him no, and I tried to stand my ground, but when your father really wants something, he tends to get it, I'm sure you know. So I went out and left them alone together. I don't know what Henry did. He said afterwards he could tell Richard knew he was there.

Oh, the candle's gone out. Have you got your lighter? I don't know where the matchbox is, I've dropped it somewhere. Thanks muchly. The story's almost over, but we can't sit here in the dark. We'll have one more cigarette, and then I'll go back to being good.

So . . . yes . . . well. I did hold his hand. At the very moment of it, I didn't feel anything, or think anything. I was just an observing consciousness with a right hand, like a manicule. The moment after, I stopped believing in God. I couldn't help it. I wish I hadn't. But my faith went out of me. I thought, That wasn't pain like Christ's, it didn't mean anything, it didn't change anything, it didn't make anything better. I only suffered because I loved Richard. I still don't know why Richard suffered. I suppose because he was selfish and cruel and narcissistic and arrogant and unforgiving and immoral and petty and frivolous and hypocritical and a snob, I suppose because he thought too highly of himself and spent too much of other people's money and loved the wrong people too much and in the wrong ways, and because he punished people for things they hadn't done, and turned people against one another, and never repaid favours, and always took revenge. I suppose that if he had lived perfectly, he wouldn't have suffered, or if he did, he would have suffered happily, knowing he hadn't deserved it.

When I left the hospital, I went to your father's house in town. You weren't there, none of the children were, you were all at school. Right up until he let me in, I was intending to be righteous, and tell him this was all his fault, and make him repent. Then I looked at his face for too long and started wanting him to like me. For about half a minute I was dead butch: I stood there in your hall and said, 'I won't come in, I've just come to tell you Richard is gone.' I thought Henry would approve of me for keeping a stiff upper lip. I thought he would be pleased that it had happened. He cried, literally, on my shoulder. I had to hold him. I could hardly have shoved him off. He said he loved Richard. He said he would pray for Richard's soul. Once he was quite recovered, he thanked me for coming to tell him and for all I'd done for Richard, and said he hoped I would understand that he would be taking things in hand now.

The last time I received the Host was at Richard's funeral mass. I had to sit in the back with my family. Henry wouldn't look at me. He wouldn't shake my hand when he thanked us for coming. Well, fine. I didn't want him to touch the hand that had been holding Richard's when he died. Can you believe Henry buried him at St Edward's? As if he could lop that branch off of the family tree just by burying him somewhere different. I'm sure if it were up to him, Henry would have put him in unconsecrated ground. He would have liked to damn him, so that if he himself were damned he could say that at least he was no worse than Richard. At first, he tried to hide him in St Mary's at Kensal Green, but they told him no, they were full up, so he had to go begging to St Edward's. I dream sometimes that someone's broken into the grave and taken his body out. *The* body – is it his, still, or is it Henry's, because he owns the plot?

I don't know what else there is to say. I loved Richard. I would have married him if I could have, if he'd have had me. I would have died for him. I think I would have. I never had the chance, and I never know exactly what I'll do. Everything I've done has been a bit of an accident: I keep asking, 'What should I do? What on earth should I do?' And nobody ever tells me the right answers.

I'm sorry that Richard left me the house in London. You should have had it, really. I had to sell up just to pay the tax. Richard knew I'd have to. It was enough for him to know the house wouldn't go to your father. If we could have been married, I could have kept it – there wouldn't have been tax on the inheritance – but he knew that too. I did live there for a few months, afterwards. I kept smelling his cologne. I didn't know if I was just imagining it. Will said he could smell it too, but it could have been folie à deux. So I sold the house and bought this one, and now Will's going to spend what's left of my fortune on a pond with a waterfall and bridge. No, I'm sorry, I'm awful to him, aren't I? I don't mean it. I think the garden is lovely.

PART SIX

TEREU

31

June passed without Hal seeing his father again. Henry and Jeanne honeymooned in St Barts; Hal woke early and had a cold shower and took the tube to Notting Hill and bought his breakfast at Pret and went to the Woodstock offices to draft press releases and email stakeholders and send templated responses to incurious apparatchiks at Conservative-owned newspapers. He picked up lunch at Itsu or Leon and ate at his desk while he sent more emails. After work he went to the pub with the other junior staff and listened to them talk about their drunken exploits at a nightclub last weekend, their drunken exploits five years ago at uni. One night, a girl from marketing caught him alone, out for a smoke in front of the pub, and asked him what he was doing that weekend. He panicked and said, 'I'm Catholic!' which apparently was enough of a turn-off that she started avoiding him. He always went home alone; he got a takeaway on his way back to his flat and ate in front of the TV. On Saturdays he played tennis, and on Sundays he went to mass at the Brompton Oratory.

He ignored Percy's calls and texts and WhatsApps and emails until the night before the anniversary of his mother's death, when Percy messaged him asking whether he was going to the memorial this year. Hal rang him and said, 'No, I'm not going this year, actually not going, so don't try to convince me. But what are you doing this evening? Say at six?'

They met at St James's Park; it was the only royal park they hadn't been to together. They sat next to each other on a bench looking out over the lake. The sun was setting on their right shoulder, throwing the shadows of the great trees over their heads and down the asphalt path that separated them from the water. Hal drank his canned G&T and thought about how ducks were apparently always raping one another with their corkscrew penises.

'Everyone has been asking about the wedding.' Percy was smoking one of his own cigarettes, hand-rolled, all-natural tobacco. 'Everyone we know knows . . . Well, they've heard something about it, not necessarily the truth. They know there was a fight. Half of them think I started it, half of them think you started it. Half of them think you won, half of them think I won.'

'Did either of us win? I think we just rolled about on the grass.'

'I'll say you won,' said Percy. 'I don't mind. I've been embarrassed so much this past year it doesn't matter any more.'

'Saying I won would embarrass me more than you. Everyone would feel sorry for you and take your side, and I'd be the psychopath who beat my boyfriend at my father's wedding.'

'Nobody's going to believe what we say about it anyway. I asked someone where he'd heard it, and he said Marguerite's friend Portia told him, so I asked Portia and she confessed she'd filled in some of the detail that was missing from the story Marguerite told her. So I talked to Marguerite and she said she'd only told a few close friends. She didn't even see it happen. She only knows what I told her, and all I told her was that we had a disagreement that got out of hand.'

'You didn't tell her what we were saying?'

'I said I'd finally had it with your father.'

'I hope you haven't been telling people you were screaming at him about me being molested.'

'No! I wouldn't. I wasn't even going to bring it up again. I get it, you don't want to put out a press release and then do an exclusive interview with the *Telegraph* that's like, *Earl of Hereford, colon, inverted commas, I was abused at Catholic school,* and then the *Mail* does a story that's like, *Aristo nonced by notorious nonce Catholics,* and then you have to establish a charitable foundation to advocate for child sex abuse survivors, and then go on *BBC Breakfast* and tell everybody the gory details so they'll let you plug your foundation . . . I just thought that if anybody in the world should know, it's your father.'

Hal said, 'I have to tell you something that I think will hurt your feelings.'

Percy looked like his feelings had already been hurt, just from that. He said, 'I'll be fine.'

'My father already knew.' Hal was laughing, not even nervously; it was just funny. 'He knew about it when it was happening. He knew from the beginning.'

'And he didn't do anything about it?'

'He pretended it hadn't happened. I pretended it hadn't happened. He didn't even have to tell me to keep quiet, I just knew. I was a good boy, back then.'

The shadows had lengthened since Hal had last looked up. The silhouettes of the trees in the water looked blacker, and the pink reflections looked more fragile, closer to disappearing. Pigeons bobbled over the path, trying to keep clear of tromping tourist feet. The ducks that had been swimming just in front of them before were specks in the further water. The sun was still an hour from setting; late spring was rounding off into summer.

'What about Eleanor Woodstock?' asked Percy. 'She didn't know.'

'I expect I could rely on her to testify in court if I ever brought charges, or to donate a quarter million to my charitable foundation. She doesn't like my father either. She's very unfair to him, actually. Philippa told me she started a massive stinking row after I left.'

'I didn't hear anything,' said Percy, 'and I stayed for breakfast.'

'No, you wouldn't have. There had been enough indiscretion for the weekend.'

'You know what I've been thinking of—Maybe I was imagining it – I was just lying in bed trying to reach you and not getting anything back, I was worrying you were going to get plastered and walk into the sea – but that night after the wedding I thought I heard something, like, scampering? Above me? Like some kind of animal?'

'How odd. Maybe you *were* imagining it.'

'I don't know if I was. I mean, I said that, but actually it was loud enough that I was like, No, I'm not going mad, there is definitely something scampering. We had rats at the lodge a few years ago. We kept hearing these noises and I was like, "It's rats," and my dad said it's just mice, and I was like, "Yeah, very large mice."'

'Did you ever find out what it was?'

'Oh, yeah, it was rats,' said Percy cheerfully. 'One of them got trapped in the wall and died and made a huge stench.'

'I suppose it serves us right,' said Hal, 'for building houses we expect to be occupied by us exclusively.'

When they finished the four-pack of G&Ts, Percy let the conversation wind down, as if they were going to go their separate ways, then said impulsively: 'Want to go for a pint?'

As they exited the park, they found themselves facing the Wellington Barracks. The yard was empty; there were no red jackets or tall hats to be seen; the tourists passed without looking. Percy was walking with his face in his phone, looking up pubs on Google Maps – 'Ugh, these all look awful, I hate Central' – and Hal, submitting to an impulse he should have suppressed, said, 'Follow me.'

He took Percy west, past the palace and the souvenir shops and into Belgravia, where they were suddenly alone. As Hal ascended the steps to the front door, Percy said, 'Oh, your dad's house. I was wondering why we were here.'

Hal led Percy into the drawing room, opening the curtains to let in the last of the light. He offered Percy a drink, and before Percy could answer he said, 'No! I know what we'll have,' and took Percy down to the cellar.

'We got everything from the cellars at the house in Lancashire before it went over to the National Trust.' Hal ran his fingers over the bottlenecks sticking out from their cubbies, then wiped his dusty fingers down the front of his chinos. 'Richard tried to drink everything good before he died, but he didn't quite get through it all.'

He chose four bottles and gave Percy two to carry. Percy looked at the labels and said, 'Gosh, 1982 and 1999 . . . Hang on, this one's 1899? Should we put this one back?'

'You'll call your father a racist at the dinner table, but you won't drink the Duke of Lancaster's 1899 Château Latour Grand Vin?'

Sitting on the rug in the drawing room, opening the bottle, Hal said, 'This is wine the thirteenth duke bought before he was exiled. Of course, he was the Earl of Hereford then. 1899 was the year he married Isobel. Now that was a wedding that went wrong. The marriage was arranged: Edward's father had gone to Isobel's father and said, "Wouldn't it be nice for us if those two got married," and the twelfth duke wasn't the sort of man you said no to. And everybody was sick of this French chap Edward had picked up. He was terribly undiplomatic, as most sons of diplomats are. He used to make up rude nicknames for all the important people whose hospitality he enjoyed.'

Poured into glasses, the wine was amber-red like Amontillado, thick with sediment. Hal swirled the glass, watching the flakes floating like sparkles in a snow globe.

'The twelfth duke died during the engagement,' he went on, 'but Edward still went through with it. He was still seeing Piers Gaveston. He invited him to the wedding, and the guests all wrote in their letters that Isobel barely got a glance. I'm sure they were exaggerating. It hadn't been five years since the Wilde trial. Now it's been a hundred years since Gaveston's trial, and everybody still thinks Edward was the worst man who'd ever lived.'

Percy said, 'He lived in the wrong time.'

'There's no such thing.' Hal took a sip and said, 'Mmm. Yeah, well, it tastes like wine.'

After they drank the last dregs of the 1899, they went out to sit on the terrace steps and smoke. The night was warm and dry, lilac-scented, and the stars were bright, and Hal had brought the other bottles with him. Percy broke his glass setting it down too hard, so Hal tossed his own down the steps and they both drank from the bottle. Two bottles in and they were gorgeously drunk, making each other laugh, telling each other blackmail material. Percy used the flashlight on his phone to give him enough light to roll his cigarettes. He rolled cigarettes for Hal, saying he owed him.

Smoking, they fell into silence. Hal, having forgotten, remembered the pity of the world.

Hal said, 'Percy,' and Percy said, 'Yeah,' and Hal said, 'I brought you here to get rid of you.'

'I thought so,' said Percy. 'It had to end sometime, didn't it?'

'That was what I was going to say. Had you been thinking it all along?'

'Not all along. At the beginning I didn't think it would happen at all. I thought you'd slap me for kissing you. Then the first time we slept together I thought, Well, we'll see how long it lasts. But I didn't think it would be forever. Which is funny because every time I date a girl I think, Oh, this is the one, I'm going to marry this one. And then when we break up, I'm terribly surprised and heartbroken and I rage at the unfairness of the world.'

'So in a fair world we two would be apart.'

'Most people only ever love people who are like them. I think that's wrong, I don't think like should go with like, I think there should always be some crucial difference. Otherwise you're just looking into a mirror and admiring your own reflection. And then you turn into a flower.'

Hal said, 'Narcissus didn't realise he was looking at himself. He thought he was some beautiful stranger. He didn't love Echo, and all she said were the things he'd said. If he'd really loved himself, the thing he knew as himself, he'd have loved her.'

'God, shut up, I literally have a degree in Classics. People who only love people who are like them don't realise they're looking at themselves either. Because they think, Well, we're different people. We think we're different people.'

'But we're not?'

'I meant it would be vain of me, it would be wrong of me, to love . . . To love . . . To love a person who's just the thing I hate about myself. I want to be different. I want to make myself different. I couldn't live with myself if I was just myself.'

'If you want to be different,' said Hal, 'you really will have to be different. What will you do? You won't be the fucking prime minister.'

'Can't I be?'

'You could be if you were yourself. There's still time, too: it's extraordinarily possible. Quit SOAS, burn your copy of *Orientalism*, join the Conservative Party, write a few pieces for the *Telegraph* about how you came to despise the paradoxical prejudice of leftism. Stand as a councillor, stand as MP, have a drink with all your father's friends, get a nice blonde middle-class girlfriend and make her go off the pill. You'll be in Downing Street by 2030.'

'God! I'd rather kill myself.'

'It's like you haven't been living in the world. You can't just be what you want to be. You went to Eton and you own a grouse moor. Don't you know your place?'

'I know where I was born,' said Percy. 'But I want to go somewhere else.'

'You can't go on crying because you'd die if you flew into space.'

'W-well, I'm going to India. I don't mean metaphorically: I'm going this summer. Some old friends are putting me up.'

'You are going metaphorically too, though. To your surrogate, underground self.'

'Don't quote *Orientalism* at me. You only read it because I did.'

'But you will come back to England.'

'At the end of August. I can't remember exactly what day. I'll miss our anniversary. What would have been . . .'

'If it had lasted longer than a year, our fathers would try to have us murdered.'

'No, yeah, totally,' said Percy. 'We've just got to . . . Nip the snake in its head. Cut the root at the pass.'

Hal – taking a final drag, watching the tobacco ignite and burn up as he inhaled, tossing the fag end down into the dark – said, 'Not that I want to.'

Percy said, 'No, I don't want to either.'

Hal lay back on the terrace and looked up at the stars. He said, 'We could hold off for now, anyway.'

'For now, until whenever . . .'

'Whenever we . . .'

'Whenever . . .'

They finished the fourth bottle and were as drunk as they had been a year ago. When they tried to get up, they struggled, slumped back onto the terrace, and Hal knocked one of the empty bottles over with his foot. It rolled down the steps and stopped with a clink against the glass he'd tossed down earlier. They followed it down into the grass and stayed there, finding it more comfortable than the stone. They held each other. Hal would tell someone everything, he thought. Not now, but at least before he died. Why not now? Because there would be time for it later. Time to redeem himself, time to become someone who did not need to be redeemed. Time for the sun to come out, to set, to come out again. And in the space between this time and that, he would live. What else would he do? Good God, you ask for too much. Tell us what you will do, Hal, tell us who you are. Do you know what you will do? Do you know who you are? Really?

The stars were gone when Hal came to. The sky was deep blue, and in the east, above the roofs of other houses, there were streaks of pink where the sun was going to rise. He was lying in the grass; his clothes were smeared with dirt. Percy lay next to him, asleep where he'd fallen. At Monmouth, Henry must have been lying awake remembering the day Mary died. Jeanne must have been next to him. In the garden, there were birds calling – robins and finches, he thought, and swallows – ordinary garden birds, singing the same songs he'd heard as a child, waking here on any morning in spring or summer.

Hal pulled himself up and took a long piss on a patch of grass that already looked a little withered, then lit one of his own cigarettes.

Waking from the smell of the smoke, Percy said, 'Hey, give me that.'

Just as the rest of the world was coming to England, crowding the British Museum and the National Gallery and the stately homes and the cathedrals, going away with 'Keep Calm and Carry On' posters and commemorative royal teacups, Percy left for two months in India. Hal tried to get him to stay – 'Your dad's right, you know, this isn't going to impress your future constituents' – but he had known, from the second Percy said he was going, that he would go. A few nights before he flew out, Percy said he didn't mind if Hal saw other people while he was gone. Hal said, 'I'll start lining up dates.' But he went out to Heathrow just to see Percy off, to kiss him goodbye-for-now in the vast gleaming atrium of the terminal. About fifteen hours later, Percy was updating his Snapchat story with videos of the Delhi streets, the night markets, the wide, low, smoggy skyline as seen from a friend's balcony. He captured himself looking at himself in the front-facing camera, spinning round to try to get his friends in the frame behind him. Percy had such a lot of friends. Hal messaged him asking if everything was going well, and Percy responded, 'SO HAPPY TO BE OUT OF FUCK-ING ENGLAND'.

There were a lot of Percy's things still in Hal's flat: books left on the tables, clothes that had got mixed in with Hal's, ginger pubes that kept appearing in Hal's bed or on his bathmat or stuck to the bottoms of his socks. For the first couple of days, Percy's side of the bed still smelled like him, and Hal rolled onto his stomach and pressed his face into Percy's pillow and breathed in. Eventually the cleaner changed Hal's bedding and the scent faded, and Hal resorted to huffing a sriracha-stained hoodie Percy had left in Hal's laundry basket. He would put it back in and let it get washed when the scent wore off.

Alone in his bed, Hal had nightmares again. He didn't remember them; he woke ten or fifteen minutes before his alarm with a sense of unease and a pain in his jaw from clenching his teeth. Images flashed, disappeared, became irretrievable. It wasn't enough to have the nightmare: his mind had to show that it was fallible, that if dreams could go, so could anything else. Well, what were dreams but genuine experiences that, lacking context and order, could not be retrieved at will? They were just like all the other memories that only came to the surface when some external stimulus tickled the right part of his subconscious. Once a real thing had passed into memory, it was just as unreal as a dream.

32

Philippa's invitation, texted to Hal in the early hours of a weekday morning, had said only that Jeanne was taking her to dinner as a reward for finishing out the term and that he was welcome to come if he liked. Tom and John would be working late, Humphrey was in Corfu on a sailing course, Blanche was in Croatia with about a dozen other girls who had just begun their gap year, and Philippa didn't have any friends.

The restaurant was in Mayfair. The interior was an uncanny fabrication of old-world elegance: the ceilings were decorated with plaster ornament and the walls were hung with gilt-framed pictures, but the seating was upholstered in neon chartreuse, and if you looked closely, you could tell that all the picture frames had come out of one batch by the same manufacturer. Hal wondered whether Jeanne had chosen this place to appeal to him or to Philippa, and when he was guided to the semi-circle booth in the back corner, he realised that Henry was there, that Jeanne had tried to choose something Henry would like and got it wrong.

Henry was dressed well and looked terrible. His eyes were low-lidded and slow, his skin was pale and moist. Philippa, in a gleaming pink satin A-line dress that uneasily reflected the chartreuse, gave Hal a questioning look. Hal returned it with a look that said, *I don't know what's wrong with him except the things that are always wrong with him, and how dare you question me when you're the one who didn't tell me he would be here,* which was sort of a raise of the eyebrow and a slight wiggle of the head.

Henry said, 'Oh, Harry's here, we'll have to get his drink order in.' Hal said it was fine, he'd just have wine with dinner, but Henry got the attention of a waiter, saying, 'No, no, have what you like. What is it that you like: lager? Gin?'

The waiter gave an onerous description of the restaurant's speciality gin cocktail. Henry said, 'That sounds decent, doesn't it, Harry? You'll like that.'

'Oh, yes, I'll have that too,' said Philippa, glancing about her to see if anyone would give away that she was still too young to drink.

The waiter didn't ask her age. When he was gone, Henry said to Hal, 'There's another one of your bad habits she's picked up.'

'I don't just do what Hal does,' said Philippa. 'Lots of girls from school drink. And smoke.'

'I've been given to understand that the girls at school do what you do, not the other way round. That's why they're so keen to get rid of you.'

Jeanne said, 'I think she deserves a treat, don't you?'

'They're my children,' said Henry.

'Of course.'

'You didn't raise them. You're spoiling them.'

'I think every child should be spoiled a little.'

'I've spoiled Harry all his life. Now I've got to trick him into seeing me. I had to trick him into coming here. Tom and John will do whatever I ask.'

'I'm here,' said Hal.

'I think it's rather too late to ask for praise.'

'I'm not.'

'Ah, yes, you came to see your sister.' He said this with a derision that baffled Hal: did he disbelieve him, or did he think there was something wrong with it, a person having an ordinary love for someone to whom he was related?

When the waiter took their orders, Henry said, 'Your name is Mateo? Are you Italian?'

'Spanish,' said Mateo, a little embarrassed.

'Oh, I see.' Henry asked him a question in well-accented Spanish.

Mateo answered dutifully, and Henry said something else, and Mateo's smile strained, though he kept up an encouraging continuous nod. 'I stayed there for a few weeks,' Henry told him, 'when I was about your age. The ocean is absolutely beautiful. And the people are so kind. I can't imagine why you've come to London.'

'Ah, I wanted to see what there was to see.'

'Well, don't let me keep you. I'm sure they're working you off your feet.'

Over starters Henry said, 'That's what Richard always did, you see.'

'Sorry?' said Jeanne.

'Tell me what to do with my own children. And when that didn't work, he'd try to win them over with flattery and presents. Well, he made them pay in thank-you notes. He expected a full two pages, front and back, handwritten, for any gift he'd given, or else he'd accuse you of ungratefulness.'

This was entirely true. Jeanne must have experienced it herself. Still, she looked at Henry as if she wasn't quite sure they had understood each other.

'Only Harry ever went over to his side,' Henry went on. 'I understand why. Richard put the most effort into cultivating him.'

'Didn't you say,' said Philippa, 'after Mum's memorial last year, that you wouldn't count sins at the table?'

Hal said, 'That was because a priest was there,' and Henry said, '*Behave*,' so unforgivingly that if Hal were a year younger, he would have shut up and been decent for the night.

But what could Henry do to Hal that had not already been done? Hal said, 'I am behaving. We're all behaving, we can't help it.'

Philippa wasn't so much behaving as exhibiting behaviours, in a clinical sense. She ate her Jerusalem artichokes with the ferocity of an eagle pecking out a liver. She left the food half-chewed in her mouth as she said, 'Oo-oh, this is so good! Mmm! Wow! This is fantastic!' For her main, she had veal. Henry tried to dissuade her, and she insisted. She aided her digestion with three large glasses of red wine, for which the sommelier had another onerous description, as if he really thought she was a discerning epicure and not just a teenage girl trying to get off her face. When Henry made a comment about her healthy appetite, Hal watched for her cringe and saw that instead she projected manic satisfaction.

'I'm brilliant!' she said. 'I had such a good time in Sussex. I'm so-o much better now.'

Henry had fish, and pulled the flesh off the bones without putting any of it into his mouth. Jeanne asked whether he wasn't feeling well, and he said, 'It doesn't matter.'

'It's funny.' Hal held his fork aloft and jabbed with it for emphasis. 'You tell me the same stories from school over and over again. I haven't heard a new one since I was in the sixth form. So I thought I'd heard everything. But you never told me anything about Robert de Vere. Did you know he's in Quebec now? Banished to the colonies.'

'For heaven's sake.' Henry looked physically repulsed. 'Who have you been talking to?' He realised the answer as soon as he posed the question, and the repulsion gained in confidence. 'Well, if it's Edward Langley, I see why you've come away with misunderstandings.'

Jeanne said, 'Have you seen Edward? I haven't kept up with him. I think the last time I saw him must have been at one of Richard's parties.'

'I'm sure,' said Henry, 'that he hasn't had a thought worth verbalising since then. He's a machine built for the sole purpose of dispensing attention to the highest-ranking person in the room.'

'I thought he was sweet,' said Jeanne.

'I've no doubt he was, when he did deign to talk to you. But didn't you ever notice that he only did talk to you when there wasn't anyone else there he thought was better?'

'So was it you,' asked Hal, 'who got Robert chucked out? It must have been someone.'

'I'm sure that's the story Edward told you. Richard never told a story that made him look bad. And Edward never stopped to think whether his mind was his own or whether he had leased it out in exchange for invitations to parties he wouldn't have otherwise been asked to.'

'So the monk just happened across them?'

'They all knew boys went off to misbehave. If a boy was caught, it was because he knew the risk and took it anyway. The only bad thing that ever happened to Richard that he couldn't possibly have avoided was his father dying, and I don't think he thought of that as a bad thing at all. He was happy to be bumped up the line of succession.'

'Like you were?'

'Robert de Vere,' said Henry, 'wasn't the first boy who left school because of Richard. There was a boy in our year named Francis Green. He was a local boy – he was there on a music scholarship. He had the most sublime voice. Richard liked people like that. Sort of shabby people, but with talents and charms. I liked Francis too. I would happily have been his friend if Richard hadn't got to him first. But by the end of our first year of senior school Francis was growing his hair out like Richard's, even though our house master kept telling him he looked untidy.

'What really spelled his doom, in the end, was that Richard had made an enemy of the history master. It was true that Mr Sellar was a tedious disciplinarian, but even at the time I felt sorry for him: you could tell he just couldn't cope with life. Richard, of course, took everything as a slight against him. There was a time in year 11, just before Christmas, when Mr Sellar took a letter Richard had been writing in class and crumpled it up and put it in the wastebasket. It was Richard's fine French stationery, so he stood up and told Mr Sellar he had no right, and picked the paper out of the wastebasket again. Mr Sellar told him to put it back and he said no. It went all the way up to the abbot, and the abbot had Richard stay behind for a day after the end of term to clean the classroom and help Mr Sellar finish his marking. That was one day fewer for Richard to spend in Lancashire with his mother and Robert de Vere. It might have ended there if he hadn't been caught at it again in January. That time, Mr Sellar took the letter and sent it on to Richard's mother. And there was something about the letter that apparently wasn't quite proper – not obscene, just close enough that Richard was embarrassed.

'So then one weekend they got drunk at the pub in the village – I mean Richard and Francis and Edward Langley – and they came up with this sort of comic strip, this caricature of Mr Sellar with this sort of wingèd baby, and a limerick about how the baby was glad to be in heaven because it had had an ugly pervert for a father. And that was meant to be Mr Sellar's son, who had died of leukaemia. I haven't said the worst part yet: the worst part is that then Richard and Edward told Francis to go in early on Monday morning and slide the paper under the door of the classroom. Apparently the Latin master came round the corner just after he'd done it. He'd thought he'd got away with it, because he didn't say anything to him then, but once word got out among the staff that Mr Sellar had found this picture, the Latin master realised he knew the culprit. They asked Richard about it, and he said he had no idea what had happened. He said yes, he'd complained to Francis about Mr Sellar, they all complained about him. Francis must have thought he'd curry favour with Richard, attract his notice, you know. And Edward said nothing. It was one of the worst acts of cowardice I've witnessed, I think. Francis wasn't expelled, they only retracted the scholarship, but they knew he couldn't have stayed on without it. I went to the abbot to intercede, and he said there was nothing to be done. Did Edward tell you that?'

Hal said, 'That seems quite mild for Richard.'

'It was. But it was just enough to make everyone who wasn't in absolute thrall to him feel that something should be done to put things to rights.'

'Getting rid of Robert didn't put things to rights.'

'Not in the least. If Richard could have spoken on the day he died, he would have said that he'd never forgiven anyone for it.'

'You think that's hurting his chances of getting into heaven?'

'God knows. I do still pray for his soul.'

Jeanne was sighing, bored. 'When I was at school, there was a girl we all hated, and once when we were at Cannes I pushed her off the deck of a yacht.'

Philippa said, 'You mean you murdered her?'

'Do you think I would be telling you about it if I did? No, she could climb back up. There was a ladder . . . But I'm sure we're boring you, Philippa.'

Philippa had the placid farm-animal look of one who has reached a level of intoxication at which they are content with merely absorbing sensation. She had eaten all of the veal, and the leafy garnishes also. The plates had been cleared away; she was waiting for her pudding, which the others had declined.

'Philippa is eminently capable of registering a complaint,' said Henry, 'if she has one.'

She said, 'I don't. Only I do think sometimes you haven't considered whether there are things you've done that Richard wouldn't have.'

'Like what?'

It was wrong, thought Hal, that a man who paid so little heed to his youngest daughter, the last child of his first and best wife, should know her well enough to be certain she had enough self-preservation to retract her provocations when punishment seemed imminent. Well, that was why Hal had come the closest to telling Philippa, out of everyone.

'Lots of things,' she said. But it had all the bite of the pouting 'No, *you*' she would visit upon her brothers.

When Mateo arrived with the pudding, Henry said, 'Oh, thank you, Mateo, you've made my daughter very happy.' Then he said something in Spanish, to which Mateo replied, 'You're very welcome, sir.'

Philippa did make her complaints known, when she wanted to, when she thought she could get something she wanted. Once Henry had paid the bill, Jeanne looked Philippa over and said, 'I think it's time for you to go home,' and Philippa said, 'No! Hal promised to take me out afterwards.'

'Out where?' asked Henry.

'Drinking,' she said.

'Better that you didn't.'

'Why? What are you afraid of? That I'll become a fallen woman? We're all fallen.'

'It's bad enough you're acting like your brother. You needn't talk like him.'

Jeanne said, 'We can let her have one night out, can't we?'

Philippa said, 'Oh, do get your nose out of it, Jeanne. If my father were going to let you change his mind, he wouldn't have married you.'

'You've made your mother very proud,' said Henry.

'If she had lived till now, she'd say it was better if she died.'

Philippa was pink, trembling, gazing hungrily at the impossible near future in which she let her self-loathing turn outwards, towards its proper target. Henry had stolen her pleasant ambivalence; he didn't even frown.

'Jeanne is right,' he said, 'you should go out. You're young. I suppose I've forgotten what it was like. I suppose that if your mother were here, she'd be telling me so.'

If Hal had really wanted to show Philippa how he lived, he would have taken her to Camberwell; he would have taken her back to the townhouse, or to Wales. Instead he took her where she wanted to go, to a private members' club that was just as overdecorated as the restaurant. Hal had had to text several acquaintances to find someone who would let him in. She sat on a velvet sofa, a knock-off Louis XIV, and drank a frothy pink drink from a martini glass, failing to bring herself into the conversation of Hal's acquaintances. Eventually she excused herself and swayed off in the direction of the toilets. She had been gone for fifteen minutes when Hal texted to ask if she was alright. She texted back, 'yes im FINE'.

She returned bloodless and watery-eyed, asking if he would give her a cigarette. Outside, Hal marvelled at the city, the street, the rows of lamps. If it were 50,000 years ago, he would have only been able to follow her by moonlight. Tonight the sky was overcast, the low clouds lit from beneath by the city glow. Fragments of darker sky suggested nothing, no other world beyond.

'Did you have anything in the cloakroom?' he remembered to ask.

'No. Is it going to rain?'

Hal checked his phone. 'Thirty per cent chance of rain. I've been chancing it.'

She was veering off-centre, reaching out to cling at the bars of the wrought-iron fence that kept them out of a private garden to which they did not have the keys. She swayed and groaned. Her cigarette hung like a red electric bauble between her index and middle fingers.

'I feel so bad,' she said. 'Hold on—It'll be over in a second—'

'If you've got to puke, just do it. The pavement is at your service, Lady Philippa.'

'Ugh, no, don't! You're embarrassing. I'm not going to, I can't, that's what everybody else thinks I do.'

'What, you were going to eat all of that and not vomit it up later? I only eat that much if I'm absolutely certain I'll be puking my guts up.'

'And everyone says, "Oh yes, there's Hal, there he goes again."' She put her weight against the bars. As her hair fell forward it hid her face from Hal's view. 'Oh, I feel so-o ill.'

Hal reached out and put his hand on Philippa's shoulder; he felt the muscle and bone shift beneath his palm. He wasn't sure if he should actually try to rub her back or if that would be weird, so he refrained. He pulled away when he heard high heels on the pavement. There were young women approaching, and Hal wondered whether they knew him. In a loud, bland Hollywood accent, one of them said, 'Are you okay? Do you need to go home? Do you need us to call you a cab?'

They were talking, in fact, to Philippa, reaching out to her without touching her, as if they expected her to lurch gratefully into their arms. What were they doing? Did they think he was trying to rape her? If they were English, or a little less stupid, they'd have just stepped aside.

Flipping round to face them, Philippa said, 'Do I know you?'

'If he's bothering you, just tell us. We'll take you home. Where do you live?'

'Oh my God! Who do you think you are? Do you do this to everyone?'

'Oh my God, I'm sorry. You looked like you needed help.'

'Thank you for thinking of me!' said Philippa, ungratefully.

One of the girls who wasn't talking was looking at Hal's face: looking at his scars, not recognising him. When he looked her full in the face she looked away. She was already angling herself in the direction they'd been walking. Presently her friends followed her, giving one another commiserating glances: what fucking freaks!

'Dad's going to send you away again,' Hal told Philippa. 'At least wait until term time, so you can get out of school. There are better things to be doing on your summer holidays.'

'It won't matter where I go if I've got to keep coming back, if I've got to keep being me. Isn't it just the worst thing ever, that I've got to keep being this for the rest of my life? I don't think I could make it to thirty, I'd be so sick of it. I already am. I don't want to be Lady Philippa any more. I don't want to be a Lancaster any more. I don't even want to be a Philippa.'

'What does that leave you with? I think you tried to castrate the last person who called you Pippa.'

'God!' Philippa tossed away the fag end without crushing it out. 'Is that all I can have, this name or a variation of this name? This body or a variation of this body? In this country? Where everyone chooses each other's lives for them, and everything we'll ever do is measured against whatever we were when we were born, and there are bells over our heads that are set to go off if we even dream about being someone else, so that when the bell tolls everyone else can come and club us like a baby seal? I had more hope for life when I was still in the womb. At least there I was alone and there was nobody to call me anything. I must have thought there would be such good things on the outside. But what is the outside? It isn't this. Is it heaven? And then what if it isn't? What if we're like an explorer who thinks the world is flat and tries to sail off the edge and sails all the way back to where he started? Even if I left the planet, I'd still be in the same body. And even if I left my body, I'd still be in the same soul.'

Hal said, 'I don't know what you want. You have more than you need already.'

'I haven't, have I? That's what wanting things is for: to tell you you need something. How do you live with it? When you always know there's something you haven't got, and you won't ever get it, and all you can have are the things you can have?'

'Feelings come and go,' he said. 'All I can hope for is to make it through to heaven.'

'Another kingdom!' She was striding ahead, her arms swinging at her sides, her hair tossing with the forceful forward motion of her body. She was headed in the direction of Regent's Park; Hal didn't know if she knew where she was going, or if she intended to go anywhere in particular. Without looking back, she asked, 'Do you think you'll still be the Duke of Lancaster, in heaven?'

'If I inherit before I die.'

'If the angels call me Lady Philippa,' she said, 'I'll ask to be let out.'

She spent the night at Hal's flat. She slept in Hal's bed, in one of his t-shirts, and he stayed up in the front room. He took a couple of Xanax and drank whisky and watched *Barry Lyndon*, wondering whether he'd have been that legendary in the eighteenth century or if, in the absence of any other drugs, he'd have just been a miserable drunk. Once every couple of hours, Philippa shuffled from the bedroom to the bathroom and back again. He asked her if she was ill, and she said no, she just kept waking up having to pee.

Hal was still awake when the credits rolled, having been reduced in his boredom to scrolling through Instagram posts he'd already seen. There was Percy, at a glitzy nightclub with his good-looking Delhi friends. There was Humphrey, sunburnt in glittering water. Poins had posted a candid of his co-stars vaping in their Tudor costumes, laughing, the whole scene blurred in motion, as if the person taking the picture was shaking laughing also. Yes, thought Hal, but you can't be having too much fun, can you? Don't you wish you could be somewhere else? Don't you wish you could go to the places I can go? A boy Hal had known at school was being held up on his mate's shoulders, the moon a grainy white spot half an inch above his head.

*

When Henry rang him, Hal thought: He broke first. Weeks had passed. Hal had thought of his father rarely. He had hoped Henry and Jeanne were happy. Summer had come and the world lived visibly around him. But Henry was not really breaking, he was exercising a right, and Hal, accepting the call without thinking, was submitting himself to this celestial order. If they were an unrelated man and woman this would have been pathetic. Thank God Hal was literally made of Henry's sperm.

'I don't feel well,' said Henry.

It was a weekday evening. Hal had come straight back to his flat after work to drink gin and tonics in front of the TV. For dinner he'd had a ready-meal beef Wellington.

'You see, Jeanne has left me,' Henry went on.

'No, she hasn't.'

'She's in Geneva, with her parents. That's what she's said. She's said her father's ill, but she told me I couldn't come with her, so I don't know what to believe.'

'I've never known her to lie.'

'I can't think . . . I've taken these tablets.'

'The sleeping pills? Well, "Early to bed, early to rise, makes a man healthy, wealthy, and wise." That's Benjamin Franklin. I doubt he was rising early after all those nights at Parisian brothels.'

'Please. I think I might have had too much. I've been drinking whisky, and I had the wine before that . . . I was enjoying myself rather. Listening to my records. Then I started to think about the past.'

'Shall I dial 999?'

'No, no, please, don't. Don't tell anyone. Not Dr Bradmore. Not your brothers. Whatever you do, don't tell Jeanne.'

'You're alone in the house?'

'Yes,' said Henry.

'All by yourself in that big, expensive house with the enviable address?'

'Harry, I'm afraid.'

Hal thought this was the beginning of a reprimand: 'I'm afraid you'll have to do better than that,' or 'I'm afraid you've gone too far this time.' Then he realised Henry was actually talking about fear. Hal felt that his father was beneath contempt. The image of him, young and handsome, had been totally defaced, so that Hal pitied him just as he would pity a person who had always been his lesser.

Hal said, 'You should be. Hell is real.'

'Harry, I hope you have been happy, sometimes.'

'You hope I've been happy.'

'I do love you. I've loved you since I knew Mary and I were going to have a child. I've never loved you any less than I did then.'

If Hal had been there with Henry, he would have said, 'You liar.' But he wouldn't want to say it if he couldn't see Henry's face, so he said, 'Okay.'

Henry said, 'I do love you. I do. I love you. Can you love me, please? Can you forgive me?'

'I don't even know what that means.'

'No, neither do I. I believe in it anyway.' Having made Hal silent, Henry said, 'I'll ring off. You go on. Goodnight.'

'Well—' Hal opened his mouth to say goodnight and instead he laughed.

The night, when Hal went out, was cool and dry, with just the slightest bit of light left in the west. How many people lived in London: 8 million? He imagined the hundreds of thousands who were setting out tonight in search of pleasure: putting on their make-up and their smart shoes and cologne, texting their friends that they'd be there soon, queuing for the clubs, meeting their dealers, stepping out onto the pavement and breathing in the unhealthy air and thinking, *This is it! This is life!* He envied them; he envied himself for having been happy too, on nights like these. As he climbed into the black cab, his body gave him that lightness he'd felt then, that sense of safety, of mastery, of faith: an echo of that three-pint drunk, that three-line high, convincing him of his own worth. Really, he was sober. He hadn't even finished his last gin and tonic, and as the drive went on, the feeling went away.

33

The door to the house was unlocked and inside it was darker than the night. Leaving the door unlocked, Hal turned on the lights in the hall and went up the stairs. The second-floor landing was dark. Henry's bedroom door was open, and the bedside lamp illuminated the empty bed, the duvet pulled back, the sheet wrinkled. There was an empty tumbler and several prescription bottles on the table next to the lamp, along with a decanter of – what was it, whisky? – with the stopper in. There was a lovely scent in the air: roses, thought Hal, not one of Henry's usual scents. The lights in the en suite were off, but the door was open. Henry lay across the threshold, ungracefully arranged, his face in the Afghan rug. His hair was damp; he was in a threadbare white bathrobe gone greyish with washing, different from the one he had at Monmouth, but with bloodstains on the elbows also. His knees and shins were freshly bloody, raw and pitted. It looked like he'd torn the scales off and took the outer layers of his skin with them, leaving the deeper flesh exposed. The crevices were filled with a slow glinting ooze of blood.

Hal checked for Henry's pulse and couldn't tell if he felt it: maybe he felt his own pulse in his fingers. Henry's breathing was shallow and slow. Turning him onto his side, Hal saw that his face was pale, his lips colourless. When Hal got out his phone to dial 999, he found the cracked screen unresponsive. He mashed his fingers against the 'slide to unlock' button and effected nothing. He turned the phone off and tried to turn it on again. The screen was black, without even the blinking complaint to recharge. This is a sign from God, he thought, then made a prayer in apology for having used God as an excuse to do what he liked. He put the phone down. He bent to hook his arms under Henry's, and dragged him like a corpse onto the bed. The blood from Henry's knees smeared on the linen. Hal turned him onto his back, then remembered being dead drunk at some schoolmate's house party, just conscious enough that he was aware of a boy he barely knew rolling him onto his side on the plush carpeted floor of his parents' drawing room, saying, 'Get him on his side, that way he won't choke if he vomits.' Hal heaved Henry up so that his head was on the pillow and shoved him onto his left side, then opened the windows to let in the night air.

There was a faint, distant rushing noise, the accumulated hum of traffic from several streets over, or the breeze passing unimpeded through Belgravia's empty passages. Ringed by light and sound and life, they stood in the numb unoccupied centre of the world. Looking over the garden to the houses opposite, he saw that very few lights were on. He thumbed through the vinyl Henry had brought in from the study – the favourites, the original pressings hunted down and bought at high prices – and put a good LP on the record player, pleasing himself with the delicate work of setting the needle into the groove. He poured a bit of whisky into the cup Henry had drained. He took off his trainers and lay back on the bed, against the headboard, his feet crossed at the ankle. He was on Henry's side of the bed; beneath him was an indentation in the mattress where Henry had lain. This had been Mary's side: when she was gone Henry lay where she lay. There was nothing of Jeanne here, no half-read book or discarded jumper or earrings left lying out, no remnant of her scent. Twenty years ago, before Hal was aware of his own existence, Mary must have come to this bed and lain down beside Henry and seen what Hal did now: the line of his cheek, the curl of hair at the crown of his head, the smooth, susceptible slope of his neck. She must have looked at this with love, leant over and kissed his cheek, put her hand on his arm, woken him briefly and said, 'Go back to sleep.' And in another postcode Edward Langley sat up with Richard under the blue canopy, playing Bezique with him, reading him the gossip columns. When you pass the night in bed with a person you love, their body becomes the surrounding darkness, and you feel no need to leave because you believe that if you do, you will only be going into their extremities, away from their heart and mouth but within the reach, still, of their gaze, which might reproach if it catches you straying. There was something in Hal that reached out for attachment; it could have been the part of Henry that lived on in his son, yearning to prove loyalty to the precedent. Here Henry had nothing but the bare fact of his life. Unmoving, unspeaking, unseeing, he could do nothing to Hal, or to anyone else, not even himself. He lay still and existed, and Hal did things to him. This was what it had been like for Richard, dying. This was what it had been like for Hal, yielding control of himself without question or resistance: because he was Henry's creation, allowed life only on the condition of total obedience. Hal felt no joy at the reversal. Henry had ceded power to spare himself the pain of having it taken from him, to spare himself the pain of having it. If he were dead, he would not have to live, he would not have to be good, he would not have to be sorry, he would not have to let Hal go.

Seven cigarettes were left in Hal's packet. There would be cigarettes of Henry's somewhere, Hal didn't know where; Henry hid them from himself. The longcase clock on the landing was chiming ten, which meant that to make it through the night he would have to limit himself to one per hour. He drank his whisky slowly and listened to Henry's music and waited until eleven to smoke, then picked at his scars and waited until midnight to smoke another. The clock chimed the West-minster Quarters. The breeze was gentle, dampened by the heavy humid night. The curtains stirred so subtly that Hal, staring, couldn't tell if they were really moving. The damask spiralled outwards, past the fabric, merging with the chinoiserie, with the light and shadow, with the specks in Hal's vision, until everything was foreign and form-less, indistinguishable from the patterns on the inside of his eyelids. There was that boundless perpetual fear that always seemed, however long he bore it, to be unbearable.

Hal turned Henry onto his back, ran a hand towel under hot water, and washed Henry's bloody knees and elbows. The blood had congealed, but not quite hardened into scabs; when Hal scrubbed at the wounds, he reopened them and got the blood flowing again. He soaked it up with the towel, watching the breaks in the raw flesh welling up with fresh red. He leaned down and licked the blood until it stopped. There was gauze in Henry's medicine cabinet; Hal wrapped Henry's wounds. He clipped Henry's fingernails down to the quick. He combed his hair. Strands of hair, brown and grey, came away in the teeth of the comb, and Hal let them fall onto the pillow. Henry was still breathing; Hal still felt a pulse, whomever it belonged to. Hal had had enough whisky to put him down for at least an hour or so, and he wanted badly to sleep. It would be nice, wouldn't it, if they could sleep together. When Christ died on the cross, his father could have taken him home straight away, or let him lie alone in the quiet dark. Why have him rise again, and save all the rest of us sorry sinners? Hal could only suppose that it was sadism, the same impulse of any man and woman conceiving. When Mary still had Hal inside of her, she and Henry must have thought they were making the closest thing possible to perfect life. Mary was good, Henry was good, their eldest son would be tall and fair and healthy and pious and clever and honourable and clean, and live for nothing but the name. Could he still? Could he have ever? There was always sin. All this nonsense about increasing and multiplying: all this nonsense about creation. Make life, make life, make life. What sort of life? We can prune and water and weed ourselves, but we can't stop the rot once it gets in. Then we suffer, we wail and we moan. Well, we know what we've done. Henry, pale and quiet on the wrong side of the bed, lived no better than the beasts of the earth and the creeping things. So let the tree wither, thought Hal. Let the floods come, let the beasts and the creeping things eat of our corpses and live. Deus vult.

The clock chimed five. Hal pulled the curtains back from the left-hand window and saw the secret beauty that belonged to very early risers and those who had not slept. The sun was mounting the far side of the earth, tossing lines of light above the horizon. He turned off the lamp and watched Henry sink into darkness. The light from the window drew faint blue lines over the folds of the linen, the edges of the furniture, the highest, sharpest points of Henry's body. The lines trembled; there were a few deep breaths.

Henry said, 'Who is it?'

Hal, looking down at his father, said, 'Remember me?'

'Is that Harry? Or someone else?'

'It's your son,' said Hal.

'Why are you here?'

'You rang me.'

'Did I . . .'

The shadows in the bed lay still, glistening with streaks of light, like dark paint varnished till reflective. Henry sighed. Besides that, there was no motion. He said, 'I thought I might not live.'

'You've only slept about nine hours.'

'What time is it?'

'Does it matter?'

'Is the sun rising?'

'It should be. I suppose one never knows.'

'What sort of day will it be? Wet or fine?'

'I couldn't say. It isn't raining now.'

Henry stirred again, then was still again. There was not enough vitality in him, not enough desire, to sustain his movement. Without the strength to enforce a command, he pleaded: 'Come nearer. Sit down.'

Hal came to the side of the bed where Henry lay. Henry reached out for Hal's hand, his fingers brushed Hal's, and Hal stepped back.

Henry looked so sorry. He looked like a child who had just been born, who was just about to start crying, Oh God, oh Mother, why has this happened to me? What have I done to you, to make you do this to me? Hal remembered what Mary had looked like after Humphrey and

Blanche had been born: she had seemed happy, she had seemed to love them, she had held them so closely that they must have believed they were safe and would not be let go. By that time Hal had been let go already. He remembered that when he cried, his mother would kiss him and say, 'You're alright, stop crying, run along,' which must have been what her mother had said to her. So Hal stood at his father's bedside and looked at him without pity, thinking, You're alright, stop crying, run along.

'Last night,' said Henry, 'not just now, I mean the night before, I had this awful dream.'

'I don't want to hear about your dreams.'

'Not really a dream, one of those nightmares when you think you're awake. Monstrous. I thought Mary was downstairs so I went down and she was there, in a corner of the hall, wrapped in a sheet – lying naked, I mean dead, with sort of that look, you know, the colour. I only saw her half an hour after she had died, so she was like that, then. But in hospital she was laid out straight, and in the dream she was bent, sort of limp, like she'd been dropped there carelessly. And the sheet came unwound and I saw her body, with all the fluid coming out. I thought it was real, I thought I'd have to call the police and tell them my wife's body had come out of her tomb.'

'It wasn't in the hall when I came in,' said Hal.

'You think that by the time you're old you'll be satisfied with what you've done. You won't. It's an effect of our class: we keep the heirs subordinate for half their lives or longer. I spent the best of my youth thinking my life wasn't my own until Richard died. Then by the time he died I had grey hairs. Now I watch you, and Philippa, and the rest of you, and you have no idea. You sleep half the day, you . . .' Henry put his palm to his forehead, he closed his eyes. He swept his hair back and his eyes opened again, only halfway. 'And Richard . . .'

Richard had done everything he was ever going to do. Still the vision of him recurred, the scent of him remained. They all went on saying 'Richard' and meaning him, that person, born on Epiphany and dead on Valentine's Day, buried in the freshest grave in the graveyard of St Edward the Martyr's, moving only under the force of decomposition. Henry lifted himself up and put one hand into the opposite sleeve, feeling the gauze.

'It's starting to hurt,' said Henry. 'Did you do this?'

'I put the bandages on.'

'I'm surprised you didn't put a pillow over my face.'

'God, no. Don't you realise I've stopped doing what you want me to do?'

'You never did.'

'Ha, yes. Well, look, umm.' Hal laughed. He glanced towards the door as if someone was coming in. 'The thing is, I've run out of cigarettes. I hope you wouldn't mind if I just nipped out.'

'There are some here. I've tucked them away somewhere, I think in the study . . .'

'I'll just be a minute.'

'No, stay here.'

'Liudmila will be here in a couple of hours, if you really don't want me to call Tom or John in.'

'I told her not to come today. I thought she shouldn't, if I did . . .'

'I'll look in the study, then. Shall I turn the light back on?'

'No,' said Henry, 'I want to see the sun rise. Open the curtains.'

Hal opened the curtains. The sky was lighter, as if they had moved from deeper into shallower water. Soon the sun would be up. He went down the stairs and out through the front door, onto the street, which was caught in the cool hush between the streetlamps going out and the sunlight reaching the rooftops.

He had thought leaving was meant to feel good. This was freedom: he could do anything it was within his power to do, and though his power was not limitless, it was vaster than his imagination. He didn't want oblivion, he didn't want pleasure, he didn't want freedom: he wanted to go back into his father's house and lay himself at his father's feet and say, 'I'm sorry, please forgive me,' and do what his father told him, and never sin again, and be loved, and be good, and be clean, and then to rule forever, stainless master of his own domain.

The only thing that saved him was that it was not yet six and there was no off-licence or newsagent within a mile that would open before seven. He had learnt this at an early age, when, desperate for a cigarette, he snuck out of the house and walked for hours to find someone who would sell to him or buy for him or give him one of their own ('I've got my own light, thanks,' he would say). He walked past Hyde Park Corner and into Mayfair, to the corner shop open twenty-four hours despite not having an alcohol licence. The shopkeeper looked at him strangely, and Hal was about to ask if he'd never seen anyone buy fags at five in the morning. He glanced into the fisheye security mirror and saw that his face was spotted with blood where he'd picked at his scars.

'Shooting accident,' he said, and the shopkeeper said nothing. As Hal left the shop he wiped at his face with his sleeve. By then his desire had subsided, the sky was light. There were other people on the street, people he did not and would never know.

34

The first trailer for Poins's film was released. He posted a teaser on his Instagram, which over the past couple of years had gone from a haphazardly updated collection of party shots to a professional presence in which pictures of airports and foreign skylines and his mum's dog provided a charismatically authentic backdrop for dutiful self-promotion. He appeared for about half a second in the trailer, bowing as Tim Strong's Henry VIII swept through a tapestried hall. Still the comments on his post were filled with adoration for him specifically: people who followed Poins without being followed back, people who only knew him as 'Edward Poins the actor', telling him: 'I can't wait!', 'Excited af for this ♥', 'you look sexy in black', 'Love from Japan'.

Hal googled 'Jack Falstaff', and beneath the usual results – 'Jack Falstaff – IMDb . . . Jack Falstaff, Actor: *Tiger Squadron* . . . Jack Falstaff was born in 1961 in Maida Vale, London . . . Height: 6′ (1.83m)' – was an article, recently published, about an upcoming production of *The Importance of Being Earnest* in which Jack had been cast as Lady Bracknell. 'This marks Falstaff's first return to the stage since his turn as Sir George Crofts in Dame Philomela Spalding's 2008 West End production of *Mrs Warren's Profession* . . .'

Hal emailed Jack congratulating him on finally finding employment. Jack responded with an invitation to come by and watch rehearsals one day. 'This is your chance to see the master at work,' he wrote. Hal wrote back, 'Who is the master?', to which Jack never responded.

The day Hal went to see him was one more hot dry day in a long spell of the same. All across the island grass was going brown, skin was going red and peeling off. Even in the auditorium, surrounded by hundreds of empty seats, the bright day was printed on the dark like a double exposure.

The boy playing Worthing was one of those acting-family heirs who dream of Hollywood but find themselves too attached to the local value of their name to endure the indignities of tertiary roles as Tudor courtiers. When Jack introduced them, Hal felt the narcissist's antipathy towards any person who is too much like himself. As they worked out the first exchange between Algernon and Worthing – 'Yes, I like when you play it as if you're disgusted with him for being in love,' the director told Algernon – Hal looked the boy up on his phone. Eton, Cambridge, RADA: typical. Was this who Jack had replaced him with? Once Hal saw them on stage together, he thought not. Jack tossed out bait, an innuendo or a teasing insult, and the boy let it go cold between them, responding with a controlled charisma that made him seem as though he were practising to be a life-size cardboard cut-out of himself. Occasionally Jack looked out at Hal, sharing a wordless private joke that Hal did not interpret, just enjoyed.

Hal took Jack to lunch at the nearby Wetherspoons that Jack had made his temporary local. They were safe here, among the fruit machines and the red floral carpet and the cheap pine dragged up to parody stately-home mahogany. Nothing was wanted of them but the purchase of a pint, and even that only cost three quid. It had been half a year since Hal had been to the Boar's Head, and he remembered it like his mother, missing it achingly and knowing that if he returned, it would only disappoint.

'Do it with me,' Hal said to Jack. 'I remember all my lines.'

'I thought you had given it up.'

'I had, but I can always count on you to enable a relapse. Go on. "Thank you, Lady Bracknell, I prefer standing." Pretend I'm standing.'

Jack said, 'I am quite ready to enter your name, should your answers be what a really affectionate mother requires. Do you smoke?'

'Well, yes, I must admit I smoke.'

'I am glad to hear it. A man should always have an occupation of some kind. There are far too many idle men in London as it is. How old are you?'

'Twenty-nine.'

'A very good age to be married at. I have always been of the opinion that a man who desires to get married should know either everything or nothing. Which do you know?'

'I know nothing, Lady Bracknell.'

'I am pleased to hear it.'

The voice Jack put on, the physicality, made a perfect mockery of everything about a gentlewoman except her femininity. This he conveyed with an earnestness that Hal suspected would undermine the intended point of comedy, which was that in fact he was a man. It brought Hal back into that first thrill of realisation that if you wanted to be someone else, you could, just by being them. Some actors were only good if they were playing a character who was essentially themselves. Hal was the opposite. When he did *Earnest* at Oxford, the director said he'd make a good Algernon – 'You've got that swagger, that insouciance, that élan, that devil-may-care attitude, that sense that you've got a really juicy secret' – but he had demanded to play the other one, the fool, who knew nothing and could not commit to a lie.

Coming out into high noon, Hal moved more easily; he felt no pain. The red brick of the West End stood in perfect contrast to the blue-white above. Hal put on his aviators and looked at the sun. He remembered being four or five and looking at the sun on a fine clear day and being told by his nanny to stop, or he'd ruin his vision. But he'd been doing it for eighteen or nineteen years now, and he still had his vision, so he kept doing it. Maybe that was why he had floaters. Remembering, he saw them again, sliding lazily across the sky.

Hal said, 'Have you really got to go back?'

'Go back where?'

'To rehearsal.'

'Oh, rehearsal. Yes, I have absolutely got to go back to rehearsal. I'm not in high enough demand that they wouldn't replace me. How

many fat, white-haired old men are there in London who would mem-
orise a few lines and carry a parasol round the stage in exchange for a
few thousand pounds?'

'It's the leading role,' said Hal.

'But think of all the other plays in which I haven't been cast in the
leading role. Think of life! Could I not have played a better part in
that?'

'Come, come, you've still got time to be explosively famous. If all
else fails, you can start committing crimes. More interesting ones than
you already do, I mean.'

'You do it. You've got more life. I'm old, and when I was young the
world was unkind.'

'You didn't suffer that badly, did you?'

'Only vicariously, and then from absence.'

'What, when you tried to get sober?'

Jack said, 'I'll be sober when I'm dead, and death will come soon
enough.'

The theatre was a late-Victorian neoclassical wedding cake: very
little of the exterior had escaped ornamentation. The lights lining the
awning were lit up, a little embarrassed by comparison with the sun.
Jack bypassed the grand entrance and went round to an unmarked
side door, where a middle-aged actress of moderate accomplishment
was loitering in a kimono-style dressing gown, smoking a clove
cigarette.

When Jack opened the door, Hal hung back. Jack said, 'Coming?'

'No, I'm sorry, I can't stay, I've got to, umm . . .'

'Go on, then. It's too fine a day to stay indoors. I'd offer you a ticket
to opening night, but I think you should pay for it.'

Hal did go again, that summer, to the London house. Henry was going
to be alone. Jeanne had gone with her people to the South of France,
and all the children except Hal and John had fled London again. Even
Tom had taken a week's holiday, to Mykonos, with his lads from
Durham. Jeanne had rung Hal first, saying she didn't think he would,

but he could stay with Henry if he liked. Hal had said, 'Yeah, no, John can do it, but thanks for thinking of me.'

Then one Sunday after mass, Hal texted John and said, 'Take the day off, I'll come see him. Go play tennis or something'. John took this literally, and arranged a match at the courts in Holland Park.

The epistle had been 1 Corinthians 15, a smugly self-effacing chastisement of converts whom the apostle Paul felt were not taking things seriously enough: 'And last of all, he' – Jesus Christ, that is – 'was seen also by me, as by one born out of due time. For I am the least of the apostles, who am not worthy to be called an apostle, because I persecuted the church of God. But by the grace of God, I am what I am.' 1 Corinthians 13 was the bit that everyone knew – 'When I was a child, I spoke as a child', et cetera – and one had the sense that, by the fifteenth chapter, Paul was impatient to get to the end of the letter. Hal sat under the great dome of the chapel and looked up to see the sun lighting the gold lettering: 'GLORIA IN EXCELSIS ET IN TERRA PAX HOMINIBUS . . .' The ceilings above the crossing and the altar were painted in white, gold, and a blue that was almost Richard's.

Hal had gone to confession the day before. However unworthy, he was in a state of grace. He knelt at the rail and received the Body of Christ, and felt the helpless love-hatred of the child towards the father who has caused him to suffer. This was what Christ had felt, dying. The love came with the blood, and the hunger. It reached its height in the last second before death, between the final doubt and the final conviction, when he saw his father opening his hands, waiting for him to give up the ghost. Hal swallowed. The priest leading the mass prayed for the body and blood to stick to his guts and cleanse him of his stains. To Hal it was just like fucking: having the mortal body of a man who loved him living for a time inside of his own mortal body, keeping him company till the day there is no more need for touch.

It was another fine day. There were fresh-cut lilies in a vase on the table in the hall. Sun was fading through the fanlight, through the open doors of rooms in which all of the curtains had been tied open. Why would there be lilies in the hall, he wondered, if Henry wasn't leaving the house? There was the new live-in housekeeper, a young French Catholic who had worked for Jeanne before. Perhaps she had put them there for herself. But did she go through the front door?

Approaching Henry's bedroom, Hal called out, 'Hello! It's me!' Nobody heard it: Henry wasn't in his room. His bed was made. The knitted blanket was tucked neatly over the sheet, and the pillows were fluffed. His reading glasses lay folded on the bedside table. The room still smelled like him: not the body-scent of a sleepless night, but like he'd put on cologne after a bath and then walked through. Hal looked in all the rooms on the upper floors, even his own, where the bed had been stripped. He called out, 'Hello! Hellooo! It's Hal!'

As he came down the stairs to the lower ground floor, he encountered the housekeeper, who flinched.

'Hello!' she said. Her thick hair struggled to escape its plait. She was holding a basket of Henry's laundry.

'Sorry, am I in your way?' Hal got clear of the staircase, but she didn't go up. She seemed to be hesitating over how to address him. She was looking, Hal noticed, at his scars. He said, 'I'm Hal, I'm the eldest. I've just come to see my father. I'll try not to bother you.'

'Have you been looking for him? He's outside, on the terrace. Your brother told me you would come, but I didn't realise you were here already.'

'Go on,' he said. 'Really, that must be heavy.'

'A little. Tell me if you need anything. I'll be upstairs. His Grace said he wouldn't have lunch, but I'll make something for you, if you like.'

'Oh, you haven't got to call my father "His Grace" in front of me. Call him Henry.'

'If you like. I might make a mistake when I'm talking to him.'

'You ought to – it'll be good for him. Now go! Wait—No, don't stop, you can keep going up. Just tell me your name.'

From halfway up the flight of stairs, she said, 'Sorry! I thought you knew. It's Marie!' Then she kept going up. The stairs creaked under her step.

Hal entered the garden through the door at the end of the lower ground floor corridor. The terrace was above him. He ascended the steps and saw Henry sitting in the wrought-iron chaise longue, facing the garden, with a cup of tea on the table beside him. He was still wearing his woollen trousers. The sleeves of his white shirt were rolled up; the top button was undone. He wore loafers without socks, baring his ankles and the thin-skinned dark-veined tops of his feet. His hair was combed. All around him there was green, then a few late blooms.

'Sit down,' said Henry. 'Would you like tea? I think Marie is in there somewhere. She's a very pretty girl, isn't she? . . . What's in that?'

Henry was indicating the folder Hal carried, which he chose to rest on the wide, flat top of the balustrade rather than place within Henry's reach. Leaning back against the balustrade, Hal said, 'Papers.'

'Ah,' said Henry. He was slow and undemonstrative. It seemed to pain him to speak too loudly or make too fast a movement, even a hand-raise or a head-turn. 'Thank you for coming to see me.'

'I only did because I want something from you.'

'I thought so.'

So here he was, Hal's father: a man sitting in his garden. Hal should have left Henry to himself. It wasn't that he didn't need his father any more: he needed him more than anything, and knew that he would not have him, so would just have to do without. It hurt: well, yes, it always hurt. If he was lucky, he would only feel it sometimes. If he was good, he would go to God.

'Well?' said Henry.

'Will you give me what I ask?'

'If I can give it.'

'Why would you? I could ask for anything. You haven't done what you've done just to give up and let me have what I want.'

Henry was looking past Hal, who turned his head to see the trees summer-green, having long since lost their flowers. The pears were in fruit, and would be plucked in the autumn.

'It's awful to be awake. It's awful to sleep.' Henry shut his eyes. 'I want to be with Mary. I want to be with Richard. I want another child.'

'Sorry,' said Hal, not quite with feeling.

'I want to go to Jerusalem again. I think I will. Next year, in the spring.'

Hal put the folder on the table next to Henry. There was a cheap ballpoint pen clipped on; Hal unclipped and uncapped it. He said, 'Just sign the blanks.'

Henry blinked at the papers, held them further and closer, struggling to read without his glasses. He said, 'Oh. Human remains. Well, aren't we all.'

Full name of the deceased: Richard Edmund Francis
    Lancaster
Date of death: 14/2/07
Age at death: 37
Was the deceased: [x] Single
Did the deceased have any children? [x] No
Please indicate whether the remains are: [x] Not cremated
If the remains are not cremated, please state the cause
    of death: Pneumonia
Following the exhumation of the remains, is the intention to:
    [a] Return the remains in the same grave [x] No Or another
        grave in the cemetery: [x] No
    [b] Remove non-cremated remains to another cemetery in
        England or Wales: [x] Yes
    [c] Please indicate whether the remains will be re-interred
        in ground consecrated in accordance with the rites of
        the Church of England: [x] No

GRAVE OWNER'S DECLARATION
I am the registered owner of the grave plot in which the
    deceased is interred and give my consent to:
The opening of the grave: [x] Yes

Any necessary removal of the headstone (if applicable):
    [x] Yes
Name: Henry Lancaster
Signature: _____
Date: 9 Aug 2015

_____

The birds in the garden were quieter at noon than at dawn. Still there was a robin singing somewhere. Here in this beautiful place Hal felt the fear: his head was light, his heart was fast, his guts ached, his fingers prickled, his ears rang. Nothing was going to happen. Henry was still seated. He was signing the papers. His hand trembled, and the lines of ink trembled on the page, rendering inanimate his living frailties.

'You know I used to come out here and smoke,' said Hal, 'when I was younger.'

'I could see you from the window in the study. You would hide under the trees when you knew I was in. But when you came in again you smelled of smoke.'

'I thought I was getting away with it.'

'You were,' said Henry, closing the folder, clipping the pen back on. 'I let you get away with it, every time.'

A breeze came through; hundreds of living things rubbed their surfaces together, making noise. There was still a robin singing, perhaps a different one. A sweep of Henry's hair was very gently swaying against his forehead.

'When Richard told me,' he said, 'we were at Oxford. It was Hilary term. It was cold. It was snowing. It was late at night. We got drunk in his rooms and then we went round throwing rocks at the windows of people in college we disliked. He rolled in the snow on the front quad. In the morning we walked to Blackfriars for mass, and then we had breakfast in hall. What a night. No more of that, now.'

Hal said nothing.

Henry said, 'You're sure you don't want tea?'

Hal said, 'I was going to go.'

'Your brother isn't back yet, is he?'

'Not yet. You'll be alright; he won't be long.'

He took the folder and went back down the terrace steps, back through the lower door, down the corridor and up the stairs. The upper ground floor was quiet. Hal listened for steps above and heard none. He stood in the hall and watched, for a moment, the dust floating in the bright midday light coming down through the stairwell.

On the porch, with the door shut and unlocked behind him, he lit a cigarette to ease his way to the bus stop in front of Holy Trinity Sloane Street, which was a huge red-and-white offence to God. Fucking Anglicans, he thought. In all the years he'd been taking buses from this stop, Hal had never entered it. He wouldn't today: the 22 was here. He sat on the top deck next to the window and watched the King's Road pass beneath him. He couldn't rest for too long – he would be in Fulham in twenty minutes – but he shut his eyes and watched the inside of his eyelids turn yellow or black as he passed in and out of shadow. Presently someone sat down beside him. He didn't look to see who it was; he only felt their shoulder pressing against his. He fell half-asleep, and even as he felt himself moving and heard voices around him, he dreamt. The person beside him got up. There was the noise of their footsteps as they descended the stairs. When Hal opened his eyes, the bus was just coming up on Eel Brook Common, so he rang the bell and went down.

35

Nobody knows exactly when Lancaster Castle was built; everyone who did know is dead. It was probably sometime in the late eleventh century, during the Conquest. Nobody knows who built it, either, except that it was not a Lancaster, because it was seized by a Lancaster in the early twelfth century. For the next 400 years the Lancasters fortified and expanded it, and on occasion – when they were not in more important parts of England, or in Wales, Scotland, Ireland, France, or the Holy Land – lived there. Then, in the late sixteenth century, the sixth Duke of Lancaster was imprisoned for treason, and the castle was confiscated by the Crown. Catholics (not Hal's ancestors) were executed there. It was a prison for as long as it had belonged to the Lancasters: HM Prison Lancaster was not shut down until Hal was at Oxford. It became a tourist attraction, like the ruins in Monmouth, like the family seat, which stood about three miles north-east of the castle, further up the River Lune.

Lancaster Park, so called because it was set in a deer park of about 400 acres, was a minor masterpiece of the English Baroque, a long thin symmetrical line of limestone with a monumental fountain in front and an Italianate garden in back. It had been constructed at the end of the seventeenth century, on the site of an earlier manor: in 1687, James II had restored the dukedom, making Henry Lancaster, born 1661, the seventh Duke of Lancaster. In 1688, James was deposed and fled to France, and Henry put his big new house, still under construction, into the care of a Protestant relation. The chapel was added after the Roman Catholic Relief Act of 1829 was passed.

There was no graveyard: throughout all this gaining and giving up and regaining of lands, the Lancasters were laid to rest in St Michael and All Souls, which was just north of the castle and had once been the family's parish church. They had gone on burying one another there through the Reformation, saving the church from a forced conversion by claiming it as private property. Nineteen generations of Lancasters had been entombed there. The two who were missing were the sixth duke, interred in St Peter ad Vincula in the Tower of London, and Richard, who wasn't missing any more.

Hal and Philippa went to St Michael and All Souls first, because it was within walking distance of Lancaster station and they wanted to get somewhere dry. The rain had been pleasant enough on the train; out on the street, the wind was strong enough to make their cheap umbrellas fold into themselves. They fell into the church gratefully, shaking themselves out, taking off their overcoats and leaving them to dry on a pew. The church was open to the public – there were placards detailing the architectural history, and a donation box beseeching visitors to contribute to the upkeep – but they were alone now, conscious that all the echoes came from their own steps and voices.

The oldest tombs were topped with life-sized stone effigies. There was the first duke in his plate armour, his praying hands having long since been broken off; there was the third duke lying next to his wife, the protrusions of their faces crumbled but not yet worn away entirely. One of the heirs who had been so unlucky as to live and die while the dukedom was forfeited knelt upright with his ruffed wife opposite, another pious mirror image of the husband. Some of his ancestors Hal identified only by the numbered labels on the laminated guide he'd picked up in the vestibule, which solicited him to 'Put me back where you found me, please!'

Pointing to an effigy, he said, 'Look, Philippa, this is the one that had its head stolen, and then forty years later someone returned it in the middle of the night.'

Philippa was taking a selfie with the third duke and duchess, sticking her tongue out and flashing the victory sign. She looked at the picture once she'd taken it, said, 'Ugh! No,' and tried again at a different angle.

'Do you want me to take one for you?'

'No, you're terrible at taking pictures.' She looked at the second attempt and said, 'Ugh! Why do I look good when the picture is mirrored and awful when it's the right way round? Is this really how everybody else sees me? How sad.'

Most of the Lancasters past the seventeenth century had been buried under the floor; their tombs were marked with inscriptions that had been worn faint by footsteps. Hal trod upon them once more as he went down the aisle, turning left into the north transept, where a fifteenth-century window of the Archangel Michael looked over a black granite tomb with a surface as smooth and reflective as still water. Richard's name, and the dates of his life, were inscribed in fresh gold. Down there, thought Hal, beneath that black box, was the body that was Richard's. Was there still flesh? Eyes, fingernails, hair? What about the lungs, the heart, the brain? Would he keep his insides when he was resurrected, or would he be hollow, full of light that shone when he opened his mouth?

The west doors – last replaced in the 1860s, he had read – groaned open, and at length thudded shut. There were footsteps in the nave, respectful sightseeing murmurs: 'Shame we can't see the stained glass in the sunlight. Have you got a pound to put in the box?'

Before Hal and Philippa left, they crossed into the south transept to see their mother, who had been interred beneath an unostentatious white slab:

HENRY

LIONEL ST MICHAEL

LANCASTER

OBIIT

AETATIS SUAE

MARY
ELIZABETH
LANCASTER
OBIIT XXVI JUNII MCMXCIX
AETATIS SUAE XXIX

STELLA MATUTINA
ORA PRO NOBIS

Philippa kept her hood down as they left the church. She turned her face up against the rain and looked for so long at the sky that she didn't look where she was going and stumbled over a crack in the pavement.

'Fuck,' she said, then, 'Sorry,' then, 'What a lot of bodies!'

The long approach to the house was designed to impress a visitor arriving in a horse-drawn carriage. Hal and Philippa arrived on a bus that dropped them off at the gated entrance to the park, near a brown sign indicating 'Lancaster Park' with a helpful arrow. They walked in the rain along the side of the road, passed occasionally by a car going in or out. As they came closer to the house, Hal saw that the fountain had been turned off, its enormous basin half-filled with cloudy rainwater.

At the ticket booth, Hal paid £15 for himself, £12.50 for Philippa, who said, 'Did you not tell them we were coming?' Hal shushed her and gave her the sticker that would show the ticket had been paid for. He paid an extra £3 for a map.

A guided tour had just begun – 'You can run along and join this one, or there's the next one in forty-five minutes,' the woman at the desk explained – and they kept turning corners to find themselves impeded by a mass of sightseers and pensioners and families with bored children, crowding around a picture or a statue or a significant piece of furniture, sparing an occasional glance upwards to the crown moulding and the rosettes.

In the gold room at the end of the enfilade they found the tour staring with bored deference at a late-fifteenth-century depiction of the first Duke of Lancaster, who had been imagined in furs and a red chaperon. The tour guide, a thin, large-eared old man in a polka-dotted tie, glanced over at Hal and Philippa as if counting his sheep. He returned his attention to the duke's exploits in Ireland, then faltered as he looked at them a second and third time, just on the verge of recognition. Hal pulled Philippa out of the room. The door through which they exited led onto the first-floor landing of the west staircase; a picture of Richard hung over the half-landing. Philippa said to it, 'Oh! It's you!'

The figure was an uncanny half-size larger than life; the canvas was twice as large as the tomb. Richard lay on the bed with the blue canopy, expanding himself, the reflective folds of his white silk dressing gown merging into the matte white of the linen. He was propping his head up with a pale hand done in quick, fluid strokes, reddish in the shadows and blue-white where the light fell. Around his long nose and thin mouth and the curls of his hair there was beautiful imprecision, blurring, as if the artist had meant to give the picture its own sovereign motion. The thick brushstrokes did seem to shift as Hal descended. But what if Richard had lived? What if he were here, now, with Hal? Somewhere else – then, there – he was: he lay in that bed, and Hal stood at the foot of it, being looked at.

Hal had to set on. A door was opening behind him, there were footsteps on the landing above. Philippa was ahead of him, going down two steps at a time, saying, 'The rain's lighter now. Let's go out and look for the deer.'